WILD

ALEX MALLORY

HARPER TEEN
An Imprint of HarperCollinsPublishers

HarperTeen is an imprint of HarperCollins Publishers.

Wild
Copyright © 2014 by Saundra Mitchell
All rights reserved. Printed in the United States of America.

Library of Congress Cataloging-in-Publication Data
Mallory, Alex.
 Wild / Alex Mallory. — First edition.
   pages cm
 Summary: "When Cade, a boy who has lived in the forest his whole life, saves a regular teen from a bear attack, he is brought into modern civilization for the first time" — Provided by publisher.
 ISBN 978-0-06-221874-2 (hardback)
 [1. Nature—Fiction. 2. Civilization—Fiction. 3. Orphans—Fiction. 4. Love—Fiction.] I. Title.
PZ7.M29535Wi 2014   2013043190
[Fic]—dc23   CIP
                                                                      AC

Typography by Michelle Gengaro-Kokmen
14 15 16 17 18   LP/RRDH   10 9 8 7 6 5 4 3 2 1
❖
First Edition

For Jim McCarthy, who deserves a lot more

PROLOGUE

There's a secluded camp deep in the heart of Daniel Boone National Forest.

It's not a summer escape. There's no tent here. This is a living space. Comfortable. Tidy. Laundry hangs on a line, and Brendan Walsh sits in the open, scraping a hide. He's brown from the sun; his skin is the same shade as his earth-worn jeans and buckskins.

Beside him, Cade, a toddler, plays in the dust. With his dark hair and brown eyes, he can fade into the forest completely. Hide-and-seek is the most terrifying game Cade can play. He's small enough to fit inside stumps or inside the belly of a bear.

His chubby fingers grip his clay animals. They're artlessly made, suggestions of a bear, a cat, a cow. Their owner doesn't care. He marches them up his mother's leg, then down it again.

When he looks at her, he laughs. She smiles, but it doesn't quite reach her eyes.

Liza Walsh is ever aware. Ever watching. Ever listening. Even as she braids reeds into a basket, her eyes dart. They linger on shadows, on shapes. It's summer, when the shade beneath the canopy turns the forest to perpetual twilight.

Interrupting his wife's thoughts, Brendan says, "I thought we might hike to the falls tomorrow."

"That'll be nice," Liza says. "We'll check the hives on the way back."

In high summer, the bee hollow flows with honey. The Walshes feast on rabbit and wild parsnips, cattail roots and dandelion greens, and for dessert, blackberries and mulberries, and honey. Honey raw on fingers. Honey thinned in ginger water, honey drizzled on the creamy, custardy insides of a ripe pawpaw.

Fall brings big game, but less honey. Winter is hunger season, and spring, near starvation. So the Walshes visit the bee hollow as often as they can in the summer. They have to be careful. If they damage the hives, the queens will fly away. They'll be left with nothing but sagging, empty honeycomb and the memory of sweet days lost.

When a crack rends the air, Liza jumps to her feet. She plucks Cade from the dust. As unfamiliar voices ring out, she stuffs Cade into a recess in the cliff. It's not quite a cave, just big enough to hide in.

A man says, "South by southwest."

"Quadrant clear," a woman replies.

Hands on Cade's shoulders, Liza leans over to whisper, "Stay here, baby."

Then she rushes outside. Moving as a team, she and Brendan dismantle their camp. The laundry comes down. They haul blankets made of leaves and vines from the underbrush. A hollowed rock rolls over their fire pit. They can do nothing about the smoke. Its sweet scent hangs in the air, but there will be no more white, wispy fingers curling toward the sky.

They don't stop to admire their work. Once the camp is erased, Brendan and Liza duck into the hiding place with Cade. Picking him up, Liza smooths his head against her shoulder.

Outside, two rangers tramp by. Their olive-and-khaki uniforms don't blend into the forest. They're highlighted against it. A streak of light glitters on their badges.

Murmuring, rocking, Liza tells Cade, "Don't ever let them see you, baby. They'll hurt you. They'll infect you."

Liza presses herself close to the mouth of the cave. The rangers hike on. She listens until she hears nothing but the forest. When the birds start to sing again, when the frogs join in, that's when it's safe to come outside again. Pushing aside the leafy camouflage that hides them, she turns back.

"We can't ever go back. They're all dying. We're the only ones who are safe. Remember that, Cade."

Cade's eyes are wide and frightened. He's four years old, and he understands that their forest is the only world that's left. When outsiders come through, and they almost never do, they're dangerous. They'll make him sick. Sick means he'll die. Cade's not sure he understands dead, but he knows it's bad.

Past the park rangers, who only hiked in to check on the big-eared bats living among the caves, past hikers trying to orient themselves to find the next trailhead; out of the woods and onto a highway, past cars on the road, and down a long highway—beyond a sign that says Makwa Town Limits, down the main street, into the heart of a town green.

Hundreds of people mill the square. Laughing. Eating fair food. Going from booth to booth, ducking helium balloons and stuffed animals tied in plastic. A little boy Cade's age throws a Ping-Pong ball and wins a goldfish. His parents curse under their breath; their neighbors smile and turn toward the band-stand.

Older boys cruise the festival. Their gangly gaits take them past clutches of girls who either watch them or pretend to eat their funnel cakes. Everyone is happy—young and old, diverse and energetic. They bask in the sun and share treats, and walk arm in arm, around and around.

What they are not is sick. They're not dying.

ONE

Watching two outsiders build a camp, Cade felt a particular hum run through him. It was a sting from the inside. It warmed him, conquering the cold that rose from the ground.

Below, an exotic, gold girl hammered stakes into the ground. Her hair bounced in a ponytail. Her clothes were green and blue and bright, and when she laughed, she threw her head back. Her front teeth were flat, and the canines jutted forward.

Cade wanted to touch her pink lips. Even though the cliff soared above the alien camp, he scented her. Sweetness, and flowers, but not the kind that grew near there. Mint, too, and something else he couldn't place. It was sharp. It burned his nose.

Quiet, Cade pressed his fingers into the cold, damp earth. Spring had come early—the timid, budding part of it. Just warm enough that the trees had knobs on them. Soon, they'd become buds, then tendrils, then leaves. The queen bees were waking their hives. Bears stumbled into the sunlight to break their fast.

And now, these outsiders. With their glowing skin and quick smiles, their strange clothes and music, they were alien. No uniforms like the rangers. No sickness that Cade could see. They weren't starving or desperate.

A hollow ache throbbed behind Cade's temple. He was supposed to be the last. The rest were dead. Or dangerous.

It was too big a thought to wrestle with. So Cade kept watching, noting the things that did make sense. The boy had his own scent. Sweat and more of the sharpness. Juniper and meat; it was overpowering. Cade wondered if they realized that everything in the forest could smell them.

"No, put the cooler in the little one," the boy said.

He pulled a box from his pocket, then tapped it until it chirped. It was too small to hold a bird, and that didn't make sense anyway. Why would he need a bird in a box? Why would he just stand there poking it?

The girl dragged a red-and-white cooler into a tent. Cade had a cooler hanging outside his cave. It was old, but the same color, the same shape. He kept fresh meat in it so he didn't have to eat pemmican and jerky and dried fish all the time.

Something cracked inside the tent, and Cade lifted his head.

When the girl came out again, she carried a silver can. Drinking from it, she wandered to the boy and leaned against his arm. Looking at the bird box in his hand, she frowned. "I was afraid of that."

"It's the cliffs," the boy said. "It'll be fine, we just have to climb or something."

The girl turned to look. She raised her face to the sky, then pointed at Cade. "Maybe there?"

Exhaling, Cade melted against the ground. He made himself flat, he made himself still. He watched the boy sweep his gaze all along the ridge.

The boy's jaw was broad, his shoulders, too. Solid and confident, the boy saw nothing at all. Then he slipped his arm around the girl and leaned down to kiss her neck.

Cade's sting turned to fire. There weren't supposed to be people left. Rangers . . . a few survivors maybe. He hadn't seen many, but now there were two, a half day's walk from his camp. One of them was beautiful.

The other one touched her, and Cade fought the urge to throw a rock at him. Instead, he pushed onto his hands and started a careful slide down the hill. Distracted by too-big thoughts, and red-hot emotions, he carelessly broke a branch on the way down.

"Did you hear something?" the girl asked.

The boy was quiet, then hummed. "Probably just a squirrel, Dara. I wouldn't worry about it."

Cade slipped into the trees, invisible on his light feet and in his warm, tanned furs. Cold seeped through his deerskin boots, though. Time to grease and cure them on the fire again.

A chore for later, when darkness fell. There was nothing in his cooler for dinner, so it would be jerky and roots if he didn't get back to hunting. Besides, he'd learned exactly enough about them.

The girl's name was Dara.

There were cornflakes everywhere. Dara let her hiking bag slip from her shoulder and stared at the chaos in camp.

The zippered doors on their food tent flapped. A river of half-melted ice and Diet Coke cans flowed out, mingling with empty cookie boxes. Rice dotted the ground, and a bottle of ketchup leaked from a mortal wound in its side.

"What happened?" Dara asked.

She answered her own question when she picked up the ketchup. A white haze of tooth marks surrounded the gaping hole. It wasn't broken open—it was bitten.

"I didn't know raccoons could work a zipper," Josh said. He knelt down to save their eggs. Then he groaned when they collapsed in his hand. Something had gnawed the end from each shell and sucked out its contents. It was fine, meticulous work. More complicated than opening a nylon tent, for sure.

Dara grabbed the latrine shovel. They didn't have a rake, so she scraped the grocery garbage toward their fire pit. "See how much is left. You're cute, but I'm not going to starve for you."

They could have been in Orlando. That's where the rest of the senior class was for spring break. Hanging out with their friends, riding rides, and eating food on sticks . . .

It wasn't hard for Dara to imagine her best friend, Sofia,

wearing souvenir ears and soaking up the sun. She'd probably come back with one of those photo key chains. Everybody smiling in it, wearing shorts and sandals instead of coats and boots.

But Josh had offered Dara an adventure. A place she'd never seen and probably never would again. Time alone, together, before senior year ended and they headed to different colleges.

The plan was simple. A real forest, untamed and unmonitored. Past the paths, into places found only on survey maps. She could take her beloved camera. Get pictures of mysterious, wondrous places.

When Dara was little, she camped with her parents. Though her memories were faint, they were fond. Wood smoke and hot dogs roasted on a fire. It didn't matter that her parents' tent stood twenty feet from the next one, pitched on grass. Or that she swam in an over-chlorinated pool instead of a lake. It was the wilderness to her.

So when Josh busted out the plan, she pulled his arm around her and said yes. They'd fought a lot lately. But the arguments were safe. About things and places, instead of feelings. The actual words flew over college plans that didn't match up. Dara wasn't interested in following Josh, and Josh didn't understand why his top pick wasn't good enough for her. Neither of them wanted to admit they'd changed since freshman year.

Back then, photography was a hobby for Dara, and Josh was still planning on saving the world. Now, she wanted to shoot the world and make great art. He wanted to get a business degree and specialize in finance.

Dara said yes to the trip because she wanted things to be okay. She said yes because thinking about the future was just too hard. It was hard to be happy on an expiration date. Running away was exactly what she wanted. What they needed. Their parents thought they'd be in Orlando, their friends would cover for them.

The weather agreed with them: go, be on the land. Be free, be outside. They left Makwa at dawn, stripping their jackets off first thing. It was unseasonably warm, and they didn't feel like sweating for the whole two-hour drive to the protected wilderness area.

They left Josh's truck in a parking lot near the easiest trailhead. Hefting bags and duffels, they stepped off the pavement and into an otherworldly paradise. Waterfalls cast mist and rainbows into the air. A few early flowers teased with color.

The trails grew steeper, and they had to strip their top layers to cool off.

According to the maps they'd downloaded, there was a good place to leave the trail just ahead. Dara hesitated, looking back at the dirt worn smooth, the way it wound through the forest. It wasn't an easy path, but it was visible.

"Come on," Josh said, tugging her pack straps. "Almost there."

With one last look at the known world, Dara followed him into the woods. There was less room to marvel as they struggled through underbrush and downed trees, unexpected sinkholes and cliffs that came out of nowhere. They pressed on, though, and around noon, they found their perfect campsite.

A high, mossy wall of sandstone shielded them to the north. A sloping expanse of forest surrounded them on the other three sides. They even had a foundation for their tents, smooth plats of rock revealed by eroded earth.

Though spring had only started, they had green-filtered shade during the day. Thin leaves and buds stretched for the sky above them. The river was a close walk, the clearing big enough to settle in.

But it was colder than they expected. They'd shivered through the last two nights. And the wildlife was more cunning. Dara plucked a pudding cup out of the mess. Some clever creature had peeled the lid from it. There wasn't a scrap of foil left on the edges.

Tossing that into a bag, Dara called to Josh, "How do they even know what's in a pudding cup?"

"They can smell it?"

"Through the plastic?"

Emerging from the tent, Josh presented her with a leaking honey bear. "Yep."

Dara rolled her eyes. "Put it in a bag and save it. Next time we go camping, we're getting a lock for the cooler."

"Next time?"

They both laughed. With a long step over the pile of trash Dara had collected, Josh slipped behind her. Binding her in his arms, he rubbed his face against her hair. Taller, a little possessive, he curled around her. His warm breath skated along skin, and she softened, leaning into him.

With a shrug, she let the shovel go. Tangling arms in his, she tipped her head against his shoulder and smiled. "I think we're really bad at this."

All their friends were in Orlando, but Dara decided she and Josh were having a much better time.

TWO

*H*er throat was smooth as a doe's. She was golden, her own light in the forest. That's what Cade thought as he trailed Dara to the river. And she was loud. That made her easy to follow.

Climbing from tree to tree, Cade stopped when Dara stopped.

It was as quiet as she had ever been in his woods. All day long, she sang or talked to the other one. They banged pans together. Music jangled inside the tent. At night, the other one drummed on empty pans, and Dara sang. When they were surprised, scared, delighted—anything, they filled the forest with sound.

Now, everything was quiet. Even the birds had settled pensively, and it seemed to put Dara on edge. Proof, Cade thought, that she wasn't oblivious. Her keen eyes darted along the tree line.

When he moved, she stilled—there was intelligence there. Sharp. Innate. The boy with her was blind to it all. But *she* knew something was in the woods. She realized something was following her. And he had been for a couple of days now.

Cade was fascinated by the way she moved over the land. She carried a box around her neck. It clicked when she held it to her face. Most of the time, she let it hang. But when a flash of color or shadow caught her eye, she followed it. Down ravines, into creek beds, beneath the old mill road that looked like nothing but stone arches from below now.

Fearless, curious, she had found the pond where the spring frogs had spawned. Hundreds of tadpoles squirmed in the water. She sank onto her side to watch them at play. It was a well-hidden watering hole, shielded by mossy rocks and overgrowth. Somehow—by listening? By looking?—Dara found it effortlessly.

Then she basked in it before she made her black box click. It was like she was filling herself with every long look. Drinking up details and secrets.

So Cade wasn't surprised when Dara stopped in the silence now, turning slowly within it. Her eyes keen, she searched all around her. Arms held wide to keep her balance, she breathed in relief when she finally made it all the way around. She hadn't seen anything on the ground, so she kept going.

That was a good way to get hurt or killed.

It was too early for snakes in the trees, but just the right time of year for bears. Coyotes, too, though they were more likely to spring between the trees than out of them. Cade might have been dangerous too, up in the canopy. He wasn't; all he wanted to do was study her.

The last woman Cade had seen was his mother. Dara was nothing like her. Mom had kept her hair in a thick brown braid. Her skin was brown, too, baked and freckled from the sun. And her eyes—she always looked up first when she heard an unfamiliar sound. Aware. That was the best way to describe her.

Dara wasn't aware, but she wasn't oblivious. She didn't hear Cade twist a hand in the thick bittersweet vines that clung to the oaks. She had no idea he ran above her head, anticipating her path. She never heard his feet, silent, running along thick branches as easily as she did the earth.

When she reached the river, she didn't know he watched the pale expanse of her neck as she bowed her head.

"Getting some water," she sang.

She pulled a huge water bladder off her shoulder, dumping it on the bank. Then, she walked back and forth, leaning down to look at the shore. She twisted the cap from the bladder. Tipping its mouth into the water, she frowned.

Puzzled, Cade slipped from his perch to a lower branch. His skins camouflaged him against the tree's trunk. If Dara looked up with the right eyes, she'd see him. But he was brown hair and deerskin against a dark and barely budding forest. He was hidden from her.

And it was better that way. She fascinated him, but she

frightened him, too. His mother had told him few of their kind remained. The ones that did were poison.

"Avoid them as if your life depends on it," she'd told him. "Because it does, my little wolf."

Dara didn't look like poison. She fascinated him; her lips were pretty. Her hands flashed like swimming fish when she talked.

But as he watched her gathering water, she confused him.

"Come on, come on," she muttered.

Her distress made no sense at first. Her lips moved. She talked to herself, just loud enough to hear. Bending, she splashed water at the mouth of her bottle, then sighed. It took him a moment to realize the bladder wasn't filling fast enough for her.

If she'd followed the silty riverbank a ways upstream, she would have found a deeper pool. Animals had trampled this bank smooth, creating shallows. It was obvious. Or it should have been.

More proof she didn't belong there. She should have known. Would have seen.

Unexpectedly, she stood. Peeling off her shoes, she stepped into the water. As soon as she did, she spun around, yelping. "Cold, cold, cold. Oh my god, so cold."

Cade couldn't help it. He laughed.

"Josh?" she called. She froze. Her eyes were sharp again. The wind carried her scent away. It made her hair wave, sunlight freckling her like a fawn. And this time, after she'd looked around, she looked up. "Where are you?"

Drawing a thin breath, Cade melted against the tree. He wore its nearly bare twigs for hair. Made his fingers knots, his back just a strange turn of trunk.

When her gaze burned across him, it lingered. He thought she might see him. Part of him wanted her to. To see that he was tall and strong. Smarter than the Josh crashing around at their camp.

But sadly, her gaze drifted by, and then she stopped playing. She waded deep enough to gather her water. Instead of singing or splashing, she stood. Throwing looks over her shoulders, she watched the underbrush. Even when she put her shoes back on, she peered east then west before hiking back to her tent and fire.

She had become aware.

Cade was disappointed. If she'd really belonged, she would have seen him.

He followed her through trees and treetops, all the way back to the clearing. Their tents huddled beneath the ridge, small and obvious in the open. Cade sat in an oak's forked arms, peeling spring green buds from the branches to chew.

"There's somebody else out here," Dara told Josh, the other one. She hung the bladder on a hooked branch, only a few feet below Cade.

"Where?"

Jerking a thumb over her shoulder, Dara said, "By the river. I heard someone laughing."

Crouched by the fire, Josh barely looked up from the embers. He pushed them with a stick. Little flames licked up, then sank into the glowing coals. He fed it no kindling, no air. He just stirred it like a raccoon.

"It was probably a bird," Josh said.

"I know the difference."

Josh gave up on his fire. He tipped back to sit on the ground and shook his head. "Maybe you imagined it. There's nobody out here for miles. That's the whole reason we came."

When he reached up to hook a finger in hers, Dara brushed his hand away. "It's a wilderness area, not the moon."

Cade leaned his head against the tree trunk and sighed. Dara was smart. Too smart for the other one. He couldn't even start a fire. When strange sounds crackled around him, he never looked up. Cade thought if a wolf walked into their camp, Josh would probably try to convince her it was a dog. Maybe he would try to feed it.

Smiling wryly, Cade melted into the shadows again. He listened. From below, Dara and Josh sounded perfectly normal. Not even a little sick. But, Cade reminded himself, he couldn't tell just by looking.

"It feels like the moon," Josh said. "I'm dying for a burger."

Dara hummed a neutral sound. Cade had heard his father do the same a hundred times. When Mom rambled too much about the outside world. When she got too vehement about the death and destruction that lay outside the forest. As far as Cade could tell, it was a sound that meant, "I hear you, but I'm not happy about it."

"You mad?"

Turning his head, Cade peered down from his perch. Dara

sat across from him, the fire between them. Holding her clicking box between both hands, she touched something that made it flash. Curious, Cade measured the forest around him, trying to decide if there was a way to get a better look at the light without being seen himself.

With a sigh, Josh hauled himself to his feet. "I'll get some more wood."

"You do that," Dara replied.

Now alone in the camp, Dara put the box aside. She didn't watch Josh walk into the coming dark. Instead, she stretched her legs, then her arms. She dragged herself closer to the fire. Its light gleamed in her hair. It gleamed on her skin, too, when she reached out to hold a hand above it.

Passing her fingers through the flame, she turned them, curled them. It was like she was daring it to burn her. Cade shifted his weight, and the branch groaned. Like that, Dara stiffened. This time, she did look up. Her gaze passed right over Cade and stopped.

A shadow lit on her brow. Leaning forward, she narrowed her eyes. Just when Cade was sure she'd spotted him, Josh crashed back into camp. He dumped a meager armful of wood on the ground. The logs drummed the dirt, silencing the forest around them once more.

"That'll do us for tonight, you think?"

Giving up her contemplation, Dara nodded. "I think so."

"Hey, c'mere," Josh coaxed. Brushing wood chips off his hands, he trailed his touch up her arms. Watching him touch her lit a different fire in Cade's skin. This one was swift and furious. His teeth felt molten and his stomach, too. For some reason, Dara pressed closer instead of pushing away.

Cade didn't understand it, but he knew he didn't like it. He liked it even less when Josh put his mouth on Dara's and clasped the back of her neck. She twisted her hands in his shirt; to Cade, it looked like she wanted to put space between them.

When Josh's hands slipped lower, Cade couldn't help himself. Cupping hands around his mouth, he keened like a hawk. The cry echoed, was answered. The forest rose up, other birds arguing. Squirrels rushed to safe perches. The owls would question soon. Their low, booming calls would go on and on.

Scrambling away, Cade didn't try to go quietly. He just went. Back to his home; back to the last safe place in the world. With nimble steps, he bounded through the narrow valley. A maze of grape vines hung like a wood curtain.

His path was nothing but a trace in the brush. Cade saw his own ghostly footsteps. Hints of him left behind in broken twigs and soft earth, leading to the cave he called home.

The red cooler swayed in the wind, the only evidence anyone lived there at all. Trees, full of beehives, hummed when he slipped past. They gave off heat, the faintest bit, because they were alive.

Cade found the mouth of his cave unerringly. The cool vault greeted him, sharp with just a hint of still-smoldering moss. Picking up the box that held his kindling, he breathed it back to life. It glowed as he started a new fire, illuminating the place where he lived. That fast. That easy. Josh was an idiot.

A rough-hewn table and chair stood nearby. There were

boxes, some with peg-locks, and a shelf to keep his few books dry. In the back, a carved bed frame held a thin mattress off the ground.

Fir branches sweetened the mattress from below. Tanned deerskin and beaver pelts covered it. It was stuffed with goose down. Cade needed to get more to fill it out. Once this season's goslings were hatched and grown, he'd do just that.

But for the moment, he satisfied himself with dinner and pride. Pulling two thick fish from his pack, he wrapped them in wet hide and laid them on the fire. He stepped over the pit, trailing his fingers through the shell chime he'd made. It was a little bit of music, and if he got it started, the heat from the fire would keep it going.

Sprawling in the light, he reached for his clay animals. He'd lost the giraffe years ago, but he still had a cat and a bear. Holding them over his head, he turned them until they cast giant shadows on the wall behind him. With just a trick of the light, they came to life.

First, he made the cat chase the bear. He swirled it in lazy circles, its shadow growing and shrinking by turn. Then the bear fought back, chasing the cat until it was tiny and disappeared. Tucking the cat into his shirt, Cade savored its stone coolness against his skin.

The bear, he held over his head, studying it by the light of the fire. Pressed into one side was a faint fingerprint. Its whorls had smoothed over time, now barely visible. But Cade knew it was there. Fitting his finger into the impression, he discovered that it fit now. His hands were as big as his father's.

His gaze trailed back to the little cairn by the wall. It was just smooth stones, stacked together. Behind it, he'd scraped figures into the wall. A woman, a man, a boy. He'd drawn it right after Dad died, on his first night completely alone. Handprints surrounded the figures, painted with wet ashes that same night.

That was such a long time ago. Twelve seasons, at least. All those days and months and years alone. His own company was starting to drive him crazy. Tucking the bear figure into his shirt, Cade turned back to his fire. The fish crackled; they would be delicious.

While he waited for his dinner, the stone animals weighed on his heart. They cooled his skin and turned his thoughts deliberate.

He made a deal with himself. If Dara and Josh were fine by the full moon. If their eyes were still clear, their skin smooth. No coughs or sneezes or spots—maybe then, he'd walk into their camp and say hello.

His parents wouldn't like it. But his parents hadn't been there for a while. Maybe it was time to make some decisions of his own.

THREE

*S*ince he hadn't slept much, Josh found it easy to wake before dawn.

He crept from the tent in his boxers. Instantly chilled, Josh slapped his chest for warmth, then scrubbed his arms with his hands. Though it had been cold other mornings, it shouldn't have been on this one. He was sure of that enough to roll out without getting dressed.

He approached the fire pit, looking for an explanation, and groaned. Black and cold, the embers had died.

Which was deeply unfair. Because instead of dumping water on it last night, Josh had left it burning. There wasn't an open fire or anything. The flames had faded to an orange glow in the ashes.

Since they'd built the pit up with stones, Josh felt safe leaving it. The river rocks kept the sparks in, and it had been raining a little at night. If the wood was too wet to start the fire in the first place, they weren't gonna burn the forest down. He was getting a head start on morning, he reasoned.

Or not. The pit was so dead, it didn't even smoke. An acidic smell wafted from it, though. Slapping his chest again, Josh returned to the tent to get dressed. Sweatshirt, jeans . . . He pulled the latter on, then lay back on his bedroll. Shifting to face Dara, he smiled. Her hair threaded across her face. It wavered when she breathed.

With a careful touch, he smoothed it away.

Lashes flickering, Dara crinkled her nose, but she didn't wake up.

When she was awake, she was gorgeous. Bright and loud, and too smart for him. Since she didn't care, he tried not to. But every so often, she'd go off about something and he'd wish he had a Wikipedia chip in his head.

She wasn't perfect. She was insanely bossy, and sometimes lost in her own world. That evened it out, some.

But right now, when she was asleep, she was beautiful. Quiet and elegant, even. Not just her face. The way she curled her fingers in her T-shirt. The perfect angle of her eyelashes, sort of golden, sort of brown. The roundness of her knee, tenting the sleeping bag as she slept.

He loved her. Most of the time, it was a regular feeling, a ticking clock in the background. Steady. Reliable.

Here, in the forest, on their own? With no one watching, and nothing between them—when the only, best thing he had to do all day was look at her and listen to her laugh? It was a roar. A storm inside him, distant and immediate at the same time.

How his skin contained it, he didn't know. But he kissed her shoulder, and rolled to his feet at once. He needed a breath, some cold air. Space. With one last look, he ducked outside. He felt bigger. Stronger.

Grabbing his pack, he squared his shoulders. Time to conquer the fire.

Dara peeked out the tent window, then curled up again.

Bright and frigid, dawn transformed the forest. It was too cold for dew. Instead, there was fog. It made silhouettes of the trees and softened the sunlight. A blue cast hung in the air, darkened by smoke.

Metal tapped against metal by the fire—Josh making breakfast. Instead of sliding from her sleeping bag, Dara burrowed deeper. Warmth washed around her. The red nylon tent filtered morning to a pleasant crimson glow, but she hid from it.

Sleeping late was part of a vacation. She wasn't ready to strip in the cold, and she didn't want to do it by the fire. Even if Josh wasn't, *she* was convinced. They weren't alone in these woods. Not the way Josh thought they were.

Anyone was allowed to hike into the wilderness area and camp.

Last summer, she and Josh had hiked a short stretch of the Appalachian Trail. They walked miles of beautiful solitude, but they weren't alone. No matter how far they got from town, no matter how far between stations, there were still people.

Stubbornly, to herself, she insisted. She heard somebody laughing at the river.

And that weird bird scream last night . . . Every single horror movie she'd ever seen came to mind. Strangers lurking in the dark. Getting lost in the woods. Girls running through backlit trees, tripping at the worst possible moment.

Of course Josh laughed it off. He was six five, athletic, and oblivious. He'd never parked his car under a light so he wouldn't have to unlock it later in the dark. When Dara carried her keys with one spiking between her fingers, he thought she was playing Wolverine. Josh wasn't oblivious on purpose. He was just fearless in a way she never could be.

The tent zipper sang, and Josh slid inside. "I have cocoa."

"Really?" Sitting up, Dara let the sleeping bag bunch at her waist. She took the mug, warming her hands on it.

With a sweet smile, Josh sank next to her. His eyelashes glinted in filtered sunlight. The red glow from the tent made his eyes seem lavender instead of pale blue. Stealing a kiss, he said, "And I knocked the spiders out of your boots."

Dara wasn't afraid of them, but Josh was. Melted by cocoa and gallantry, Dara leaned into him. Dipping cold fingers down the front of his shirt, she pulled him closer and thanked him with another kiss.

Last night's irritation had passed. She felt more than a little guilty, because even she could tell she vacillated between come-here and go-away with him. In her head, it was an irrational carousel that turned and turned. We're together, we're in love;

we're doomed, this time is wasted.

And even now, it turned again. He was warm and tempting, but they only had so much daylight in the forest. She'd come to the wild to be with him, but also to capture it with her camera. The forest had so many secrets; if she could just catch them, print them with light . . .

Gently breaking away, she said, "Mmm, okay, I have to get dressed now."

"Go ahead."

"I will as soon as you let yourself out."

"You sure?"

"Josh," Dara said, warning.

Amused, he sighed and rolled away. On his feet and already at the tent door, he looked back. "Because if you're not sure . . ."

"Can you get the extra batteries out of the cooler, please?" she asked, changing the subject. "I don't want to miss anything this time."

Stepping into the cold, Josh pushed his head through the tent flap to smile at her. "You're never going to get over that, are you?"

Dara shook her head. She had no pictures from their day trip to the Appalachians. All because of a pair of dead Duracells. The camera had hung heavy in her bag, chastising her with every step. This time, she had a pack of forty batteries in the cooler and eight more in her jacket. Just in case.

It didn't take long to dress, or to bolt down the sparse break-fast. She filled their canteens while Josh hauled the cooler into the tree. It dangled listlessly against the trunk, like it had fallen out of a plane and gotten stuck. But it was up high now, and tied with bungee cords. The raccoons would have to find dinner somewhere else.

With their camp secured, Josh and Dara set off for the falls. The woods were sweetly manipulative. They tempted with strange and beautiful sights. Dew clung to a spiderweb canopy, a veil of diamonds overhead. New vines crept up the trees. Old, thick ones dangled from above.

And then, the forest opened.

Dara put her camera case on a mossy log. She couldn't tear her eyes away. They stood at the foot of a cliff. It was obvious on the topological maps, but maps hadn't prepared them for the sight.

The stone rose in curved walls, thirty feet high, at least. They were shaped like a horseshoe. No, a broken bowl, and she and Josh stood in the open end. It was like a giant had dropped a bowl in the forest, and the forest had grown in around it.

White, lacy water spilled over the far edge, a perfect waterfall. It filled a pool, never smooth, never glassy. Above, spindling trees stretched toward the sky and left a clearing in the middle to reveal it. Fog lingered above the water, and early frogs peeped in their hollows.

"A gate to Avalon," Dara murmured.

A scarlet bird burst into the air. It didn't cry out. Just streaked from beneath the stone ceiling and disappeared.

"Look at that," Josh replied.

He let his pack slip from his shoulders. It made a good chair, and he stared into the alcove. Pulling his phone out, he held it above his head. There was still no signal. The stone probably blocked it.

Freeing her camera from its case, Dara edged the pool carefully. There was so much to capture there. Too much. She angled up, stopped to focus on velvety moss and water-smoothed ledges. Then, down with the macro lens, to capture the fine sheet of ice lining the walls.

Despite the cold, she shed her shoes and waded into the pool. Not to get wet, but to get a picture of the mist in the air, and the water spilling into the pond. Aching from the frigid water, her toes curled over stones beneath the surface. The camera sang, clicking again and again.

It didn't stop—she couldn't stop. Not until she had the picture. The perfect moment. The gate to Avalon, captured forever. Everything else, home and camp, the noises in the woods and even Josh, fell away.

She was alone in the world with this strange altar to nature, and her camera.

As he checked his traps Cade chewed a sweet gum twig. It cleaned the night-taste out of his mouth. His mother said it protected his teeth, too, but he didn't know from what. Every day, he did things she'd taught him.

Mixing ash with fat for soap. Rubbing crushed yarrow on his cuts and burns. Chewing willow leaves when he hurt.

His head was full of practical things. And the rabbit skin pouch at his waist was full of early herbs and greens. Dandelion shoots and parsnips, mostly. He broke into a smile when he found a patch of field garlic. Before he pulled it up, he stopped to study the land.

He wasn't the only creature who ate greens. Better to let the rabbits have it, and then have the rabbits. As soon as spring bloomed, he'd have to leave the animals alone for a while. They needed time to grow their families and to grow fat.

But this garlic, and the trails of it that disappeared into the underbrush, lay untouched. No pellets or scat nearby. The tree trunks bore no marks from nibbling deer. So Cade claimed it for himself, then hiked on to his traps.

The woods were quiet, but not silent. Birds sang this morning. Daredevil squirrels flung themselves from tree to tree. Just at the top of the hill, a doe quivered. Alert, she slowly turned her head. She bolted. Wind whispered, trees crackled.

And Cade's own footsteps rattled through dry leaves and underbrush. No need to be stealthy today. Dara and the other one had hiked to the pool.

It made him anxious. They were in his forest. He knew they were there, all the paths they walked on. They touched things, and left their scents everywhere. They weren't like the rangers who sometimes appeared. The ones who took samples of the water, and the earth.

When he was little, Cade had to hide when the rangers came. His mother insisted on it. She tucked him in caves, in burrows, and once inside a hollowed tree. She would whisper, "Shh, shh," and wait for them to go.

Dad followed the rangers when they moved away from the camp. Then he and mother would pack their things. That night, always that very night, they moved. Up the ridge or down it. Sometimes into the stone ruins left by ancient people. Never into the ruined hunting lodges or old mining town.

"Too many people remember these are here," Mom explained.

It was the truth. Cade knew because he remembered where they were. When he was little, he loved to sneak back to them. Though the forest had swallowed the edges, the spaces between, Cade could still see the town in it. The houses fascinated him. They had windows. They had doors.

In one house, the floor had rotted away. It revealed a cellar, and in that cellar, people's things. A doll, its face marred by crackled paint. Photographs faded close to nothing. In a fine box, he found a half-rotted Bible. Most of the pages were ruined, slick with mold. But he could make out spidery handwriting inside the back cover. Names. Jedediah and Hepzibah. Ann and Charles. Mary and Oren.

There were lives in that town. Their ghosts filled the ivy-choked walks, drifted through crumbling walls. This wasn't the world his parents had described. It was an antique version of it. No Mustangs or telephones in the mining town. No televisions or escalators. He had the hardest time imagining an escalator.

Once, with a bit of charcoal, his father drew stairs to explain. His mother described the belts and the pulleys underneath them. The motor that made them go. She claimed the stairs would flatten into a metal band at the top. That gears would pull it inside. Then it would reappear at the bottom to turn into a step again.

"But how?" Cade asked.

His parents exchanged a look, then shrugged. He'd asked for more than they knew. It happened a lot. More as he got older.

Though they both swore escalators were real, he never quite believed them. And it didn't matter anyway. They claimed it was all gone. Forgotten, just like a mining town in a forest. Just like him.

A small scream jolted Cade from his memories. The cool air wrapped around him, the cool earth pressing from below. Winding down an uneven slope, he found a rabbit in his snare. It was fat, its fur shimmering in shades of brown and grey. Paws beat at the air. Black eyes darted, wild and frightened.

Cade picked it up with both hands, and gently turned it over. He stroked his thumb over its belly, then sighed. There was a litter in there already. He pulled out his knife, and cut the snare. Setting the animal free, he smiled ruefully.

No rabbit for dinner, and probably not for a while. Fish would have to do, and if he got lucky, he might find a wild hog. They rooted mercilessly, devoured turkey eggs, gobbled down roots and greens. It was never a bad time to take down a wild hog, and the meat would last if he cured it. The salt lick wasn't far; it would be worth the trip if he took down a hog. It would get him through till summer. His stomach rumbled in anticipation.

But maybe soon he'd walk into Dara's camp and say hello. Maybe she would feed him from her pot, and sit next to him. Close to him.

Maybe, beneath the full moon, he'd find out what color her eyes were.

FOUR

Morning glow flooded through the walls of the tent.
Rolling over in the sleeping bags, Josh pulled a pillow over his head. He disappeared beneath the nest of bedding with a grunt. It didn't look like he planned to get up for a while, so Dara dressed quietly. Jeans, boots, sweatshirt, jacket—and lots of batteries. The zipper rumbled as she eased it open.

Several times now, she'd had the sensation that she wasn't alone in the woods. At camp or nearby, there was no way to prove that she wasn't just noticing Josh's presence in the forest. Pulling the topo map out of Josh's pack, she unfolded it by the banked fire for a quick look.

The river where she'd heard the laughter wasn't far. Then there was the tadpole pond. She hadn't heard anything there, not exactly. It just felt like something—someone—had been nearby. A couple of times at the camp now, too. Josh could blow it off all he wanted.

And since he wasn't interested in investigating it, she could do it herself.

Twice, something had drawn her attention by the water. That made sense—another camper would need to refill his canteens, too. Orienting herself by compass and map, Dara looked into the forest. Pale light filtered through the canopy, just streaks of it. Just enough light to make her feel confident.

Stepping on one of the logs they'd dragged to the fire, she opened the cooler in search of something breakfasty. The animals had already eaten the tastiest, easiest things. No yogurt, no pudding, not even a hot dog that she'd shamelessly eat cold since Josh wasn't awake to give her a hard time about it.

Fishing around, she produced a bag of dried apricots. Little, fleshy disks that sat fuzzily on her tongue. The sensation made her shudder, but it was better than hiking off on an empty stomach. Slinging the water jug across her chest, she took one last look at the camp before setting off. It was so peaceful. No alarm clocks or honking horns. No banging cabinets or garage doors grinding open.

Wind through leaves, and birds in trees—that's what made a morning in the forest. Almost out of reflex, Dara raised her camera and took a shot or six. Unremarkable photos, but they'd be memories. This is what serenity looks like. As much as she enjoyed hot and cold running water, the internet, walls, there was something about this place that made her feel whole.

As Dara started into the woods, her eyes flickered from color to color. On the other side of a fallen log she heaved herself over, red bloomed across the forest floor. A field of mushrooms had sprung up overnight. With thick red caps and white spots, they looked straight out of Wonderland.

Dara sank to her knees. Slinging the canteen around to her back, she picked up her camera. Crawling through the moss, she ignored the cold seeping through her jeans. There was a long column of light streaking through the trees. If she could line the mushrooms up with it just so . . .

Dignity would have to wait for another day. Dara slid onto her belly to find the right angle. The fresh, clean beam suddenly filled her viewfinder. A flare danced in the corner while she adjusted her settings. Now lying almost flat, she had an upward view of the mushrooms. The sun rose behind them. They seemed mighty, scarlet giants in perspective.

Her heart pounded, a wild, fluttering beat that rushed blood to her ears, and into her fingers and toes. She tingled everywhere, drunk and dazed on pictures she couldn't have taken anywhere else. That's what photography was to her. The essence of it, the soul: discovering unseen things and revealing them. Though she knew she could probably find thousands of pictures of these toadstools online, none of them would look like hers. This was her moment, a place in space and time that no one had ever seen but her.

"Eat me," Dara murmured, firing off shot after shot. "Was that to get small or big?"

She made a mental note to look it up when she got home.

— —

Up early to collect ice from sheltered water, Cade stopped when he heard Dara's voice. Grabbing a supple hickory branch, he scaled the tree swiftly. Its budding leaves didn't rustle around him so much as whisper. They weren't big enough yet to provide cover.

Moving carefully along the branches, Cade resisted the urge to grab hold of the bittersweet vines left from last year. Usually, they were sturdy enough to carry his weight. They were better for swinging out over lakes and jumping into deep waters than anything else. But when the branches were big enough, aligned enough, he could zip from tree to tree. It was still too early in the season, though.

Sometimes, the only things keeping the vines up were the shoots that tangled through the trees' canopies. Once fall claimed those, the vines were dangerous. Without warning, they could snap, and he'd plummet into whatever lay below. Usually, it was brush.

Once, memorably, it had been a sharp bit of quartz jutting from the ground. It sliced through his flesh as cleanly as any knife.

His mother had sewed that wound closed with a fish-bone needle and thread she pulled from a worn shirt. Even now, Cade instinctively reached up to touch the scar that furrowed across his scalp. That was a lesson learned the hard way.

The tick-tick-tick of Dara's box acted as a guide. Walking well above the ground, Cade almost passed over her. Only the ticking box stayed him. Curling his toes into the branch, he held on with one hand and leaned over the clearing above her.

Today, instead of tadpoles, it was mushrooms that delighted her. When she reached out to stroke one, he tensed. They were pretty, but poisonous. He collected them in the hottest part of summer to keep the flies away. Chopping them into bits, he left them in bowls of walnut milk. Flies swarmed them, drank, and drowned. It was too bad there was nothing that worked like that on the mosquitoes.

He almost spoke to warn her, but she took her hand back at the last moment. Relieved, Cade pressed his lean body against the trunk of the tree. He didn't understand the ticky box. Or why he kept catching her with it, staring so hard at things in the forest.

But when she put it aside, she always took a few minutes more. Trailing her fingers through the tadpole pond; petting the mushroom with a gentle touch. It was more and more obvious to Cade that she wasn't sick. And she was a little bit like him. She saw things with keen eyes.

As if to prove it, Dara suddenly arched her back. The sun reflected off a bit of glass in her box, the telltale ticking a threat in the quiet. Exhaling all of his breath, Cade closed his eyes and tried to disappear against the tree's bark.

Not yet, he wasn't ready to say hello yet. He wanted to—he was close. But he was waiting for the full moon. That was the rule he made for himself. He was going to honor it. Saying hello at all broke so many of his parents' rules, he couldn't stand the idea of shattering one more.

After a moment, Dara stopped squinting into the tree. She put her box down and brushed the dirt off her chest. Then, consulting a sheaf of paper, she hiked on into the forest. This time, though, she looked back—and she looked up. His pulse raced; he bit his own lips because he didn't dare move.

Perhaps she wasn't aware yet, but almost.

When Josh had gone to sleep, everything was fine. When he woke up, he was alone. And when Dara got back from her picture hike, everything went to pieces.

Josh heard Dara before he saw her. Running through a forest wasn't quiet. It sounded like she'd slipped at the top of a hill and was hitting every tree on the way down. The only reason he didn't panic was because she was yelling at the same time.

"Josh! Josh, look! Josh!"

Standing slowly, Josh dumped his stick in the flames. His stomach twisted with hunger. Since they had to ration everything out, breakfast for him was a cup of instant coffee, four Twizzlers he found in his coat pocket, and some peanut butter scraped onto crackers. They had canned stew and chili; those had to wait for dinner.

He felt like one of those starving cartoon dogs, looking around and seeing nothing but T-bone steaks. If they'd started hiking out after breakfast, they could have been in the truck no later than two. Any town in any direction would have a diner or a drive-through, and he could have that burger he'd wished for last night.

He could just imagine Dara's face if he suggested it. She'd gnaw off her own arm before she gave up a place full of so many pictures. Though he kept it to himself, Josh thought all the pictures looked pretty much the same. A really big butterfly in one shot still looked like a really big butterfly in another. She insisted what she was doing was art.

Dara finally came into view. She held her camera above her head and stared at her feet as she ran. Probably not the best plan, but it seemed to work for her. Gasping for breath, she all but stumbled into camp. Red splotches darkened her cheeks. Sucking in a deep breath, she went to say something, but doubled over instead.

"Dara?"

"Cramp. Oh, oh god, cramp."

Helpfully, Josh said, "Walk it out. What's going on with you?"

Circling the fire, Dara inhaled, then flapped her hands as she exhaled. It looked like she was trying to learn how to breathe and talk at the same time. When the words finally came, they spilled out in a rush. "I was right. You were wrong. There's somebody out here besides us."

"How does that make me wrong? I said it was probably hikers."

"No." Shaking her head, Dara stripped off the canteen and her pack. Each step staggered, she fumbled her camera before righting herself. Exhaling like a horse, she flipped the screen toward him. Thumbing through her pictures, she jittered when she reached one. She almost took his nose off when she thrust the camera at his face. "Look. Look."

Leaning over, Josh squinted. He saw a mash of brown and touches of green, some wavy motion lines, some sunlight. She said he had a bad eye for details. It pissed him off, but there was no point fighting her about it. Once Dara decided she was right, that was it.

Kinda like then. She kept shuffling and huffing. Annoyance came off her in waves. It was like it was killing her to wait for him to get it. Digging in, Josh raised the camera to his face. Inwardly, he bristled but he finally had to give up. He rolled his head to look at her.

"I don't get it. It's just some trees."

Dara jabbed her finger at the screen. "No. Right there. That. That's somebody in the trees, Josh. Wearing, like, I don't know, camouflage? It didn't look like camouflage."

Now that he knew what he was supposed to see, Josh looked again. It shouldn't have been hard. When she pointed out the shapes of rabbits and dragons in the clouds, he noticed. When she shoved a picture under his nose to show him the old woman's face in the bark of a tree, he saw it.

But there was nothing on this screen except blurry trees. Telling her that was gonna start an argument, so he hedged. "Maybe. It's blurry."

"I told you," she exclaimed.

Stomach growling, Josh handed back the camera. "So what? It's a free country. He can be out here if he wants to be."

"That's the thing," Dara said, turning away from him. "I don't think he's just camping."

Since she couldn't see him, Josh rolled his eyes. "Why not?"

"His clothes, for one." Dara stepped onto the log, and started rooting through the last of their supplies. "And he's quiet. I don't think we're that quiet out here, do you?"

Josh thought he might be, but she sure wasn't. Shrugging, he sat down by the fire again. Propping his booted feet on the rocks, he toasted them until he smelled the leather. "I have no idea, Dare."

"Josh, come on."

"What?"

"I'm telling you that there's some guy living in the trees out here, following us, and you're all huh huh huh, no idea, Dare."

Nostrils flaring, Josh dropped his feet and leaned over the fire. "What do you want me to say? I don't know. I don't even see anything. And I think it's hilarious that you think you do see something, and you're not screaming at me to take you home."

"Why would I do that?"

Sarcastic, Josh said, "I don't know. I'd be kinda scared if the ghost-footed monkey-stalker was following me around the woods."

Dara's face fell. Wrapping her arms around herself, she looked like she was trying to shrink, which always made Josh feel like crap. Even though she was blonde and sunny, she could turn dark on him.

Pursing her lips, she glared off into the distance. "Why do you have to be like this?"

Wrenching himself to his feet, Josh snatched up the big canteen that she hadn't even bothered to fill while she was out.

"I'm gonna go get some water," he informed her coldly.

"I am not crazy," she called after him.

Josh was going to have to respectfully, and silently, disagree.

FIVE

Cade woke early.

Yesterday, he'd done something stupid. So stupid that it crept into his head and poisoned his dreams. They had tumbled end over end through the night, waking him long enough to worry, then dragging him into the depths again.

Snatches of his parents' faces melted into shadows. The tick-tick of Dara's box pursued him. Fire swept through his camp; it devoured everything in the cave. His figures swelled and shattered in the heat.

The morning's rain was a relief after a whole night of burning. It deadened his footsteps, not that he had to sneak up on the river. Still in the shadow of the big trees, the water was frigid to the touch. Silvery fish darted in the deepest part, and that's what Cade had come for. Pulling his knife from his belt, he re-sharpened the tip of his gig.

Sitting all day with hooks in the water was fine in the hottest part of summer. But in the colder months, gigging was a better bet. As long as he was faster than the sluggish fish, he could take care of a whole day's meals in an hour.

He'd cut down a green maple branch a little thicker than his thumb. He stripped the bark to make it smooth, then whittled two points onto one end. With careful strokes of the knife, he shaped them. Then he reinforced the joint with long strips of leather to keep it from splitting. The gig looked like a two-pronged spear. That's how Cade hefted it as he walked the bank of the river.

The water hissed, splashing on the banks. Cold seeped through the air, and into Cade's clothes. Even as he steadied himself, his thoughts started to swim. Dara had seen him. That's not how it was supposed to go at all. He hadn't made a sound. Not a broken branch, not a foot out of place. But somehow, she knew to look up, and she saw him.

Cade balanced the gig, then plunged it into the water. It bounced uselessly off a rock. The vibration went all the way up his arm, and ached into his shoulder. Readying the gig again, he tried to clear his thoughts. Though he saw his prey, he hesitated. His mind was just too scattered. He couldn't wait for the full moon now. Or could he? Maybe it was time to change camp.

When he was little, his parents changed camp every couple of weeks. Or, if the rangers strayed too close, there was another move immediately. That was how they stayed safe, his mother insisted. Usually, they circled out from the bee hollow, which was too rich to give up. But it was a big circle, sometimes a whole day's walk and back.

Even after Mom died, they kept moving. Just the two of them, until Dad got sick. He was pale for a long time. After long walks, his lips would turn bluish.

"Just getting old," Dad would say with a smile. "Try not to do it. I don't recommend it."

Always, Cade smiled back. "I won't. I'll live forever."

"You keep thinking that."

Each time Dad said it, it sounded more and more forlorn. Before Cade's eyes, he grew thin, the shape of his skull beneath his skin uncomfortably obvious. Without Mom to insist, they stayed in one place a whole summer, a whole autumn, a whole winter.

Slowly, Cade took over all the hunting, all the gathering. By the time spring came, he did everything but tan the deerskin and cook the meals. Dad could do those without getting up. The tanning left him breathless, but he refused to give it up.

Until he gave up everything. One rainy day, he pulled a fur over his head to catch the heat as he sat by the fire. He closed his eyes and soon was dozing. It wasn't until Cade went to wake him that he realized that the sleep was permanent.

Stunned, Cade lay beside him that whole day, and that whole night. He understood that Dad was dead. That he wouldn't be coming back. They had buried his mother together; he'd hunted enough animals. Death wasn't a mystery to him, but solitude was. He knew as soon as he put his father in the ground that he'd be alone. Completely. Marooned in an empty, devastated world.

The next morning, Cade didn't hunt. He went to the river and cut down huge bundles of cattails. He didn't have time to cut a tree and carve it into a box. So Cade wove two long mats from the reeds, then sewed them together with leather. He tried not to cry as he slid his father's body into it. He was so cold. So heavy. It was almost a relief to sew the top of the mats closed, because then he didn't have to look at Dad's empty face anymore.

By himself, he dragged Dad down to the cairn where they'd buried Mom. He scraped away the dirt beside her to make room. His fingers bled, because he had to dig deep. Animals had keen senses; if the grave was too shallow, they'd find it and unearth it.

Tears slicked Cade's face, as he pulled the body in, covered it with his fir-branch mattress and a full deerskin. Then dirt, then rocks, like he had to weigh him down to keep him beneath the ground.

Without words, Cade stumbled back to the cave. Mixing water into ashes, he darkened his face then pressed handprints to the wall, as high as he could reach, as far back as he could. It was endless, mindless—something to think about so he wouldn't have to think about his father. His family.

He broke his mother's first rule, because he never left that camp again. When he couldn't sleep, he counted the hand-prints. When he was lonely, they kept him company. Bit by bit, the camp became permanent. Only now, Dara had seen him. Now, instead of walking into her camp, she might stroll into his.

Because last night he did something stupid. The full moon had seemed so far away that he sought out their camp to listen to their voices. Instead, he heard them argue: Dara knew he was here. The idiot Josh refused to listen to her.

His voice, his attitude—they infuriated Cade. He knew what love looked like. His parents had it. They never raised their voices. Even when they disagreed, they spoke thoughtfully. They worked things through, together. Dad never would have spoken to Mom the way Josh did to Dara.

So, angry, Cade decided to prove Josh wrong once and for all. He cut one of the carved antler pendants from his shirt. His favorite one, the one with two bees on ivy. It was his finest bit of carving, rich and lifelike on the creamy buff interior of the antler. Pulling a thin length of leather from his kit, he threaded it through the pendant and tied it off.

Then, when they were sleeping, he walked into their camp. Planting a stick in the soft ground, he hung the pendant from it. Left it there, dangling, for them to find. He was all the way back to his own camp when he realized what he'd done. What he'd really done—not taught Josh a lesson, no.

He'd told two strangers, two dangerous strangers, that he was there. He was real. Now, instead of idly stalking Dara, he felt like prey. That's why the nightmares came. That's why he couldn't settle his thoughts. Usually the rain soothed him, but not this morning. This morning, he was raw and exposed. And what if he was infected?

That thought distracted him so much that he missed the next two throws.

The whisper of rain on nylon woke Dara.

A fresh, green scent filled the air, but it was cut with something bitter. The smell was familiar, but still half-asleep, Dara had a hard time placing it. The light didn't glow through the sides of the tent this morning. Dara shifted, stroking her hand through the sleeping bags to find her sweatshirt. She pulled it over her head.

Breath hazing in the air, she considered going back to sleep. The best pictures would come after the rain, when droplets still hung from leaves and spiderwebs; when water flowed down surprise falls. But she'd let the cold into her sleeping bag, and now she was hungry.

"You want breakfast?" she asked Josh. She prodded his shoulder, but he rolled over and burrowed deeper. "Guess not," she mumbled as she picked up her boots and knocked them together. Nothing living in them, so she shoved them on her feet. Without bothering to tie them, she ventured outside.

She pulled her sweatshirt's hood over her head. The rain was more a mist, but it gathered on the leaves above, and fell in fat splashes. As soon as Dara approached the fire pit, her nostrils burned. Now that she stood over the source, she knew exactly what the smell was: wet ash.

That was a problem. They had some dry wood in the tent, but she didn't know if she could get a new fire going while it was still raining. In fact, she wasn't sure she could start a fire at all.

She didn't know where the matches were, and she wasn't sure where Josh had stashed the newspaper they used for kindling.

Disappointed, Dara straightened up to consider her options. And when she did, she saw it: a stake in the ground, straight and deliberate. A chill streaked up her spine. She hadn't put it there, and neither had Josh, she was sure of it.

With deliberate steps, she approached the stake. Something dangled from it; when she crouched down, she realized it was a necklace. Gingerly touching the pendant, she shivered again. Two bees swirled around an ivy leaf on the disk. When she rubbed it, it felt warm, strangely alive. Definitely not wood or stone. She wondered if it was bone.

Her breath slipped out of her. This was proof. She wasn't crazy. She might have missed the shot, but she'd definitely seen someone in that tree. And that someone knew where she and Josh were camping. Suddenly burning from the inside out, she snatched the necklace from the stake. Stumbling to the tent, she nearly fell into it as she tried to unzip it.

"Josh," she said, kneeling down to shove him. "Josh, wake up. Look at this."

"What?"

Thrusting the pendant at Josh, she refused to let it go. She didn't know why, but she felt possessive about it. Like it was meant for her alone. Still, she had to let him look at it, otherwise he'd never believe her. "He was in the camp last night. He left this by the fire."

That woke Josh up. Without hesitation, he sat up and craned to look outside the tent. He'd gone from sleepy to bristling in an instant. "What the hell? Dara, we're leaving. Let's start getting this stuff together."

Dara surprised herself when she said, "No."

"Wait, what?"

"No," she repeated. Tugging the necklace away from him, she tucked it in her pocket. "I'm not afraid. I'm curious. I mean, if he wanted to hurt us, he could have slit our throats last night while we were sleeping."

"That's real comforting."

"That's the point," Dara said, scrambling back to her feet. "He didn't. And I told you, there was something about him. The way he walked, his clothes . . . I don't know what it is. But I want to find out more. What if he lives out here? What if he's got a story to tell?"

Setting his jaw, Josh glared at her. "What if I tell you I'm packing my stuff and you can stay out here on your own?"

That sounded like an ultimatum. If she'd had doubts about staying, that would have burned them away completely. Since she didn't, all it did was fire her resolve. "Go for it," she said. "Have fun explaining to my dad why I didn't make it home *from Orlando* with you."

There was just enough threat in that. Josh said nothing. Instead, he turned over in his sleeping bag. Punching the pillow a couple of times, he dropped his head into it. Pointedly, he put his back to her, and pulled his hoodie over his head.

Fine. If that was how he wanted it, then that was okay by her. Grabbing an extra pair of socks and an extra sweatshirt, she ducked out of the tent again. Heading for the water had worked yesterday, so that's what she would try today. Somebody was out there, and he wanted her to find him.

So that's exactly what she was going to do.

The pile of fish on the riverbank grew.

After a while, sheer cold had quieted Cade's mind. Once he had silence inside and out, he found his balance again. His body remembered how to do this. He found a regular, steady pleasure in forgetting everything and just working.

Still, he should have stopped three fish ago. He could only eat so much in a single day. There was still ice to be found in some of the sheltered ponds, but he hadn't brought his cooler with him.

Sprawling on the ground, Cade tossed the gig aside. He rolled back, laying on the cool, clay earth. Rain kissed his face, and he smiled. Steam rose off his skin. It happened sometimes, when he worked too hard in the cold. Though it wasn't mystical at all, it seemed like it. There wasn't a lot of magic in his life. Plenty of beauty, but no wonders or marvels.

At least, not until Dara came. She had music in a magic box. Her ticky box. Fire in a tube, lamps that glowed without flame or smoke. In his heart, he knew it was technology. His parents had talked about the world before the fall. But to him, it was stories. To see it working—magic.

Suddenly, the brush crackled. Rolling over, Cade plastered himself to the ground. He held his breath so it wouldn't reverberate in his ears. There were a hundred sounds the body made that could distract a tracker. Gritting teeth dimmed sound;

grinding them blotted it out. Sharp breaths muddied the direction. Swallowing could obscure it completely.

Breathless and motionless, Cade listened. It only took a few seconds to figure it out. It was human, and it was heading that way. Panic roared inside him, but outwardly, he stayed calm. Grabbing his gig, he pierced three of the fish. Two more went inside his shirt. That left two on the ground and he hesitated.

That was good food. Even if he couldn't preserve it, he could stuff himself with it tonight. But he had one free hand left. That meant no way to climb if he needed to. No way to catch himself, to fend anything off. Eyes darting, he peered through the hazy morning in search of motion.

Footsteps, light, purposeful. Just one. It was Dara; it had to be. The rangers always came in pairs: their boots thumped, their radios crackled, they talked. It couldn't be them. It moved too keenly to be *Josh*. He tramped around behind Dara with feet of stone.

Any other time, Cade would have already been gone. Some wandering bear would have found a treat in the abandoned fish, and nothing else would have happened all day. But a small, senseless part of him wanted to see her. He wondered if she'd found the pendant yet. Probably; it was impossible to miss.

What did she think of it? Had it scared Josh? So many new emotions spilled over in his skin. Cade's heart pounded. It washed the cold away again, sweeping him with a shock of heat and sweat.

Dara broke through the tree line, let out a little cry and froze. Clutching her hands to her chest, she stared at him. Her eyes were so wide. The dim light meant Cade still couldn't make out the color. He forgot all about that when she took one step toward him and spoke.

"Who are you?"

Cade's throat seized. It clamped down on his breath, his voice. She was too close, and it wasn't the full moon yet. This wasn't a glimpse, maybe one she could have forgotten about if he'd quit coming around. This was face-to-face.

When he didn't answer, she talked more. "What's your name? Where are you from?"

Raising the gig, he looked past her. There were a hundred ways to escape. He needed both hands for most of them. One of the fish in his shirt flopped helplessly and he shuddered. There had to be a way out. He wasn't ready to say hello. He wasn't ready to stand this close to someone from the outside.

Frowning, Dara approached again. She held out his pendant, the leather wrapped around her hand. "You left this for us."

Somehow, it had led her straight to him. Shaking his head, Cade stepped into the river. Icy water burned around his ankles. The cold sank in bone-deep. When he found his voice, he waved the gig at her, and at his leftovers on shore.

"You're hungry," he said, the words coming out in a growl. "Take those."

Blinking at the fish for a moment, she shook her head. "I wouldn't know what to do with them."

It was Cade's turn to be surprised. There was nothing more basic than cooking a fish. There were lots of ways to do it. He liked to steam them, scenting the whole camp. But there were easier ways. Pointing at them again, he said, "Push a stick in the mouth. Hold the fish over the fire."

Vaguely green, Dara curled into herself a little. Dragging her attention back to him, she lit from the inside. Her face said she remembered why she came in the first place. Holding the pendant out again, she said, "I know you've been following me. I just want to know why."

That question was too hard to answer. Because he was curious. Because she was beautiful. He was lonely; she was there. He thought the world was mostly dead. She proved it wasn't. But he could hear his mother's voice in his head, sharp. Furious.

We're the only ones who are safe. The rest are sick.

Planting the gig into the river bottom, Cade backed away. He wanted to talk to her, but he couldn't. It was too soon. She could be dangerous. This was all a bad idea. He needed to move camp. His head buzzed, too many thoughts at once. Too many feelings to settle on just one.

So he told her, "Eat the fish."

Then he ran.

SIX

"**H**e reminds me of those people on the trail last year," Dara said, slitting the sides of a black plastic trash bag.

Now she knew for sure that someone was nearby, watching, that meant no more trips just out of camp to relieve herself. Turning trash bags into makeshift curtains, she kept her fingers busy as she talked.

"Which ones?" Josh asked.

"The ones who basically lived there?" Looking over, she watched as he turned the fish on the fire. "They followed the weather and didn't have a home to go to?"

Skeptical, Josh craned around to look at her. "You mean the homeless guys."

With a roll of her eyes, Dara tied the first two bags together into a single sheet. That was so very Josh. In record time, he could reduce anything to the most negative interpretation possible.

Admittedly, there had been some people out there who'd frightened her. The ones that talked too loud and too close. Or the ones who liked to show off their guns and knives. It seemed like their stories always had police in them, or jail. Usually both.

But there had been several people on the trail who lived there because they wanted to. One was a guy not much older than them. Soft-spoken, his blond hair twisted into braids, he liked to quote from *Walden*.

Then there was a couple who'd met hiking there in college and spent every good weather day on it. They had a dog with a bandanna, and banana bread in their packs.

Those were the people Dara meant. The ones who had decided that city-job-tech kind of life wasn't for them. The boy at the river reminded her of them. He had to be a survivalist or something.

There wasn't a stitch on his body that came from a retail store, as far as she could tell. Seriously, the clothes were just bizarre. Like he walked out of an old movie about the frontier.

Then there was the bee pendant. She still didn't know what it was made of. When she rubbed it with her thumb, it felt buttery and warm—not plastic, not glass. And finally, who fished with a sharpened stick? Only somebody who wasn't planning on getting into town for new hooks and bobbers, was her guess.

Everything about him fascinated her, from the dark, wary tilt of his eyes, to the thick fall of his dreads. "He needs water like anybody else," she mused aloud. "And he's probably going to avoid the river. Where are the maps?"

Now irritated, Josh frowned. "Just leave it alone, Dara. Some crazy guy in the woods is following you around, and you want to find him? Have a sense of self-preservation."

"Don't start with your mom and dad's actualization stuff," she retorted.

It was a low blow. Josh couldn't help his weird parents any more than she could. The new agey, attachment-parenty stuff was totally out of Josh's control. Already, Dara felt bad for saying it. Flushed, she stopped knotting her bath curtain. "I'm sorry."

Lips flattened, Josh turned his back on her and poked at the fish. "How am I supposed to know when these are done?"

Swallowing down her guilt, Dara shook her head. "I don't know. Let me find the guidebook. It had a chapter about cooking in the wild."

With a quick tug, she unzipped the tent and ducked inside. Sinking to her knees, she felt the cold in the sleeping bags, and the cold outside pressing in.

Their unseasonably warm spring had turned into just plain spring. Damp, chilly, grey. This wasn't the trip she'd hoped for. No doubt, Josh felt the same way. Their mismatched edges didn't line up any better in the forest than they did back in Makwa.

A surge of emotion tightened her chest. Josh was a good guy. He was generous and friendly. He was thoughtful and steady and true. He was exactly the guy she'd fallen in love with freshman year. What had happened to the rush of infatuation she used to get when she looked at him?

Smoothing her hands over his sleeping bag, she pressed her face against his pillow. It smelled like him, and once, that would have given her such a thrill.

She had a whole drawer at home, filled with pilfered sweatshirts. She tucked them into her bed, to breathe and dream against. Even when they lost his scent, she couldn't bear to give them back.

But lying there with her face on his pillow, she realized something. She couldn't remember the last time she'd taken one of his sweatshirts home.

There was a time when lying on his sleeping bag would have driven her nuts. She would have had to flail around just to handle it all. At that moment, she felt nothing but a wistful pang.

Probably just the weather, she told herself. The fact that raccoons had eaten all the really good stuff. That the guy out in the woods was making him act like an overprotective jackass. No, that wasn't right. Josh didn't seem overprotective at all. He just seemed annoyed. As if the boy by the river was a neighbor playing his radio too loud.

Josh's voice interrupted her thoughts. "Did you find that guidebook?"

Sitting up, Dara scrambled through the bags until she produced it. "Got it," she called back. Then she made herself climb back out of the tent to sit beside him. Even shoulder to shoulder with him, the cold crept in. He didn't put his arm around her. He just kept turning the fish, slowly blackening them in the flames.

This wasn't the trip she'd hoped for at all.

— —

His fire flickering, Cade lashed sturdy branches together. Shoulders knotted with concentration, he tied off two long ones, crossed at one end, to make a V-shape.

Then he twisted vines around smaller branches, connecting the V in several places. It looked like a crooked ladder, but it wasn't for climbing.

Grabbing each branch, he shook them hard. One by one, tightening the vines where he needed to. When everything stayed in place in spite of him, he dropped the frame on the cave floor.

Spreading out his largest fur, he centered his cooler on it. Then, he dropped his animal figurines into a leather pouch. That went onto the cooler, too, followed by his kit of herbs and the last scraping bits of salt he owned.

He planned to roll up his bed in the morning. Not the frame; he'd make a new one. But the down mattress and the furs, the leather pillow stuffed with dried grass. Everything he owned would fit in this bundle.

And that bundle, he could tie to the travois he'd just made. The long ends of the V would rest on his shoulder. Dragging his gear was easier than carrying it all.

And he had to drag it a long way tomorrow. Outside the circle around the bee hollow. Past the old mill town, probably even past the old Indian village. He'd follow the river south, as far as he could.

Though he'd never been there, he knew the hills gave way to mountains. His family had always stayed inside the ring of cliffs. The valley was safer, darker, or so Mom said.

Once, studying their worn map, Dad had called him over. The paper was streaked with red lines, crossing and tangling with each other. But he skimmed his fingers over little triangles scattered across the page.

"That's the Cumberland Mountains," Dad told him.

Pursing his lips, Cade considered the page. "What do they look like?"

"Green and rolling." With a faint smile, Dad sank back. His gaze trailed away, settling on Cade's mother plucking stems from a basket of berries. "There are oceans out there, too. So much water you can't see the other side. And it's salty. It tastes like the water out by the lick."

Wrapping his arms around his knees, Cade pulled them to his chest. "Have you been to the ocean?"

"Once. A long time ago."

"Can I see it?"

Dad hesitated, just long enough for Mom to interrupt. She didn't sound upset. Still, something in her voice sounded final. "I need someone to spread these berries with me. Which one of my handsome boys wants to help?"

Cade did. He always did. He loved the things she whispered when they worked. Strange stories and fairy tales, secrets to keep until the end of time. She always said that, *keep that secret until the end of time.*

Dragging himself back to the present, Cade sprawled in his bed. The firelight made the handprints dance. They reached up and up above him. They floated into the dark, just like the smoke. They took his heart with them. This was the last night he'd sleep under them. Maybe the last time he'd ever see them.

Emotion welled, knotting in his chest and his throat. His parents slept beneath the stars not far from here. Side by side, always together, always near. Now he had to go, and it was his own fault. He'd been too curious, and for what?

For thirty seconds of conversation about nothing. Dara got close enough to infect him. If she was a carrier, it was probably too late. He wondered what might be growing inside him now. If his immune system was already starting its change. If it would make the slightest bit of difference.

Despite it all, he still wanted to touch her. Just skate his fingers down her cheek. Find out if she was warm. Soft. Throwing a forearm over his eyes, he tried to blank everything out. The past and the future, Dara's gold hair, everything. All of it.

In the morning, he would lose everything. He only had one night to let go.

Josh let Dara sleep alone.

He wasn't trying to punish her or anything. There was somebody out there. Somebody who came into their camp while they were sleeping. All those times Dara swore she heard somebody in the woods? Josh believed her now. And now he felt like he had to sit awake by the fire with his hunting knife close by.

Throwing more wood onto the fire, Josh recoiled from the smell. Wet wood, with mold or something on it, it stank. The smoke burned the inside of his nose. One thing was for sure, nobody else would want to get close with that kind of smell hanging in the air. To make it bearable, Josh threw on another log, this one drier and smoother.

It cut the acrid stink, but not by much. Josh had a feeling that it would linger like burned toast, or microwave popcorn. Settling in his canvas chair again, Josh went back to work. He'd cut down a thick branch and started carving the end of it. He wasn't sure what he needed a stake for. But it felt like he was doing something to protect both of them, so he kept going.

Arguing with himself, he blustered inwardly. What he ought to do is pack up all their gear, get everything all ready. That way when Dara woke up, she had no choice but to hike out with him. Without the tools and the food and toilet paper, she wouldn't last on her own. She wouldn't even try.

A more reasonable part of him pointed out that she was just stubborn enough that she might. And what kind of jerk would he be to abandon his girlfriend in the middle of nowhere. With some weird homeless guy already on her scent, at that. Where was all her careful-at-night, parking-under-the-lights, asking-security-to-walk-her-out defensiveness now?

It was like she took one look at this guy and forgot who she was. And Josh didn't know if that pissed him off or made him jealous. She hadn't been real specific about what he looked like. Maybe he was an old man in weird clothes, climbing in trees. No, that *would* have left her wary and ready to get right out.

He had to be young. He had to be something to look at, because she kept pointing her camera into the trees. She'd be standing there, and a noise would crack in the underbrush. Whipping around, she shot off a bunch of pictures. Then she studied the camera's screen like it was a crystal ball.

Glancing at his watch, Josh pushed to his feet again. Knife in one hand, stake in the other, he circled their camp. The fire kept his eyes from adjusting too much to the dark. But he stared into it anyway. He waved the stake slowly, careful with each step. Surging with bravado, he talked to the night—to whoever was listening.

"I know you're out there."

Nothing answered. Josh continued this patrol around the camp. When birds suddenly flew up, he turned and stabbed into the dark. "I'm not afraid of you," he said. And it wasn't a lie. He wasn't afraid. In fact, he was pumped up. Excited in a way. He hoped the guy would show his face. Then Josh would have an excuse to knock him down in the dirt and explain how it was.

Dara was his girlfriend. This was his camp. And he didn't care that his stomach was full of this guy's fish. He could catch fish, too. They didn't need his help. They didn't *want* it. Sweeping his stake into the dark again, Josh turned slowly with each step. He saw shadows, shapes, but nothing he could identify.

Maybe he *would* pack everything up tonight. Dara didn't know it but he had an emergency credit card in the truck. It would pay for a hotel room for a couple of days. A couple trips through a drive-through. Probably a real restaurant if that's what she wanted. As he backed toward his place by the sour fire, he wondered why they hadn't gone to Orlando with everybody else. This had been a good idea, once. Something private and special.

Anger licked through Josh. It built until he felt full of fire and acid. Drawing his arm back, he heaved the spear into the forest. Nothing cried out. It didn't crash into anything. It just fell into the soft brush. No more impact than throwing a pebble in a lake.

Squaring his shoulders, Josh glared into the fire and waited for morning.

SEVEN

The sun rose, and Cade walked to his parents' graves. They were nothing more than slight mounds in the forest floor now. His body fit between them comfortably. Sitting there, legs crossed and arms draped over them, he stilled his breath.

Sweet wind played through the trees. Somewhere, early honeysuckle bloomed. When light slanted through the burgeoning leaves, it took on a hundred shades of green. Motion surrounded him, rabbits bounding and birds diving, the river rolling on to places he'd never been.

Today, he'd follow that river and who knew what he would find. The world used to be full of life. Maybe elephants and alligators had survived. Would he recognize wheat if he saw it?

Tucked away with all his other information, Cade was sure he knew what to do with wheat. Grind it, discard the shells.

Add water and honey, let it stand uncovered to find the yeast in the air. His stomach growled. He'd never tasted bread, but he wanted to.

His mother tried not to talk about the world before the fall. Every so often, though, she'd turn to his dad and say, "White Wonder Bread." Then she'd sigh and lean against him. Cade wanted to try this Wonder Bread, the thing that lasted in Mom's memory and made her wistful. It had to be amazing.

He should have been excited. All his life, his mother had chosen the next camp. They moved on her command, and settled at the same. She favored the dark, cramped, and tomblike recesses.

Always near a cleft in the stone walls that surrounded the valley—but never the deeper caves. Bears liked caves, that was the most obvious danger. But bats did, too, and she had a litany of diseases bats might carry.

So what if he followed the river to the mountains, the ones his father called green and rolling. What if he made his camp on the top of one, in the sun. That couldn't be wrong. There was no one left to tell him no.

There were other mounds in the forest. Subtle coils and heaps, with shells scattered around them. The Indians followed the river, too, or so his father said. They left their dead in the woods, sheltered by time and trees and shells. All Cade had were the disks he carved out of antler. Dara had the one with his bees, his favorite.

Carefully, Cade cut the pendant with a doe carved into it, and pressed that to his mother's grave. On his father's, he left the moon and the stars. Climbing to his feet, he scaled the nearest tree. It soared high above the ground, and soon Cade stood at its spindling peak. The wind made him sway, but he wasn't afraid.

This was his favorite view. He saw his camp and his river, the ponds where he fished water and ice alike. The land had shape and form, a blackberry patch darker and denser than a string of birches. A single coil of smoke thinned into a fan by the wind: Dara's camp.

He wondered how long she would stay. Did she live here now? He worried that she would starve if that was the case. He hadn't seen Dara or Josh looking for food. It was the thin season, but there was fish and ramps, henbit and redbud pods . . . But she probably didn't know to avoid the plants that smelled like almonds. She'd touched the red cap mushrooms thoughtlessly; did she know to avoid things with thorns? With milky sap? It took longer to climb down a tree than to climb up it. The whole way, he fretted over Dara left alone. As good as alone. Left alone with Josh, Dara might starve in a week.

So instead of gathering his things and heading south, Cade grabbed his gig. Tomorrow, he'd leave at dawn. He swore it to himself, and to his parents. It didn't matter that he loved the bee hollow, or the falls, or the mill town. It was too dangerous to stay, so he promised it again. To the handprints on his walls and the drawing of his family he'd scraped into the cave long ago.

But today, he needed to fish and gather and leave something for Dara to eat when he was gone. Just one more day.

— —

"Let's go somewhere," Dara said.

She had to break the tension between them. He'd let her sleep late, long enough to let the sun break through the canopy. But breakfast was tense. Cereal without milk, biscuits burned on the outside and mushy inside, all washed down with silence and warm Diet Coke.

Torn, she considered a surrender. They could salvage some of their spring break. Maybe even make it home as a couple. They had tickets to the prom. There were graduation parties waiting for them.

It seemed like such a sudden, ugly slide into the end—this, on a trip that was supposed to bring them together. The end was coming anyway. She really didn't want to rush into it.

But as she scooped the insides out of a badly made biscuit, she stole a look at Josh. He seemed so angry. So far away. Honestly, it surprised her. As much as they'd both changed since freshman year, she never would have expected this.

Tossing the rest of her breakfast, Dara stood. She dug the pendant from her pocket and placed it by the fire. Carefully, because she wanted to keep it. But firmly, because she had just decided: they were making a new start.

Then she curled a hand on Josh's shoulder. Slipping up the back of his neck, she rubbed there gently and tried to catch his eye. "Come on. Yesterday sucked because of the rain. Today will be better."

Josh didn't look convinced. But he got up anyway. Swinging his arms, he took up so much space in the camp. Popping and stretching, he looked like he was getting ready for a fight instead of a hike. Dara ignored that, ducking into the tent to get her camera.

"Maybe we can try to climb up one of the cliffs," she called to him as she rummaged.

Josh called back, "If that's what you want."

Something in his voice made her still. He wasn't happy. Neither was she. So she tucked her camera back into its case. Instead of disappearing behind the lens, she'd be there. Present. Right there next to him, so he didn't have a choice but to see her. Determined to fix this, at least as much as it could be fixed, Dara emerged from the tent empty-handed.

"Actually," she said, measuring steps until she came up to him, "you said you wanted to see the falls. Why don't we hike up that way?"

Frowning, Josh looked her over. "Where's the camera?"

"I don't have to take pictures of everything."

Disbelief crossed Josh's face. But he didn't question her, not out loud. And that was good, because Dara felt like she was making an effort. He had to, too. It would never work if they weren't both trying. Plucking up a long, thick stick, Dara tested her weight against it. Sturdy, a little springy, it would make a great walking stick.

Trying to coax Josh out of his darkness, she nudged him. "If it's warmer when we get there, we could go skinny-dipping."

That made him laugh. It was a thin, brief huff, but it counted. "There's no way it's gonna be warm enough for that. You just wanna see my junk crawl up."

Now with a more genuine smile, Dara tugged on his shirt.

"Maybe. It's kind of hilarious."

She put the tension from her mind. The boy in the forest, too. Everything out there was temporary. A handful of days out of a lifetime. As curious as she was, it wasn't worth it. Not to ruin senior year. Not to break up with a genuinely good and decent boyfriend.

Handing Josh the topo maps, she held up the compass. Once they had their direction, they walked into the woods together.

It was too cold at the falls to swim. Too cold to wade, too. But Dara convinced Josh to take off his boots and to try. After just a few steps, his teeth chattered. She looked miserable, clutching herself with her arms and trying to be sunny.

It was just like Dara to make the best out of it. She was always the devil's advocate. Always the one trying to see it from both sides. That's why she liked pictures, she said. The image was the truth, but what interested her were the things people put into it.

To be honest, Josh wasn't sure he understood the point. A picture of a tulip was a tulip. A picture of kids in a fountain were kids in a fountain. Once, she'd shown him a painting of a pipe. In cursive, in French, the painter wrote *This is not a pipe* under it. Josh didn't get that either, but Dara thought it was freaking genius.

So he felt bad watching her try to splash with stiff, cold hands. Every time she laughed and tried to get him to play, he felt worse. He wanted to go home. He wanted a hot shower and a hot dinner and a real bed to sleep in.

Most of all, he wanted things to get back to normal. He was big enough to admit that his idea for a romantic spring break had failed.

Josh couldn't relax. For the whole walk to the falls, and the whole time they'd been there, he'd been waiting. For that guy to show up out of nowhere, or to finally see some evidence of him tracking them. Instead of taking in the scenery, Josh scanned the trees and the shadows warily.

Because he *was* out there. And he *was* watching. Stepping from one smooth stone to another, Josh tipped his head back. Squinting against the light, he searched the upper branches now. Was that how he'd gotten away with it so long? Climbing through the canopy like a monkey?

Dara broke his concentration. Flicking water at him, she asked, "Where are you?"

"I'm standing right here." Even though he knew what she meant, he played dumb. Like he expected, she pursed her lips. Like *she* expected, he backed up. He answered her disapproving silence with a defensive, "What?"

No longer playful, Dara stalked out of the water. Though rainbows drifted through the air around her, she stopped marveling. Instead, she snatched up her hoodie and tugged it over her head. If it was possible to be passive-aggressive by putting on a pair of boots, Dara managed it.

Rather than argue with her, Josh sat down a few feet away. He put his boots back on, too, silent. With silence, she couldn't box him in. She wouldn't talk him in circles with logic . . . but that prickled at him. There was nothing logical about any of this. Raising his head, he stared at her. She looked the same as ever, pretty and golden. Even the furrow in her brow was cute.

"If there was some guy following you around back home, you'd lose it."

Dara sighed and closed her eyes. "Josh."

"Am I wrong?"

Though she didn't answer right away, she did answer. "Probably. It's different."

Leaving his boots untied, Josh leaned toward her. "How?"

Josh watched her struggle with the question. Her expression twisted and pulled. Her whole body twitched in subtle ways. It was like she was fighting with herself to come up with an explanation that made sense. But there wasn't one. They both knew it.

"Are you hot for him or something?"

Dara exploded. Whatever struggle she'd been having burned right away. Josh immediately realized his mistake, but it was too late to take it back.

"That's the best you can come up with?" she demanded. "There's some guy living in the middle of nowhere in clothes from the 1800s, fishing with a spear, disappearing and reappearing anywhere he wants to, whenever he wants to, and the only reason you can come up with that I'm interested is that I might want to *do* him?"

"Well, why not?" he shot back.

"Because it's ridiculous!" Dara dragged wet hands through her hair. Twisting it into a ponytail, she shook her head. She was done arguing, so the argument was over. That was just like her, too. Grabbing her walking stick, she started for the trees. With a glance down, she informed him, "Your boots are still untied."

Furious, Josh stalked after her, still untied. Sometimes she could be a pain. Sometimes he didn't get her, or the stuff that made her tick. But he loved her. He loved her stupid, crooked toes and the sound of her laughter. He loved the way her head fit right under his chin when he hugged her. The way she smelled. The weird emails she sent when she couldn't sleep. He loved all those things about her.

So he said nothing. He watched the curve of her shoulders and the sway of her hips, and said nothing.

EIGHT

Dara clung to her walking stick. Planting it a step ahead, she used it to haul herself up the hill that led back to their camp.

It was a subtle slope. Just enough to make her muscles burn with exertion, and her breath come hard and fast. Josh was two steps back, pretending he wasn't winded. The fight at the falls lingered, and the return was a struggle. They were tired, tempers frayed, and both of them were hungry.

Dara tried to make a mental list of the food they had left. Dried and reconstituted and canned, ugh. Her thoughts drifted to mashed potatoes, hot bread and butter, meat loaf. Heavy things that tasted like home.

She almost laughed at herself. It's not like they were *stuck* in the woods. And it wouldn't kill her to have thin pancakes and stew. It was easier to concentrate on that than the reality: it might kill her relationship to spend much more time alone with Josh.

The awkward quiet between them had its own flavor, sour and dry, like ash on the tongue. Nothing could wash that away, so Dara thought about sausages, scrambled eggs, and French toast instead.

Grabbing a fallen tree for balance, Dara crinkled her nose when she touched something slick.

There, among the brush, was a half-eaten stick of butter.

Her amusement died. It wasn't possible. They'd locked up the food since the raccoons had helped themselves last time. The cooler was up a tree. Everything had bungee cords wrapped around it. And yet, none of that mattered, obviously. Heart sinking, she stopped. Shouldering back into Josh, she pointed out the butter.

"They got into the food again," she said, dismayed. She still had plans. There were pictures she needed to take of things. Of *people*.

"A motel room wouldn't be so bad."

"I'm not ready to go, Josh."

"You don't have to flip out on me."

Annoyed, Dara plunged ahead. She wasn't flipping out, she was worried about leaving. She hadn't raised her voice or whined. She'd pointed out the obvious. Without food, they'd have to leave. Despite that, she wasn't ready to go.

As she rolled the possibilities over in her head, her stomach churned. If they were going to leave, it had to be soon. It was dangerous to hike through the dark. Animals. Obstacles.

Even with the topo maps and a compass, the forest felt bigger at night. Wilder. The GPS gave out completely after dark, like it knew better.

They took a few more steps, and a flash of yellow caught Dara's eye. She snatched a box from the ground and the last of their breakfast cereal bounced through the underbrush, fleeing like mice.

She shot Josh a look, then crushed the box to shove in her pack. They'd done a lousy job locking the rest of the food down.

Without a word, she trudged on, more frustrated with each bit of trash she discovered. Something had scattered a bag of rice. The red peak of their tent appeared in the distance, but not before a final insult.

A few feet away, a jar sat on a tree stump. It wasn't broken— the thief had unscrewed the lid and dug tiny fingers all through the peanut butter.

"Seriously?" she asked the sky.

Dara stalked toward camp. Once again, the clearing was a disaster, wrappers and bottles scattered everywhere. The cooler hung upside down—still on its rope, completely empty.

Furious, Dara started for the sleeping tent. Just then, the smaller tent shook, something rustling behind it. The little monster was still there!

"Hey!" she shouted. She threw the walking stick toward the tent, expecting a furry, black-masked bandit to streak into the woods. The rustling stopped, but nothing moved. Plucking a rock off the ground, she hauled back to throw it.

She let it slip from her hand when the bear stood up.

Its muzzle and paws were white with biscuit mix. With dark eyes fixed on Dara, the bear flared its nostrils, huffing at the air. A low creak rolled from it. Not really a growl. Another kind of sound, almost thoughtful. It shifted, like it was trying to get a better look at her.

Blank with shock, Dara fumbled for her camera. It was stupid; she didn't even have it with her. Even as she reached for it, she knew it was stupid. It was like she was too afraid to think about the threat. To remember any of the things she'd read about bear encounters before they hiked into the woods. Her fingers knew the shape of her camera; her body knew how to take a picture out of reflex.

"Run," Josh said behind her. That broke the spell and brought her to her senses.

"I don't think we're supposed to. I think we're supposed to make noise and scare it away, or back away slowly. Oh god, I can't remember."

Josh clapped a hand on her shoulder. "Dara, come on."

The bear popped its jaw, the sound grisly and echoing. Its fur bristled as it rose to its full height. Everything about the beast was aware, especially its eyes. Now it did growl. Its breath fogged the air, the growl turning to a roar. Yellow teeth flashed, curved like claws. And then, it charged.

Dara screamed.

Something struck her in the ribs. It knocked the breath out of her. Suddenly, she was flying. Everything came at the wrong angles. The top of the ridge was sideways. The trees, too.

She looked down. An arm clutched her. It belonged to the

boy from the river. Her stomach dropped, and her head swam. Then suddenly, she was on the ground. Hard roots banged into her ribs. She scrambled to sit up, leaves and dirt clinging to her.

Slapping her hair from her face, she saw the boy soar over the clearing. His body cut between the trees gracefully. Strong hands clung to a bittersweet vine. And then, he let go. Dropping in a perfect arc, he landed on his feet. He was fearless.

Scrambling to the edge of the ridge, Dara stared down in horror. The bear swung toward the boy. It barked; she had no idea bears could bark. Panic turned everything on edge. She searched for Josh.

Where was he? He had been right beside her. Right before she flew. Scanning the ground, a hysterical thought occurred to her. What if the bear had already eaten him? Then she realized Josh had flattened himself on the ground. Half covered by the brush, he didn't move at all.

Drawing a deep breath, the boy roared. It was a human sound, but unearthly. It rippled through the woods. It seemed to vibrate on the trees. Animals everywhere went quiet. Even birds stopped their calling.

The bear hesitated, lowering its head. It backed away, sharp shoulder blades poking through its fur. As it moved, it knocked a lantern over, then the pot that sat by the fire. Snuffing at a package of dried fruit, the bear stopped. The forest went silent, the air electric with possibility.

Then, there was a telltale flicker of muscles along the bear's flank. Slapping the ground, the bear growled again. Then it charged. Thundering across the ground, the great beast moved impossibly fast. The first lunge missed, but the boy lunged back. Then the beast rose up. It twisted in the air, almost graceful. Then it struck, clawing the boy across the chest.

The boy cried out, but refused to fall. Staggering, he reached for Dara's walking stick. Blood poured down his chest. It soaked the skins he wore. The color drained from his face, making his eyes black coals among the grey.

With another roar, he brandished the stick, then attacked. This time, he surged forward. With feral strength, he struck the bear in the head. A crack rang out.

The bear growled, trying to shake off the blow. Oddly human, it pawed its own ear. The boy struck again. Roared again. And though he grew paler by the moment, he did not stagger.

Terror ran through Dara. He'd saved her and he was going to die.

Heart wrenching wildly in her chest, she turned and searched the brush. The forest was full of sandstone: cliffs and ravines, chunks of it broken off or thrusting through the earth. It only took her a moment to find a big, sharp piece of it.

Adrenaline coursed through her. She dragged the stone from the ground. It caught on her skin, its pocked texture unpleasant and alien. Dragging it to the edge of the ravine, she summoned her courage. Her strength. She raised the stone over her head. Its weight made her wobble.

The first time she tried to roar, no sound came out. It was humiliating, and her skin flamed. She tried again, immediately.

She opened her mouth and screamed. This time, the cry tore free. It was a raw, bloody sound. Her throat burned with it.

At once, the boy and the bear looked up.

Dara dropped the stone. She couldn't help it; she cringed when it hit the bear. It was a living creature. She wasn't accustomed to hurting things, not on purpose. But she celebrated when the beast hesitated, then fled. It galloped, a dark shadow against the forest. Trees shook in its wake. The boy, left behind, swayed on his feet.

"Are you okay?" she called, trying to find a way off the ridge.

Finally, she slid, rough stone tearing her jeans, pulling her hair. Halfway down, she fell the rest of the way. It was ungainly, and her knee protested. But she ignored that, running to the boy. Hands flying, she caught him, and pushed him to the ground. He was so cold. So pale.

"Josh, help me!" she cried.

He was right there, the last time she saw him. Pressed into the dirt, his arms over his head. Why didn't he appear? Pulling her sweatshirt off, Dara rolled it and pressed it to the boy's chest. As brave as he'd been facing the bear, he looked absolutely terrified now.

Her head buzzed, like it was full of bees. A constant sound that threatened to overwhelm her. Her brain tried to break free, but nothing made sense. She had flashes, half thoughts. Bear. Boy. Dying. Help.

"We're going to get you some help," she told him, then lifted her head again. "Josh!"

The boy reached up. His cold fingers slid across her cheek,

slick with blood. Grey lips parted, and he murmured, "Dara."

Startled, Dara jerked back. "What?"

"You're Dara," the boy said. "I'm Cade."

And then he slipped away.

NINE

*N*othing held back the clouds.

Cade blinked through a haze and saw the sky. Only the sky. No trees stretching across it. No birds or cliffs. He felt untethered like the stars, floating in a vast expanse of nothing. Then the ground jolted beneath him, and there was pain. Weight. Across his hips and his chest.

Dara leaned over him, blotting out the sky. Her eyes were green.

"You're awake!"

His dry lips cracked, and he moaned when the ground jolted again.

"Sorry," she said.

This time, he managed to speak. "For what?"

She shifted, her eyes darting but her hands sure. She

straddled his hips, holding him down. And she kept her weight on a bundle of cloth on his chest. His heart struggled beneath it. It hurt. But she didn't move, even though the wind tore at her. Her hair was a whip, snapping around her face. "He's being as careful as he can."

Something roared beneath them. Cade gasped when gravity shifted. It pulled them to one side. His stomach turned. It was hard to focus, so he reached out. Catching Dara's arm, it confused him when his fingers wouldn't tighten. "What's happening?"

Dara looked at him again. She knit her brows, her expression softening along with her voice. "Do you remember getting hurt?"

With a croaking laugh, Cade winced. "Hard to forget a fight with a black bear."

"What about after?"

"Somebody carried me?" His thoughts foggy, Cade shook his head. "No. You're too small."

"I'm not that small. But yeah, Josh did most of it. Now we're taking you to the ranger station. They can land a helicopter there. You're going to be okay."

Fear slipped through Cade. He remembered his father saying that once, but it was a lie. They'd stood over his mother's body, her color turned to ash. Her skin cold, her body stiff. They dug her grave together, beneath the tree with all the trumpet vines. The dried bushclover wavered in the wind, and it was not okay.

Even though they'd wrapped her in furs to keep her warm,

he couldn't bring himself to cover her with earth. He grabbed the lowest branch of the scarlet oak, and climbed. Climbed until the tree was slender and dangerous, until he could see the bare sky. There, he howled until his voice gave out. It was not okay.

Dara touched his cheek, startling him. Her hair washed around her face again, gold and tipped in blood. His blood. Worry creased her brow, and she pressed harder on his chest. "Talk to me. Kay, you said your name is Kay?"

He floated, inside his head. All of a sudden, she felt very far away. The pain a distant ache. Flexing his fingers once more, he caught her coat sleeve. His grip was weak, but the red plaid between his fingers was real. "Cade."

"Cade what? What's your last name?"

Shaking his head, he closed his eyes. He snapped them open again when she patted his cheek, hard.

"How many people are left?" he asked.

"What?"

Cade struggled to shape his mouth. It felt like the words were slipping away, his thoughts, too. Haze filmed across his sight. Drifting again, a pleasant warmth surrounded him. Then Dara's sharp hand on his cheek wrenched it away. "In the world."

Surprised, Dara laughed in disbelief. Looking up, around, she shook her head then said, "I don't know. Seven billion?"

That was a lie. Throat closing, Cade shivered. It started on his skin, then dove into his bones. His jaw clenched then spasmed, teeth rattling together. Before he could ask more, she unzipped her coat and sank down to cover him. She lay across the bundle on his chest, pressing it down with her weight.

Curling her arms around his head, she pressed her hot brow to his temple. She breathed on him, hot breath skating his skin. His flesh welcomed the warmth, but inwardly, he recoiled. Voice thin and panicked, he asked, "Are you immune?"

"Shh," she said. She stroked his head. Her voice was soft and low. "I think you're in shock. Let's talk about . . . I don't know. Let's talk about something happy. Do you have a happy place? Mine is mostly in my head. An imaginary darkroom. Nobody uses them anymore, not really. But I like to think about the process."

Breath draining, Cade drifted again. "I don't know what a darkroom is."

"That's okay. That's just mine. What's yours?"

Her breath kissed his jaw. Skimmed the corner of his mouth. Slowly, he relaxed, but his thoughts stayed close. "The bee hollow."

"That sounds nice," she said. "Tell me about it."

In the dark, beneath her warmth and weight, Cade pictured it. He breathed and tasted the sweetness of the air. He saw the shapes of the trees, their trunks twisting and elegant. Their branches twining together overhead. Their bellies full of honeycomb, bees dancing with them in clouds.

"Still with me?" Dara asked.

Cade nodded. "I'm there. In the summer, you can drill a hole. The honey drips out. Not too much, I don't want to ruin the hive. Just a mouthful, and there's an apple tree that fruits early. Apples and honey by the falls."

"Do you swim?" Dara asked.

"Sometimes."

Gravity shifted again. She tightened around him, but their smooth flight turned rough. They shook and bounced, little shocks knocking them together. She raised her head to look at him, apologetic. "Gravel road, sorry."

Before he could answer, the sky turned dark again. A white helicopter swept over them. Its propellers looked like hummingbird wings: moving, but not moving. Cade had seen one, once. At a distance. He hadn't realized how loud they were. It was an inverted rumble, the sound of stone on stone underwater.

Dara choked up, a sob of relief. "They beat us here. You really are going to be okay."

Cold swept in when she sat up. It burned, vicious like fire. Suddenly, the motion stopped, and she climbed off of him. Dropping his hand on the bundle on his chest, she promised him it would be all right again. Then she stood, she jumped over a wall he'd just now noticed, and disappeared.

Too tired to follow her, Cade slumped. The voices in the distance tangled to noise, so Cade didn't try to listen. Instead, he closed his eyes and lingered in the memory of her body on his. She'd left traces behind. All the sweetness and strange flowers on her skin perfumed his now.

His struggling heart thrummed.

Shoving her hands in her pockets, Dara made herself stand back.

The paramedics were in charge now. They'd swarmed Josh's truck. With all their weight in it, the tailgate dangled perilously close to the ground. They'd carried their huge kits over on the stretcher, because it wouldn't roll on the gravel.

Now they moved purposefully. Slowly. It bothered Dara that they didn't run over, barking out orders. They didn't flash or hurry. They had to know how serious this was. Why weren't they acting like it? Her grandmother would have said they were taking their own sweet time.

"Did you get any information from him?" one of the paramedics asked her, interrupting her worried thoughts.

His name tag said Raheed, and he had the kindest face. Maybe that was his job, she mused. To be calm and kind, to get information out of hysterical people. But she wasn't hysterical in the least, just concerned. Dragging her gaze away from the truck, she shook her head, then nodded. "His name is Cade. Um . . . He likes honey."

"Great," Raheed said, actually typing that into his tablet. "Does he have a last name? Is he allergic to anything?"

"No. I don't know."

Raheed put a gentle hand on her shoulder. At first, she didn't know why. Then she realized she was crying. Not great, heaving sobs or anything. She didn't feel sad. Just swallowed up and shaking everywhere. His blood was so dark and she was soaked with it. Their camp had seemed so safe. Infested with raccoons, but safe.

What would have happened if Cade hadn't come out of nowhere? She and Josh would be dead. Missing and dead. Sofia knew where they were, but no one else did. There wouldn't have been anything left to find. Just their tents and their stuff, abandoned. No one would have ever known . . .

But Cade had come out of nowhere. And now he was bleeding to death in the back of Josh's truck.

"Why are they going so slow?" she asked, swiping her face dry.

Raheed's tone never changed. He was calm, smooth. "So they don't make any mistakes."

That made so much sense. And it started the tears again. It was awful, there was nothing wrong with her. She didn't understand why she couldn't control herself. Inwardly, she told herself she was fine, and to stop. But that only made it worse.

"Hey, Dara," Raheed said. He clipped his tablet to a carabiner on his belt, and put his other hand on her shoulder. Squaring her gently, he leaned down to make eye contact. "You did a good job. You got him here, he's going to be okay."

Her chest hitched when she took a deep breath. It was hard to believe him. She'd told Cade the exact same thing, not because she knew. Because he was upset. He was slipping away from her. He'd needed to hear it.

She swabbed at her face again, embarrassed. "I'm all right. I'm fine. Sorry."

Giving her a gentle shake, Raheed stepped back. "No need to apologize. You've had a crazy day. But did he say anything else to you? Anything that might help us take care of him?"

Shuddering with another breath, Dara shook her head. He

hadn't said much of anything, not really. Nothing helpful. But the question dug into her brain. It twisted around, obvious and present. Then suddenly, she remembered. "He asked if I was immune."

Concern crossed Raheed's brow. The tablet came off the carabiner again, and his fingers danced across its screen. "Did he say to what?"

"No," she said. She turned when the truck's shocks protested.

They'd hefted the gurney from the bed. Strapped to it, Cade looked so small and helpless. His strange clothes littered the ground, furs and leathers all cut and bloodstained. The flight nurse held an IV bag over her head, and leaned close to Cade, to listen to him.

Raheed tapped the screen again. "There's an ambulance on the way. You and your boyfriend need to wait for it, all right?"

"I'm fine." Dara watched the gurney, following it anxiously.

"How about you let the docs decide that?" Raheed said, gentle but firm. "They're gonna want to check you out. Probably give you some medicine in case he has HIV. You can't be too careful when you're dealing with somebody else's blood."

The flight nurse maneuvered with the gurney, then called out, "Hey! Dara! Come here!"

Adrenaline surged through Dara, flavored with fear. She couldn't think of a good reason for the nurse to call her. Leaving Raheed behind, she jogged across the lot. She wasn't ready for the shock. It had been terrible, seeing him struck. Sitting on him, trying to stanch the blood. Trying to keep him alive.

But seeing Cade wrapped in pristine white sheets made it worse. He seemed so much sicker. The bandage on his chest was already striped with blood. She recoiled when she realized his eyes were closed, and his face was impossibly smooth. Was he dead? Would they really make her look at him like that?

"Tell this boy," the nurse said, demanding Dara's attention, "that you can't go with him, but you're going to see him at the hospital."

Dara slipped her hand through the bars to touch his hand. "Cade?"

His eyelashes flickered. "There you are."

The nurse shot Dara a meaningful look. One that told her to get on with it.

"You need to go with them," Dara said. She curled her fingers around his, then added quickly, "They're going to take me to the hospital, too, so I'll see you there. I'll be there, all right?"

Wincing, Cade squeezed her fingers, a touch barely perceptible. "Swear it."

"I swear."

His touch fell away. "Okay."

"On three," the nurse said. She shouldered Dara out of the way, filling the space where she'd just stood. "We're going up. One. Two . . ."

Josh's hands spread on her shoulders. She recognized his touch. She leaned into him, the familiar shape of his body, but didn't look back. She had to concentrate on the helicopter. It was wishful thinking, a prayer made up on the spot. If she watched until they took Cade away, he would be all right. Her heart pounded as the paramedics signaled the pilot.

Come on, come on, come on, she pled.

Just then, Cade lifted his head and looked. For her. Dara knew it was for her. Because as soon as his gaze met hers, he settled. And he watched her until the white doors closed between them.

Josh led her away. Gently, he repeated, "He's going to be okay."

"I know," Dara said, and looked back one last time.

TEN

Everybody talked about how clean hospitals smelled. Twitching at the end of her bed, Dara picked at the plastic bracelet around her wrist. After nearly a week in the woods, she could still smell sweat and Cade's blood—even though they traded her a blue hospital gown for her ruined clothes—and smoke. The smoke clung to her hair.

But just beyond her own skin, everything was tangy and chemical. Alcohol, hand sanitizer, filtered air. Soap on the gown and even the plastic of the trays and tools and machines around her. A few curtains away, someone had a tray of food. It wasn't identifiable as one single thing. It was just a mishmash, hot, meaty, starchy.

The hospital didn't smell clean, it smelled industrial.

It was loud, too. Even with people keeping their voices low, there were just so many of them. A baby cried; a nurse tried to trade an overnight shift with someone else. A doctor—it sounded like a doctor—kept complaining that her attending had pulled a vanishing act on her. Dara didn't know what that meant, but she recognized irritation when she heard it.

Then, heavy footfalls approached. A jingle of keys, a certain sway in the step. Before the curtain opened, she knew exactly who it was. Making sure her robe was pulled all the way closed, Dara wrapped her arms around herself. She took a deep breath and when the curtain opened, she forced a smile.

"Hey Daddy."

He was in uniform. Of course he was. His beige tie was tucked into the crisp chocolate-brown shirt. Gold pips glittered on his epaulets, competing with the gleam of his badge and commendation pins. The gun belt crossed his waist heavily, and his radio hung from it, silenced. At least for the moment. When EMTs brought the county sheriff's daughter in, he was allowed to ignore everything else for a while.

Sheriff Porter clasped her face in his hands. He was a cop, he had a good poker face. But even he couldn't hide his relief when he looked her over. "Are you all right?"

"I'm fine."

"Your mother's going out of her mind," he said, taking a step back. Smoothing a hand over his head, he seemed to be at a loss. Like he had been prepared to be devastated, except she was just fine. Tired. Still hungry. A lot shaken up, but fine. When he finally recovered, he asked her incredulously, "Why aren't you in Florida?"

"I'm sorry."

"That doesn't answer the question, Dara. What's is going on?"

Suddenly tearful, Dara swallowed hard. "We just, Josh and I wanted some time alone, it's—"

"I shoulda known this was Josh's idea."

"It was my idea, too," Dara said. "I wanted to take pictures."

Clapping a hand to his chest, Sheriff Porter said, "It's my understanding there's scenery in *Florida*. You were out in the forest? What do you know about the woods, Dara? Arlene in dispatch said you got attacked by a bear."

Dara's head felt so hollow. "I didn't. There was a bear in our camp. Cade, this . . . this other camper, he tried to scare it off. He got hurt. He's really hurt. He lost so much blood. I put pressure on it like you taught me, but it was—I thought he was going to die. He might still die."

With that, Dara started to cry. It was all just too much. When she closed her eyes, she saw Cade bleeding beneath her again. Heard the roar of the bear and felt the gravel road jolting beneath her as she tried to hold Cade together. It had happened so fast. Now it kept happening, in her head, over and over.

Suddenly, her father abandoned the interrogation and wrapped his arms around her. Emotion choked his voice as he rocked her. "Shh. Shh. We can get into it later."

"It could have been me," Dara sobbed, pressing her face against his polyester shirt. "It almost was. He saved us, Daddy."

Stroking her hair, Sheriff Porter sighed. "You all got lucky."

"I don't feel lucky."

"I do."

Sheriff Porter leaned back, pulling a packet of tissues from his pocket. He always carried them, along with hard candies and breath mints. Carefully, he wiped her face for her, like she was still little.

The poker face was gone, completely. He furrowed his brow and worry played through his eyes. He was just a dad, and he looked sick with worry. Overwhelming guilt spilled through Dara; she was the reason he looked so human. So afraid.

With a hand swept beneath her eyes, she choked out an apology. "I'm sorry. I'm really sorry. For all of it; I scared you. I scared me. I lost my camera, I . . ."

"We'll go back and get it. And you can be sorry later. Calm down."

Dara hiccuped. "Okay."

Her father handed her the rest of the tissues. Taking a deep breath, he glanced toward a buzz building in the hallway. "I need to go talk to a couple people. I told Harland that putting emergency calls on Twitter was a bad idea."

Shrinking, Dara apologized again.

Makwa was a small town. Nothing much happened there, so the Twitter feed was usually as exciting as oatmeal. Shoplifters at the mall, stolen bikes, vandalism. A kitchen fire, and twice last summer, kittens down a storm drain. For weeks, that's all anybody talked about, Lightning and Thunder, the kittens down the storm drain.

It was embarrassing to realize that she was one of those calls now. She waited until her dad walked down the hall to dig out her phone. It was weirdly pleasurable to see full bars again. Pulling up the county sheriff's account, she didn't have to scroll far to find her fifteen seconds of infamy.

@PCSD_911 Three campers vs. bear in DanBoone Nat'l, Park Services on scene, Lifecom, EMS en route

Closing her phone, Dara slumped in relief. At least it was generic. No names, no details. Hikers had weird animal encounters all the time. It was bad enough living in a small town when regular stuff happened. The last thing she wanted was to be the new Storm Drain Kitten.

Not when things with Josh were so tenuous. Not with Cade in surgery, probably still in surgery, right that moment. Fortunately, half her school was in Florida and wouldn't be back till Sunday. That was plenty of time for something else mildly interesting to happen. Anything. Anything at all.

Dara slumped back on the thin pillow and covered her eyes. The sounds of the emergency room rose up around her. So loud. So busy. And yet, it all managed to blend together to a white noise. Soothed by the blankness, she finally drifted off to sleep.

— —

Shortly after noon, three teens camping in Daniel Boone National Forest were surprised by a bear that entered their camp. Though they managed to scare the animal off, one of the youths sustained an injury to the shoulder. All were transported to local hospitals; two have been released. The third has been admitted and remains under observation.

Their identities are being withheld pending notification of their families. The Kentucky Department of Fish and Wildlife Resources encourages everyone to treat all bears as wild animals. If you encounter a bear . . .

After signing off on that press release, Sheriff Porter headed upstairs. His deputies knew where to find Josh at home. They had already driven out to get his version of the story. What interested the sheriff was the third boy in the mix.

Dara called him a camper, but the EMTs called him Davy Crockett. They'd cut buckskins off of him, and he was bare underneath. It was their job to stabilize him and find out as much as they could. And what they found out wasn't much.

The boy was afraid of the helicopter. Afraid to go to the hospital. Wouldn't give up anything but a first name. He didn't know if he was allergic to anything, and he wouldn't give them contact information.

"Made me wonder if he was a runaway," the flight nurse said.

It made Sheriff Porter wonder a lot of things. If the kid was in trouble, or if he was trouble himself. He was all kinds of prickly that Dara was involved at all. That meant he had to step lightly. Do everything strictly by the book—right up to the point of stepping away entirely. That wasn't going to happen unless he absolutely couldn't avoid it.

Stopping at the desk, Sheriff Porter waited to catch someone's eye. He smiled at the nurse who came over, smoothing a hand on the counter. "How's John Doe doing?"

The nurse tapped on the computer, pulling up a few records.

Ticking his tongue behind his teeth, he scanned the screen. "Out of surgery, and according to this, he's awake. Do you want to talk to him?"

"If you wouldn't mind," Sheriff Porter said. "We're still trying to contact his parents."

The nurse pointed him in the right direction, and Sheriff Porter made his way to a room at the end of the hall. Looking through the window, he tried to get a feel for the boy before he spoke to him.

To him, he looked frail and small. Way too young to be sitting there in the hospital alone. And he had to be in pain. The bandages covered most of his chest; he hadn't been out of surgery that long. He stared blearily toward the window, lips moving. Was he talking to himself? Knocking on the door, Sheriff Porter let himself in.

"Mind if I come in?" he asked.

Cade rolled his head toward him. It lolled heavily. His eyelids drooped; his lips barely moved. "I want to go home."

That was a good start. Sheriff Porter walked lightly, pulling a chair closer to his bed. "I'd like to help you get home, son. My name's Sheriff Porter. What's yours?"

"Cade."

"You have a last name, Cade?"

To Sheriff Porter's surprise, Cade shook his head. He had one free hand and he raised it, just long enough to drop it against his mouth. It was like he was trying to shush himself. Ordinarily, the sheriff wouldn't bother with a minor drugged to the gills. But figuring out who he was and where he belonged was more than a little important.

Settling in the chair by the bed, Sheriff Porter tried another tack. "I expect they're worried about you, your parents."

"Shhh," Cade replied.

With a frown, Sheriff Porter leaned back. It took a lot of strength to be stubborn on that much morphine. It made him suspicious. He could send a deputy over with a fingerprint kit later, try to run him that way. But things would be a lot easier if the kid would just talk.

"Is there somebody I can call for you?"

Eyes widening, Cade stared at him a moment. Then he slumped down, all the tension melting from his expression. Fingers twitched on the pale sheets, and he murmured. "You're all dead. I think. That's what they said."

Was that a threat? Or was he just talking out of his head? Sheriff Porter didn't want to overreact, but if there was something bigger going on here, he had an obligation to figure it out. He had a county to oversee, and innocent people to protect. Clearing his throat, he deepened his voice just a little. "Who said that?"

"Mom," Cade murmured. "Just Mom. Have you seen Dara?"

His daughter's name on this stranger's lips made Sheriff Porter stiffen. "She's fine."

"She was hungry. Now I'm tired."

With a sigh, the sheriff stood. This was pointless; he could admit that. Patting the bed rail, he said, "Get some rest. We'll talk again tomorrow."

Leaving the boy to surrender to sleep, Sheriff Porter closed the door quietly behind him. It was already a long night, and it had barely started. He hoped somebody at the office had managed to pull up a missing persons to match this kid. The sooner he had some parents to claim him, the better.

Sheriff Porter didn't care for complications. Especially not when his daughter was involved.

The next day, Josh folded himself in the corner of his couch and tried to blot out his parents' voices. They hovered over him, holistically concerned, fully understanding, and insisting that he cooperate with the police. Again. This was the third time in twenty-four hours that he had to explain the disastrous ending to their camping trip.

This time had the added bonus of Dara's parents mixed in, Mrs. Porter and Sheriff Porter, who was definitely on the clock and on official business. Dara kept shooting him sympathetic looks from her end of the couch. It was the smallest consolation that she looked as miserable as he felt.

Stroking his digital recorder, Sheriff Porter kept repeating things they'd just told him. This time, he fixed his gaze on Josh. The man had never liked him, and Josh knew it. Mostly, he didn't care.

"So you're saying you didn't know anyone else was out there."

"Not until the guy left a button in our camp."

"It was a necklace," Dara interrupted. "Like a charm on a piece of leather."

Josh's mom, Mrs. Brandt, fluttered in her seat. "Why didn't you leave then?"

"People do stuff like that out there," Josh said. He didn't know why he was defending any of this. If they'd left when he wanted to, none of this would have happened. No bears, no strangers, no police. Pushing a hand into his hair, he waved the other one around. "People talked about it on the Appalachian Trail last year. You pass by a camp, you leave something behind. It's friendly."

Sheriff Porter wasn't convinced. In fact, he looked at Josh like he was brain damaged. "Then what happened?"

"I ran into him by the river." Dara crossed, then uncrossed her legs. The whole couch shook as she shifted anxiously. "He gave me a couple of fish. That's what we had for dinner."

"And he just handed them to you."

"Yes!"

Quietly curious, Mr. Brandt raised his hand. It was embarrassing the way he waited to be called on in his own house. When he finally spoke, his voice was soft like powder. "I feel like there must have been some conversation at that point."

Defensive, Dara twisted herself around. "I mean, yes, I asked him if he was camping near us. I noticed his clothes were kind of weird. And he was skittish, you know. Nervous. He didn't want to talk, but he gave me a couple of fish and that's it. It was like, a minute-long conversation. If that."

Josh broke in. "Is there something you guys want to ask us? Do you think we're lying about something?"

Hand raised, Sheriff Porter shook his head. "Nobody said that."

"We're just trying to process," Mrs. Brandt added.

Frustrated, Josh said, "That's everything, then. We knew he was out there. We didn't hang out with him. We didn't see his camp. *I* didn't see him until we walked up on the bear. Maybe Dara had some deep conversation with him in the truck, but I doubt it. She was trying to keep him from bleeding to death."

Mr. Brandt murmured a distressed sound. Reaching out, he smoothed a hand over Josh's shoulders. Sympathetic, he said, "I'm sorry you two had to go through that. That's a lot to unpack."

"But we're very proud of you," Mrs. Brandt added. "The right thing isn't usually the easy thing to do."

"We weren't gonna leave him out there to die," Josh said.

That was true, but Josh wished he meant it more. Not that he wanted Cade to die. In fact, if Cade could be healthy and happy and back in the wilderness area tomorrow, that would be Josh's fondest dream. Let this all fade away. Let him turn into a memory. A weird story to tell in twenty years, half remembered.

Keys jingling, Sheriff Porter stood up. Offering his wife a hand, he looked to Mr. and Mrs. Brandt. "I thank you all for your time and your cooperation. If there's anything else that comes to mind, Josh . . ."

"We'll call," Mr. Brandt assured him. "He's going to have some consequence time coming up. I imagine there'll be a lot of thinking involved."

Mrs. Porter waited for Dara to stand. Though she'd been quiet for most of the talk, her presence suddenly filled the room. Bold and firm, she slipped her arm around Dara's shoulder and looked her over. "Yes, Miss Independent's going to have some thinking time of her own."

The parents shook hands and chatted themselves out. Josh, however, focused on the carpet. He didn't know where things stood with Dara. And since they weren't gonna have time to hash it out, it made more sense to pretend she was already gone. He didn't even risk a glimpse of her silhouette; when the front door opened, he closed his eyes.

When he opened them again, she was gone.

ELEVEN

It felt strange to be at home.

Dara opened the fridge and stood in front of it. As silly as it sounded, she found it remarkable. All the bright light. All the food, just waiting there. It was packed so full that she didn't know where to start. While she stood there in awe of the Frigidaire, her younger sister slunk in behind her.

"Lose something?" Lia asked snidely.

Plucking a box of leftover fried chicken from a shelf, Dara finally closed the doors. "I missed you, too."

Lia rolled her eyes, texting away on her phone. It ticked like a bomb, little bloops punctuating finished thoughts. Without ever raising her head, she managed to sneer at Dara at the same time. "I don't know what makes you so special. If I ran away with some guy, I'd be grounded for life."

That was Lia's gift, making everything sound shadier than it was. Dara wasn't sure when her little sister had turned all goth bitter. It wasn't an overnight thing. But now she was full-blown in black eyeliner and combat boots.

Dara figured she had two choices. She could ignore Lia, which would tick Lia off. Or she could reply, which would also tick Lia off. There was no winning with her.

So, Dara picked the latter. "Mom and Dad knew I was spending spring break with Josh. They just didn't know where. And FYI, I *am* grounded. Happy?"

"No," Lia said sullenly. "My phone is blowing up because of you."

Taking out a plate, Dara shot her sister a look. "I'm sorry?"

"You should be. I get enough of Dara-Dara-Dara at home." Fingers flying, Lia sent another text, then slapped her phone down so Dara could see the screen.

Abandoning the chicken, Dara reached for it. That was the first thing her parents had taken away: technology. She'd spent a week trying to get a signal in the middle of nowhere. Now that she had one, she wasn't allowed to use it.

Lia snatched the phone back. "No, no. You can look, but you can't touch."

"Quit being a weasel," Dara said.

"If you don't want to see . . ." Lia replied. Her voice was a singsong, full of sisterly threat.

Dara was trapped. She didn't want to give Lia the satisfaction of giving in. But Lia was making such a big deal out of it that Dara was dying to know what was going on online. She probably had a million emails and a wall of texts. Her best friend, Sofia, *had* gone to Florida. There had to be news about hookups and breakups and drama. Now Dara was practically vibrating to find out.

Raising both hands like she was being robbed, Dara said, "Okay, fine."

A satisfied smile touched Lia's lips, just briefly. She was pretty anti-smile lately. Laying the phone down, she scrolled to the top of her text scroll. "My friend Kit wants to know if you got the attack on video."

Mouth dropping open, Dara blinked at her sister. "How does he even know it was me out there?"

"Duh," Lia said. "Everybody knows."

"Dad didn't release our names," Dara insisted.

Disgusted, Lia rolled her eyes again. "Um, okay, but everybody knew you bailed on Florida. And everybody knows you're home early. Everybody knows who *didn't* leave town for spring break. Gee. I wonder how people figured it out?"

Ugh. Dara slumped on the kitchen island. "Fine, whatever. Of course there's no video. What kind of idiot takes video when there's a bea— Hey, don't tell him that!"

Lia hit send and shrugged. "Sorry, too late. Okay, so that's Kit. Sofia wants to know why you haven't called her. She wants to know that approximately four hundred times. And she asked if you were the one in the hospital. I told her no. I'm not a total monster."

A chill raced Dara's spine. The whole Florida crew knew about it? There was no way she was getting out of being a Storm

Drain Kitten now. Reminding herself that it made her a bad person, she actively hoped somebody would come back from Florida pregnant. It was the universal rule of gossip: your drama stopped being interesting as soon as better drama came along.

"Anything else?"

Touching the screen, Lia gave it a sharp swipe. Text bubbles flashed by, far too fast for Dara to read any of them. But that wasn't really the point. It was the sheer number of them. The scroll went on and on. "Do you have any idea how obnoxious this is?"

"Yeah, I kinda do."

"Then do me a favor," Lia said, pocketing her phone. "Sneak online and update your Twitter. I'm not your digital secretary."

With a quick look to make sure their parents were out of earshot, Dara leaned in. Her hands itched to take the phone now. Something that had been an annoying ache, being without the internet, suddenly consumed her. "Just let me text Sofia real quick. She'll clear everything up. People will quit bugging you."

"Nope."

Surprised, Dara reared back. "Why not?"

Plucking a soda from the fridge, Lia waved it at her sister. "Because you're grounded. It would be *wrong* to go against Mom and Dad's rules. Wish I could help! Sorry!" Then, with a gloating laugh, she breezed out of the kitchen.

Dara didn't have anything to throw at her. So she bit into a cold chicken leg and scowled instead.

— —

Strangers kept coming. Kept going.

Cade could barely keep his eyes open. He felt buried under a pile of stones, and nothing really made sense. The sun never went down here. Maybe he was dead. That seemed possible. The sky never changed. It was grey squares next to grey squares every time he woke up.

But if he was dead, and he was aware, where were his parents? Forcing his eyes open, forcing them to focus, he looked for them. They should be close. They should hold their hands out and welcome him home.

Instead, the man in the hat stood over him. His voice wobbled. It sounded like he was talking underwater, the words slowly washing closer until Cade could hear them. When they finally spilled into his ears, he shook his head.

"No last name," he said. Slow sparks built beneath his skin. When realization struck, Cade raised a hand. Wagged a finger. "Sheriff Porter. Sheriff. Sheriff of Nottingham."

The sheriff frowned. Sitting beside him, he leaned forward. This man was a grey man. His hair, his skin. Just grey, everywhere. He didn't look like Dad. Maybe because he was sick? Curling away from him, Cade considered holding his breath. Then he forgot to.

"That's right," the man said. "You know who I am. How about you tell me who you are? I bet your parents are worried about you."

"I bet they are not," Cade said with a drunken smile. They didn't worry about anything anymore. They were two perfect mounds by the river. Or they were souls somewhere else. Not there, obviously. They definitely weren't there.

Weight tugged Cade's hand to the mattress. Eyes rolling back, he almost fell asleep again. Something kept him right on the edge of it. Dry mouth. His mouth was so dry.

Struggling to sit up a little, he winced at the sharp pain in his shoulder. Reaching with his other hand, he dropped it before he managed to get the cup in front of him. It was pretty. Made of something thin and pliable, it didn't have a taste.

Standing again, the sheriff poured more water into the cup. Then he held it to Cade's mouth to help him drink. When some of it spilled, the sheriff cursed, but Cade didn't mind. It was cold and clean. It reminded him of his river. His river, where was it? He couldn't see it. Didn't smell it. Where did they put his river?

The sheriff replaced the cup, but stayed on his feet. "Son, I don't know if you're just out of it, or if you're trying to give me a hard time. You should be aware, we're gonna put a name to you sooner or later. If you can help us, it'll be easier all around."

With a sigh, Cade sank into his pillows again. Pillows. So soft. Softer and crinkly, his pillow never made sounds. Everything in this room made sounds. Beeps and scratches, crinkles and whooshes. No wind, though. No birds. No rabbits racing through the brush. No bees. No owls. No waterfalls to whisper all night long.

The sheriff leaned over him. "What's your name, son?"

Dragging a hand down his face, Cade peered over at the sheriff. "Cade. Just Cade."

"What did you mean when you asked my daughter if she was immune?"

Cade curled a finger in the air. "Probably an H1. That's what did it. Spanish knocked out five percent, knock out twenty and the world ends."

That answer didn't please the sheriff. He stood up straight. He huffed, like a bear. Bears huffed to warn you away. Cade had never seen his father do it; maybe this one did. Maybe other people were strange and mutated. Hard to say, hard to say.

"You'd better explain yourself."

"You must be immune, too." New footsteps sounded and Cade tried to turn to look. It made his head swim. But he smelled sweet chemicals and heard papers rattling. Guessing aloud, he said, "That's a nurse."

"That's right," she replied. "I just need to get your vitals."

She was going to touch him. Recoiling a little, Cade winced when she grabbed his arm anyway. Her fingers were cold. They pressed hard into his skin. Suddenly, she was all over him. Something wheezed, something ticked.

Struggling to sit up, Cade only managed to smash himself against the metal bars on the other side of the bed.

"Open your mouth," she said, tapping a stick against his teeth. Screwing up his face, he twisted his neck from side to side. He didn't know what that thing was, but he didn't want it in his mouth. Unfortunately, that much motion wore him out. After a moment, he slid back down and she pushed the stick under his tongue.

"In your opinion," the sheriff asked the nurse in a very low voice, "in your medical opinion, how much of this is he putting on?"

To Cade, the nurse said, "Don't chew on it. Just hold it under your tongue." To the sheriff, she said, "Hard to tell. He's on a lot of pain meds. If you're not used to them, they can make you pretty loopy."

"I'm fine," Cade said, spitting the stick out. "I'm tired."

"Let me get your blood pressure and you can get back to sleep," she said.

There was something magical in those words. She whipped out a black band and tied it around his arm. And without another question, the sheriff slowly backed from the room. He was a tiny, grey shadow and then nothing, all gone. Now Cade loved the nurse, because she made the sheriff go away.

He only had one answer, and the sheriff didn't like it. Woozy, Cade clutched the side of the bed as the ground rolled beneath him. His stomach lurched, and then he felt like he was floating.

One of the machines let out a sigh, and warmth spread through him again. He barely noticed the black band on his arm tightening.

With one more uneven smile, he said, "Hi."

If the nurse answered, he didn't hear it.

It was the perfect crime, really. Nobody used the landline anymore, so nobody thought to take it away from her. Threading it into her closet, Dara sat down and pulled the doors closed. Light slanted through the lattice.

She was cramped in there. It was barely wide enough for the hangers, let alone her whole body. But it was the only place she could think of to hide. Quiet, out of the way, no one else would think to look inside and the clothes would muffle her voice. Perfect.

On the other end of the phone line, her best friend, Sofia Cruz, said, "Seriously, you saved this guy's life and they ground you for it?"

"Ugh," Dara whispered back. Wrenching an arm behind herself, she pulled out a bent hanger. No wonder she was so uncomfortable. "I think that's the only reason I'm not going to boarding school."

"Were you scared?"

"Terrified. My brain went on vapor lock."

Somewhere behind Sofia, a party raged on. Laughter, music, it all rolled through the line. Probably the last blast before everybody came home, tanned or faux-tanned.

Somebody would have a tiny dolphin tattoo—it was like a requirement of Florida spring break. Dara guessed Sofia would be the one who came back with *mehndi* looping up both hands. Their friend Tyler would probably show up with fifty percent less hair than he left with.

None of them had nightmares splashed red with blood. Not a single one of them had sudden, random flashbacks to the sight of that bear rising up. But Dara wasn't sure she would have traded her spring break for theirs, either.

Sofia shooed someone away, explaining that she was talking to Dara. Then she said, "You're lucky you're not dead."

"I know, right?"

"How's Josh doing?"

Pressing herself against the wall, Dara tried to fold herself smaller. "I don't really know. We went over to their house so Dad could grill us together. He looked miserable. You know they're going to make him do an interpretive dance about his behavior or something."

"He's so normal," Sofia said. "His parents are so bizarre."

"He's weird, too," Dara replied.

"Are you kidding me? He calculates interest for fun."

Clapping a hand over her mouth, Dara held back a laugh. When the urge passed, she whispered, "You don't think that's weird? I do. And you know what? Even when I had proof that there was somebody watching us in the woods, he was like, whatever, can we make pancakes if we don't have any more eggs?"

Sofia hummed curiously. "Really? He didn't go all macho he-man on you?"

"Not really. I mean, once he knew he'd come into our camp he wanted to leave. But I'm like, he's out there spearfishing and walking around in trees, you're not the tiniest bit curious?"

"I'm curious." Sofia hesitated, then asked, "This isn't relevant at all, but . . . what does he look like?"

Covering her eyes with her hand, Dara tried to summon his face, as it was at the river. When he wasn't grey turning ash, when he wasn't dying. Her pulse stuttered, chest tightening. At the river, she reminded herself. By the water, when she really saw him for the first time.

"He's probably our age. Brown eyes. Really dark hair, I don't know if it's black or brown. But it's in dreads. They go past his shoulders, for sure. Maybe as tall as Josh, I don't know."

A high-pitched tone lingered on the line. It resolved into Sofia asking, "And?"

"And what?"

"Is he hot?"

With a sigh, Dara dropped her hand in her lap. "Seriously, Sof. I'm still traumatized, for real. He was torn to shreds. I was literally holding pieces of his chest together."

Immediately penitent, Sofia apologized. "Sorry. Sorry. My whole week has been is she hot? Is he hot? Who's hot? Am I hot? Brain is still engaged in OrlandoVision, obviously. Is he okay?"

She only wished she knew. "They won't let me go to the hospital to see him. Family only, can you believe that?"

"I can't, that sucks."

"It really does," Dara said. Her promise to Cade at the ranger's station haunted her. Was he sitting up at the hospital, waiting for her to arrive? Was he afraid? Was he awake? She didn't even know that for certain.

Her dad wasn't all that forthcoming when she asked about him, and there was nobody else to fill her in. Every so often, he'd ask her again, did she know his name? Did she know him? That told Dara something important: they hadn't found Cade's family yet.

That meant he was all alone in the hospital. No one to sit next to him, or hold his hand. No one to reassure him that everything would be all right. It made her stomach churn.

Eager to change the subject, Dara asked, "Anyway, whatever. Is Orlando awesome? Tell me stuff. Are you having the best time ever?"

"Oh my god," Sofia exclaimed. "The closest beach is an hour away. An hour away. Did you know that?"

"Are you telling me you haven't been to the beach even once?"

"No!"

"You went all the way to Florida for spring break and no beach?"

Practically yelling, Sofia said, "No! And I'm furious!"

Suddenly, Dara laughed. It rolled from her, low and soft. It felt so good, like it had released a pressure she hadn't realized was building inside her. Tucked into the sweet, dark corner of her closet, Dara escaped in her best friend's vacation for just a little while.

For the time being, that was the only escape she had. She wasn't about to let it go until she had to.

TWELVE

It was too bright, and everything stank.

Struggling to sit up, Cade winced. His chest hurt, his shoulder, too. He started to rub it, but tubes jerked him short. They coiled around him, unnatural vines. They trailed from his arm to a metal hook above the bed.

Bags of yellow liquid hung there. One drip at a time the contents slipped into him, through needles fixed with filmy white tape.

He understood he was in a hospital. The buzz from the helicopter rotors still filled his ears. Bright flashes from the emergency room came back when he closed his eyes.

Chaos—his head was chaos. The memories were disjointed. He remembered people asking him questions. Pushing needles into him. Rubbing his hand when it got dark again.

Until then, he hadn't felt anything. It was rush after rush. Bleary awareness followed by black nothing, unconsciousness instead of sleep.

Well, he was awake now.

Sliding to the edge of the bed, Cade stared at the floor. It was so smooth. Blue and brown tiles, triangles. They fit together in a pattern, and they were cold under his bare feet. A wave of nausea hit him and he lifted his feet a moment.

His mother had said that hospitals were the best place to get sick and die. *Staphylococcus aureus, Pseudomonas aeruginosa, Acinetobacter baumannii*—Mom made diseases in Latin sound like music.

They weren't musical anymore.

Eyes darting, Cade reeled. There were so many things he couldn't see. The bandages on his chest could have already been contaminated. The needles taped into his flesh might be feeding infection right into his veins.

Shuddering, Cade took a step. The motion reverberated in his chest. It hurt to move, but Cade ignored that. Carefully studying the tangle of equipment tethering him, he stripped himself clean. Piece by piece—the clip on his finger was easy enough. It shook right off. The IVs were trickier.

With a hiss, he peeled the tape off and flicked it from his fingers. Blood welled around the needle and a bone-deep hurt spiked through his arm. Better fast than slow, he pulled the IVs out. Sticky patches on his skin came off last, and that's when the alarms blared.

So many lights blinked. The sound punched at him, unnatural, mechanical cries. He had to get out; his skin crawled. Throwing the curtains open, Cade slapped his hands against the windows. Greasy, bloody handprints smeared the glass. Scrabbling, he dug around the frame, then realized the only way through it would be *through* it.

When he turned, a nurse strode into the room. Both startled, their screams combined. She rushed toward him.

"You need to get back in bed," she said. She was young; she looked afraid.

Scrambling back, Cade knocked over the IV stand. A new alarm sounded, and set off a chain down the hall.

The nurse stopped. Her fear showed on her face, in the shadow on her brow. And the way she had to start twice before she managed to say, "Let's just lay down, okay? You're bleeding, let me help."

Cade felt caged. Backing into the wall, he jerked away from it and measured the height of the bed. Could he jump it? "I have to go."

"You need to lay down."

She sounded more certain. Like she'd worked up her nerve. She walked toward him purposefully. Voices in the hallway rose and footsteps spattered. In a panic, Cade grabbed a chair. That broke her bravery—she screamed and ducked.

Cade felt a fleeting sense of guilt. He wasn't going to hurt her. He just needed to get out. The chair was for the glass; surely it would break the glass and he could climb down. He could get out, get back home to his cave by the bee hollow. Lie in running streams and let them wash him clean. *Home.*

But that thought was erased by the blinding hot pain in his chest.

Instead of throwing the chair through the window, Cade dropped it. The crash echoed—down the hall, and in his ears. Head pounding, vision blurring, he stumbled. It seemed like the world had turned on its side. Catching the edge of the bed, Cade fell hard. Darkness swept up, soothing, sweeping away his sick stomach and his pain.

Just then, the tray table tipped. Ice water sheeted across his back, a clear river, cold and hard. His eyes snapped open when the cold shocked him back to awareness. He grabbed the bed again. He had one thought: get up. But the floor was slick. Skating, sliding, Cade fell again.

Before he recovered, strong arms hauled him off the floor. When he hit the bed, he screamed. The pain in his chest blotted out sense and thought. Hot sweat rose on his skin. All he could do was pant. Gasp. Try to ride it out.

"Thorazine," somebody said.

Somebody else said, distantly, "Get some restraints and the biohazard team in here."

Cade roared. He knew what biohazard meant. He wasn't safe. The room wasn't safe. He tried to wrench himself off the bed. A hard hand slammed him back down. Someone, a man, broad and imposing, hovered over him. Though his scrubs had little blue ducks on them, he wasn't friendly at all. His wasn't a sweet, familiar weight like Dara's.

Dara. Throat raw, Cade rasped, "Dara, where is she?"

"Quiet," the man with the blue ducks said.

Suddenly, Cade was cold. He shook, his teeth chattering. The last of his adrenaline sputtered out. He was cold, and hurt and the weight on his chest made it hard to breathe. Everything blurred. No matter where he looked, he couldn't focus. Smeared, doubled people stood over him. Their voices were a jumble.

He heard someone telling him to hold still, and someone else yelling at him to calm down. *Calm down.* That confused him, because he *was* calm. He *was* still. Wasn't he? He was floating, didn't that mean he was still? A bright, silvery pain slipped into his hip. It was like an anchor. It tethered him to the bed.

"Please," he said. But his tongue felt thick. And he didn't know what the please was for. Please let me go? Please help me? Please don't let me die? Whatever it was, he didn't have long to consider it. A new dark came over him. One that slipped over his eyes, a mask of blue.

He floated, dreamlessly, in space.

Sometimes, talking to her dad felt like a police interrogation. In this case, it actually *was.*

Dara pulled her sleeves over her hands. "Dad, for the millionth time, I don't know him."

"But you know something *about* him."

It hadn't been a million times, but it was pushing fifty, at least. Nobody—not even her family—believed her. A stranger swooping her away on a vine, it was ridiculous. It was a story that belonged in old books and cartoons. And boy, what a mistake to mention that she thought Cade might have been following her.

Slumping, Dara said, "He told me his name. He wanted to know how many people were left. And that's seriously, really, totally all I know."

Dara's dad pushed his chair back. He had keen eyes. They weighed people's words, their expressions. He liked to tell Dara and her friends that he was a human lie detector. Which explained why Dara got invited to parties, but nobody ever told her the address. It was pickup and delivery only for the sheriff's kid.

An old clock ticked away on the wall. It buzzed, competing with the fluorescent lights. The itchy, tingly sound went on and on while Sheriff Porter peered at her expectantly.

This was a tactic, Dara realized, called "let the other guy talk first." Unfortunately for her dad, she didn't have anything to say.

Slumping a little more, she let her gaze wander. The police station was almost as familiar as her living room. In December, a wobbly plastic Christmas tree stood in the corner. She used to make presents to put under it. Now, she brought cookies. People only needed so many tin-can pencil holders.

The bulletin board hung on the other wall. Lots of FBI fact sheets and Most Wanted lists. But weirdly, now a police sketch of Cade and a picture of his bloodied clothes hung there, too.

He wasn't dangerous, but he *was* most wanted. Since they'd come out of the forest by helicopter and ambulance, official people had a lot of questions. Like what Cade's last name was. Where his parents were. How they could be reached.

Dara didn't know. Cade wasn't telling.

It seemed to Dara like her dad, the human lie detector, should have realized she wasn't holding back on him. No, Cade was as mysterious to her as he was to the social workers and the police. And the rangers, and the Parks Department. Get attacked by a bear in a national forest, and a lot of people want answers.

The worst part was, school gossip was slowly turning into news. Lia's idiot friend Kit was running a Tumblr now. He'd cobbled together some of the stuff the police put out trying to identify Cade. There were pictures, of his face and his blood-ied deerskin clothes. Somehow, Kit got ahold of an email from the Pulaski County Sheriff's office to another department in Nashville.

Nobody was supposed to see the email except for other police. So it looked pretty terrible, their theories written out in black-and-white. They thought Cade's babbling about infec-tions and sickness meant something. Maybe he was a terrorist. It was obvious he'd been living in the woods for a while; was he growing drugs? Hiding a bomb lab?

Kit added his own messed-up spin on all of it. He turned it into a sideshow, complete with macros. They were all the same picture, some guy in a coonskin cap on an orange-and-red star-burst background.

The first one read STEP ONE: FIGHT BEAR. STEP TWO: ??? STEP THREE: PROFIT!! Another one read BREAKING BEAR: ALL NATURAL METH. There were more, each of them stupider than the last. Dara made the mistake of asking Lia to get Kit to lay off. Two hours later, somebody added a stick-figure girl to the macro with the caption, LEAVE MY PRIMITIVE BOY ALONE.

Sheriff Porter pulled a folder from his desk. "He trashed his hospital room today."

Dara's pulse stilled.

"The whole time, he was screaming for you."

She felt sick. She'd sworn she'd see him, and she hadn't. Not for days, not since the paramedics had closed the helicopter doors between them. No matter how many times she asked, even when she explained her promise, the answer was always no. Guilt and responsibility nagged at Dara. She raised her head to meet her father's gaze. "Is he okay?"

"What's it matter if you don't know him?"

What a jerk. Gathering her bag, Dara stood. "He only saved my life."

Pointing at the chair, Sheriff Porter said, "You're grounded. It's you and me until your mother gets off work."

It wasn't a little bit of grounded either. Sneaking onto the landline was probably the last contact with the outside world she was going to have. They'd confiscated her car keys and her phone, her laptop and her iPad. The only reason she knew what Kit was up to online was because Lia couldn't stand keeping the hilarity to herself.

Dara wasn't sure why her parents had cracked down so hard. She was a good student. She didn't get in trouble; they never had to worry about her—not like they did about Lia. And what's more, they *knew* she was spending spring break with Josh. Sure, they thought it would be at Disney World, not

Daniel Boone National, but so?

"I have homework," she said, raising her bag.

"On the first day back?"

She ducked out of his office and planted herself at the empty desk near the filing cabinets. She lost herself in a book. Occasionally, her thoughts would interrupt. She really did want to know how Cade was. Screaming for her? Her dad could have been lying, but Dara wanted to see for herself.

Unnoticed at the back of the station, Dara read and plotted. What she needed to do was get her mom to volunteer for guard duty. Things were always so busy at the Pulaski County At-Risk Outreach. Even when Dara went in to help her mom with month's-end paperwork, Mom barely noticed she was there. Dara could break out for a visit, easy. No problem getting back in time for the dinner run home, for sure.

Dara turned a page of her book. She found herself looking over it, though. Glancing at the bulletin board again. Something in her chest tightened. The sketch was bad, but the pictures of Cade's ruined clothes made it all too real. The heat of his blood felt fresh on her hands. His wild, terrified look pierced her again.

She *would* get to him. Soon.

THIRTEEN

Sofia had been Dara's best friend since third grade. That meant she had special privileges. For example, torturing Dara for details about anything. The big rescue in the woods had been the topic of conversation since Sofia had stepped off the plane from Orlando. Unfortunately, there was more to say about Sofia's mahogany tan than there was about Cade.

That didn't seem to sink in for Sofia, though. As they walked from the parking lot to Pulaski County At-Risk Outreach, Sofia took advantage of her free pass again.

"If I'm going to cover for you," Sofia said reasonably, "I need information."

"Fine," Dara said. She knew what Sofia wanted to hear. Pressing a hand to her chest, she lowered her voice. A sexy, late-night podcast voice. "Okay, just this once. He's six five, brown dreads, brown eyes, incredibly hot."

Sofia brightened up. "Really?"

"Oh yeah. Built like you wouldn't believe."

"Are you serious?"

"Absolutely. When I was sitting on him, trying to keep him from bleeding to death, I was so turned on."

Realizing she'd been punked, Sofia rolled her eyes.

Dara understood that as her best friend, Sofia really did deserve the most details. She knew more than anyone else, but there were some things Dara wasn't ready to share. The nightmares, she kept to herself. When she was asleep, she was there again in the forest. The bear, the collision . . . then all the blood. It always came back to the blood.

Even awake, she had to shake those thoughts off. Sometimes physically. The less she talked about it, the better she'd feel. With her head full of it again, she had to surface.

Back to the real world, where she was safe and fine and she nearly shrieked when a man stopped in front of the office doors.

"Dara Porter, right?" he said, thrusting a business card in her face. "I'm Jim Albee with the *Makwa Courier*, hi. How are you feeling?"

"I'm good, thanks."

"Glad to hear it, you've been through an ordeal," Albee said. He dripped with fake sympathy. It was a thousand times creepier than real sympathy from strangers. "Do you have time for a couple of questions?"

Confused, Dara shook her head. Her father had been the sheriff for a long time. He'd drilled it into her, no matter what the reporter wanted, she didn't have a comment. Some of them weren't above trying to get information about him through his children. Trying to reach past him to open the door, Dara said, "I don't, sorry."

"Just one quote about the Primitive Boy."

"Don't call him that," Dara snapped. Hearing Kit's stupid Tumblr name for Cade coming out of a grown man's mouth shocked her. How did this guy even know about it? Why was he *using* it? Pulse pounding furiously, Dara tried to reach for the door again to escape.

"Do you know who he is?" Albee asked anyway. "Did he confide in you?"

Sofia swiped her thumb across her cell phone. "I'm calling the police."

Albee moved, but he didn't leave. He stood there like he owned the place. Or like he realized he only had a few more minutes to ask questions before the sheriff rolled up. "What do you think about the hospital putting him on a psychiatric hold?"

The path clear, Dara grabbed Sofia's arm and rushed inside the building. Their footsteps echoed on the back stairs. Heat flashed through Dara. It made her dizzy and sick at the same time. She didn't realize she was waiting to hear the door latch, until relief flooded her at the sound. The reporter didn't follow, thank god. Only the sound of their panting breath filled the stairwell.

On the second-floor landing, Dara let Sofia go and slumped against the wall. It was marble, nice and cool. She looked to

Sofia, still carrying her phone.

"Haven't they answered yet?" Dara asked.

Sofia turned the speaker on. "Thank you for calling Kentucky 811. *Para continuar en español* . . ."

"I thought . . ."

Hanging up her phone, Sofia sat on the bottom step and waited for Dara to recover. Her dark hair swung in its ponytail, ironed smooth and bright. "Easier to sneak out if your dad's not in the parking lot in his police cruiser, am I right?"

Relief bubbled through Dara. "You're the best."

Sofia shrugged. "I know. Go out the other door, I'll tell your mom you're in the bathroom."

Already halfway up the next flight of steps, Dara looked back when Sofia called her name. Her head was already in the next step. The next move she had to make. Was it true? Was Cade under a psychiatric hold? Her dad said he'd trashed his room—was that true, too? Had he really been screaming for her?

Emotions already winding tight in her chest, more questions spilled out in her head. Why would a reporter be interested in this at all? Gossip was one thing at a high school where literally nothing happened. Didn't the real news have something better to cover? It took Dara a moment to realize that Sofia was talking to her. Shaking her head, she asked, "What?"

"*All* the details," she said, wagging a finger at her.

Dara crossed her heart with one finger, then disappeared down the back hall.

— —

Sneaking into the hospital was harder than sneaking out of her mom's office.

Dara made the mistake of going to the ward desk first. The nurse on duty typed forever on the computer, then shook his head.

"I'm sorry, no visitors allowed," he said. He didn't sound sorry at all.

At a loss, Dara scrubbed her free hand on her jeans. With the other, she clutched a balloon. Static electricity kept making it drift toward her hair. It crinkled in her ear, a lightning storm just in her head.

"Could I leave a note or something?"

The nurse didn't roll his eyes. He should have, because it was obvious he was annoyed. He slapped around the desk, opening drawers, and making his life's work out of finding a pad of paper and a pen. The WHILE YOU WERE OUT pad right in front of him wouldn't do, it seemed.

Dara wrote a generic note, *sorry I missed you, give me a call,* and signed it with her phone number. Then she dropped the balloon's gold weight on top of it.

"Thanks," she told the nurse, then started to walk away. She stopped, like she suddenly realized she had a question. Turning back, she asked, "Um, the bathroom?"

The nurse pointed the way, and Dara thanked him before hurrying down the hall. To make it look good, she went inside. Washing her hands twice, she stared at herself in the mirror. Pulling her fingers through her hair, she straightened her spine and pulled her shoulders back.

She'd learned a lot of things listening to her dad. The previous summer, he'd chased a ring of shoplifters all over town. They weren't the usual pack-of-gum, box-of-smokes shoplifters. They strode into electronics stores and walked out with flat screens. After every hit, the store clerks were embarrassed to admit they let it happen. The guys acted like they were supposed to be there, they said. They seemed like they knew what they were doing.

Proof you could get away with anything if people thought you belonged.

I belong, Dara told herself.

Pulse quick and chest tight, she walked that hall like she was the CEO of Lake Cumberland Regional. When she turned a corner, she smiled and nodded at the cluster of nurses gathered around a cart. They smiled back. And they said nothing when she caught sight of Cade through wire-laced glass, and let herself into his room.

The rush of pulling it off died when she realized two things. First, he was asleep. And second, he was tied to the bed.

It struck her, a hammer directly to the chest. This boy, who'd done nothing wrong—who'd gone out of his way to feed her, and then to save her—they had tied him to the bed like an animal. The reporter was right. Someone at the hospital had talked; medical records were supposed to be secret. That nurse wouldn't even let her in to visit, but a reporter knew?

A hot spike of anger pierced through her. It seemed to fire her from the inside out. They were monsters, treating him this way. He was a hero, and he didn't have a friend in the world here.

No, that wasn't true. He had her. And she had promised they would take care of him. She'd sworn it, because at the time she believed it. Making sure the door closed tight behind her, she pulled the curtains closed and approached his bed.

He'd been afraid of the helicopter. Of the truck. And he was only here because she convinced him to come. The thick leather bands around his wrists and ankles tormented her. They may as well have put him in chains. He was still so pale. There were so many tubes and wires surrounding him—the bandages stretched across his chest, and IVs dangled from the inside of his arm.

Throat knotted with tears, she reached out carefully. Touching his brow, she smoothed her thumb against the furrow between them. She had to fix this somehow. She had to make it right. What could she do? As a plan slowly unfolded in her thoughts, she started with the most logical place.

Leaning in, she whispered, "I'm so sorry."

Breath touched his ear. A whisper slipped into him.

Cade blinked, drawn out of the dark. He wasn't really awake. Just sort of aware. It took a few more blinks to make out the shadow hovering over him. Leather tongue rattling in his mouth, he struggled to speak. "Dara?"

"What have they done to you?" Dara asked.

She pulled at the straps around one wrist. When she freed that one, she leaned across to get the other one. That woke Cade more than anything. Her sweet scent covered him, her weight, too. Raising a tingling hand, he caught her arm. His fingers slipped off her skin, too weak to grip.

"I need to go home," he managed to say. Then he winced. His throat hurt, and suddenly, he was so, so thirsty.

Dara bustled around him, tugging at his ankles. "I'll take you there right now. I can't believe they're treating you like this."

"The windows don't open," Cade volunteered.

"I'm not surprised."

Golden strands of Dara's hair floated as she unlatched the last of his restraints. They drifted in the air, glittering like dust in the streak of late-day sunlight. The same beam of light raced across her face. Shadows chased away, her eyes glittered like clear water. Useless fingers waving, Cade lifted his head to try to get to her.

The drugs in his system pulled him back down. He drifted back into the dark, only to surface when Dara appeared at his side. She put her cool fingers on his forehead, and it felt so good. So familiar. Trying to catch her arm again, his hand glanced off her wrist but he managed to look up.

"Take me home?"

"First, we get you up."

Dara looped an arm beneath his neck. He felt like he was floating when she pulled him to sitting. Swaying against her wasn't terrible. He could breathe her in. He had a reason to hold on to her. Cade had no idea where Josh was; he didn't care. Maybe he was far away. Maybe he was just a bad dream he'd had. Everything was hazy, but Cade felt possessiveness just fine.

And embarrassment. Dara hadn't seen him at his best yet.

Afraid at the river. Bleeding to death, then crying like a baby, afraid to get in the helicopter. Now this, limp and dozing. Searching his head and his mouth and his throat, he managed to meet her eyes. It was like a dip into fire after a long winter hunt.

"Are you stealing me?"

Dara laughed. It was high and shrill, like a blackbird's call. "I think so. Shhh, we have to get out of here. Two steps to the wheelchair, come on."

When he dropped into the seat, he hissed. He'd ripped open the doctor's first careful stitches. They were worse the second time. Deeper, maybe. Tighter thread. His flesh felt like raw meat, chewed and gnawed at the edges. At night, the only thing that dragged him out of his sedative coma was the pain.

Trailing her fingers over his shoulder, Dara whispered, "Sorry."

"I like it," Cade said through gritted teeth.

"Uh-huh," Dara replied. She lifted his feet and dropped them on the metal rests. When she leaned over him, her hair parted and bared the nape of her neck. Her flesh was golden, creamy like the inside of a pawpaw. Fingers twitching, he longed to touch it to find out if it felt like it looked.

But he blinked into darkness. And when he opened his eyes again, they were moving. The hallway stank of antiseptic and sickness. Recoiling, Cade pulled into himself. A hot sweat rose on his skin; his heart beat like he was facing that bear again.

"Taking him to X-ray," Dara told someone. They were nothing more than a blur.

They moved so quickly that the breeze chilled him. It kissed his face, and rushed into the open hem of his gown. The hair on his thighs prickled. Gooseflesh swept his body, and he lolled his heavy head back to try to look at her. "They took my clothes."

"I know," Dara said. There was hurt in her voice. Worry. She rolled to a stop, then pushed the wall until little disks on it lit up. Staring at illuminated numbers above her head, she didn't seem to realize the strange magic she was working.

Cade had heard of elevators, of course. They went with the escalator lesson, and automatic doors. It was nothing he'd ever expected to see, though. His parents said that world was gone. Electricity and cars, and little rooms that could slide up and down a shaft, carrying people from floor to floor.

The people. The people were all supposed to be gone. He wanted to ask Dara about them, but just as the doors slid open, his eyelids fell again.

Drifting back into the dark, he missed his first elevator ride completely.

FOURTEEN

*J*osh Brandt's house was usually an oasis. His father taught yoga; his mother taught philosophy at the university. They spoke softly and lived quietly. The TV never blared, and everyone wore headphones to listen to music. That made the pounding on the front door even more jarring.

Hauling himself off his bed, Josh walked out of solitary confinement to go answer it. His parents hadn't banished him to his bedroom. No, they had both been very *disappointed* in Josh for the secret camping trip. They had *concerns*. Since they made himself define his own consequences, Josh had grounded himself. It was better than writing an exploratory journal about his actions.

Dara stood on his porch, close to collapsing under Cade's weight. A sheet wrapped around his shoulders, Cade looked like he was going to a toga party. Or, from the way he listed and could barely raise his head, had just left one. An abandoned wheelchair sat forlornly on the walk, the porch stairs too steep to mount.

"Help, please." Dara sank down, starting to wobble.

Slinging Cade's good arm over his shoulder, Josh hauled him up. Then he dragged him inside and dropped him on the squeaky leather couch. He didn't like it, but what else could he do? Knotting a hand in his own hair, he stared at Cade, then turned to Dara.

"What even, Dara?"

Jittery and talking too fast, Dara paced. "He wanted to go home, and I . . . and I . . ."

"You brought him to mine?"

"He passed out. I didn't know where to take him." Dara stopped, putting a hand on Josh's arm. Looking up at him, she really did seem sorry. "Dad took my keys. You can only wheel somebody through Makwa for so long before somebody notices."

Josh looked at Cade again. He could tell he was awake. Listening, even. Yeah, he had a gorked-out look on his face. But under heavy lids, his eyes followed them as they talked. Creeped by that, Josh covered Dara's hand and pulled her into the dining room.

"It's just until I can figure something out," Dara swore.

"He can't stay here." Josh glanced toward the back door. The door his dad would be coming through anytime. "I'm grounded. And he's . . . you kidnapped him!"

Dara shook her head insistently. "I didn't. He wanted to go."

Leaning to look at Cade on his couch, slumped and pale in his sheet, Josh raised an eyebrow. "Uh-huh."

"They tied him to the bed," Dara said. She touched Josh's face, making him look at her again. She looked wounded, like she was the one in restraints. Considering she'd just broken a guy out of the hospital, Josh mused, maybe she needed to be. Her fingers curled, skimming down his chin, his throat. "I couldn't leave him there."

"Okay, great, but . . ."

Cutting him off, Dara said, "I know. He can't stay here. Can he borrow some jeans, though?"

Josh wanted to say no. After a moment of hesitation, he headed for his bedroom. Agreeing didn't make him agreeable, though. The irritation came through when he asked, "Where are you taking him?"

"I'll figure it out," Dara said flatly. She crossed her arms, standing in the doorway of his room.

Three weeks ago, she would have sprawled on his bed. Distracted him from his homework by taking his picture from a hundred angles. Wrapped her arms around his neck, and kissed him until they couldn't breathe.

In his closet, Josh had two antique baseball cards—his college fund, his parents joked. He would have sold them both to take back the camping trip. The box with the cards rattled as he threw open his closet doors to find his oldest jeans and his least-favorite T-shirt.

"Why are you so mad?" Dara asked. She slid into his room.

Leaning against the wall, she kicked at a pair of old sneakers.

Bristling, Josh tossed some jeans to the bed. "My dad's on his way home."

"I'm sorry, I didn't know."

She did. Or she should have. They almost always came back to his house after school. For homework, or photography, or whatever. And at five thirty, when his dad rolled in from work, it was always back to homework. Three years, going on four—Dara knew. Josh grabbed a threadbare T-shirt from his shelf, then a pair of socks to go with. He thrust them at her.

"There."

Dara took the clothes, but she didn't move. "He saved our lives, Josh. You could be a little more grateful."

Sweeping an old pair of sneakers off the floor, Josh dropped those on the pile of clothes in Dara's arms. He didn't answer her, except with a look. One that told her she needed to get the Primitive Boy dressed and out of his house as quick as she could.

Because he wasn't grateful.

Josh had kind of hoped the guy would get patched up and go back to wherever he came from. That he'd never have to see him again, or hear about him, or talk about him. Every time he saw his stupid picture on the news, Josh remembered. Every time he checked his email, he remembered. On Twitter, on Skype, his friends couldn't stop talking about this guy.

For them, it was just some weird story. Something interesting to take the boredom out of Makwa.

But for Josh, it was a lot more. When that bear stood up,

his thoughts came fast and clear. He'd put his hand on Dara's shoulder. He was going to drag her away, throw her over his shoulder if he had to. But before he could, Cade swooped out of nowhere.

Like some backwoods Batman, he saved the girl and left Josh facedown in the dirt.

If he'd been one second faster . . . if he'd moved one second sooner . . . Since he'd gotten home, Josh lay awake at night, chewing the insides of his cheeks raw.

That's why he'd decided to ground himself. No phone calls, no more internet, no dates, no company. He didn't want them. It was easier to hide than to look at her. It devoured him from the inside, because he was the one who took care of her. Who bought her batteries, and found new places for her to photograph.

Since freshman year, he was the one who held her hand. Who walked on the outside of the sidewalk, closest to the cars. That's who *he* was. Josh Brandt, Dara Porter's boyfriend. Her protector. He should have hauled her out of the woods the first night she thought they were being followed. All the arguments after that would have never happened. Cade the Primitive Boy wouldn't have swept her away.

Pounding a fist against the wall, Josh bellowed, "Hurry up!"

Dara ignored that outburst.

Instead, she pressed her cheek to the bathroom door. It had gone quiet in there. She was afraid Cade had passed out— wouldn't Josh love that? Things were so strained now. Except for the joint interrogation, she hadn't even seen him since they got home.

To be honest, she hadn't been desperate to, either. She'd realized too many things about herself during the camping trip, and maybe too many things about Josh, too. The distance was there and it grew.

The door shook and Dara jerked away in time for Cade to open it. This was probably the view Sofia had been hoping for. He'd managed to get the socks, jeans, and shoes on. But his chest was bare. His waist tapered into the jeans; his skin everywhere was bronze and smooth. His few scars trailed his muscled body like silver vines.

Holding the T-shirt out, he said, "I can't raise my arm."

Glancing down the hall, Dara was relieved to see Josh had gone outside to wrangle the wheelchair. He was already mad; watching her put a shirt on another guy couldn't possibly improve his mood.

It should have made a difference that Cade's chest was heavily bandaged. There was nothing sexy or fun about the spots of blood seeping through. Now that Cade was steadier on his feet, did that mean his pain medication was wearing off, too? As she pressed into the bathroom with him, she wondered how badly it hurt.

Bunching the shirt up like panty hose, she pulled it over Cade's head. "Arm through there, good."

Hands beneath the shirt, she pulled the collar down his shoulder, then stretched the sides and sleeve as far as they would go. It was a 3D puzzle, and she reached through the armhole to grab Cade's wrist.

"Push," she said.

Cade lifted his head. His jaw was hard, and he pressed his lips together tight. It was like he was trying to trap a cry in his throat. His brows knitted with the exertion. When Dara straightened his arm, his nostrils flared and he sucked in a sharp breath.

Wavering, Dara pulled the shirt down. Maybe he *needed* to be in the hospital. What if the restraints had been for his own good? But she shook that thought off. Nobody deserved to be chained to a bed. What if there had been a fire, or a tornado?

"I called my friend Sofia," Dara told him. She turned on the tap, rinsing her hands with cool water. Then she pressed them against his face, trying to soothe him. "She'll be here in ten, tops. It's going to be fine."

Cade grimaced. "I want to go home."

"I know. I'm working on that," Dara said. "I promise. Come on, can you walk?"

She led him from the bathroom and through the kitchen. Sunlight spilled through the French doors. When Cade slowed, Dara squeezed his hand, tugging him a little. "What?"

"What is all this?"

Dara looked around, confused. It was just an ordinary kitchen. To be fair, a nicer than average one, with black countertops and cabinets that went up to the ceiling. There even a built-in wine refrigerator, half full of Coke. But nothing unusual, down to the totally ordinary microwave and can opener.

"What's all what?" she asked.

Slowly, Cade considered the room, then pointed. "That. What's that?"

Was he seeing things? Dara followed the line of his finger, but there was nothing there. Confused, she pointed with him. "You mean the stove?"

"It's inside . . . ," he said. It wasn't a question. To Dara, it sounded like *wonder*. Maybe he still had more medication in his system than she thought.

Tugging him gently toward the doors, Dara nodded. "Yep, it's a stove inside. Sofia has one, too, you can check it out. But we have to get outside so she can pick us up, all right?"

"You're talking down to me."

"I am not!"

He laughed a little, the first time Dara had heard that since the harrowing ride to the ranger's station. His resistance melted away and Dara led him out the back doors. A small alley ran behind Josh's house, just wide enough for one car. It was the perfect escape route; Dara had used it more than once.

As she unlatched the gate, Dara stiffened. She heard sirens in the distance. It wouldn't have taken them long to discover Cade was missing. Had they already pulled the security cameras? Was somebody from her dad's station watching her roll Cade out under the noses of every single guard in Lake Cumberland Regional?

Stop it, Dara told herself. Those sirens could have been for anything.

From nowhere, Cade smoothed a hand over her shoulder.

Though his skin smelled sour, mixing badly with the scent of Josh on the borrowed clothes, his presence was comforting. Warm, even. "What's wrong?"

The crunch of tires on gravel drowned out the sirens. Relieved, Dara patted Cade's hand and slipped from under it. "Nothing. Okay, okay. We're going to Sofia's first. Her parents are out of town, so we can catch our breath and get everything situated."

"You said you'd take me home."

"And we will! I mean, do you live near here?"

Confused, Cade frowned at her. "I don't know."

"Well, what's your address?"

"I live near the bee hollow," he explained.

"Quit messing with me," Dara said. "I don't have a lot of time here."

"I'm not. That's my home." Cade raised his brows, like he was waiting for her to get it. To understand.

But Dara didn't. People had addresses. Houses. Except when they didn't. She was right; he *was* one of those people on the Appalachian Trail. But now that she'd actually seen him, talked to him . . . There was something deeply sad about that.

He wasn't old enough to go to the woods to live deliberately. He should have been in school. He should have had a home. There were so many terrible possibilities that would explain why he didn't. She saw them all the time through her mom's job, to a lesser extent through her dad's.

Twisting her hands, she looked away, then back at him plaintively. She wanted this to be a joke. She hoped he was just playing around with her, for whatever bizarre reason. "Seriously, Cade."

"I'm very serious."

A car horn blared in the alley. It was a break in her churning thoughts. The next step was Sofia's, to get him out of Josh's hair and somewhere he could rest. Settling him in there, that would give Dara time to think. And to figure out the truth. Grabbing Cade's hand, she pulled him toward the steps. "Sofia's here. Time to make a break for it."

"Okay," he said.

For a second, Dara suspected he had no idea what that meant. But she didn't have time to worry about that. She had to figure out how to pack him into the backseat of Sofia's car before anyone saw them.

It didn't sound complicated, but it was. Sofia had the world's largest collection of fast food bags back there. A purse wouldn't fit back there, let alone a towering, broad-shouldered guy on the lam.

When the car stopped, Sofia leaned her head out. "Dare! What the hizzy?"

Dara shrugged as she helped Cade to the car. "Hey, you wanted details."

FIFTEEN

Cade sat in a very blue bedroom. The walls and carpet, a trash bin, a desk—all blue.

Though he couldn't help it, he heard every sound in the house, including Dara talking to her friend in another room. He was used to listening for much smaller things. The footfalls of squirrels, the rustle of a single bird in a bush.

"He lost a lot of blood. He could be confused, or . . ."

"Most people know where they live," Sofia said. "Ooh, unless he has amnesia."

"Really, Sof?"

He didn't have amnesia. A bad case of his skin crawling, sure. There were so many people here. Crammed together, constantly touching. Breathing on each other.

"Just go get the stuff."

"You're sure he's going to be okay here?" Dara asked.

Of course I am, Cade thought, and peeled off his socks. Already, he hated them. How was he supposed to keep his balance without his toes? In *sneakers* that didn't bend like supple leather boots? Once his feet were bare again, Cade stood.

He hadn't heard Sofia's answer. It was probably the same. He was fine in this blue, blue bedroom. Not nervous. Not anxious. Nope. He'd already learned something about this new world. Panic didn't help. And he'd panicked at the hospital.

When his parents had told him about the world outside the forest, Mom started with the hospitals. How they were full of disease, of dying. They sealed the walls and windows against the wind. The water only came in cups and pitchers. Instead of healing, hospitals harmed. That's where the infections began . . .

Yes. He'd panicked, and it wouldn't happen again.

Standing, Cade crept around the edges of the room. Touching everything. Looking at everything. Bottles full of blue liquid sat on top of the dresser. A musky, chemical scent radiated from them—the same scent clinging to the curtains and carpet. Cade picked up a few coins; not interesting. He'd seen money before.

The pictures didn't hold his attention either. Back in his cave, in a box he'd built himself, he had a few photos of his own. His mother, young and dazzling. His father, lovesick and consumed by her. In a few snapshots, they held a baby—Cade. They stood inside a house Cade didn't remember, with people Cade didn't know.

Ranging across the artifacts on the dresser, Cade found a

small box wrapped with wires. There was a switch on top of it, and tentatively, he pushed it.

A screen lit up and Cade nearly dropped the thing. A tinny sound gushed from the wires, from little buds at the end of each one. Tentatively, he brought one to his ear, then reared back. It was music, but nothing like he'd ever heard. It pulsed, loud and hard, with a rhythm he felt in his fingertips.

He shook the box, and the music changed. Something slower. Sweeter. As an experiment, he pushed a bud into one ear and smiled. The music seemed to play inside his head. It was too loud, but too novel to abandon just yet.

Hooking his fingers in a drawer pull, he slid it out slowly. Clothes, mostly socks, bathed in a pleasant but artificial scent that made Cade's nose twitch. The drawer under that contained shirts like the one *Josh* gave him, then more jeans . . .

"You better stop before you find Javier's porn," Sofia said.

Startled, Cade slammed the drawer shut. He had no idea what porn was. It was the surprise that unnerved him. There were so many scents in this room. When he pulled the blaring bud from his ear, the house's sounds flooded back in. "I didn't see anything."

Sofia shrugged. "I told him to take it with him. Maybe he actually listened for once."

"Where's Dara?" Cade asked.

"Hitting up the drugstore." Studying Cade, Sofia made herself at home at the desk. Spinning the chair around, she gazed up at him. It was like she could measure him with a look, even the unnameable stuff inside of him. "She wanted to change your bandage."

"Then she's taking me home."

Sofia started to say something. Then she closed her mouth, squinching her lips to one side.

Muscles tight, Cade froze. "Isn't she?"

"As soon as she figures out where you live, yeah."

"I told her."

"Right, the woods." Sofia rubbed her hands together. "You don't really live there, do you?"

Drawing the answer out, Cade said, "Yes . . ."

"All by yourself," Sofia said. She spun again, her hair washing over her shoulders in black waves.

Cade kept his mouth shut. Until recently, his life was normal. As far as he knew, the cities were deserted. Towns, farms . . . all empty. The people that were left, of course they lived in the forests. The caves. That's where it was safe. He didn't understand why *they* didn't understand. Pressing his lips together, he shrugged.

"Honey, seriously, I don't bite." Sofia smiled, then snapped her teeth playfully. "Unless you ask me to."

"Why would I do that?"

Spinning to a stop, Sofia perched at the chair's edge. Her playfulness faded. Instead of measuring him, she examined him. In the forest, animals would have hushed—freezing, waiting. That same uneasy, near quiet filled the room.

"It's a joke, Cade." Then, thoughtfully, Sofia laced her hands together. "Is English your first language?"

Uncomfortable, Cade grabbed a bed knob, used his good

arm to swing onto the mattress.

He landed in the middle of it. Springs protested under his weight, shrill, metallic birds. A chemical cologne scent puffed into the air. Dragging his wrist and hand beneath his nose, he finally peered back at Sofia.

"It's my only language."

"Hm," Sofia said. She deflated, touching her toes to the ground.

Used to the quiet of his own company, Cade watched Sofia, but didn't say anything. Beneath him, the bed squeaked then groaned. A shift in balance, and it almost sang. Curious, Cade put his weight into a bounce, just a small one. Metal hummed inside the mattress, echoing on through the coils.

"Having fun?" Sofia asked.

"Yes."

"Can I be rude?"

Cade considered this. "Probably."

"Aren't you worried your parents are freaking right now?"

At once, Cade stopped. Sitting heavily, he draped his arms over his knees. Even that little movement made his chest hurt, but he didn't change positions. "No. They're dead."

Sofia blushed. Squirming right out of the chair, she stretched toward the door. Confident before, she'd turned skittish. A fawn realizing its mother is out of sight. "I'm sorry, I didn't know. Who do you live with now?"

"No one."

"You're what, like sixteen?"

"Almost seventeen," Cade corrected. He didn't know his

exact birth date. But he knew it came in the hottest month. Usually when the birds started to flock to head south. It had been three autumns since his father made the last honey-cake for his birthday. That was his thirteenth year.

Sofia considered this. "But, your grandparents or your aunts or . . ."

"They're all dead."

This time, Sofia didn't blush. In fact, his blunt response seemed to strengthen her. Counting her fingers off, she approached him. "Foster parents?"

Cade grabbed the bed knob again. But he forgot, and tried to haul himself up on the clawed side. Instead of landing gracefully on the footboard, he collapsed in the middle of the mattress. Clutching his chest, he hissed a breath through his teeth. He'd obliterated the low-grade ache in his chest. Now, new, vicious pain burned through him.

"Oh crap, are you okay?" Sofia rushed over.

Eyes closed, Cade nodded.

"Should I do something?"

He shook his head and retreated into himself. He was tired of questions, tired of answers. Tired of puzzling out what made Sofia uncomfortable, and what made her bold. He wondered if Dara would be back soon. If she'd bring supplies, and take him back into the forest tonight.

If she stayed, he could show her all the things she didn't know about the wild. Maybe he could touch her hair; maybe she would let him smell the back of her neck.

Those thoughts, and his silence, sustained him.

Waiting at the back door, Sofia threw it open the second she saw Dara approach. She'd stuffed her hair into a hoodie, like that wasn't the most obvious disguise in the world. Jogging half down the steps, then back up with her, Sofia started in.

"I think he's on drugs."

"Yeah, they pumped him full of them at the hospital," Dara said, slipping inside.

Oh, Dara, so sweet, so completely missing the point. Sofia took the drugstore bag and dug inside it. Gauze. Peroxide. Ointment. Incredulously, Sofia said, "I have all of this stuff in my house."

"Well, I'm sorry," Dara said, annoyed. She tugged the hood off, her hair falling into her face. "I don't usually have to liberate people from the hospital, okay?"

"Dial it back," Sofia said.

Following Sofia upstairs, Dara lowered her voice to a whisper. "I'm freaking out, Sof. I have no idea where I'm taking him next."

Cade called down the hall. "Home!"

"Which he swears is in the woods," Sofia said, putting a hand on Dara's shoulder. "I know I said he could stay here . . ."

Shocked, Dara shook her head. "No. Sofia, no, no, come on, you can't . . ."

It was Sofia's privilege to torment her, but her responsibility to protect her. Whether that was from jocks with too many beers in them at a pool party, or the loonbox currently hanging in her brother's old bedroom, it didn't matter. Best friends, sacred duty. "Look, I'm here for you. Always."

"But?"

"I don't know. We had the weirdest conversation."

"I hear you," Cade called.

Sofia whipped a look down the hall. If Cade had been in the path of it, he might have even shut up. "That's why it's called talking *about* you, not *to* you. Hush!"

Something thumped in the bedroom. Sofia's guess was that monkey boy in there tried to climb the ceiling fan. Because trying to climb the footboard had worked out so well. Lowering her voice a little more, Sofia turned her back on the hall so she could face Dara. "He swears he lives in the woods. He says his whole family's dead."

"Oh no," Dara murmured.

"And he doesn't have foster parents. Or a social worker. Or basically . . . anything."

"Seriously?"

"Also, he was humping the bed."

At that, Dara pulled a face. Apparently that was her tipping point, because she rolled her eyes. Reclaiming the bag from the drugstore, she brushed past Sofia. "If you don't want him to stay, that's fine. You can just say that."

"All I'm saying is that we don't know anything about him . . ." Sofia trailed off, watching Dara stalk into Javier's room fearlessly. Now she was the one eavesdropping, trying to make out Cade and Dara's quiet conversation from the top of the stairs.

It was her house, so she could barge in if she wanted to. But the problem with Dara was that she was a pit bull. Once she decided to dig her teeth in, she'd hold on until somebody pried her jaws open with a crowbar.

Still blocking the hall, Sofia wasn't sure what she could say to call off the pit bull. The weird thing was, she wasn't afraid of Cade. She really wasn't that worried about him staying there while her parents were away. In fact, she thought it might make her feel the tiniest bit better, not being alone all week.

But Dara had already done one crazy thing. Two, if you counted trading spring break with the Mouse for spring break with a bear. (And she did.) The possibility of more irrational insanity was extremely high. Therefore, it was Sofia's job, sacred duty, etcetera, to save Dara from herself.

Pushing the bedroom door open, Sofia sighed. "That is not how you put on a bandage. Now I remember why you dropped out of Girl Scouts."

"I joined the photography club," Dara said.

"Whatever," Sofia replied. "Just let me. You don't want him to lose a nipple to gangrene, do you?"

To Sofia's delight, Cade and Dara both squirmed.

SIXTEEN

*f*lattening herself, Dara tried to slip between her back door and the frame, like a note left between classes.

Her head buzzed, thoughts fast and distracting. Maybe she shouldn't have left Cade at Sofia's. He was in good hands, but it wasn't the same. As soon as she got inside, she turned the knob to silently close the door.

Sunlight slanted in the west, the same shade as a split peach. It spilled around the door, casting long shadows on the kitchen floor.

Dara could sneak all she wanted, but she was undeniably late.

The latch whispered closed, and Dara's sister cleared her throat. Spine stiffening, Dara turned to face her. On a good day, a bribe could shut Lia up. Or a tradesie; now that Lia had her little sophomore social club, she needed big sis to cover from time to time.

"Loser," Lia said. She didn't give Dara the chance to negotiate. She polished off the milk in her cereal bowl and tossed it the sink. It clattered, rattling against breakfast dishes and OJ glasses.

The noise worked as expected.

"Is that Dara?" their mother called, her footsteps approaching.

"Thanks," Dara hissed.

"Stop stealing my sweaters," Lia snitted. Then she raised her voice. "Yeah, it's her!"

Now Mom's footsteps thundered. She stalked into the kitchen, then stopped abruptly. Phone in one hand, she waved the other. "Nice of you to finally waltz in!"

"It was more of a shuffle." Even though she knew better than to deploy sarcasm in her parents' general direction, Dara winced when she heard herself say that.

"Funny," Mrs. Porter said. Into the phone, she said, "Yes, it's her. Do you want to talk to her?"

Lia stage-whispered through a smirk. "Dad's pissed."

Dara muttered back, "No, really?"

Mrs. Porter hung up and tossed the phone on the counter. She exhaled heavily. "So let's hear it. Where were you?"

"Sofia's," Dara said.

Mrs. Porter narrowed her eyes. "Sofia was at work, where she was supposed to be."

"It's too loud at your office to do trig. I went to Sofia's to finish it."

Lips pursed, Mrs. Porter glanced over at Lia and caught her

making a face. She jerked a thumb at her. Dismissed, without even a word.

Skulking from the kitchen, Lia shot Dara another dirty look before ducking around the hallway door.

"She's listening at the door," Dara said.

Barking, Mrs. Porter shouted, "Go finish your homework, Lia!"

Feet pounded on the stairs, and Mrs. Porter pinched the bridge of her nose when Lia's bedroom door slammed. Nostrils flaring, she took a long, calming breath, then turned her attention on Dara once more. "Let me see your book."

"What?"

Holding out a hand, Mrs. Porter approached her. "Your trig book. Let me see it."

Ugh, Dara should have known better. Never lie without backup. The book sat in her locker, the finished assignment pressed between the pages. She liked to knock her homework out during lunch when she could.

"Okay, I didn't."

"You," Mrs. Porter said, angling to point toward the door, "are grounded. You go to school, you come home. That's it."

Dara looked away. "Fine."

"I'm *this* close to canceling Sofia's internship. I don't appreciate being lied to."

Panic replaced Dara's irritation. Sofia loved working at At-Risk Outreach. She was sickly addicted to policy and spreadsheets, do-gooding and causes—Mrs. Porter had plenty. One day, Sofia fully expected to spend her days changing the world at her own environmental nonprofit, so the internship with Mrs. Porter was her mini holy grail.

It was low to threaten Sofia's internship. But Dara knew better than to mouth off about the injustice. There were other ways to protect her friend. Pretending to be contrite, Dara bowed her head. "She didn't want to cover for me, I made her. I wanted to see Josh."

Exasperated, Mrs. Porter sighed. "That's what I thought." Slumping to lean against the kitchen island, she waved an impatient hand at Dara. "Go. Finish your homework before dinner." Then, she turned the phone on, already dialing.

Dara took the escape gladly.

These windows opened.

Cade rubbed his fingers against the bare screen. It tickled, and a buzzing filled his ears. Back home, the bee hollow would be making the same sound. Sleepy drones woke; the queen walked among them. It was almost time for them to swarm. They'd leave the hive in the hollow to a new queen, and she had so much work to do before there would be summer honey.

An unfamiliar exhaustion blanketed Cade. Everything inside his chest felt heavy, and his muscles longed to curl and still. He'd felt that way before, when his mother died. Then, after his father. Too tired, too heavy to do anything but mourn. This was a smaller version of that. He didn't know it was called homesickness.

Pushing the screen, Cade jumped back when it popped. He didn't know where Sofia was. If she was close enough to hear.

There were no trees to camouflage him here. Standing still was his only defense, and he waited against blue wallpaper until he was sure it was safe.

Then, with another testing touch, Cade realized the screen was fabric. Its edges were frayed. A cord secured it to the frame. With a quick zip, Cade pulled the cord out. Now the screen hung loosely, and Cade put his whole arm through it. Perfect!

Cade climbed through the window. His bare toes clutched at the brick sill; he reached out to frame himself in it. It wasn't so far up. He'd jumped from higher, though at home, he had branches and vines to slow his descent, and outside Sofia's window there was nothing but smooth grass.

Considering the house, Cade lit up. A rail ran near the window, attached to the roof. It wasn't a vine, but it would do. Cool wind touched his skin. It called to him, urging him to follow it to the woods again. *Back home, come home,* it said.

The rail felt sturdy. Metal, maybe, with grooves pressed into it. It fit neatly into his hand, so Cade dug in and jumped. For a second, he clung to the house, steady and deft as a squirrel.

Then, the rail cracked. Dust flew up, burning Cade's nose. Crumpling under his weight, the rail pulled away from the house. At first a little, then completely. Twisting in the air, Cade braced for the impact. When he crashed to the ground, he fell on his good side.

His thoughts and breath flew out of him. Blood roaring, he heard nothing but his own heartbeat. Lights went on everywhere. In Sofia's house, and the houses next to hers. A shadow appeared at the back porch, so Cade scrambled to his feet. He ran.

The night loomed strange and unnatural around him. The concrete bit at his bare feet. Splinters dug into his palms when he hopped a bare wood fence. Greenish lights cast sickly shadows as he ran beneath them. His first thought was to find Dara.

But there was no way to track her. No broken twigs, no footprints. City smells burned away any scent he might catch. They were greasy and heavy.

At the corner, Cade stared down one street, then the other. It all looked the same to him. Stunted trees stood in the middle of green flag lawns. The shoots without blossoms huddled in beds, plucked and pruned and docile.

A heady waft of honeysuckle decided Cade's direction. He followed that smell, cutting through alleys and side streets. It was a real scent, a familiar one. Veering through someone's backyard, he knocked over a trash can. Hurrying to right it again, he fled when that house lit up, too.

Sprinting through the neighborhood, he lost the scent. Seized with fear, he stopped in the middle of the road. The city tried to blot the honeysuckle out. Closing his eyes, Cade turned a slow circle. Cold wind prickled on his skin. It cut through his clothes. Shivering, he turned and breathed in again—it couldn't have disappeared. He had to find it.

Just then, a car turned onto the street. Its lights swallowed Cade. Squinting, he held up a hand to try to see.

"Get out of the road," the driver yelled from the window.

Then a terrible siren sounded, and Cade bolted. The mechanical roar behind him quickened his pulse and his pace. The scent, where was it? Safe against a tall fence, Cade centered himself, drew another inquisitive breath.

There it was. Bright and sweet, cutting through the greasy wall of city night. Cade followed it through a clearing, one with wood chips instead of grass, and strange metal frames. The streetlights played tricks with their angles. They threatened, chained seats twisting slightly in the dark.

Cade cut wide around them, and broke out running when he saw a great grove of trees. They weren't his—too short, too close together. But they were familiar enough. Plunging beneath the canopy, Cade finally slowed.

A worn path led into the trees, but Cade avoided that. Paths meant people.

The overgrown brush snatched at his clothes. Cold crept beneath them, and Cade shivered in spite of his exertion. His real clothes would have kept him warm. These let every element in and kept nothing out.

Still moving, Cade tried to adjust to the half light. He would have done better by the moon alone. The lamps stretching above the park only confused the geometry. Holes were deeper than they looked. Trees closer together.

Cutting his own path, he cried out. A jagged, bone-deep pain pierced his heel. That new pain added to the old, raising a cold sweat on his skin. Teeth chattering, Cade grabbed a low branch. He clutched it harder than he had to. Dew shook from the budding leaves, showering him with icy flecks.

Winching himself to the ground, he propped himself against the tree's trunk.

He pulled his foot up and shuddered. A thick triangle of glass jutted from his flesh. Hazy with filth, the glass was thick and curved. Blood seeped around its edges. Though the pulsing ache urged him to pull it out, he didn't.

If he pulled the glass out now, his blood would flow. He had nothing to stop it with. Lifting his head, he drew a deep breath. No water in the air. Nothing to clean the wound, either. A dirty, open wound meant infection, and he couldn't even prevent that. The paramedics had taken his pack, the one with honey and yarrow and other medicinal herbs in it.

As much as it hurt, the glass had to stay.

Considering the threadbare T-shirt, he tore the hem from it. The fabric was so soft, it practically melted. Cade tore off more than he intended, a wide triangle of cotton.

"Josh is not getting his shirt back," Cade muttered.

He panted a thin laugh at that thought, a grim anesthetic. It cleared his head so he could do this properly. Gritting his teeth, Cade tied the shard in place. An overwhelming agony raced through him. With measured breaths, Cade leaned his head back against the tree. As soon as this wave passed, he'd keep going.

Maybe after the second wave, he decided. His teeth chattered painfully, and he wrapped his arms around himself. As the cold and the pain melted together, he decided again: after the third wave, for sure.

SEVENTEEN

When the phone rang, Dara looked at her bedside clock. It was two in the morning.

She tensed. Nobody called with good news at that time of night. And it was weird to get a call on the house phone. Everybody had their own cells. Grandma Porter was the only one who used the regular line anymore.

Weird as it was, something told Dara she should answer. Jogging downstairs, she caught it on the third ring. Sofia's voice spilled out before Dara could say hello.

"Okay, the police are on their way, so tell me what to say!"

"What?" Dara yelped.

"Your primeval boyfriend escaped. He destroyed our gutters; they're laying in the middle of the yard. My mom's going to murder me."

Tucking herself into an alcove, Dara kept watch for her parents. "Calm down, okay?"

"Calm is dead," Sofia proclaimed. "And I will be, too. I'm not even lying. He ripped them right off the house. And he trashed the screen in Javier's window."

"You're sure he's gone?"

Dara didn't have to see Sofia. The sound Sofia made, a mixture of disgust and frustration, was plenty vivid. It always came with the gonna-have-to-stab-somebody face, complete with deadly side-eye.

"Yeah, I'm pretty sure," Sofia said sarcastically. "Mrs. Goldstein next door called the police. She's waiting for me on the porch."

"Oh crap."

"Yeah right, oh crap. I hear the sirens, Dare. I snuck back in to call you."

Someone was definitely moving upstairs. Leaning over the rail, Dara watched to see if the bathroom light turned on. Maybe it was just Lia. Please be Lia, Dara prayed. Lowering her voice a little more, Dara huddled over the phone. "Any idea where he went?"

"Oh, well let me consult the parchment note he left, oh my god, he has the best handwriting, NO!" Sofia's patience failed. "I'd appreciate a tiny bit of concern for me, Dare. The cops. Are on. Their way."

This was a disaster. All Dara's regrets about leaving Cade alone returned. They were an unholy choir, screeching in her head. In a horror movie, it would have meant that she was about to be stabbed by a stranger in the dark.

Since it was real life, she was perfectly safe and freaking out. Cade was out there, alone and not right in the head. Sofia was losing it at home—both Dara's fault. *Panic helps no one*, Dara told herself.

"Okay. Okay. Okay, tell them you didn't see anything. You didn't. It's not a lie."

"But Mrs. Goldstein . . ."

"Didn't see anything, either." Dara peeked into the kitchen. Her car keys hung where they always did, on the rooster hook by the back door. She was grounded from driving, but this was an emergency. "I'm going to drive around and see if I can find him. Then I'll be over to help you with the gutters."

Sofia sighed. "I am so screwed."

"You're not," Dara said. "I promise. I'll fix this."

She just didn't know how.

Cade missed his bed.

A wooden frame kept it off the ground. Tanned deerskin smoothed the platform. The shell of the bedroll was more deerskin, sewn together to make a deep pocket. Rabbit fur lined the inside of it.

Sometimes, it got so warm, Cade had to slide out to cool off. In the summer, he slept on top of it, covered only by a reed blanket.

All he had now was the rough bark of a willow tree against his back. Arms pulled inside his shirt, Cade dug his icy fingers into his own armpits. Forming an uneven bundle, he breathed into his own collar. Every bit of warmth counted. Though he didn't want to admit it, he was in trouble.

Back home, he would have been fine. He lived deep enough in the forest that he rarely encountered garbage. In the mining town, he'd found a few broken bottles, a shard or two from an old lantern.

But sitting in this grove, all he saw was garbage. Fading cans glinted in the low light. Plastic bags hung in the trees. Some were so worn, they'd turned into threads. They dangled and swayed, dirty white vines that would never bear fruit. It looked nothing like his home.

His home, so far away. His bed. His clothes, his things. He wanted them all so badly. He just had to check on Dara one last time. He should have been long gone . . . but it hurt to think about the alternative. If he hadn't gone to see her again, she'd be dead.

Hot tears rose up, but he blinked them back. They'd turn icy, too, if he let them fall. Trying to stave off the cold, he sent his thoughts back home. Back in time, when everything was exactly right.

Every few weeks, his mother sat him on the cave floor to work on his hair. She cut out the knots with a knife, and smoothed clarified deer fat into the dreads. It took all afternoon, and Cade had learned this was a good time to ask questions.

"What was the world like?" he asked her once.

Pinning his shoulders between her knees, his mother twisted his curls into plaits, plaits into bundles. Sometimes she wove in fragrant herbs or flowered vines.

"He looks like a bird's nest," his father said. He had his own chores by the fire, rubbing bones into fish hooks and cloak clasps, and all sorts of useful things.

His mother laughed. "He's my pretty bird. Aren't you? Pretty bird!"

At that command, Cade peeped, and both his parents laughed. It was a good, warm sound. It radiated around him, the same as the heat from their fire. Safe with them, content, Cade leaned back and asked again, "But what *was* it like?"

His parents exchanged a look. There were stories in it, secrets. But Cade couldn't translate them. He had to believe his mother when she answered, after a long quiet, "It was beautiful and terrible."

"Tell me the beautiful parts."

"Well," she said. "People built pyramids, once. Smooth, gleaming ones in Egypt. And some with rugged steps, in Mexico and Guatemala. They're so handsome to look at, but do you know what made them beautiful?"

Lulled by her voice, Cade had to be nudged to answer. "No," he said dreamily. "What?"

"The Maya and the Egyptians never met each other." She picked up her knife, and gently shaved a knot from his neck. "There was a whole ocean between them. But they both built pyramids, reaching for the heavens. Trying to get closer to their gods."

Cade knitted his brow then. He knitted it now, remembering. "I don't get it."

"What made the world beautiful," his mother said, "were the people in it."

Oh. The emptiness of the forest sprawled around them, and Cade looked into it. Except for the occasional ranger, *they* were the only people in the forest. Some of the few left in the world. Though Cade understood this was tragic, he didn't really understand it. He'd always been content with his mom and dad. They were enough, just the three of them.

"Dara," Cade murmured. A twinge of pain brought him back to the present, and he licked his dry lips. "Sofia. Idiot Josh. Three in the helicopter. People at the hospital. The man in the car . . ."

He tried to count all the new people he'd seen. They blurred together. Everything blurred, mixed with cold and hurt—his stomach rumbled—and hunger, too. He should have taken the slice of pizza Sofia had offered him. Even though it was greasy and unfamiliar, it had been warm. He wanted something hot right now. Boiling broth, stew, soup. Roast meat and wild potatoes, something. Anything.

Wracked with cold, he shook so hard that dead leaves fluttered from the tree above him. They kissed his face as they fell, so gentle. He could almost imagine his mother was still alive. Once the sun rose, he'd be able to find his way. He only had to make it to morning. A few more hours, he just needed to hold on. So he clung to his best memories. They lulled him away from this foreign, frigid place.

Home, he reminded himself. *Think about home.*

EIGHTEEN

Makwa was a quiet town most of the time. There were other parts of the county that kept Sheriff Porter busy, but his own stomping grounds barely did.

He had a lot of calls around homecoming, prom, and graduation, when the kids at the high school spent the night TPing the teachers' houses. Every so often, he had to break up a bar fight at the Ski-Kay Lounge.

Mostly, Makwa was traffic tickets and noise complaints. So eight calls in one hour about an intruder was bizarre. So bizarre that the dispatcher called Sheriff Porter personally on his cell. Whatever happened overnight, usually, the deputies on duty would handle it.

"I just thought it could be connected to that kid," the dispatcher said. "You know, the one . . ."

"Thanks, Arlene," Sheriff Porter said.

She didn't have to elaborate. He knew which kid. The one that had walked out of the hospital and disappeared in the middle of the day. The one that his daughter claimed had saved her life. It sounded like a fairy tale. This kid literally flies in on a vine to beat the crap out of a bear? With his bare hands.

Yeah, right. Sheriff Porter had to admit he wouldn't have believed it coming from anyone but Dara. It was just too far-fetched. Sounded too much like covering something up. Especially with him up and leaving. Without clothes. Without money. Where was he going?

Of course, nobody knew. Nobody had gotten jack out of him. Just a first name, Cade. Nothing else. Not a last name, no social security number, no address.

Dutifully, Sheriff Porter fed the name into a bunch of different databases. Nothing came back, but he didn't expect it to. There were thousands of Cades in the United States, but none of them sixteen, six five, and living in Kentucky.

He was a mystery. And just to be an absolute thorn in Sheriff Porter's side, he was a mystery that all of a sudden the newspaper wanted to write about. Jim Albee turned up at the station after the kid went MIA from the hospital. Sheriff Porter shooed him off because there was nothing to tell—and that was the truth. But the newspaper getting interested meant complications.

Buckling his belt, Sheriff Porter then tucked his hat beneath his arm. All his girls were sleeping, and he hated to leave in the middle of the night. But the job was the job, so he kissed his sleeping wife and headed out.

Since he was still half-asleep, Sheriff Porter didn't realize where the first call was taking him until he got there. Slowing to a stop in front of Sofia Cruz's house, Sheriff Porter steadied himself. The dispatcher said nobody had been hurt, but it didn't matter. Getting calls to familiar addresses scared him every time.

A few squad cars sat in front, their lights attracting gawkers like moths. It seemed like every house on the street was lit up. Sheriff Porter was used to being watched at work, so he ignored the silhouettes in the windows. Up the front steps, he knocked on the door before letting himself in.

Sofia and an older woman Sheriff Porter didn't recognize sat on the couch. They were flanked by two of his deputies. He couldn't get over how young Sofia looked, and at the same time, how grown-up.

"Everything all right?" he asked.

Blanching, Sofia stared down at her feet. "I think somebody tried to . . ."

It was curious, the way she trailed off. Her eyes cut away, and Sheriff Porter took a step closer. This one time, being the guy in the kitchen, making post-sleepover pancakes, had an advantage. He watched his daughter's best friend shift uneasily. Gentle, he said, "Tried to what, Sof? Are you all right? Your mom and dad still out of town?"

"No," Sofia said, too fast. "I mean, yes. But you don't have to bother them, I'm fine."

Raised eyebrows were Sheriff Porter's reply.

Abruptly, Sofia stood. "Can I talk to you in the kitchen?"

Sheriff Porter waved the deputies off, stepping past them smoothly. He didn't like where this was going, not a little. But he liked that he was going to get there quick. Sofia opened the fridge door, then pulled out a Coke. Cracking the cold, red can, she took a sip, then remembered herself. "You want one?"

"Not right now, thanks." Keeping his distance, Sheriff Porter nudged her. "What's going on, Sofia?"

She took another sip of her soda, then turned around and dumped it down the sink. Completely out of sorts, she fidgeted like Sunday school had gone on just a little too long. Finally, she slumped against the counter. Whatever war she'd been fighting had ended. She met his eyes miserably.

"Nobody broke in," she said. "Cade was here, and he broke out."

Sheriff Porter blinked. "Excuse me?"

Looking like she wanted to melt through the floor, Sofia shrank into herself. Shoulders rounded, head bowed, it was obvious she didn't want to say anything else—and just as obvious that she knew she needed to.

"Please don't be mad," she finally said. "Dara said she needed to see him. To make sure he was okay, you know? But when she saw the restraints, she flipped out. It's not really kidnapping, is it?"

Since Sofia thought he knew what she was talking about, she left gaps in the story. Sheriff Porter had to piece it all together, and he wasn't happy about where it was all going. Dara being late, Cade disappearing . . . Looked like he didn't walk out of the hospital alone after all.

170

Hours of unwatched surveillance footage lurked on his computer at the office. With the rest of Makwa going crazy, he hadn't had time to look at it. And now, he did. Sheriff Porter wasn't sure what came after grounding, but whatever it was, Dara was about to find out.

But he couldn't let Sofia see that anger. Choosing his next question carefully, he tempered his voice, gentle. "Honey, did he hurt you?"

"No. God no." Sofia shook her head adamantly. "He barely even talked to me. The last time I saw him, he was asleep. Maybe he was plotting his big escape, I don't know. Like it would have killed him to use the front door."

"He didn't?"

"No! He went out the window and climbed down the gutter. Which, by the way, is trashed. I'm so screwed."

"I can't disagree with you."

Sofia sighed. "I'm sorry they woke you up for this. Now Dara's out there looking for him and it's all my fault."

That was news to him, too. The house had been quiet; it was the middle of the night. It was reasonable to think all of his girls were asleep. Grinding his teeth, the sheriff shook his head. "I think Dara's old enough to make her own bad decisions."

"I'm really sorry," Sofia repeated. Whether it was for harboring a fugitive or for getting her best friend in trouble, it was hard to tell.

Sheriff Porter patted Sofia on the shoulder, reassuring her. "I'm glad you're all right. I'll send the boys home, you lock up, all right?"

"Thanks," she murmured.

Leaving his deputies to finish up, Sheriff Porter strode back to his cruiser purposefully. Makwa wasn't a big town. It wasn't hard to map, he just had to string the emergency calls together in order.

The first call came in near Sofia's. Then a few doors down, a block away, through the alleys—it made sense on foot. The last call placed him at the park, so that was the path to follow. Turning off his siren, Sheriff Porter pulled onto the street.

If he was lucky, he'd catch Dara *and* the kid.

Driving aimlessly, Dara watched for signs of Cade. She felt stupid. What did she expect to see? Was she hoping he'd just jump out of the bushes and ask to hitch a ride?

She had to admit, if only to herself, that she had no idea what to expect. She'd been running on adrenaline and insanity since she'd stepped into his hospital room. For an honor roll student, she'd veered wildly off the sensible, intelligent course. And she wasn't sure when, exactly.

As she turned down a new street, Dara's heart started to pound. A police car had turned down the opposite corner. Now it glided toward her slowly, a silver shark in the night. All at once, Dara went cold. And weirdly, she had to pee. It was like every uncomfortable thing in her body decided to strike at once.

None of the alleys were big enough to drive down. Turning into a driveway would give the cop an excellent view of her and her car. Since she and her car were supposed to be at home, tucked into bed and garage, the last thing she needed was a close encounter with the county sheriff's department.

Red and blue lights burst to life. They blinded her, and she hit the brakes, right in the middle of the road. The cruiser angled to stop in front of her. A very familiar shadow stepped out of the driver's seat.

Leaning into her window, Sheriff Porter smiled darkly. "It seems to me I remember grounding you."

"I can explain."

"Pull up to that corner and park," Sheriff Porter said. "I'm taking you home."

It was always important to know the difference between a setback and defeat. This was definitely the latter, so Dara did as her father told her. Somehow, she suspected it would be a long time before she saw the inside of her car again.

Locking up, she trudged toward her father's cruiser. "Okay, Daddy, I know you don't want to hear it, but this is important. I think Cade is out here somewhere . . ."

"No doubt he is," Sheriff Porter said. He keyed the mic on his shoulder, barking arcane orders at someone on the other end. They responded in kind. As she climbed into her father's car, Dara regretted never learning all the radio codes.

"You have to find him. I've tried, and I haven't . . ."

"You know more about him than any of us," Sheriff Porter said. "Where did you look?"

"Everywhere. I've been driving around for an hour . . ."

Cutting her a look, Sheriff Porter raised his brows. "Aimless won't help anybody. Think about it. Anything you didn't bother to tell me? Put the pieces together."

"I can't, I don't . . ."

"You know how I got here?"

Dara shook her head.

"Bunch of disturbance calls. Started at Sofia's house, led me right here. Haven't had one since the one that led me here. That means he came this way, and then quit bothering people. Now what am I missing?"

Scrubbing a hand over her face, Dara shook her head. She didn't know. If she did, she would have found him already. But if he came this way . . . Dara swallowed hard and looked out the window. There were swings at Clayton Park. And woods, too. A copse of trees, not far from Sofia's house. If he really did live in Daniel Boone National, then he might have mistaken their town park for the edge of his forest. Hands flapping, she talked so fast, the words spilled out in a rush.

"That makes so much sense. He said . . ."

"What?"

She felt like she was giving up secrets. Sour acid sloshed in her belly. "He said he lived in the forest. That that was his home. So he . . . look, Daddy. The woods. He came here, he thought he was going home!"

Sheriff Porter made a thoughtful sound. Pulling the cruiser over, he left the lights running as he climbed out again. It unnerved Dara, the way he automatically unsnapped his holster. As far as she knew, he'd never fired the gun on duty. Still, he put his hand on it, ready to draw.

Dara rolled out of the passenger side after him. "He's not dangerous."

"Get back in the car," Sheriff Porter said.

Dara zipped her jacket. Summer was coming, but it was still a ways off. Her breath frosted gently in the air. Falling into step with her father, Dara shook her head. "If I'm right, if he's in there, you'll scare him."

"Dara," he warned, but she refused to listen.

If he wanted her back in the car, he'd have to throw her over his shoulder. Then handcuff her. Then lock her in. He must have realized that, because he took one look at her defiant face, then shook his head. Instead of giving her permission, he let her disobey. Probably so he could hold it against her later.

Walking ahead of Sheriff Porter, Dara followed the path into the woods. The grove wasn't very big, but it was a good place to drink a beer or smoke a joint without getting caught. Since it was full of poison ivy, it was a terrible place to make out. Every year, a new freshman couple showed up at school with matching rashes. It was hilariously predictable.

"Cade," Dara called softly.

Something rustled in the distance. It was so dark, she couldn't place it. It was probably a squirrel anyway. Or a house cat chasing a squirrel. The other end of the path led right into a housing development. It wasn't much of a woods, to be honest.

"Son, you need to come on out," Sheriff Porter said.

Whipping around, Dara glared at her dad. "If you think that sounds reassuring, you're wrong."

"I'll send you back to the car," he replied, arching a brow.

Dara dug her hands into her pockets, pulling her hoodie around her a little tighter. As small as it was, as harmless as it seemed, the pocket of trees scared her so much more than the entire national forest had. It was like this place didn't belong. It was unnatural, just for existing.

Stop it, Dara told herself. Venturing farther down the path, she called again, "Cade, where are you? Everybody's worried. Come out."

"Nobody wants to hurt you," Sheriff Porter called.

"Shhh!"

Dara held up a hand and turned toward a new sound. It might have been a moan, it could have been human. Heart pounding, she took a step off the path. Twigs snatched at her hair and clothes. The underbrush smelled bad, like rotting leaves and something worse. But she was sure that sound wasn't an animal.

"Cade," she said. "It's me. It's Dara. Where are you?"

After a moment of fearsome silence, a small voice replied.

"Help me."

NINETEEN

*S*lender branches became whips. They tore at Dara as she crashed through the underbrush. Thorny vines clung to her ankles. But she followed Cade's faltering voice. It led her through the mazelike jumble of the woods. She didn't remember it being so frightening in the daylight.

Dara heard her father behind her. His footfalls were heavier than hers. The mic on his shoulder hissed, an electronic snake. Though he ordered her to stop, Dara refused. She didn't look back—she had to find Cade.

He was a grey smudge. Almost smoky, and if he hadn't raised his head just then, Dara might have passed him completely.

"Cade!" she cried.

Fighting her way through the brush to him, she dropped to her knees. Even in the low light, she could tell he was pale. His wispy breath clung to charcoal lips. His eyes barely opened. Perhaps sensing her, he turned his head toward her. "You're bad luck."

Frantic and overwhelmed, Dara laughed. "I know, right. Come on, you have to get up."

Cade shook his head. "Can't walk."

At the same time, they looked at his outstretched leg. A bandage jutted at an awkward angle from his heel. It definitely didn't match the shape of a normal foot. Dara wasn't sure what it was covering, and she was afraid to find out.

Instead, she offered a little black humor. "It's just a flesh wound. How lazy can you get?"

"Lazier," he murmured, and burrowed closer to her. "Watch and see."

A trembling thrill rushed through Dara's veins. It was something about his voice, about the familiar way he pressed against her. It was like he fit her shape. Like they matched, somehow.

If she wanted proof that she was a terrible person, she had it. What kind of sicko got crushy over a guy in hypothermic shock? She wanted to believe it was *concern*. Even guilt—he wouldn't be holed up in the Clayton Park woods if it wasn't for her.

But guilt and concern didn't explain how protective she felt. They definitely didn't excuse the wild, stray thoughts playing in her head. The best way to keep someone warm, her brain helpfully informed her, is to get skin to skin.

Mortified at herself, Dara shucked off her jacket. Fact: she had to warm him up. Secondary fact: she didn't have to get naked to do it. Especially considering she heard her dad behind her, talking to dispatch. Sirens wailed on the other side of town.

"Here," she said.

Blanketing him with her jacket, she did her best to tuck it under his back. Then she wrapped her arms around his shoulders.

Gentle, she pulled him against her chest. Rubbing his arms, she tried to press warmth into him through her palms. His skin was stiff and cold.

Cade's lips rasped against her skin. "Have you ever seen an escalator?"

The question jolted Dara out of her thoughts. Knitting her brow, she tried to look down at him. She could only see his hair and the curve of his ear. There was no way to tell if he was joking, or worse, raving. "Lots of times."

"I'd like to," he said. Another wave of shudders ripped through him.

"I'll show you one," she promised. "Just hang on."

Cade sighed. His breath slipped into her shirt, shockingly present. Dara felt him clutch and unclutch his fingers beneath the jacket, like he was trying to catch the cold and strangle it.

Turning her head, she saw her father approach. He was a silhouette against the trees. If she hadn't known it was him, he might have been frightening.

The worst part was realizing his hand rested on his holster. It certainly wasn't because he was afraid of Dara. No, he was ready to shoot Cade if he had to.

Before he could speak, Dara said, "He's hurt."

"I see that," Sheriff Porter replied. Moving closer, he snapped his holster and crouched before them. With his knuckle, he pushed his hat back so he could get a better look at Cade.

"He's afraid," Dara continued. He hadn't said so, but wasn't it obvious? "I think he should come home with us."

Sheriff Porter jerked his head up. "Absolutely not."

Tightening her arms around Cade, Dara drew strength from deep within. She wasn't afraid of her father. But she was afraid to let Cade go.

The people at the hospital had proved they couldn't take care of him. It had been wrong to ask Sofia to step in. No. Cade had saved *her* life. The least she could do was protect him until he could go home.

"Daddy, please," she said. "What if it were me? What if I were alone, far away from home? Would you want me in a straitjacket?"

Sheriff Porter frowned. "He wasn't straitjacketed."

"Practically," Dara replied. "He didn't do anything wrong. You can't lock him up because he's confusing. He needs somebody to care about him."

"That's what the social worker's for."

Bristling, Dara rubbed at Cade's arms again. "We can't give the social worker our address?"

"Dara, I'm the sheriff!"

"Yes, you are. You're supposed to protect people." Dara looked him right in the eye. Probably, it was wrong to ask him for this. But she was going to ask anyway and he had to see she wasn't kidding. "He needs to be protected, too."

The pullout in Dara's basement was about as perfect as a bed could get, Cade decided. Tucked beneath a thick stack of blankets, he basked in the warmth. Mingling with the heat was the pleasant buzz of painkillers. Those were a gift from the paramedics.

They'd carried him out of the woods. They tried to put him in an ambulance, but he wouldn't get in. Wouldn't go back to the hospital. The hospital was a bad place and he was never going back.

He fought so hard that the sheriff stepped in.

With his booming voice, the sheriff directed the paramedics to patch him up. Then he made them pack him into the back of his car. There were lots of promises about following up, and other things Cade couldn't follow. He didn't understand any of it.

Cade wasn't sure he wanted to anyway. As much as he wanted to go home, he knew he couldn't hunt or forage like this. He used an incredible amount of energy just gathering his daily water. Better to recover in a place where the water came from silvery knobs, and warmth spilled from vents in the walls.

Here, he had the luxury to wonder if his parents had lied to him. The world was full of people, and none of them were sick. The cities weren't deserted. The doctors weren't hidden in secluded mountain labs.

Why not? That was the question that kept coming back. Everything they had told him was *wrong*, and he didn't know why. Were they lying? Confused? The thoughts made his head ache, and the painkillers only took the edge off his physical pain. Careful of his new bandages, Cade sat up in bed.

"Where do you think you're going?" Sheriff Porter asked from a dark corner.

Turning toward his voice, Cade said, "Nowhere. Just trying to get comfortable."

The sheriff replied with a skeptical grunt. He didn't have to say it out loud, Cade understood perfectly. Sherriff Porter had let Dara talk him into bringing him home, but he wasn't going to let a stranger stay alone in his basement. Not with his family upstairs, not in a million years.

Lying down again, Cade threw an arm over his eyes. He had to stay on his back, his ankles uncrossed. The position made him uneasy. That's how he'd buried his father. His father, who'd given him history lessons while they fished. Were all those stories untrue, too?

"Sheriff Porter?" Cade asked.

Flatly, Sheriff Porter said, "Go to sleep, kid."

Instead, Cade let his arm slip, and his gaze drift across the room. There was a box in the corner—Sofia had called it a TV. Beside that, shelves full of books. Cade had never seen so many. His parents kept a small stack. Treasured them, actually.

Every time they moved camp, Mom wrapped the books in tanned leather. Tying them tight, she tucked them in the bottom of their satchels, to keep them safe and dry. Cade had read them all, probably a hundred times each. He didn't like *The Decameron* or *A Journal of the Plague Year* all that much. They were about misery and illness.

Gulliver's Travels was better, and he liked *Little Women* just fine. But he couldn't help being curious about all the books on these shelves. There were so many more stories in the world than he realized. There was so much more to the *world* than he realized.

Except for a few creaks, the house was quiet. Locked up tight, sleeping. At least, Cade assumed they were all sleeping. There was a chance Dara lay awake above him, tossing and turning the way he wanted to.

He still smelled her on his skin. In his hair. Trying to picture her face, he couldn't decide if she stared at the ceiling, or covered her face to invite sleep. His blood stirred. It wouldn't be hard to find her room. After all, he'd tracked her through the forest back home, by scent alone.

"Go to sleep," Sheriff Porter said suddenly.

The command startled Cade. It was like the man had read his mind. Or, more likely, was listening to him breathe. Though he longed to ignore Sheriff Porter, to go creeping and find Dara, he closed his eyes instead.

I'll see her tomorrow, he told himself. *She'll see me tomorrow.*

TWENTY

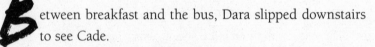etween breakfast and the bus, Dara slipped downstairs to see Cade.

It was funny the way his presence transformed the space. It felt different down there, like she was walking into someone else's house. The hair on her arms prickled, and she suppressed a shiver that had nothing to do with cold.

He sat on the back of the couch, framed by light and curtains from the half window. His hair trailed down his bare shoulders, accentuating the sculpted muscles there. Built like a gymnast, his back tapered to a narrow waist and slim hips. Before Dara could consider too much of the rest of him, he turned around.

"Good morning."

"Hey," Dara said.

Clasping her hands behind her back, she wandered toward

him. He'd left his shape in the pullout bed, the covers rolled like a sleeping bag. It looked like he could slip back into it at any moment, instantly tucked in and comfy. She had no idea why she was thinking about him, or his bed, or—enough, stop.

Shaking her thoughts out, she offered a smile and asked, "Are you hungry? We have pancakes."

A furrow appeared on Cade's brow. "I don't know."

Teasing gently, Dara said, "You don't know if you're hungry, or you don't know if you want pancakes?"

Shifting on the back of the couch, Cade sank against the wall comfortably. His borrowed pajama pants fit a little too well, in Dara's opinion. His bandage didn't do much to ruin her view of his chest, either. Dusted with dark hair, cut like Italian marble, he seemed more naked than most guys did without their shirts. Spreading his good arm against the windowsill, he considered her. "Both."

Stepping onto the pullout bed, she sat next to him. Not exactly beside him, because she was already off balance. Nevertheless, the couch had never seemed smaller. Bringing her brain back to the topic, she said, "They're really good, even though Lia made them."

"What are they?"

Being next to him this morning was so different from last night, when he was so cold and so small. Now he filled the space around him with heat. A hint of wood smoke clung to him, and his eyes were unusually sharp. It was scary how long his lashes were, and she really had to stop staring at him.

"Okay, well," Dara said, slipping an elastic from her wrist to bind her hair. "It's bread. Sort of. More like a cake that you fry in a pan. Butter, maple syrup, crazy delicious?"

Cade cracked a smile. "Never heard of them."

"How?" Dara demanded. "Haven't you ever been to Bob Evans?"

"Nope."

Last night, she'd lain awake thinking about him. Trying to put all the pieces in the right place. Convinced she could make sense of him, she went over his few details until they blurred together. Right before she'd fallen asleep, she'd composed a mental list of questions. His ignorance of all things buttermilk and fluffy reminded her.

"Why haven't you ever seen an escalator?"

The white bandage on his chest quivered slightly at the edge, giving away his pulse. "We don't have them where I come from."

Dara glanced over her shoulder. Then she lowered her voice. "Do you really live in Daniel Boone National?"

"Is that what you call it?"

"Yeah, because that's its name. It's a national park."

With a frown, Cade nodded. "Yes. I really live there."

"You told Sofia your parents are . . . gone."

Nostrils flaring slightly, Cade looked out the window again. The tape on his bandage pulsed faster, and his shoulders rose with his breath. "It's true. Does this matter? Let's go back to *pan* cakes."

Now Dara was surprised; she pursed her lips. His pronunciation was off; he'd *really* never heard of them. If he'd been

Sofia, she might have reached over to pet him, to reassure him. Instead, she dropped her hands in her lap. He was showing way too much skin. She didn't trust her hand to land someplace acceptable.

"They're yummy, and you should have some." Braving the space between them, Dara slid closer. "The social worker's coming today. I don't know if they'll let you stay here anymore."

"Why not?"

It was a good question. Dara started to answer a couple of times. It was hard to find the right words. She'd grown up understanding the system, and her parents' place in it. Disadvantaged kids and group homes and foster care came up on a regular basis. But if Cade really didn't understand any of it, she didn't know where to start.

"It's complicated," she finally said. "You're not old enough to live on your own. Nobody knows where you live. And, um . . . if your parents are gone, then you need somebody to take care of you."

Cade dropped his gaze, and his hand. His fingers curled and he brushed his knuckles against her shoulder. "I take care of myself."

Toes curling in her sneakers, Dara shivered. "For how long, though?"

"Three summers."

If he was telling the truth, Dara found that terrifying. People didn't just *live* in the wilderness. They didn't leave their kids there alone. When she was thirteen, her mom wouldn't let her take the bus downtown. Trying to make sense of his facts, Dara asked, "How long were you in the park? The forest, I mean."

Cade frowned. He uncurled one finger, idly tracing the seam of her sleeve. His other fingertips flickered, a soft rhythm that danced across her skin. "Always."

Before his touch could spread, Dara hauled herself off the couch. The floor felt uncertain beneath her feet, her insides turned upside down. Yes, he was mysterious, and sexy, and half dressed in her basement. But everything she felt, it was just gratitude. That's all. Nothing else.

"Okay," she told him. "I'll assume that's the truth."

"You should."

Dara backed toward the stairs. "Well, I'm going to be honest with you. People are gonna think you're a liar. Or worse . . . they'll think you're crazy."

"Why?"

"There are laws, Cade. I mean, the county takes kids away from parents who don't have running water and electricity all the time. And they live in actual houses."

"I see."

"So what's going to happen is, they're going to think you're a runaway. Or wanted for a crime somewhere. Or mentally ill. Because people don't grow up in national forests. It just doesn't happen."

Curling into himself, Cade pulled his knee to his chest. He perched on the back of the couch effortlessly, and turned to look out the window. Then he looked back at her, shadows caught under his dark brows. "It does."

Just then, Lia leaned into the basement door. "I'm telling

Dad you're down here," she said.

Dara glared at her. "Why do you have to be evil?"

"Why do you have to be ugly?"

A timer went off in the kitchen, their five-minute bus warning. Dara turned her back on her sister. One hand on the rail, she anchored herself on the steps. Cade still sat on the back of the couch, coppery skin gleaming, his brows furrowed. Against the lacy curtains and the damask upholstery, he was wildly out of place.

Clearing her throat, Dara waited until he looked at her. Heat coursed through her when his brown eyes turned her way. No one had ever looked at her like that. So sincerely, so earnestly, like he needed her to believe.

"I'm not lying to you," he said firmly.

"Okay." Her voice fell to a murmur. "I believe you."

Then she fled upstairs.

The reporter was back.

He stood on the edge of the school property, right next to the sign that said all visitors needed to register at the office. Dara saw him as the bus pulled in. He held his iPhone up like he was taking pictures, or video. Ugh, maybe both. What a freak.

Of course, she knew exactly what he wanted. He'd probably listened to the calls roll in from the police radio last night. The only surprise was that he hadn't turned up at their doorstep. Facing off with the actual sheriff might have been too much. Maybe he was only brave enough to corner the sheriff's daughter.

A spidery sense of unease crawled down her back, and Dara

slid from her seat. Her sister sat in the back, with a couple of guys from the Spoken Word club. Hurrying to her, Dara leaned over so the whole bus didn't overhear. "Hey."

"What?"

Lia didn't appreciate being interrupted. Most days, Lia didn't appreciate admitting she knew Dara at all. They used to be best friends, back in the days of playing Barbies in the backyard.

Once they both hit high school, though, Lia couldn't shed her older sister fast enough. They were both popular in their own groups, but wow. In the Venn diagram of social order, their groups didn't remotely overlap.

Oh well, Dara thought. *This is more important than sibling rivalry.* Leaning past Lia, Dara pointed at the reporter. He wasn't even trying to be subtle. As the bus skimmed past him, he tracked it with his phone.

"See that guy?"

Reluctantly, Lia looked over. Then she frowned. "Yeah. Freak."

"He's from the newspaper." Dara tried to balance on the edge of Lia's seat, but she didn't make it easy. "Cornered me at Mom's office yesterday, asking questions about Cade."

Scoffing, Lia said, "Freak number two."

"Just . . ." Dara trailed off; she wasn't sure what to say. It's not like the reporter had threatened her. Seeming skeezy wasn't against the law, but she wanted Lia to be careful anyway. "Avoid him if you can, okay? I don't trust him."

Lia hauled her bag off the floor and bumped Dara off the seat. "Whatever."

Leave it to Lia to be obnoxious about something important. Dara straightened, brushing off her jeans. Through the window, she watched the reporter pace his line. Then, fearlessly, he approached the security guard directing traffic. Somehow, that made Dara more nervous than before.

The bus driver threw the front doors open, and everyone stood at once. They weren't in a rush to get off, although Lia was definitely in a rush to blow past her sister. Pulling her bag onto her shoulder, Lia pressed right into Dara as she squeezed into the aisle.

"By the way," Lia said smugly. "Mom wants Mowgli out. She told Dad she'll have a placement for him by noon."

"What?!"

Carelessly rolling her shoulder, Lia said, "Too bad, so sad. No more stray boyfriend in the basement for you."

Lia's friends snickered. Dara pushed herself between them and her sister, half to keep an eye on Lia. And half, Dara had to admit, just to be mean. *They* were sophomores, she was a senior. And there *was* a social order to uphold.

TWENTY-ONE

*E*nticed by the books, Cade pressed himself close to the shelves to examine them.

First, by touch. He ran his fingers over the spines. Some of them wore paper sheaths. Others were cloth and leather—he recognized the scent. Brushing his nose against a matching set, he inhaled. Dictionaries smelled wonderful.

Slipping a slim volume from the shelf, he flicked it open. Poetry, Walt Whitman. Pristine pages crackled as he turned them. The paper was so smooth that the black letters left an impression. Cade skimmed his hand over them, smiling a little. He'd never seen a book so new.

He tucked it under his arm, then dug into the shelves again. He wondered if Dara would let him keep one if he had to leave. He didn't like the sound of these laws. These strangers who stole children from their homes. A new story would be nice. Something to remember her by.

Footsteps echoed on the stairs, and Cade bounded back to the couch. It quavered under his weight, but he found his balance. It was harder with one foot bandaged, and one arm weak.

But if they tried to take him away, he'd run for home again. It would be harder to get by, but summer was coming. The river would be fat with fish. He'd have apples and honey, soon, plenty of roots to roast. If he stuck to foraging, he'd be fine. He'd be healed by autumn, just in time for hunting season.

"All right, son," Sheriff Porter said. He stepped into the room, followed by a brown, mousy man with glasses. Gesturing for the man to sit down, Sheriff Porter put his hands on his hips and stared at Cade for a minute. "This is Branson Swayle. He's a social worker, he's here to help you."

Cade folded the book against his chest. "I don't need help."

"Just call me Branson. And you know, that's very admirable," Branson said. "But everybody needs help sometimes. Can we get to know each other?"

Sheriff Porter shifted uncomfortably. He looked at Cade, then the couch cushions. It was obvious he was trying *not* to say something, but the struggle was too much. With a nod, he said, "How about you sit down and give Mr. Swayle ten minutes. I'd say that's fair."

Wary, Cade slid from the back of the couch. He felt penned in, claustrophobic. If something came from behind, how would he know? Shifting his gaze from Sheriff Porter to Branson, Cade licked his lips and waited. In silence.

Branson didn't seem to mind. He flipped open a thin rectangle, and its surface glowed. When he touched it, it chittered like a chipmunk call, or a particularly nervous squirrel. Leaning slightly, Cade tried to get a look at it. The thing was obviously a machine, maybe like the light-up box that played music in Javier's room.

"Nifty, huh? I just got it last week," Branson said. He turned the rectangle toward Cade, then nodded at him. "Go ahead, take a look. I'm still not used to it."

Cool and heavy, the rectangle fit neatly in Cade's hands. There was a picture inside it, two kids with Branson's nose. Cade knew they weren't really in there. Still, he touched their faces. They were so clear, so bright. Not like the faded photos he had back home.

The picture jiggled, and when Cade jerked his fingers back, the image slid away. Rows of boxes replaced it, each with a letter of the alphabet in them.

Curious, Cade turned the device, and the boxes spun. They landed at the bottom again, so he touched one. He didn't feel anything move, but the thing ticked anyway. Then suddenly, grey filled the screen.

Search web, the screen read. There was a compass beside the words, but nothing happened when he touched it. So he turned the rectangle, and the screen followed.

Branson chuckled. "Your first tablet, too, huh?"

Cade glanced at him. Then he turned his attention to the rectangle—the *tablet.* If it was like the box in Javier's room, Cade could make it sing.

Swiping his fingers back and forth, he made the children's picture appear again. Little pictures obscured their faces when he turned it over. It took him a moment to realize the small pictures had labels.

Carefully, he pressed the one that said MUSIC. But all that did was bring up more pictures.

The tablet taunted him. He turned it, watching the pictures spin. That didn't help, so he patted at them. Hand swabbing the screen, he muttered to himself. Different images flashed. Bits of the screen leapt around.

The music had to be in there somewhere. Cade shook the tablet, and just before he slapped the screen, Branson reached over to still him.

"I feel the same way, sometimes," he said with a smile. With a gentle hand, he flattened the tablet to lie on Cade's thighs. Pale fingers swirling, he cleared the screen. Then he touched one of the small pictures, and a white page opened.

Moving too fast for Cade to follow, Branson wiggled his fingers and opened a page. It had lines, questions on it. The top read Intake Form. "Why don't you help me with some of this paperwork? Use your finger like a pen, you can write on the screen like this."

He demonstrated. Drawing on the screen by the line that read Coordinator, he smiled. His strokes glowed, a firefly flitting across the screen. Then, with a chirp, they turned into text, like the inside of a book.

"See? Go ahead, put your name and address in there."

Cade stilled. Though he didn't look up, he felt Sheriff Porter watching. He knew how to make block letters; he just couldn't bring himself to do it. Dara's warning plucked at him. *Crazy,* Dara said. *Or lying.* It was a needle beneath his skin, piercing and pulling the movable parts in his arm.

Sheriff Porter would never let a crazy liar near his daughter.

His expectant expression fading, Branson considered the screen, then Cade's face. Radiating warmth, he reached for the tablet. He didn't just grab and take. He waited for Cade to relinquish it.

When he did, Branson asked, "Do you know how to read or write, Cade?"

There was no judgment in his tone, but Cade bristled anyway. Of course he could read and write. During his earliest winters, his mother spent hours teaching him the letters. Dad took turns with him, reading one line of a book, then handing it to Cade to read the next.

But if he *couldn't*, they'd make him stay until he could answer them. All Cade needed was time to get better. Time to sit with Dara, just *time*. Forcing down his pride, Cade shook his head.

"That's very brave of you," Branson said. He scribbled on the tablet's screen. "Can you tell me what your last grade of school was?"

"No."

"Did you drop out?"

Cade felt Sheriff Porter's eyes boring into him. He refused to be smaller than him, so he looked up. Without wavering, trying to make him look away, Cade said, "I never went."

Almost to himself, Branson said, "Going to have to get some testing . . . all right, Cade. I'm going to start at the very beginning, so be patient with me."

Slowly straightening his back, Cade held Sheriff Porter's gaze. He didn't waver. He wasn't afraid. There were bigger things in the forest he'd stared down. Greater beasts, far more dangerous. This was just a man, with weaknesses and doubt. Cade told the social worker, "All right."

"So tell me your whole name, including the middle name if you have one."

Filling the corner of the couch, Cade smiled slightly as he answered. "Only Cade."

"What's your address?"

"Daniel Boone National Forest," he said. The words felt unfamiliar on his mouth, but their effect on Sheriff Porter was unmistakable. He narrowed his eyes, and a muscle ticked in his jaw. Did he think it was a lie? Because he was sure Sheriff Porter considered him sane.

Branson wrote it down dutifully, the tablet chirping and beeping. "And how long have you lived there?"

"Always," Cade said.

At that, Sheriff Porter snapped. He looked away, cursing under his breath. When he paced away, his belt jingled. His footsteps echoed, and he turned back abruptly. To Branson, he said, "Can I get you a cup of coffee?"

"Thank you, I'd appreciate that," he said.

Sheriff Porter offered Cade nothing. After losing such a basic challenge, he was embarrassed. It showed in the flush on his cheeks and the tips of his ears. And he revealed it, when he took another look at Cade before disappearing up the stairs.

Comfortable as the temporary alpha, Cade turned to Branson. Because he wanted to—because he wanted to stay—he waited for the next question.

Through the crush in the hallway, Josh made his way to Dara's locker. There were all kinds of rumors going around. He didn't appreciate having to tell his boys he didn't know what was going on with the freak from the woods and his girl.

Dara's blonde hair glimmered, falling to her shoulders unrestrained. What happened to her usual messy ponytail? She never wore her hair like that. Something else new and different to put him on guard. Excusing himself, he pressed himself between Dara and the guy at the next locker.

"Well?"

He didn't want to get too specific. That way, anything she felt like she needed to confess would bubble out of her.

"Hey," Dara said. She looked trapped. One brow danced up, like it always did when she was trying to figure out the right thing to say. Usually, that happened after they got in a fight. She didn't believe in apologizing unless she was sure she was wrong, but she hated getting the silent treatment.

"What's up?" Josh asked.

Pulling a couple books from her locker, Dara finally shook her head. "You wouldn't even believe me."

That was bad. Anytime Dara got cagey, it was bad. In spite of his annoyance, Josh took her camera, holding it while she shoved her books into her backpack. "Lia's telling everybody you've got him socked away in your basement."

"My *dad* kept him there. It was that or jail, because he wouldn't go back to the hospital."

His own jealousy caught Josh by surprise.

She must have noticed he was too quiet, because she stopped packing her bag and squinted at him. "What?"

"Nothing."

"What, Josh? What?" She slung her bag over her shoulder. Grabbing her camera from him, she looped the strap around her neck, then gestured at it. "I have to be down in the west pod for club pictures in five minutes, so please. Just . . . whatever it is, say it."

It was scary, how she'd gone from distracted to pissed that fast. Holding up his hands, Josh said, "Nothing. I'm just hearing this stuff . . ."

Dara closed her locker. "Since you couldn't keep him, I took him to Sofia's. Sometime after midnight, he decided to walk home. Which, by the way, *is* Daniel Boone. He *does* live out there, yeah. Only, we're sixty miles away, I don't even think he knows what a mile is. He definitely doesn't get the concept of Nikes, because he was barefoot and got all cut up at Clayton Park."

"Look, never—"

She ignored him. Her hands waving, she stepped away from her locker. "Rather than dump him in the countryside like a puppy nobody wants, my dad brought him to our house. He's probably talking to the social worker now. Anything else?"

Josh hesitated. "Is he okay?"

Temper dissolving, Dara sighed. "I think so. I'm sorry. I barely got any sleep, and this reporter from the *Courier* keeps showing up. He was outside the school this morning."

"Slow news month or something," Josh said. He smoothed a hand over her shoulder, pulling her closer. The big bad reporter, that was something he could help with. He could watch out for anybody with a notepad and a gleam in his eye, and run them off. It felt good to have a purpose. "You mad?"

Shaking her head, Dara said, "No."

"You sure?" Josh coaxed her, tipping her chin up so he could kiss her. Her soft lips tightened, and she broke away a little too fast. "Dare?"

"Totally sure. I have to run, I'm going to be late."

Before he could catch her, Dara had slipped his grip and was already bolting for the stairs. He raised a hand, calling after her. "I'll drive you home!"

She answered with a half wave, code for *I heard you, but I'm not saying yes.*

It didn't make Josh feel better.

TWENTY-TWO

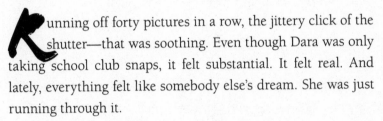unning off forty pictures in a row, the jittery click of the shutter—that was soothing. Even though Dara was only taking school club snaps, it felt substantial. It felt real. And lately, everything felt like somebody else's dream. She was just running through it.

"Say cheese," she told the Forensics Team.

Ten rictus smiles filled her viewfinder, and she took that picture. She always did; parents liked those for some reason. Those were the pictures she handed off to the yearbook staff.

But she kept snapping, because that's when people relaxed. When their real selves appeared. Those were the ones she slipped into her digital portfolio. Photography wasn't about capturing people in poses. It was about stopping time. Saving it. Keeping a moment fresh and alive, to savor again later.

Once she'd run off enough shots, she lowered the camera. "You guys are painfully sexy, thank you."

A couple of the girls laughed, and one of the guys rolled his eyes. But they wore real smiles as they filed out, making room for 4-H and Future Farmers of America. There was so much overlap, Dara insisted on shooting them at the same time.

Dropping a new memory card into the camera, Dara waited for everybody to gather. These pictures would have a second life on the pages of the high school yearbook. People would scribble names, love notes, secrets on them. Mustaches. Devil horns. They were meant to be touched.

Unlike the photos from Dara's camping trip. She had a folder on her computer desktop full of them. No idea if they were any good, Dara hadn't looked at them yet. She'd plugged the camera in, saved them with a nice, neat time stamp, then closed the file.

The pictures should have been special. Their trip away, just the two of them. Except, Dara was pretty sure *they* weren't in any of them.

Fog clutched by the trees, the horseshoe waterfall, yes. Rainbows reflected off the mist in the air, definitely. But not them. Not even the obligatory shot, holding a camera at arm's length and trying to cram into the frame.

It was like she knew. Not out loud; she hadn't been ready to admit it. But maybe she knew.

Josh had a partial scholarship in New Orleans. Dara had student loans lined up to take her to New York City. Except for the *new*, their colleges had nothing in common. They didn't either, and they hadn't since freshman year when they started "going together."

A bleat dragged Dara's attention back to the present. Izzie Wells hefted a bundle of squirming legs, and smiled.

"Tristan won first place at the fair. Principal Tran signed off on it."

"Okay," Dara said. Nobody had prepared her for a pygmy goat, but she could deal. In fact, it was nice to focus on something solvable. Something easy. Like getting the goat to look at the camera when all the people did.

Everything else in her life was suddenly complicated, and completely unfixable at the moment. So Dara crinkled a bag of Sun Chips to get Tristan's attention. Then she lost herself in the rhythm and tick of her camera.

When Sheriff Porter appeared with a greasy bag, Cade watched him, wary.

"Here," Sheriff Porter said, digging into the bag. He pulled out a paper-wrapped package, and tossed it in Cade's direction. "You want fries?"

Turning the package over, Cade sniffed it. Meat of some kind, cooked. Since he didn't know what fries were, he shook his head. What he wanted to do was take the food to his perch on the back of the couch. But instead, he unwrapped it where he sat, on the floor by the bookcases.

"Thank you," he said, which surprised Sheriff Porter.

He actually stopped unpeeling his package to look over at

him. Now distracted, the sheriff kept unwrapping, and kept staring.

Animals smelled fear; Cade wished he could. His nose was only so sensitive. He had to watch instead, trying to read raised eyebrows and sharp hand motions. It made him uncomfortable to have Sheriff Porter so close, and watching him. They weren't family. He didn't know what he might do next.

"You'll be glad to know we found a place for you," Sheriff Porter said. "Right here in town."

Though his stomach growled, Cade put the food down and retreated to the couch. "I'm not interested."

Sheriff Porter seemed distracted by the food on the floor. His attention kept drifting toward it. "That's too bad. Because that's the way things work. Until you start being honest with us . . ."

"I am."

". . . I can't do a thing to help you," Sheriff Porter finished. It was like Cade hadn't said a word at all. "But don't worry. I'll find out who you really are."

Slowly, Cade unfurled. He pulled his feet into the couch, then crept up to sit on the back of it again. He didn't need a better sense of smell or more experience with people to recognize that. It was a threat. Rather than reply, Cade turned his attention to the window.

"What if I told you I thought you were out there in those woods cooking meth?" Sheriff Porter asked.

Through slim windows at ground level, Cade watched the sidewalk, the people walking by. There were so many of them.

A woman dressed all in blue stopped at the front walk.

Opening a bag at her hip, she took something from a black box, then shoved her own bundle in. A delivery of some kind, but Cade would have to get into the box to find out what.

"Or something worse." Sheriff Porter's cup rattled when he shook it. "Biological weapons?"

The woman in the blue uniform moved down to the next house, and Cade kept his silence. He knew a lot about biological weapons, actually. Anthrax had to be inhaled; it wouldn't spread person to person.

Bacteria were delicate—living creatures, prone to dying themselves—no good on the battlefield. Viruses were tricky. Almost perfect, as long as they bound with the right strand of DNA. A global disaster if they collaborated with the wrong one.

Cade remembered his mother's face. The way it would go hard when she talked about things like this. When she explained vectors and vaccines, diminished herd immunity, useless antibiotics. She'd stroke Cade's brow, murmuring sadly, "The end of the world, contained on the head of a pin."

Irritated, Sheriff Porter nudged the couch with his boot. "How about you sit the right way when I'm talking to you?"

Lifting his head, Cade replied, "There's a man in your yard."

Sheriff Porter didn't wait for an explanation. He bounded up the basement stairs two at a time. A door opened, and Cade felt the slightest breeze coming in. It carried the sheriff's voice smoothly. The stranger's, too.

"You mind telling me what you're doing on my property?"

"Good to see you again, Tony. Been a while since I covered

your election," the stranger said. "Jim Albee, ringing any bells?"

Shifting, Cade pushed the curtains out of the way. All he saw was feet and pants legs. They shuffled, shifting weight. Dancing uneasily. Just by the way Sheriff Porter set his heel, it was obvious he wasn't happy. Their conversation spilled out, water over stones. They interrupted and flowed together.

Most of it made no sense, until the stranger said, "Just let me talk to the boy. Five minutes."

"Jim," Sheriff Porter said. His feet moved. They overlapped the stranger's gait—he was leading him away from the house. "I've got no comment. He's a minor, you're well aware."

The stranger stopped. "Is he, though?"

"You have a nice day," Sheriff Porter said.

It was the second time Sheriff Porter had confused him. First with the food, now protecting him again. Cade couldn't read him. He wasn't easy and open like his own father. Or even layered and complicated like his mom. Most confusing of all, he had Dara's eyes—the shape, the color. But not the softness.

When he was with Dara, it felt like she saw him. Maybe even knew him a little. Sheriff Porter didn't. His gaze cut through him, trying to take him apart by pieces.

And since he was coming back, Cade slid from the back of the couch and reclaimed his food from the floor.

TWENTY-THREE

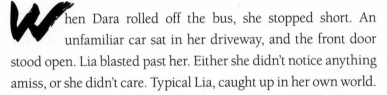hen Dara rolled off the bus, she stopped short. An unfamiliar car sat in her driveway, and the front door stood open. Lia blasted past her. Either she didn't notice anything amiss, or she didn't care. Typical Lia, caught up in her own world.

Before Dara could head inside, her dad stepped onto the porch. A woman followed him, and then Cade. He wore new clothes and new shoes. Clutching a bundle to his chest, he slunk behind them. Eyes darting furtively, they rested on Dara for a moment, then slid away.

"What's going on?" Dara asked. She tried to sound chill, but her heart was already racing. Stupidly, she'd believed that the hard part was talking Dad into keeping Cade one night. That the next, and the next after that would be easier.

Sheriff Porter closed the door, then clapped a hand against

Cade's back. "Good news. Your mom had a chat with Ms. Fourakis here this morning. She's willing to take Cade in for the time being."

Plastering on a smile, Dara shifted her bag from one shoulder to the other. "I thought he was staying here."

"He'll be more comfortable with me," Ms. Fourakis said. Charm and warmth surrounded her like a halo. She had bright brown eyes, and they crinkled at the corners when she smiled. Genuine. Looking to Cade, she went on. "His own room, some privacy. I think we'll get along, don't you?"

Stiff, Cade cut a look at Sheriff Porter, then nodded. "Yes. Thank you."

Protests ran wild in Dara's head. There were so many, and they came so fast, it was hard to figure out where to start. Stammering, she groaned inwardly when she picked the least important one. "How far away do you live, though? I'm really the only person Cade knows."

Ms. Fourakis touched her chest, as if she found Dara absolutely adorable. "Your father has my address. It's just a few blocks from here. Close enough to walk or bike . . ."

Poor Cade's face was a mask. A little pale, incredibly stiff. Coming closer, Dara ignored the way her father loomed over them.

"Are you okay with this?"

Resentful, Cade nodded anyway. "For now."

"We don't want to keep Ms. Fourakis waiting," Sheriff Porter said. That not-so-friendly hand on Cade's bag nudged him down the step.

"Can I ride over with you?" Dara asked. She shucked off her bag and dropped it by the door. Pressing herself between Cade and Sheriff Porter, she offered a sugared smile. "That way I know where it is."

Sheriff Porter started to shake his head. "Dara . . ."

"Why don't we let Cade get settled in?" Ms. Fourakis said. She fished her keys from her pocket and nodded toward the car. "Come by tomorrow. You can map it online, you won't have any trouble finding it."

Stonewalled, Dara slipped her hand into Cade's. Fingers lacing, she squeezed, trying to reassure him. And she moved slowly. New sneakers covered the bandage on his foot. She didn't have to see it to shudder at the memory of glass buried deep in his flesh. His palm was hot and dry, and when she glanced over at him, she noticed his lips were pressed almost white.

"Are you okay?" Dara murmured.

Rubbing his thumb against hers, Cade kept his eyes forward. He marched like he was going to jail. Stiff steps, shoulders blocked. His jaw was hard and set, but he answered her gently. "I'll be close to you."

Strange currents threaded between them. Something electric and liquid at the same time. They teased a sting across Dara's skin, tingling on the back of her neck. Before they reached the car, she squeezed his hand again. It frightened her a little. When he squeezed back, her heart pounded.

With a subtle pull, she made him stop. Made him look at her. "I'll come right after school, tomorrow. I'll be there first thing."

At that, Cade did nod. Then he leaned down. His cheek grazed hers as he whispered in her ear, "You were right. They think I'm a liar."

The misery in his voice made Dara ache. She didn't know what the truth was, exactly. Except that *he* obviously believed that he grew up in a forest, had never seen an escalator or a light switch. That he was utterly alien and lost in a world that seemed completely normal to her. It was so clear to her that he was afraid and hurting. Why didn't anyone else see it?

Covering his hand with hers, she turned to look at him. Their noses almost brushed. It was too close. Too intimate. But she didn't pull away. "I'm sorry."

"I don't understand what they want."

"We'll figure it out," Dara told him. She reluctantly let her hand slip from his, then leaned past him to open the car door.

Cade loosely hooked his fingers in her collar. There was no pressure. He didn't pull. Plaintive, it felt like a gesture. A way to hold on to her a little longer.

When Dara swallowed at the knot in her throat, she felt his knuckles graze her skin. Heat trailed there. It bloomed and blossomed through her, making her bolder. Raising her head, she told him with a lot more certainty than she felt, "I mean it. We'll figure it out."

In reply, Cade brushed his finger against her pulse. His touch settled there. It lingered on her throat, alive, insisting. For one, impossibly brief moment, she felt *his* pulse, an answer to her own. Dara's breath thinned. She felt his on her cheek, the world a distant roar.

Then, without another word, Cade pulled away and climbed into the car.

The house phone rang for the fourth time in an hour.

Mrs. Porter fumbled with an ancient answering machine, plugging it in just in time to catch the latest call. She stood over the machine, listening to ten-year-old Dara and eight-year-old Lia giggling and inviting people to leave a message. The machine clicked, and an unfamiliar voice spilled through the speaker.

"Hi, this is Lucy Faul. I'm a researcher from WTHR in Indianapolis. We're interested in running a piece about the Primitive Boy. We'd like to get a quote from you or a family representative."

Sheriff Porter stepped into the hall. Walking up behind his wife, he wrapped his arms around her waist. The reporter left her name and number, then hung up abruptly. With a frown, Sheriff Porter pressed a kiss to his wife's shoulder. "Indiana?"

"And Ohio, and Missouri, and Illinois." Distracted, Mrs. Porter untangled herself. She turned the answering machine down, then looked back at her husband. "I don't understand this. As many at-risk kids as I work with, this one's the one that gets all the attention?"

Sheriff Porter leaned against the wall, and sighed. "I don't know. If it was just the bear, it probably would have blown away. But now you've got the bear, and the missing identity, and the idea that he's some caveman . . . Jim Albee's story in the paper sure didn't help."

Mrs. Porter frowned. "No. No it didn't."

Sheriff Porter leaned against the wall. "We'll figure out who he is, and they'll get bored. He's probably just some runaway trying to hide from going home. The paper's only interested because it's weird, and there's nothing else going on right now."

Mrs. Porter replaced the answering machine. "I don't know why they have to bother us."

"Like I said—" Sheriff Porter started. Another call interrupted him. The phone's clang exploded the quiet in the house. It was an unnatural sound, now that they all had custom ringtones. It was like an invasion, people walking into their house uninvited.

Glancing at the caller ID, Mrs. Porter smiled mirthlessly. "The *Tennessean*. That's all the border states."

There were more calls coming in at the police station. The two newest recruits sat at desks, answering the phone over and over. They had colored Post-its spread before them.

Yellow was for media calls, that stack was the largest. Orange for other police departments trying to match up their runaways with Makwa's mystery kid. Day-Glo pink notes boasted tips from psychics. Later, those would be pinned up in the break room, for everyone to enjoy.

The last batch was the smallest, only two messages scribbled on bright green.

One came from Martha Pond in Corbin, Kentucky, who called every time someone ended up on the news. She was sure she recognized any given subject, whether they were black or white, red hair or bald, old or young. She thought the sketch of Cade was her long lost niece, Elena. It wasn't important and the deputy knew it. But someone needed to touch base with her before she showed up at the station in her house dress. Again.

Slapping down two more yellow squares, the deputy on phone duty covered up the other green note.

That one came from somebody claiming his name was Dr. Jupiter O'Toole, which is why he got put into the possible fruit bats pile. But his information was interesting enough that the deputy at least wrote it down. He'd only pretended to take messages from Elvis Presley, Shirley MacLaine, and J. Edgar Hoover.

Dr. Jupiter O'Toole, however, wondered if he could talk to the police about a colleague who'd gone missing sixteen, seventeen years ago. She and her husband had vanished without a trace, along with their infant son. He was sure it was nothing, but the boy was just the right age. . . .

By the end of the shift, the break room boasted twenty-four calls from psychics, one hundred twenty-seven calls from the media, eight runaway idents from other departments, and just the two green, possibly loony, tips about Cade's possible identity.

Those two notes, on the bottom of the stack, got separated from the rest. They never made it to the assistant's desk. No one entered them into the station database.

They went out in the trash, with crumpled coffee cups and used tissues, forgotten.

TWENTY-FOUR

Cade followed Ms. Fourakis inside.

The new house smelled good. Plants hung from hangers at the ceiling. They spilled out of pots in the windows. In the kitchen, a particularly ambitious vine climbed the tops of the cabinets, and dangled down by the door. It was a forest in miniature, and it almost made Cade feel like he was at home.

"You can help yourself to anything you find," Ms. Fourakis said, dropping her purse on the table. "If you want something special, just add to the . . . well, you tell me, and I'll add it to the grocery list."

Cade followed her as she flung open cabinets and drawers, and a cold box that glowed with gem-colored bottles. Quick as lightning, she explained all the contents. Cade wouldn't remember most of it, because he recognized none of it. Perhaps after dark, he'd experiment.

Curly hair swaying cheerfully, she led him down the hall. "Dining room, I use it for scrapbooking. Living room, TV, right down here is my craft room. I could teach you to sew," she said with a twinkle.

"I know how," Cade replied.

"A man of many mysteries."

It seemed to amuse her, so Cade just nodded. Unusual scents filled this house. Spicy, herbal scents. Some he recognized, garlic, field onion, peppermint. Others eluded him, but they all came together pleasantly. It made this house feel familiar, even though it was ceilings and walls, glass and carpet.

"This will be your room," she said, pushing open a door.

"Thank you."

The floors here were bare, and the walls had paintings of trees and birds and butterflies. A woven blanket covered the bed, and everything shone in comforting shades of blue and green. At the foot of the bed sat a basket stuffed full of small bottles and tins. Tentatively, Cade touched the edge of the basket to peer inside.

"Everything you need, deodorant, soap . . . do you need anything special for your hair?"

What a strange question. Cade shook his head, still faintly smiling.

"Razor, shaving cream . . ." Ms. Fourakis lowered her voice, confidentially. "You're looking a little shaggy there, my friend."

Smoothing a hand down his face, Cade nodded. His skin

was rough, his whiskers starting to vaguely resemble a goatee. He wasn't sure how he was supposed to fix that, though. They took his knife at the hospital. His pot of deer fat, sweetened with mint and geranium, moldered away in his cave. Ms. Fourakis gestured at a plastic stick and a can, both baffling.

"Okay," he said anyway.

With a nod, she led him out of the bedroom. Leaning into a half-open door across the hall, she flipped the light on. "This is your bathroom. You can aim or you can clean up after yourself, I don't care which."

Cade nodded as if he understood. He had a little experience with bathrooms now. Not much. Just enough to be fascinated with flushing the toilet and the magic faucets. Hot *and* cold water poured out, and it was good to drink. No need to boil it or screen it. Last night, Dara had shown him the sink; he was curious about the tub.

"Can I try that?" he asked, gesturing toward it.

Ms. Fourakis stepped out of his way. "You bet. There are some sweats in your bedroom. We'll see about getting you some jeans and pajamas and whatnot when my boyfriend gets home."

Once she walked away, Cade crept into his bedroom. Plucking up the basket, he carried it to the bathroom. Leaning against the door to close it, he studied his surroundings. The mirror unnerved him.

Though he understood it was only his reflection, it was frighteningly clear. He knew his own face from still pools of water or the shining edge of his knife.

This glass revealed his whole body in blinding light. He

stripped off his shirt and his pants. The bandage on his chest wasn't as big as it felt. A mottled bruise radiated outside its edges though, mostly black but fading toward green.

Peeling the bandage off, he hissed at the sting. The wound beneath looked strange. Puckered and pressed together with thin black lines. Reaching up to touch his head, Cade traced the scar beneath his hair.

He had other bruises, all mysterious. Climbing trees and cliffs could be brutal work. It wasn't unusual for a vine to give way. They were only so sturdy, so he was used to hitting the forest floor. Stretching, he lifted his good arm. His ribs appeared, then melted back into the definition of his muscles.

His back was tight, and his thighs thick. Strong, for climbing and jumping. His knotted feet seemed out of place. Bony and callused, too big for the rest of his body. But they were perfect for the way he lived. Hardened enough for his moccasins and boots. Toes dexterous enough to cling to a perch. Or to hold the fixed end while he braided reeds into baskets and blankets.

Leaning close to the mirror, he jerked back when his face disappeared in a circle of fog. Warily, he pressed a finger to the haze. It wiped right off. With a quick swipe, he smeared it all away and considered his face.

Not the features, those he knew. He had his mother's eyes, his father's mouth, and a great-uncle Junior's nose, or so he'd heard. The small details fascinated him. He had freckles, like Dad. There was a half-moon scar under his chin. A chip in his front tooth set it slightly angled against the rest.

Cade bared his teeth and barked at the face in the glass. It was a good noise, one that scared raccoons when they strayed too close. The sound echoed off the tile and chrome, reverberating in his ears. A moment later, Ms. Fourakis knocked on the door.

"Everything okay in there?"

Backing away from his reflection, Cade knocked on his side of the door. "Yes."

"Better hop in, my boyfriend's on his way."

Carefully, curiously, Cade twisted the taps. He couldn't help it. He got excited seeing all that clean water rush out. Punching a hand into the stream, he marveled that it was hot. Rather than waste it by touching it, he sucked the wetness from his fingers. Then, knotting his dreads on the top of his head, he stepped into the ceramic basin.

Crouching, he waited for the water to rise around him. When he was little, his mother boiled water to wash him by hand. But even then, it was no more than a bowlful at a time. He'd never been covered by warmth like this. Steam thickened the air, and slowly, the water inched up his back.

Water. Everywhere. He tasted it in the air. It gushed from the wall. So much of it, and no work at all. Even though the heat relaxed his muscles, his heart still pounded with excitement. Covered with a blanket of liquid heat, Cade rested against a pillow of his own hair.

So far, this was the only thing in the City World that was better than what he had at home. This, and Dara, just a short walk away.

Alone, with no internet to soothe her, and her head full of Cade driving away, Dara retreated the only way she knew how. Sitting at her computer, she finally opened the pictures she'd taken during the camping trip. They spilled out across the screen, and the vibrant colors surprised her.

In her mind, in her memories, the whole trip was blood red. But scrolling slowly through her shots, she discovered so much more.

A tiny, violet flower filled one picture. She'd gotten the focus so tight and close, she could make out the subtly, silvery rings that made up the petals. The florid purple seemed poured into the cells, a secret view.

She had tight shots of brand-new leaves, struggling to spread and green. When she got to the pictures of the gate to Avalon, she caught her breath.

It was shockingly beautiful. The shadows and light were so much deeper than she remembered. There were so many details that she had missed when she was in the moment.

The mist in the air caught the light. It folded faint rainbows into haze, and at some angles, caught the sunlight and sparkled. Vines and leaves spiraled down over the falls. Butterflies darted along the edges of the pond.

Sinking back in her chair, Dara studied the trees. Spindling, barely green, there's no way they hid a figure in them. But she couldn't help but wonder, had he been there? How many of these pictures had secrets of him in them?

His eyes had been so haunted when he insisted he was

telling the truth. Guilt that didn't even belong to her filled her chest. It wasn't her fault that she knew how people would treat him. But she felt bad for it, all the same. She couldn't help looking at her pictures and trying to see that place from Cade's eyes.

She couldn't imagine living there. When she and Josh packed for their trip, she had checklists. They'd printed tips off of websites. They had maps and GPS and it seemed like absolutely everything they needed to camp comfortably.

In just a few short days, though, everything fell apart. They were hungry, out of touch with the rest of the world. They were targets.

It didn't seem possible to live there. To be alone there. Even if Cade had lived there with parents, where did *they* come from?

Even if she was willing to suspend her disbelief that lost tribes of people could live in a national forest unnoticed, it didn't make sense. They were two people with one son—where were the others? Cade had said nothing about there being anyone else out there.

Then there were his questions. *How many people left in the world? Are you immune?* It was all connected. She just didn't understand how. She didn't have her dad sitting next to her, feeding her the one last piece of the puzzle she needed to figure things out.

With a sigh, she leaned forward to scroll through the rest of her pictures. Birds. Sunset through the trees. River. Mushrooms, then the blurry shot with Cade in it. Studying that image, she flicked back and forth between the others surrounding it. He was just a flash in the upper branches of the tree. So far up, almost undetectable.

Loading the shot onto a thumb drive, she shoved that and her camera into her school bag. She wanted to get some pictures of him, real pictures. Images that captured the darkness and depth in his eyes. Maybe a picture that would contain a piece of the puzzle. Or maybe just a glimpse of him she could keep.

He was only a few blocks away, and virtually a stranger. But there was a hollow ache in her chest that wouldn't go away. The only way she could think to describe it was homesickness. That was ridiculous, it didn't make sense. But as she tossed herself in bed to stare at the ceiling, that's how she felt.

Homesick and wildly alone.

In the morning, Cade sat in Ms. Fourakis' kitchen. Patient, he let her tape his shoulder up again, even as his eyes darted to take in new details.

Numbers on the fridge, photos tucked into the flowing plants. It seemed strange for the plants to be trapped inside. The windows were wide and bright, plenty of light poured in. But how big would they get, how far would they range, if they weren't trapped inside pots?

"As soon as we're done with this," Ms. Fourakis said, snipping white medical tape, "we're going to get you fingerprinted and take some pictures."

Cade wasn't sure what fingerprinting was. It nagged in his head, like he ought to know. Since he couldn't place it, he decided to keep that to himself. It seemed like something that a person who wasn't lying or crazy should know. Instead, he hedged and asked, "Why?"

With a thoughtful murmur, Ms. Fourakis picked up a new square of gauze. "We're having a hard time helping you, stranger."

"I told you my name."

"I know you did," she said. Then she shrugged, as if she couldn't help matters. "It's all part of the process."

Digging his fingers into his own knees, Cade stilled himself when her touch pressed too close to the center of his wounds. It was like an ember popping out of the fire, landing on his skin. It burned, deep down, but there was nothing he could do to stop it. "I just want to go home."

"And we want to take you there."

Cade clamped his mouth closed. This sounded like she thought he was a liar. Was that better than crazy? Probably, but he didn't know by how much. And it was fair.

He was a liar. He lied about being able to read and write. He hadn't told anyone but Sofia and Dara about his parents. Or the fact that *they* were all supposed to be dead. He was lying to himself, too. Because he wanted to go home. But he didn't want to go alone.

"So, police station first," Ms. Fourakis said, applying the last strip of tape. "Then we need to swing by the hospital and get your antibiotics. Your social worker wants you to get tested so we can get you in some classes for the time being."

Very still, Cade waited for her to step back. Then he struggled into his shirt on his own. He didn't want her to help him.

He could manage. "When can I see Dara?"

"This afternoon."

Sliding to his feet, Cade nodded, but then asked, "But when?"

"Kid, she's in school. I'm pretty sure they don't let out until three or four. So you've got a while."

Nodding, Cade didn't ask her what three or four meant. How long that would be. He knew dawn. He knew noon, when the sun was at its highest. He knew sunset, and midnight. But time was fuzzy for him outside that. He knew the words—he knew the year had twelve months, but only some of their names. Everything for him was seasons and sections and segments.

But that was another thing that he was too afraid to admit. There were flashing numbers everywhere. In the kitchen, beside his bed. In red and blue and even green. The numbers of the hours meant something to these people. It was so important that they kept time everywhere. No way he could admit he didn't understand it.

Ms. Fourakis jerked a thumb toward the hall. "I'm gonna go get my keys. Can you get those shoes on yourself?"

Finally, at last, something in this world he could do without help. He knew a whole host of knots. Though he didn't like the stiff shoes they expected him to wear, he did know how to put them on. The first, he tied tightly. The second, he carefully slid over his bandaged foot. No more hospitals. No more doctors. He had to take care, make sure.

After noon, but before sunset. That's how long he had to wait to see Dara again. So he followed Ms. Fourakis quietly and watched the sun drift across the blue, blue sky.

"Josh thinks you're avoiding him," Sofia said as she and Dara walked to her car.

Most of the seniors had a half period at the end of the day. That meant they could leave before the rest of the student body. They streamed into the parking lot, their voices low. It was like they were afraid if they made too much noise, the teachers would call them back.

Dara opened the passenger side door, but didn't climb in. The sun was too warm, the sky too bright. Soaking up the heat, she draped her arms over the roof of the car and sighed. "I'm not. I'm just not going out of my way to see him."

"I'm hella shocked he never figured that out."

"That I usually run halfway across the school to see him after class?" Dara shook her head. "I'm not. Josh is a really great guy, but he's not super observant."

Sofia climbed in, dumping her bag in the backseat and opening her purse in her lap. It would take her a few minutes to find her keys in that mess. Dara marveled that somebody as mentally together as Sofia could have such a cluttered . . . every-thing. Her car, her purse, her bedroom.

"You wanna know what I think?" Sofia asked, rooting through a tangle of earbuds, necklaces, and lip gloss. "I think you're breaking up with him in slow motion."

With an incredulous look, Dara lowered herself into the passenger seat. "That's crazy."

"Lie to yourself all you want. I've been watching you two since freshman year."

"Whatever, Sof."

Abandoning the search for her keys for a minute, Sofia reached over and caught Dara's hand. "I know something happened out there. And I'm not talking about Cade, either. I mean, maybe he's part of it. I don't know. But you and Josh aren't the same."

Dara surprised herself by agreeing. She wasn't big on sharing her relationship details, she never had been. It had always seemed kind of private. Obviously, she told Sofia about big milestones. But when she was mad at Josh, she didn't badmouth him. And when she was thrilled with him, well, she kept that to herself, too. It had always felt like she was protecting something special.

Gently, Sofia resumed her search for her keys. "Spill."

"He's not interested in anything," Dara said. Then, she immediately corrected herself. "I mean, he's interested in stuff. But he doesn't . . . like, for example: I found a whole field of little red mushrooms. Like, Smurf houses. Mario mushrooms."

"Cool," Sofia said.

"It *was* cool!" Dara twisted in her seat, hands dancing wildly as she explained herself. "I showed him the picture, and he didn't know what he was looking for. They were right there. The waterfall rainbows were right there, and Cade was up in the trees, and he just . . . he didn't care. He didn't want to know. He has no idea what I see when I look through the lens, and he doesn't want to. He just doesn't."

Sofia accidentally set off an atomizer in her purse. Perfume floated up in the car, and Dara scrambled to roll her window down. So did Sofia, contorting her face and trying to fan the fumes outside.

"It's your perfume," Dara pointed out, coughing.

"I don't usually spray it on my face," Sofia replied. "God, I'm never wearing this again."

"Please don't."

Tossing the bottle into the backseat of her car, Sofia turned to face Dara. Sympathetic and even, she reached out to pat her knee. There was something soothing about Sofia when she got down to caretaker mode. She could be a total lunatic when she wanted to be. But when it was time to get serious, she slipped into it effortlessly.

"I'm sorry. About you and Josh. I know and you know and probably everybody but Josh knows you guys were going to break up this fall anyway, but . . . you know, it still sucks."

Dara's emotions suddenly welled to the surface. She wanted to blame the unexpected tears on the perfume bomb, but she couldn't. Sofia was right. Even if things had been hurtling toward an inevitable end, she and Josh had been together a long time. She wasn't sure she even knew how to be herself without him. "I wanted us to be different, you know?"

"Most people don't marry their high school sweetheart," Sofia replied. Then, she crinkled her nose, smiling and teasing carefully. "You have to go to college and sleep with at least two questionable people before you can think about settling down. Maybe three."

Dara swiped at her face. "I get a lot more action in your fantasies than I do in mine," Dara said. But she laughed in spite of her tears. Some of the weight on her heart lifted. Even though it was sad to contemplate, it was good to finally admit to someone that her feelings for Josh had changed.

Now if she could only figure out a good way to explain it to *him*.

TWENTY-FIVE

Ms. Fourakis let Dara into the house. Rather than hover, she called Cade to come see his guest. She pointed first at him, then at her. "An hour, tops. I told your parents I'd send you straight home."

"Thanks," Dara said. Clutching her bag, she followed Cade down the hallway.

All the rooms had plants in them. There was a hint of humidity in the air. It smelled fresh, like rain might come through at any moment. She didn't know if Mom or Dad had anything to do with Cade's placement here, but it seemed really, really right.

Pushing open a door, Cade slid through it first then waited for Dara. Then he held up his fingers. The pads on each one were stained black. "Fingerprints. And they wiped my mouth with a stick."

"A DNA test," she explained. "They're going to . . ."

"Keep the sample on hand and compare it to the genetic loci between me and anybody who shows up who might be related to me. I know what a DNA test is."

Unnerved, Dara laid her backpack on the bed and unzipped it. "But you've never seen a stove."

"I've never seen Pluto. I still know it's a planet."

With a wry smile, Dara looked back at him. "Actually, it's not anymore. It got demoted."

The look on Cade's face was priceless. He hopped up on the chair by the window, peering down at her with utter bafflement. Tipping his head from side to side, he seemed like he was sloshing that idea around in his head. Finally, he shrugged. "It's still a planet to me."

"You're not the only one," Dara said, laughing. Taking a deep breath, she turned and sat on the end of his bed. Pulling her camera into her lap, she took in her surroundings with her eyes, first.

It was comfortable. Neutral, kind of hotel-like, really. But that was probably a good idea. If Ms. Fourakis did a lot of temporary fosters instead of permanent ones, it made sense to keep the room blank. There were plants in here, too, though. Probably because there wasn't room for them anywhere else.

Cade leaned forward. "What do you see?"

The question startled her. A flush stung her cheeks and she raised her shoulders, uncertain. "Well. It's a nice room. Not too big. Nothing fancy. Sort of generic art on the walls, which would be weird if one person slept in here all the time.

But since they don't, it's okay. The plants are obviously Ms. Fourakis' thing; do you like it? Do you feel kind of like you're outside?"

"No," Cade said. He pointed up. "I can't see the sky."

"Well no, I know, but . . ."

"A house is not the same as my home."

Dara's heart ached. But she mustered up a smile for him, waving for him to come sit with her. "You're right, it's not the same. But come here. I want to show you some cool stuff here in town. Just, you know . . . so you know it's not all hospitals and police cars and stuff."

When he didn't move immediately, she wondered if she should go sit over there. Since he sat exclusively on the back of the chair, there was plenty of room for her in the seat.

What kept her from standing though, was the realization that his knees would frame her shoulders if she did. He'd have to lean over her to see. The thought alone sent a strange quiver through her belly.

Definitely not doing that. So Dara held out her hand and raised her brows expectantly. "Please. I think you'll like this."

Sliding from his perch, Cade wound back to the bed. He sat next to her, but not too close. Suddenly, he darted a hand out. His finger pecked the body of the camera, once, then twice. Dara clutched it to her chest before he tagged it again.

"Stop," she told him. "You'll break it."

"Ticky box," he said. Clasping his hands in his lap, he nodded toward the camera. "That's your ticky box. There was one at the police station, too."

Dara squinted at him. "They took your picture at the police station?"

Wiggling his blackened fingers at her, Cade nodded. "After the fingerprints and the stick in my mouth."

She felt a little cheated. It was irrational. It's not like anyone at the station had tried to capture Cade's true self on film. They just needed a record, something to show to other cops, or to possible parents. They hadn't taken anything away from her, but it felt like they had. She wanted to be the one to take his photo first.

"Okay, well, this is a camera. You know what pictures are, this is how you get them."

Holding it up, she fired off a few quick shots of him. For the first time, she really noticed the sound the shutter made. Ticky box indeed. Smiling crookedly, she leaned over to show him the LCD screen on the back. Thumbing the buttons, she made his image appear.

"See?" she said. "These aren't very good, but that's how it works."

Quiet for a long moment, Cade considered the screen. Then, his brow slowly knit. "You were taking pictures in the forest. Of the mushrooms and the trees. Why?"

Resting the camera in her lap, Dara rolled her head to look at Cade. His face was so sweet. So curious. Though he waited for her reply, his gaze kept straying toward the camera. "I wanted to see their true nature. I wanted to capture everything about them in a single picture. So that later, I could show that photo to somebody and they'd understand. They'd feel like they were right there, looking at that flower for the first time."

Cade leaned over. "Why aren't these very good?"

"Because I was just showing you how it worked. I didn't try to get you in the picture."

"I'm right there."

"Right, but it's not the same thing."

It was hard to explain. Even harder to explain to him, when she wasn't sure what he knew and what he didn't. So rather than mess around with words, she scooted closer to him. She pulled out an SDHC card, not much bigger than her thumbnail. Showing it to him, she popped the current memory card out of her camera, and slid that one in.

Running through the menus, Dara put the camera in slide show mode. Then, she reached over and cupped his hands. Carefully, she placed the camera there. She was a little bit nervous. She didn't know what he would do when the pictures started to flash in front of him. Her gaze danced from the screen to his face, hungry for his reaction to each photo.

"Sofia laughing," Cade said, trying to touch the blur of black hair and red lipstick on the screen. His touch glanced off, and then the next picture slid into place. Brows lifting, he tipped his head to one side. "I saw lights like these. Outside."

Dara nodded. "Streetlamps, exactly."

"A machine," Cade said, but he sounded uncertain.

"That's the engine of Josh's car," she told him. "He rebuilt it himself."

Cade made a dismissive sound and then leaned his head back when the screen changed again.

Slowly, the slide show introduced him to glass doorknobs in old houses, mourning doves perched in the glow of a scarlet sunrise. A stained glass window at night, and a gargoyle spouting water in broad daylight. The silhouettes of children playing on a playground, a dog barking at its own, long shadow.

None of the pictures were of nature things; that was on purpose. Dara figured he knew the forest better than anyone, so why not share her world with him? It had so many beautiful details, and most people walked right on by without seeing them. When the reel ended, Dara was surprised to find herself leaning on Cade's good shoulder.

"What do you think?" she asked, tension winding her tight. He was so close, or she was. Idly, she wondered why guys always had the nicest eyelashes, long and dark and curled.

Cade's gaze drifted downward. "You smell like someone else."

That broke the spell. With a thin laugh, Dara reached for her camera. "Yeah, Sofia accidentally sprayed me with perfume in her car."

"You smell good without it."

Now Dara's blush darkened. What could she say to that? There was no ready response for that kind of observation. Clearing her throat, she put a little space between them and busied herself with her camera. "Um, thanks. So . . ."

Cade reached out, curling a knuckle against her cheek. "You're all red now."

Catching his hand, she shook her head. "Because you're

embarrassing me. You can notice stuff like that about people, but you don't usually say it."

"Why not?"

"It's just a little awkward," she said. "What if I told you that you have pretty eyelashes?"

Frowning, Cade closed his eyes and touched his own face thoughtfully. "I never thought about them. Thank you."

For some reason, that made *her* blush more. It was a conversational trap, and she had no idea how to escape. So, she retreated into the one thing that always made her feel certain.

Sliding to her feet, she pushed a new memory card into the camera. Raising it, she pointed a toe and nudged his shin with it.

"Let me take your picture."

"You already know the true me."

An electric thrill raced along her skin. He said it so certainly; his eyes looked right into her. Swallowing hard, Dara shrugged off her body's feral response. That's all it was; something animal and automatic. He was handsome, and there was something about the way he looked at her that made her feel alive.

"But I want to see if I can capture it," she said, and raised the camera instead. Looking through the viewfinder, she felt certain she couldn't. Cade wasn't himself when he was still. Sitting next to him, she could tell that even when he didn't move, that he was ready to. That his muscles could flicker to life at any moment. She'd never get that with a single picture.

That didn't mean, however, that she wasn't going to try.

— —

After Dara left, Cade lay across the foot of the bed.

The false scent hung heavily in the air. But when he closed his eyes, when he concentrated, he could smell her skin. Her heat and warmth.

Careful not to pull the edges of his bandage, Cade rubbed the middle of his chest. Everything inside him ached, but it wasn't quite pain. It was a new kind of hunger, one he'd never felt before.

He had to learn to tell their kind of time. She promised to come back on Saturday and he didn't know how long that was. There was too much waiting here. At home, his plans were never specific. Some days, he knew he had to hunt—but he never knew exactly where. If he had to go to the lick, there were lots of paths to take.

Except when he doused his fire for the night and fell asleep, Cade never waited on anything. There was always something to do. Somewhere to go. Now, in Dara's town, it was waiting. Waiting for the police. Waiting at a drive-through to get medicine. Waiting for tests. Waiting for answers.

Waiting to see her again.

Pressing down on the ache in his chest, Cade closed his eyes tight.

Dara didn't know what she expected to see out her window. Maybe she hoped that Cade would follow her home. That was just plain ridiculous, and she put the thought from her mind. But not entirely. Even though she was supposed to be doing homework, she kept getting up to check the window.

Until that moment, she saw nothing but an empty street. But this time, when she pushed the curtains back, she frowned.

There were news vans parked in front of her house. The kind with satellite dishes that rose high into the sky above them. Two different reporters stood in the street, their camera operators revolving in their orbits. One reporter stalked toward her camera, her face incredibly serious. The other kept waving a hand, gesturing at the neighborhood.

Anxious, Dara watched them, probably longer than she should have. One of the cameras turned, angling up on her house. Probably recording her. After a few minutes, she realized the reporters weren't going away.

The neighbors had figured that out, too. They stood on their porches watching. They filled their windows and leaned in door frames. Makwa was a quiet place to live. News vans from Lexington, ninety miles away, were rare blooms.

Bounding down the stairs, Dara startled her mother when she careened into the kitchen. Holding up a hand, she said, "Sorry."

Dropping the pepper mill, Mrs. Porter slumped against the counter. "Jeez, Dara."

"There are reporters out front," Dara said.

Mrs. Porter's eyes widened. Leaving dinner behind, she walked to the front windows. Parting the curtains carefully, she peered out. Sure enough, the vans were still there. And now the reporters were branching out, talking to neighbors.

"You've got to be kidding me. I need to text your father," Mrs. Porter said, stalking back toward the kitchen. Producing her cell phone, she let her fingers fly across its screen. Electronic ticks filled the air, and Dara felt weirdly trapped.

Lia strode into the kitchen and announced, "Did you see the news trucks out front? They're talking to Sasha. I don't know why she can't just shut up for once."

Lia's honeyed hair fell over her shoulders in waves, velvety pink streaks peeking out fashionably. She looked like she'd walked out of a magazine, which meant she was probably on her way out. Or had been, before the invasion of the newscasters.

Mrs. Porter frowned. "I hope her mother's there with her."

"She is."

Turning back to a messy array of ingredients that threatened to become dinner, Mrs. Porter seemed lost among them. Dara locked the door, then pulled the shade for good measure. Then she shouldered up to the counter, trying to figure out where her mom, or more likely, her dad had left off.

"I don't get it," Dara said, dipping chicken in the electric-orange crust mix. Disgusting and tasty, her favorite kind of meal. "What do they even want?"

"To get famous," Lia said, rolling her eyes. But she slipped in on the other side of their mother and took over the salad. Chopping carrots into slivers, she cut her sister a dark look. "Don't you know what they're saying?"

Mrs. Porter excused herself to set the table. "Let's not."

Ignoring her, Lia went on. "That he was raised by *wolves*."

"Seriously?"

"Totally. It made News of the Weird on Yahoo," Lia said with relish. Pulling out her phone, she opened her browser. With a few quick touches, she found the page she was after. Then, she read aloud.

"'The Primitive Boy is a puzzle that local authorities are trying desperately to solve. Lauded for a daring rescue of two Makwa teens, he seemed to be a hero.

"'But questions abound. He claims no memory of a life before his appearance in the forest. And after an outburst in a local hospital and a rampage through small-town Kentucky, we're left wondering: who is this boy, and are we safe with him in our community?'"

"Are you . . . what?" Dara exclaimed. "Is that from Kit's Tumblr?"

Lia snorted. "He wishes. He's telling everybody he broke the story, but nobody's listening to him."

"Nor should they," Mrs. Porter snapped.

"Then where is it from? Who would write that?"

"It was in the paper, dummy. That freakazoid you pointed out at school? Mmhmm."

Suddenly cold, Dara clutched the counter. "You lie."

Still surfing the web on her phone, Lia held it up for Dara to see. She'd stopped on the website for one of the local news stations. "On Channel Ten, they're mostly going with oooh, raised by wolves boy, look at his weird clothes, is he the missing link?"

Disgusted, Dara shoved the pan of chicken in the oven a lot harder than she needed to. "This is such bull!"

"Language, Dara," Mrs. Porter said. It was obligatory; she was texting fast and furious with someone and obviously hadn't heard a thing Dara said.

Itching to check the TV, Dara washed her hands instead and started on a blue box of mac and cheese.

When they wanted to be, she and Lia could be a good team. They were going to get dinner done approximately ten times faster than their mother ever would, and twice as fast as their dad—and it would be edible. They used to joke that their parents would starve to death if it weren't for them. Which is why Dara bothered to speak to Lia at all.

Filling a pot with water, Dara asked, "Okay, then why are they in front of *our* house?"

With a snort, Lia tossed a handful of tomato slices into the salad bowl. Plucking it up, she fixed her sister with a plastic, unpleasant smile. "He saved you, dummy."

"Don't call your sister a dummy."

Sweeping around Dara, Lia glided toward the dining room. She kept her voice low enough that only her sister could hear when she mocked.

"Is the sheriff's daughter the Primitive Boy's secret lovah? Or is she the victim of a potentially psychotic drifter? Tune in at ten to find out!"

TWENTY-SIX

*S*ofia always drove too fast.

Clinging to the armrest, Dara tried to keep herself upright as they turned the corner. It took a second for the car to stop shuddering, and Dara slumped in her seat.

After the reporters, Dara spent the evening uneasy. She kept expecting them to pop back up. At school the next day, or when she walked out to the bus. So far, they hadn't, but that didn't ease her nerves.

"Media free," she said, rolling her head to smile at Sofia.

"I can't believe this is your life," Sofia replied.

She followed Dara's pointed directions to Ms. Fourakis' driveway. They left their jackets in the car. A burst of unseasonable weather made it feel like summer. A particular, perfect shade of blue, the sky was clear all the way to the horizon. The sun was tiny, but warm, burning off the lingering morning cool.

Bounding up the steps, Dara pressed the doorbell, then turned to Sofia. "I found my old laptop, by the way. Watched like six YouTube videos last night. I'm totally prepared to fix your gutter."

Sofia snorted, but didn't answer. Instead, she peeked in the curtained window. Footsteps rumbled inside, and a moment later, the front door swung open. Ms. Fourakis had braided her thick, dark hair into pigtails. They made her look crazy young—way too young to be a temporary foster mom.

"Hey girl, what's up?" Ms. Fourakis said to Dara, flicking a quick, curious look at Sofia.

With a nod, Dara said, "This is my best friend, Sofia. We were wondering if Cade could . . . if he wanted to hang out."

How fail did that sound? Dara wondered to herself. She felt sheepish, like a kid asking if their brand-new neighbor could come out to play. It was kind of like that, only way more complicated. In grade school, almost nobody had to dodge Channel 6 to get to a playdate.

"Sure, come on in." She left the door open, inviting them to follow as she walked back inside. Raising her voice, Ms. Fourakis called down the hall, "Cade, you have guests."

A splash answered, and Ms. Fourakis laughed. With a shrug, she informed them with amusement, "He's taken four baths since he got here. It's not even a good tub."

"We can come back," Dara offered.

From down the hall, Cade called, "Wait!"

Ms. Fourakis grinned, gesturing toward the couch. "Guess

you'd better wait. Want a birch beer or something?"

Sofia nodded sweetly. "That would be amazing, thank you." Then, as soon as Ms. Fourakis walked into the kitchen, she bumped her elbow against Dara's. "What is that, even?"

"No idea."

Taking in her surroundings, Dara marveled at the sheer amount of greenery contained in the living room. Her mom kept a spider plant in the kitchen, and there was a fake ficus in the dining room. But this was . . . it was practically a terrarium. Catching Sofia's eye, she nodded at the ivy that spilled over the side of the armoire.

Sofia replied with an incredulous expression that said, *I know, right?*

A door opened deeper in the house. Steam wafted out, not really visible. But it carried warmth and scent with it. New but familiar at once, it left Dara shifting uncomfortably. It smelled like Cade's skin, an introduction before he came into sight.

And when he came into sight, it was something. Even Sofia murmured approvingly. Someone had bought him jeans that fit, and his T-shirt clung to his still damp skin. Tied into an intricate knot, his dreads kissed the back of his neck.

His skin was paler, all the grime scrubbed away. But he was still golden-brown and keen-eyed. It's just that now he looked like he'd walked out of an H&M ad. If the reporters could see him, they wouldn't keep calling him Primitive Boy. He looked more like music festival boy. Or underground-indie-zine boy.

"I'm glad you came," Cade said.

With a smile, Dara said, "I told you I would."

"I know. But I thought you were grounded," Cade said, pronouncing it carefully.

A stupid flutter rose in Dara's chest. It wasn't like he'd said anything that warranted it. Some rational part of her mind could admit she was crushing. It was incredibly scientific about it, too. Fortunately, the irrational part of her brain took over and smoothed things out.

"Turns out that's kind of a state of mind," she said.

"Unless they handcuff you, they can't really make you do anything," Sofia added.

Ms. Fourakis returned with an amber bottle of birch beer. Offering it to Sofia, she turned to Cade. "You're welcome to head out with them as long as you're back for dinner. Do you want me to write the phone number down for you, in case you need it?"

Cade nodded. "Please."

Squinting, Dara waited for Ms. Fourakis to walk out of earshot, then asked, "Do you even know what a phone is?"

"Yes. It plays music in your bag, and you cuss until it stops. Then you hold it in front of your face and talk to yourself."

Sofia made an explosive sound, and handed the bottle of birch beer to Dara. Scrubbing at her face with a tissue, she started to giggle. "Are you for real?"

"Yes." Cade pressed his forefinger against Sofia's arm. "See?"

It was like a tour through a dreamscape. None of it really made sense, but Cade followed Dara and Sofia eagerly. All the people in their world made him uneasy. But as long as he avoided them, and stuck close to Dara, it was exciting to see things he'd only heard about.

Traffic lights glowed on their own. Motorcycles and bicycles sped by, both in the street, piloted by very different people. Above the street, a billboard flipped, revealing a different picture than it started with. Cade had no idea what a five point inspection was, but he stared at the ad avidly.

"Okay," Sofia said, slamming the car into park. "First stop, box store."

Cade slipped from the backseat, and turned in slow wonder. Hundreds of cars surrounded him. All different shapes and colors, some plastered with slogans and others pristine and shining. He murmured to Dara, "What is this?"

With a gentle smile, she put a hand on his back and pushed him up the aisle. "Just a parking lot."

They were strange to look at, but a little wonderful. There was a picture back home, of his parents standing beside a car. It was narrower, lower to the ground than these. But it made him feel connected. This is the world his parents came from.

But it was all supposed to be gone. His mother had told him this was over. No more parking lots, no more cars. No more safe people. No more civilization. But here it was. Strange and alive and remarkably unconcerned. It was like they didn't know . . .

"Cade," Dara said. She stood a few feet away, waiting for him, Nodding toward the building, she offered him a smile. "You coming?"

At least Dara made sense. She was warm and soft; she kept

coming back. He liked the way she blushed when he touched her skin. It was like lighting a fire in her, she glowed, her voice deepened. Putting aside thoughts of his parents, he bounded after her.

She must have been dazed, because she turned and walked straight for a glass wall. Lunging after her, Cade caught her arm. She gasped, and so did the glass wall. It opened with a wheeze, cooler air washing over them.

"Automatic door," Dara explained.

Cade twisted around. Backing onto the sidewalk, he twisted up and down. Then, carefully, he crept toward the door again. His heart pounded. Would it open again? Suddenly, it did and he jumped away.

Even here, he was aware. Sofia stared at him, Dara did, too. But how could he care? Excitement raced through him, and he approached the door from another angle. Could he sneak up on it? With a quick, mental measurement, he considered the opening. Then he leapt onto the metal rail.

"Cade, get down," Dara said.

Sofia raised her phone, following his every movement.

And he didn't get down. Instead, he waved his hand at his reflection in the glass. The door didn't move. Standing up, he considered jumping to the other rail. Just before he did, he thought better of it. His foot wasn't strong enough yet. The sneakers wouldn't let him grip with his toes.

A woman clattered up to the door with a silvery cart. She shot Cade an ugly look. "You kids need to quit playing up here. People are trying to walk."

Quickly, Dara darted in and grabbed his hand. Her touch was smooth, warm. It didn't match her icy expression. "Go ahead. We're not hurting anything," she told the woman. Rather than pull Cade down, she stood beside him fiercely.

Disgusted, the woman trundled on inside.

"She's probably going to complain to the manager," Sofia said, dropping her phone in her purse again. She smoothed her hair back and approached the door. It opened for her, and Cade wondered what the difference was. How it worked.

Dara rubbed his arm, then nodded toward Sofia. "She's right. Come on."

Reluctantly, Cade dropped to the ground. But for good measure, he waited until the girls walked inside. Then he backed away from the door and ran at it. A split second before he crashed into the glass, he saw their horrified faces inside. Then, he saw them in person as the thing finally swung open.

Head aching, he let Dara pull him to his feet. The rush of cool air from inside soothed the ache. But not his embarrassment. They both laughed. It was mixed with sympathy, but it was obvious they couldn't hold back.

Petting him, Dara asked, "Oh god, poor baby, are you okay?"

"Yes," he said. He glowered at the door from the inside. Traitor.

"If you go too fast, the motion sensor misses you," Dara said.

"I think there's a weight thing on the ground, too."

He followed them through the aisles. Too many people here, for certain. His skin started to itch again. Veering around the crowds, his heart raced—but this time, from anxiety. Too many people, strangers . . . they brushed and touched and coughed. They sneezed and barely covered their mouths.

"Yeah," Dara said, still working on the door problem. "So probably like, you have to move slow enough for the sensor to see you, and weigh enough to set it off. Otherwise the place would be full of stray dogs and cats. Birds. Squirrels."

"Squirrels are not allowed to shop here," Sofia added.

"That's good." Cade said. "They're very messy."

"Oh really?" Sofia asked.

It was a relief to talk about things he knew. It took his mind off the great clouds of people that swirled around him. "That's how I find them. Piles of nut shells. It's squirrels, every time."

"Why would you want to find a squirrel?" Sofia asked.

"They taste good."

Horrified, Sofia flung herself away. She wriggled and writhed with disgust. But not Dara. Instead, she considered him slowly. Her face was mysterious, brows furrowed and a faint, folded line above her lip.

It felt good to be under her gaze. To know she was studying him the way he'd studied her. Maybe she hadn't been aware enough to look up in the forest. But Cade suspected she was a different kind of aware, in her own world.

"What?" he finally asked.

"Nothing, I'm just . . ." Dara rolled a shoulder. Then suddenly, she smiled. "I basically want to show you everything in the world. You know, to see what it's like for you."

Closing the space between them, Cade nodded. "Okay."

Her blush wasn't subtle or slow this time. It sprung up, fully scarlet, and she took a step back. "First, we have to get the stuff to fix Sofia's gutters."

Actually, first Dara couldn't resist winding Cade through the store. He approached rows of canned goods the way she would approach a sculpture in an art museum. Except he was allowed to touch the exhibits, and he did.

"Nonononono," Dara exclaimed, when he tore open a box of cookies. "It's not yours."

"It's mine. I took it."

With a sigh, she dropped it in her basket. "It's not ours until we pay for it. We'll get these, but no more opening, okay?"

He shot her a look that said he might not agree to that at all. But he did. Down the aisle, he still picked things up. He just made no move to open anything else, which was a relief. Dara was pretty sure she only had a twenty on her.

It was interesting to watch him, though. He *smelled* everything. As soon as he picked something up, he raised it to his nose. Boxes of crackers, a bottle of laundry soap. The detergent aisle made him sneeze and toss his head. Standing in the middle of it, Dara noticed for the first time how overwhelming all the perfumes were.

But Cade kept moving, turning the aisle and stopping in front of the dairy case. Pressing a hand to the glass, he looked back at Dara. Confidently, he said, "This is a refrigerator."

"It totally is," Sofia said.

It was hard to tell what she thought about all of this. But what was nice was that she went along. If Cade was a mental patient, then later, it would be an incredibly interesting story for her to tell. And if he really did turn out to be a modern caveman then . . . it would be an incredibly interesting story for her to tell.

Cade turned, taking a few measured steps. "I smell fish."

Pointing past him, Dara said, "The meat counter's right there."

Rows of perfectly cut steak and pork led the way. They were exquisite shades of marbled red and pure pink. They sat unmarred on their beds of white Styrofoam, and they seemed to frighten Cade. He approached the case, touched some of the plastic, then shrank back.

"What's this?" he asked, then poked a chuck roast curiously. "Beef. That's a cow. Where is it?"

"What?" Dara asked.

"The cow." Cade tried to look under the shelves, but mirrors reflected his face instead. "Pork, that's pig. Are the animals out back?"

Shaking her head, Dara said, "Um, no. All this comes on a truck."

Cade backed toward the seafood department. "The fish?"

"That, too."

He turned in time to find the live tank. He turned his head to one side, then the other. Crouching in front of the tank, he watched lethargic beasts crawl over each other in the murky water. Their antennae waved faintly. With two fingers, he waved back. "It's a giant crawdad."

"Related anyway. They're lobsters, from Maine." Then,

uncertain, she added, "Probably."

"You don't know where your food comes from?"

Uneasy, Dara shrugged. "I mean, the store. It comes from the store. Sometimes Mom gets eggs from the farmers' market."

"What if the animals were sick?" Cade asked.

"They weren't."

Cade tapped the tank. "How do you know?"

Breaking in, Sofia said brightly, "Okay, I'm going to go pay. Anytime you guys wanna catch up, that'd be awesome."

Dara watched Sofia go. Now she was alone with Cade, a tank of lobsters, and questions that sounded perfectly reasonable to ask. Why did she feel so stupid that she didn't know the answers?

Peering into the tank, Dara waited for the lobsters to help her out. They were mostly green, some speckled with orange. Did that mean they were diseased? Was that what lobsters usually looked like? Suddenly, Dara realized she had no idea.

"How do you know?" Cade repeated.

She didn't. But she wasn't going to tell him that. Straightening up, Dara said, "They wouldn't sell it if it was bad. Somebody checks. I just don't know who."

Another question was coming, she could tell. The whole thing left her feeling weirdly defensive. Standing quickly, she offered Cade her hand. "Come on. We really have to get Sofia's gutters back on before her parents get home."

"Or she will be grounded."

"Or she'll be *murdered*," Dara said.

He squeezed her hand, suddenly tense.

Untangling herself, Dara smoothed out their hands and folded them together again gently. "Not literally."

Relaxing, Cade nodded. "Good. I like Sofia."

"Me too," Dara said. And she laughed, because what else could she do?

TWENTY-SEVEN

It turned out Dara was right.

She could learn to do anything from YouTube, or at least, how to do some basic home repair. It didn't even take that long. Cade held the ladder like a champ while Dara nailed in the new brackets. Sofia kept the downspout in place, and when they were finished, they agreed it looked perfect.

"Can't take your word for it, though," Sofia told Cade. "Like you'd even know."

He laughed, rolling away from her when she shoved him. Dara watched them for a minute, shaking her head. It was like Sofia had completely replaced Javier, who was kind of lame as brothers went anyway.

He spent most of his time building epic Minecraft cities. Oh, and experimenting with "extreme physics" at the lake. Stuff like making dry ice bombs, building human catapults, and one extremely memorable attempt to set the lake on fire.

It was a good thing Javier was a straight-A student, because otherwise, people would have thought he was a terrorist.

"I'll step on your limpy foot," Sofia threatened.

"I'll throw you over my shoulder," Cade replied.

Before Dara could egg them on, a flash caught her eye. A short burst of light exploded from the forsythia. It had a particular quality, blinding but brief. Holding up a hand, Dara murmured, "Guys. Stop, guys. I think somebody's watching us."

They quit moving, and Dara stood for a moment, conflicted. Common sense told her to go inside. For all of them to go inside. Call her dad, let the police sort it out. But she was already annoyed—it was probably that stalker Jim Albee, and she kind of wanted to have her paparazzi moment.

Dara raised her voice, stalking across the yard. "Get out! Get out, this is private property!"

Snatching up Sofia's lacrosse stick, she waved it like a bat. The bush started to shake, and just as she reached it, a body tumbled out. Sprawled on the grass in front of her was Kit Parson, Lia's idiot friend.

He was the guy running the gossip Tumblr. The one with all the crappy macros and leaked emails that probably got the regular media interested in a total nonstory. He was anchored by the biggest digital camera Dara had ever seen."What's your problem?" she demanded.

Kit threw his hands up. Interestingly, he protected the camera, not his face. That one tiny detail is what kept her from walloping him. Dara loved her own camera so much, she'd named it. They were majestic, elegant creatures of beauty and truth. They deserved to be protected.

"Jeez, Dara, come on," he said. "I just want one picture."

Raising the stick again, Dara said, "Oh what, you can't hack anything else from the police station so you're turning stalker?"

"I didn't hack anything!" Kit's voice turned to a whine. His fedora lay in the dirt, and he looked like he might strangle himself with his own skinny tie. "If I got a tip, I published it, so what?"

Acid roiled in Dara's stomach. If he got a tip . . . and most of his tips seemed to come straight from Dad. Nobody knew where Dara planned to head today, and it certainly wasn't common knowledge that Cade would be with her.

No. Kit had known to hide in Sofia's backyard because *Lia* had tipped him.

Though she longed to whack him, Dara nudged him instead. It was the last little bit of her patience and willpower. "Get up. Get out. And tell my sister she sucks."

Kit stood. But he looked past Dara. Arms still protecting the camera, he called to Cade. "Hey! Hey, can I ask you two questions?"

"Out!" Dara shouted. She poked him with the lacrosse stick. "Get out!"

After suffering a couple more blows, Kit gave up and jumped the fence. He only ran halfway down the alley. Then he turned back to take a couple more pictures. Just before Dara lunged over the fence to teach him a lesson for real, Cade caught her by the shoulder.

"Hey," he said. Wrapping his arms around her waist, melded against her. Like he didn't know any better, he was all up on her. Possessive and hot to the touch.

But Dara was too mad to be cosseted. Peeling his arms off, she slipped out of his embrace. She bounced, unexpected adrenaline careening through her. She heaved the stick back to the middle of the yard, and then started toward the house.

"It's lunchtime, come on!"

Cade didn't hesitate to follow.

Stirring her pudding cup, Sofia decided they'd sufficiently bonded. Wrestling and takeout from Uncle Stan's had brought them together. Plus, the glory of giving Dara a hard time for the beat-down she dropped on that idiot Kit—it brought them closer together. They were a team as far as Sofia was concerned.

That meant now she could be straight-up nosy without too much interference from Dara. She couldn't help it if she had questions. It was weird that Dara didn't have more. Swirling her spoon in the air, Sofia pointed it at Cade.

"Okay, so, where do you go to the bathroom in the woods?"

"Seriously?" Dara exclaimed.

But Cade just laughed. "Away from your camp. Not in the river."

Making a face at Dara, Sofia sucked her spoon clean. "Simple question, simple answer."

"My turn," Cade said.

His pudding cup still had its foil lid. He kept rolling the cup between his fingers, occasionally sniffing at it. Once, when Dara reached over to open it for him, he held it away. Sofia watched, fascinated. He obviously knew how to open it. He just *wasn't*. Every weird little thing about him amused her.

Since he claimed a turn but hadn't said anything, Dara prompted, "Well?"

"How many people are there?"

Unaware that Cade had asked Dara the same question, Sofia reached for her cell phone. With a few quick strokes across its face, she pulled up the answer and turned the screen to him. There was a little graph and everything. "Seven billion, give or take thirty-seven million."

The same answer as before. Seven billion. *Billion*. His head ached and he rubbed at his brow. It was an impossible number.

"Why does that surprise you?" Dara asked.

"What about the pandemic?"

Sweeping a finger to get the last bits of pudding from her cup, Dara shook her head. "Like what? Bird flu?"

"No, it was swine flu."

"SARS," Dara countered.

Sofia took the challenge, and replied with, "H1N1."

Watching them both, Cade's expression darkened. How many pandemics had there been? How could there be anyone left, let alone billions and billions. He could practically feel his mother's fingers on his brow, singing an old plague song to him, *Ring around the rosie, pocket full of posies . . .*

"Aw man, there was a 5 one, but I don't remember what it was. H5N-something?" Sofia picked up her cell phone again. "The one they gave ferrets on purpose."

Cade didn't know how it contained so much information, but he wanted one. It was like Branson's tablet, only smaller, a handheld miracle.

There were answers inside that tiny box. And YouTube videos. Pictures, and whole books, tons of books. Briefly, he wondered if Sofia would notice if it went missing. Then he felt instantly guilty, because he knew better. His parents had taught him better.

While Sofia searched the box, Dara slid closer to Cade. She kept her voice down, rubbing her elbow against his. "Why do you keep asking that?"

It was possible his mother had lied. It was possible his parents had fed him black fairy tales all his life; hidden him away from *nothing*. A seed of anger pulsed inside him. But he didn't know for sure. He didn't have enough facts—maybe if he had a cell phone, he'd have enough. He didn't, and he didn't. So he shook his head and looked past her. "Curious."

"Kind of a weird thing to be curious about."

Uncomfortable, Cade deflected. He brushed a finger against her chin, then smiled. "Do *you* have any questions? How I take a bath in the *woods*? What I do for fun in the *woods*?"

"What do you do if you get a cold in the *woods*?"

Cade shook his head. "I've never had a cold."

"You lie!" Sofia forgot her phone for the moment.

"I don't," he said. Fingers skating across the table, he drew a diagram. His fingers were so warm, they left a brief impression on the cool laminate surface. "Rhinovirus spreads person to person, mostly through physical contact. Animals don't get rhinovirus, not the kind that infects humans. Mom said that theoretically, rabbits might get it, but I've never borrowed a spoon from a rabbit, have you?"

"You had spoons?" Sofia exclaimed.

Cade mimed like he was whittling. "I carved them from antler and bone."

"Where did you—" Sofia cut herself off. "Don't even answer. If you killed Bambi for spoon bones, I don't even want to know."

Standing to throw away her trash, Dara rolled that over in her head. Never had a cold, that seemed impossible. Stepping on the lever to open the bin, Dara just stood there. Thoughtfully, she pointed out, "You lived with your parents, though."

"But away from other people. Rhinovirus doesn't just float in the atmosphere, waiting to land on somebody. It dies without a host. Like I said, person to person."

All the fascinating factoids about colds aside, Dara slowed with realization. She drew out the question, her tone funny and slightly high-pitched. "Are you saying that Josh and I were the first people you'd ever seen besides your parents?"

"No."

Sofia sprawled in her chair. She didn't say anything; she didn't have to. It was obvious from her posture that she was belted in and ready to listen to whatever he had to say, for as long as he had to say it.

"Sometimes we saw soldiers," Cade said. "I mean, rangers."

Yes, they wore uniforms, but they weren't from the military. The Parks Department sent them. He still didn't know why they'd put grates over caves, or boxes high up in the trees. Or why his parents moved camp when they saw one. So little of his life made sense now.

Raising her hand, Sofia interjected. "'Scuse me."

"Go ahead," Dara said.

"You know what rhinovirus is," Sofia said. "But you don't know what chopsticks are. Explain."

Never tell, his mother whispered in his ear. She slipped through memory so easily. Rising to the top of his thoughts, full-formed, almost alive again. It made him shiver; he felt the phantom of her touch on the back of his neck. *The survivors are dangerous. They'll take you from us. They'll hurt you.*

With a casual shrug, Cade repeated Ms. Fourakis as he finally peeled the lid from his pudding. "I'm a man of many mysteries."

Mrs. Porter let the curtains drop back in place. "They're back."

Irritated, Sheriff Porter stood and took his own look. He believed his wife, but it made it more real to see for himself. Three vans tonight, plus a photographer. A flash kept going off. It came so fast, it was like a strobe light. Setting his jaw, the sheriff pulled the curtains tight. "This is ridiculous."

"I'll work on a placement out of town," Mrs. Porter said.

Technically, that was the Cabinet for Health and Family Services' job. But her nonprofit had its own pool of volunteers.

She had connections that CHFS didn't; she was shameless about pressing them into service.

Most of the time, they worked this magic for actual runaways. For teens at risk, fleeing families rife with drug addiction and violence. Kids who didn't *want* to be part of the system, and usually for good reason.

But if she could use her powers to get the local affiliates off her lawn, she'd do it. She had Branson's number in her contact list. Between the two of them, she could get Cade moved somewhere both safe, and far, far away from Makwa.

"Don't," Sheriff Porter said. He didn't like the invasion any more than his wife did. But he also hated unanswered questions, and that's all he had right now. Slumping into the couch again, he went back to the open file he had on the coffee table.

Mrs. Porter arched a brow. "Why not?"

"I don't want Dara following him, for one." Sheriff Porter frowned, flipping through photos from the hospital. The doctors agreed the story made sense. The wound was consistent, they said, with a bear attack. (*He's the luckiest kid in Kentucky*, one doctor said. Sheriff Porter didn't see it that way, but he dutifully wrote it down anyway.)

"We can always send her to stay with my mother."

"I like her just fine where we can see her."

Mrs. Porter couldn't help herself. She peeled the curtain back a little more. A fourth van rolled into sight, and she sighed in disgust. "If that's for one, what's for two?"

Stills from the security camera told the truth about the morning Cade trashed the hospital room. Before anyone got in there, he was up on the windowsill, trying to get out. He wasn't knocking stuff over to be destructive. If Sheriff Porter had to guess, and he did have to—it was his job—he'd say he was scared.

Glancing up at his wife, Sheriff Porter said, "He talks to her."

"Excuse me?"

"He talks to her, Beth. I sat here and watched him lie to the social worker. Said he couldn't read, and Branson Swayle bought it because he's—"

"Tony," Mrs. Porter warned. She knew her husband didn't have much patience for the man, but Branson was a colleague. He had a good heart; they liked to have lunch at the Thai place that nobody else would touch.

Sheriff Porter brushed that aside. "I watched that kid go through our books. He took one, by the way. Poetry. I don't know about you, hon, but if I can't read, the last thing I'm gonna do is steal a book. I *can* read, and the last thing I'm stealing is Walt Whitman."

"All right, he can read. So what?"

"If he lies about one thing," Sheriff Porter said, "he's probably lying about everything else. To us, anyway."

Paling a little, Mrs. Porter sat heavily. "You want to use Dara as bait?"

"I want her to get us some answers."

Quiet for a moment, Mrs. Porter rubbed the back of her neck. She was torn, it was obvious. The urge to help Cade No-Last-Name; the instinct to protect her daughter. Slowly, she shook her head. "I don't like it."

"Me either."

Sheriff Porter closed the file. They had another daughter to think about. He had a town to police. And frankly, he didn't care for how protective Dara seemed of that kid in so short a time. He just didn't see another way to crack him. If he'd had something to confront him with, maybe. But he didn't. All he had was a daughter, determined to be Cade's ally. He looked up when his wife spoke again.

"But you're going to do it anyway," Mrs. Porter said flatly.

He didn't answer. He didn't have to.

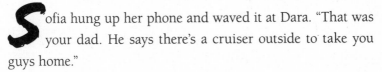

TWENTY-EIGHT

Sofia hung up her phone and waved it at Dara. "That was your dad. He says there's a cruiser outside to take you guys home."

Hopping up, Dara lifted the shades a little. Her mouth rounded, because there really *was* a police car out front. The lights weren't flashing, which was a relief. But the deputy inside looked like he was about to climb out and come to the door.

Vaguely embarrassed, Dara dropped the shades and turned to Sofia. "Did he say *why*?"

"Sorry," Sofia said.

"I'll call you later," Dara told her. "Right after I make them give my phone back."

"That would be awesome."

Cade had to be peeled away from the Wii. For somebody

who'd never seen technology before, he was a pro at Mario Kart. He was halfway through a water level and twisting the wheel like he was born driving. He veered his body when the screen shifted, and muttered when he crashed into obstacles.

Tapping him on the shoulder, Dara waited until he tore his gaze away. "We have to blow."

Cade frowned, but handed the controller to Sofia anyway. "What's wrong?"

There weren't enough words to explain it. Dara shook her head. Then she hugged Sofia at the door, opening it and waiting. It was weirdly sweet. Cade palmed the top of Sofia's head. He towered over her, and she had to tip her head back to look up at him.

She had an unexpected defense though. Poking at his ribs, Sofia reduced him to a twisted, squirming knot.

"I'm brother-proof," Sofia informed him. She shoved him out the door.

"Nice," Dara said.

Sofia answered with a wink, then watched them both head down the walk.

The neighborhood was quiet, and when Dara peered into the cruiser window, she smiled. Dad had sent Deputy Krause, one of the newer officers out of the academy. She was a walking encyclopedia of knock-knock jokes, and shared Dara's distaste for watermelon-flavored anything.

"Hey," Dara said through the window.

"Hop in," Deputy Krause replied.

Dara opened the back door and waited for Cade to slide in.

She followed him across the slick bench seat. The car smelled like old food and other people's sweat. And faintly of dog, which was odd because it wasn't a K-9 unit. Patting the steel mesh between them, Dara leaned forward.

"What's all this about, anyway?"

"No clue, kid. I just do what the sheriff tells me to do."

Sinking back, Dara snapped her seat belt, trying to settle in. Usually when she rode in her dad's cruiser, she got to sit in the front. There were no handcuff loops in the front. No boot prints permanently scuffed into the door, either. As soon as Cade buckled up, Dara joked, "Home, Jeeves!"

Chuckling, Deputy Krause flicked a look into the rearview mirror at them. "Sit back and shut up."

When the car started to move, Cade leaned over. Steadying himself with a hand on Dara's shoulder, he caught her eye. Murmuring, he said, "I could drive this."

"Uh-huh," Dara said.

"I wouldn't hit any fences," Cade said. His smile spread. It was like he was trying to lure her, tease her into pressing next to him. Even though she wanted to, it wasn't possible. Their seat belts kept them from getting too close.

Patting his hand, Dara returned the smile. "It's the pedestrians I'm worried about."

He laughed, then laid his head back against the seat. Thoughtfully, he gazed at the ceiling. His lips barely moved when he spoke, sound flickering from them in tantalizing sparks. "I had fun today."

"Me too," Dara said.

Except for the doofus creeper in Sofia's backyard, she added mentally. Cade didn't seem to understand what the big deal was. She kind of liked that he didn't care about things that made most people completely anxious.

"You should come to my house next time."

The backseat was a little too warm. It made Dara melt, spilling toward Cade. She couldn't lean on his shoulder, but their heads brushed as they both slumped toward the middle. Tapping her fingers on the soft vinyl seat, Dara said, "Tomorrow."

Cade walked his fingers toward hers. "I mean *my* home."

"Hm, I don't know," Dara said, casting a playful look in his direction. "I was really bad at camping, remember?"

"Josh was." Cade touched his forefinger to Dara's wrist. "He didn't even know how to start a fire."

Dara turned to him. "How would you know?"

"I saw you," Cade said. "I saw your tent. The animals knew where you were, and so did I."

"I knew it. You were watching us."

"Sometimes," Cade admitted. "Only a little. I was busy."

"Doing what?"

"Living."

"I have news for you, I saw you, too," she said. "I have a picture. The day I saw the mushrooms, you were up in the trees."

He nodded, fingers trailing the seat between them. "I didn't know what the ticky box was. I stayed too long."

It was confirmation, and she was so glad to have it. The whole time, she was sure someone was there. So many times, Josh told her she was crazy. Flooded with warmth and vindication, she pressed him. "Were you at the river, too? When I was filling the canteens?"

"Yes."

"I knew it!" she exclaimed. Then slowly, her thoughts turned. Strange sensations filtered through her. Curiosity and heat. A little bit of fear mixed with anticipation. Letting her fingers trail close to his, she asked, "But why?"

"You were new," Cade said. He hesitated again. It was like a switch kept flipping, his voice was on, then off. "I'd never seen anyone like you. Or Josh. And it was a long time. I was alone a long time." Cade etched his thumbnail against the soft seat. It left a faint, white trail, and he sketched it out roughly. The sun, the river, his bee hollow that was filling with life and honeycomb without him, right at that moment. "I'd never seen yellow hair."

"That's . . ." Dara started. But then she stopped. It was crazy, or impossible, but somehow, it felt true.

"My dad said when I was little, I had red hair." Cade nodded, looking past Dara now. "That was from his side. But I got older, and it turned dark. Like my mom's. I look like her."

It was a perfect moment to ask something, Dara realized. To dig in, to discover more about him. Maybe to figure out if his intentions were good, or dark, and how she fit into them. But the right question escaped her. It mocked her, like a word at the tip of her tongue, or an almost-remembered errand.

Cade filled the quiet for her. "I was lonely."

"So was I," she murmured, and watched the streets glide by.

The deputy escorted Cade to Ms. Fourakis' back door. Her boyfriend, Mr. Anderson, let him in, then quickly locked the door behind them.

"Weird day, huh?" Mr. Anderson said.

Cade nodded. He felt unmoored, drifting into the kitchen with his head full of too much information. Not enough information. The wrong kind of information. Though he wasn't hungry, he opened the fridge and peered into it. There were so many bottles and tubs and containers. Too many. Food was so easy here.

"Want some bread and peanut butter?" Mr. Anderson smeared goo from a container on a white, spongy leaf and offered it to him. "Nobody bothered you, did they?"

With a sniff, Cade considered the bread, then took a tentative bite. His mother talked about bread, usually in the fall. She'd go on about how it smelled in the oven, how delicious it was with butter. Cade had never had either, so she may as well have been talking about how much fun it was to camp on the moon.

"Someone from Dara's school took pictures of us. She ran him off."

"Seriously?" Mr. Anderson said. His laugh was laced with disbelief. "Well, you're safe at home now. We had somebody from the paper come to the door a while ago. Told him I didn't know a Cade. Or a Kelly Fourakis."

Laughing with him, Cade devoured the bread, then happily took another slice. It was incredibly soft. The peanut butter was sweet and slick on his tongue. Even though it wasn't hot, it warmed him.

After two more slices, he decided he would miss peanut butter almost as much as hot baths when he went home. When Mr. Anderson turned around, Cade plucked the jar off the counter. He had nowhere to hide it, not really. But he tucked it under his arm all the same, and half turned away. Maybe he wouldn't notice.

Mr. Anderson tied up the bread, slipping it into the cupboard. "You're kinda quiet tonight."

"I want something," Cade said.

"What's that?"

Finishing his snack, Cade brushed his hands together. He captured the crumbs in his palm, and tossed those in his mouth, too. Itching to get to higher ground, Cade considered his options.

Surreptitiously sliding the peanut butter behind the sugar jar, he hopped up to sit on the counter. It was allowed. He'd seen Ms. Fourakis do it last night. Watching Mr. Anderson, Cade folded his hands together, choosing his words carefully.

"I don't know."

Mr. Anderson laughed. "I can't help you, then, Cade. Can you describe it?"

He leaned against the fridge to watch Cade. He was so easy with his body; comfortable next to all this chrome and glass. His skin smelled like foreign spice, nothing Cade could place. It wasn't threatening at all. Pleasant, even.

It also reminded Cade that he was far from home, and had no idea how or when he'd get back. Suddenly, in his mind, it was before—when he still lived near his bee hollow and collected rain to drink. When nothing held him in because the sky was endless and too high to touch. It was a beautiful world, and boundless. Beautiful and open.

And empty.

The crushing weight returned. It filled Cade's chest and slipped over his shoulders. Somehow, it woke the aches beneath his bandages, sharp edges of pain to distract him. Everything expanded in his head, and suddenly it was hard to breathe. He'd cried before, but he was horrified by the rise of tears now.

Concerned, Mr. Anderson leaned toward him. "Cade?"

"I'll think about it," Cade said.

He snatched the jar of peanut butter and bolted from the kitchen. Feet thundering down the hall, he nearly crashed into his door. His door. That was insane, it wasn't *his* at all. None of this was. The room, the clothes, they all belonged to someone else. This place, this *world*.

And Dara. She belonged to someone else, too.

The bedroom was too bright, and too wrong. Swallowed by homesickness, Cade took in his surroundings. Then he took the plant from his (*not his!*) dresser. Cradling it to his chest, he carried it into the closet. It was dusty in there, but dark when he closed the door.

He dropped the peanut butter with the rest of his collection. A bottle of syrup, and a jar full of pickles. Crackers and cookies, and six unnaturally red apples.

Then he sank into the corner and covered his head with his good arm. He did not cry—no one had died. Things were strange. Dara was close, but far away at the same time. They kept asking questions he couldn't answer. His parents might have lied to him. But none of that was the same. He didn't cry. He wouldn't cry.

He just wanted to go home.

TWENTY-NINE

Sneaking in the back way only worked for Dara because her dad was on the front lawn giving a statement. Pressed into the front window with Lia, she cracked it open just a little and they listened to their father speak.

Surrounded by a black bloom of microphones, Sheriff Porter's voice was both clear and strong. And pretty irritated, though the reporters probably didn't know that. You had to have been grounded by him to recognize that particular strained tone.

"We appreciate the public's concern for this young man. But we also remind you that all the parties involved are minors, and deserve their privacy. Nobody's committed a crime, and things are understandably confused. But Health and Family Services is working closely with the sheriff's department and state police to identify John Doe, and to unite him with his family."

Exhausted, Dara shook her head. Though no one outside could hear her, she whispered anyway. "His family is dead."

"Allegedly," Lia replied, adjusting the curtain. "Sorry about Kit. He's an idiot."

"Oh, you know then?"

Brows lifting smoothly, Lia glanced back at her. "He says you assaulted him."

"Please. I poked him with a lacrosse stick." Furious, Dara crossed her arms over her chest. "And right now, I really, really want to hit you with it. You've been feeding him stuff all along! What's wrong with you?"

"I hate you sometimes." Lia let the curtain slip from her fingers. She didn't sound the least bit hateful. In fact, she was more matter-of-fact than she'd been for weeks. Pressing her back against the window's edge, she stretched, then sighed. "I've liked Kit for I don't know how long. And then all of a sudden, he starts texting me and hanging out by my locker. I'm really, incredibly stupid."

Slowly, Dara's brows lifted. "It wasn't your idea?"

"I was mad," she said. "You get away with everything. And then Kit shows up, and it's like . . . yay. Now I get the boy and I get you back for being perfect."

"I'm not perfect."

Lia rolled her eyes. "And I'm not getting the boy. He called me a bitch, and called *you* a crazy bitch, and then he blocked me."

Instantly protective, Dara wrapped her arms around her sister's shoulders. Now she really did wish she'd beaten him with the lacrosse stick. And kicked him a couple of times too for good measure. All this time he'd been making her miserable, and he was using her baby sister, too. "Aw, Bug, I'm sorry."

"I'm not a bug," Lia replied, sulking. She didn't exactly relax into Dara's hug, but she didn't fight it, either. Since she was taller than her older sister by a good two inches, she had to duck her head to tuck it under Dara's chin. "He's such an idiot."

Stroking her hair, Dara nodded. "In a really aggressive, hard-core way. I mean, the hat?"

"And his stupid ties?"

"Ugh, the worst."

Outside, their father was taking questions. Inside, Lia untangled herself, trying to put herself back together, and back at arm's length from Dara. She smoothed her hands over her hair. Then she swept her middle finger beneath each eye to guard against stray smudging.

Dara wasn't quite ready to let her go yet. Poking Lia's shoulder, she said, "By the way. As a photographer? I can tell you he's overcompensating for something with that rig."

"God, nasty," Lia said. Abandoning the window, she started upstairs.

"Love you," Dara called after her.

Slipping into Lia's place, Dara opened the window again. Just enough to hear as reporters climbed over each other to ask the same question. Or versions of the same question. Or the same question vaguely rephrased. *What do you know about the Primitive Boy?*

Her father's answers were the same, too. *Nothing, very little, not as much as we'd like.*

But Dara knew more. She knew Cade had a sense of humor that crept up quietly and unexpectedly. That he liked to sit on top of furniture instead of on it. That he'd watched her in the woods because he'd never seen yellow hair before. Overwhelmed, Dara sank onto the bench.

She knew he confused her. And if she was being very, very honest with herself, she knew she wanted to know other things. Personal things. If his touch on her shoulder could make her lose her train of thought, what would it be like if he kissed her? If *she* kissed *him*?

The front door opened, and Dara snatched her fingers away from her lips. Her mother ducked inside, and her father followed close behind. He locked the door and the dead bolt. Even though he'd just turned them, he checked the locks, then glanced Dara's way.

"If Jim Albee from the *Courier* comes sniffing around you again," Sheriff Porter said, hanging his hat on the door tree, "you call me."

"I would if I had my phone back."

"Here," Mrs. Porter said, resigned. She opened her purse, producing Dara's cell and waiting for her to take it. She ignored a sharp look from her husband. Dara wasn't sure what that was about, but she was happy to take advantage of it.

Taking her phone, Dara hurried up the stairs, already texting Sofia. It was good to get away from her father, from the madness out front . . . and from her own unbearable thoughts.

Cured bacon was delicious. Wolfing down strip after strip, Cade fought the urge to steal the plate from the table. Instinct told him to take it all, and take it to the highest point he could find. Safe in a tree, or on a roof, where no one could wrest the delicious spoils of Sunday breakfast from him.

Instead, he hunched in his chair and sucked grease from his fingers. In the living room, Ms. Fourakis talked to Branson. They murmured, but Cade heard them anyway. People weren't as subtle as they thought they were.

"I'm not expecting much," Branson said. "Since he can't read."

Ms. Fourakis hummed, skeptical. "Are you sure about that?"

"It was self-reported."

Carefully, like she was trying not to hurt Branson's feelings, Ms. Fourakis said, "I'm pretty sure I've seen him with books."

"Huh."

Cade snapped another piece of bacon in half and shoved it in his mouth. *Huh.* Branson was mild as a caterpillar. Soft and fuzzy, easy to divert. Picking the cracklings off the paper, Cade devoured them. They were better than the black ants that he resorted to sometimes, when the weather was too bad to hunt or fish. So much better—they didn't bite his cheeks or cling to his tongue.

Shuffling papers, Branson pressed on, though now he sounded disconcerted. Or disappointed. It was hard to tell without seeing his caterpillar face. "We'll get it sorted out. Oh, and good news. Dr. Rice can get him in soon. Check him out, get his vaccinations updated."

The word rang in Cade's head, too loud. Too bright. Abandoning the table, he crept down the hall to peer at the adults discussing him like a project.

"Great," Ms. Fourakis said. "That'll make it easier to talk to Principal Tran about getting him in some classes."

Though he wasn't sure how those two things were connected, Cade slowly rose to his full height. Tapping his fingers on the wall to get their attention, he said, "I had my vaccinations."

Two faces lit with surprise. Branson shuffled papers again, producing his glowing tablet from the mess. He tapped on it, looked down. Looked up, then squinted at Cade. His voice was gentle, coaxing. "Are you sure about that?"

Of course he was. His mother used to rant about them. How they couldn't generate some of them as quickly as the viruses could mutate, for one.

"This year's flu vaccine is our best guess," she'd say, stirring another handful of acorn meal into a pot of stew. "A mix of last year's flu, and the statistical probability of this year's. Sixty percent effective, if that. You still have to get it, but it's no guarantee. No guarantee at all."

Cade would scrub another handful of brain matter into the leather he was tanning and nod. His mother was brilliant. She knew everything. Why the sky was blue, and how the fall started.

She liked to show Cade the half-moon scar on her shoulder

where she'd gotten her boosters as a child. He always felt the phantom of his own shots, because she would tap his thigh where the needle had gone in. *MMR*, she whispered. *DTaP, IPV.* It was a song—a chant. *Hib, HepB, Varicella, boo.*

So yes, he was sure. Clinging to the wall, he leaned into the room, just a little. He wondered what would happen if he tapped the end of Branson's nose, *boo*. He didn't. Instead, he said, "All of them. Yes."

Branson tapped the tablet, then blinked up at him. "Can you tell us when? Who your doctor was?"

"No," Cade replied.

"You don't know or you don't want to?"

The first one. All his questions were exhausting, and there was still bacon on the table. Letting go of the wall, Cade backed into the kitchen again. "What kind of tests? I know my times tables. I can calculate the volume of a hole I dug to catch a wild boar."

Fighting back a smile, Ms. Fourakis glanced at Branson. "That could come in handy."

"You have to eat them before they eat you," Cade agreed.

Branson paled. And against his better judgment, it seemed, he followed Cade into the kitchen to start his tests.

Josh filled Dara's room, in a wide and awkward way.

It wasn't a war of masculine against feminine. He'd worn more than one red, lacy hat at his cousin's tea parties and had the pictures to prove it. And besides, Dara wasn't very frilly, and neither was her space. Her tastes ran to what her mother liked to call classics. Clean lines, no froth. Solid colors. *Sleek*. The same values appeared in her photographs.

No, Josh filled Dara's room awkwardly because neither of them wanted him to be there. Tipping her laptop toward him, its warm glow kept him from pressing too close. A slide show flashed on the screen. Nine thousand pictures of Debate Team and Varsity Dive and Swim illuminated their faces and cut a canyon between them.

"This is the best one, except Kristin's looking away," Dara said. "Would it be unethical to paste her head from *here* into *this* picture?"

Josh shrugged. "Dunno. It's her head, right?"

"But editorially, it's not her head in *that* moment. It's a head of lies."

Rubbing a hand up Dara's back, Josh tried to coax her attention away from the screen. "Babe, I don't know. Can we look at these later?" Maybe never, his voice said. Or maybe three thousand years from now.

With a frown, Dara flipped between them again. "I really have to get these two clubs done before I can do anything."

Withdrawing, Josh couldn't hide his annoyance. Digging his toe into one heel, he peeled off his shoe because it was obvious they weren't going anywhere for a while. Letting it drop with a thump, he cut her a suffering look.

"Don't be like that. We're both still technically grounded, we're lucky we're even seeing each other today."

"Yeah, I feel it," Josh said. Dig, peel. His other sneaker fell heavily on the floor, and he slid to his feet. He could examine the pictures on her wall again, all three million of them. Her collages took up the space that posters should have. Instead of pop stars she had inspiration boards.

Head down, Dara swapped the two versions of Kristin again. "You're always complaining I don't give you time to work on your car. If waiting for me is such a big deal, why don't you go do that?"

Josh turned furiously. "Do you hear yourself?"

"Excuse me?"

"You do remember the last time I saw you, it was because you wanted to borrow some of my clothes for another guy."

Snapping the lid closed on her laptop, Dara sat up. "Are you jealous?"

"No," Josh said unconvincingly. Then, more honestly, he added, "But I'm confused. It's like you went just a little off in the woods and never came back."

"I'm right here," she replied.

"You're all the way over there." Demonstrating, Josh walked the distance between them, then back again. His motions were short, sharp. It was like something quaked in his core, and it was all he could do to contain it. "And here *I* am."

Pushing the laptop aside, Dara looked up at him helplessly. "Maybe I did go a little off in the woods."

"Look, if you want to break up—"

"I don't!" Dara said hotly. Then she hesitated. Waving her hands beside her head, she shook with the frustration Josh felt. "I mean, you get we almost died. Right? You get that?"

"But we didn't."

"We *could* have. That's on my mind *all the time*. We almost died. And you weren't in the back of the truck. I was literally watching Cade die, like, I felt it. I felt his heart slowing down. I watched him turn grey, not pale, Josh. Waxy, it was . . ."

Josh held up a hand, talking over her. "I get it, Dare."

"Then why don't you get that I'm not *back* yet?" Slowly rising, she knotted her hands in her hair, pulling it off her face. It tightened her features, smoothing out the lines and knits and furrows. She was a mask of herself, though the shadows still showed in her eyes.

"Maybe if you let me help," Josh said.

"It's a terrible thing to say," Dara replied. She closed on him, because she was going to say it anyway. He knew it would be a bomb when she flattened both her hands on his chest. Bracing him for it. "But right now, the only time I feel safe is when I'm taking care of him. It makes the rest of this, the bad dreams, and the memories, and the reporters, and all the gossip . . . it makes it go away for a while."

She should have shot him. It would have been faster. It would have blown clean through. Instead, he had to stand there and take it. Act like she hadn't just destroyed him. Gently, he pushed her away. Then he leaned over to collect his sneakers, surprised that gravity didn't drag him straight through the floor.

Straightening up, he recoiled when she reached for him. Holding his shoes out at arm's length, a talisman against her, he threw open her door. Print photos fluttered around him, the walls sighing in empathy.

He could be calm. He had to be, because suddenly all he wanted to do was punch through the wall. Instead, he struck her with words, all he had in his arsenal.

"Call me when you get back," he said bitterly, and slammed the door.

THIRTY

Monday after school, Dara felt like psycho Betty Crocker, turning up on Cade's doorstep with a dozen cookies.

And a fake one, too, since she'd stopped at the grocery store to buy them. She couldn't remember the last time she'd actually baked cookie dough. It was made for eating with spoons in the middle of the night.

Inviting her in, Ms. Fourakis nodded down the hall. "He's in his room. Are those chocolate chip?"

Dara opened the bag for her, paying her toll before walking down the hall to find Cade. She smiled curiously to herself, because music poured out of his room. No one answered the first time she knocked. The second time, she winced, because the door rattled in protest.

The music died. The door opened, and Cade peeked through the crack. "Dara?"

"I brought cookies," she said. She shook the bag, trying to tempt him.

Pulling the door open, he stepped aside to invite her in. Dressed only in a pair of jeans, he looked like he'd just woken up. But on the bed, he had a tablet open, a can of shaving cream arranged beside it, set off by three plastic razors in a crisscross pattern. Like a little pyramid, or a hut.

Smiling slowly, Dara took in the scene, then turned to Cade. "Do I want to know?"

Torn, Cade looked from her to the bed. Then sullenly, he admitted, "I can't get the YouTubes into the box Branson gave me."

Dara tried not to laugh. Abandoning the cookies on his dresser, she reached for the tablet. Its image swirled, righting itself as she tucked it against one arm and flicked her fingers across the screen. "What are you looking for?"

Flatly, Cade repeated Ms. Fourakis, gesturing at his whiskers. "I'm getting a little shaggy. She won't let me use the knives in the kitchen."

"To shave?"

Cade nodded, then pointed at her. "That's the same face she made."

Still swallowing laughter, Dara slipped the tablet onto the bed. Then she gathered the shaving cream and razors. Nodding toward the door, she asked, "Do you have a towel?" She waited for him to grab it, then led him to the bathroom.

To be fair, she'd never shaved a face before. But she'd tackled enough legs, armpits, and bikini areas that she felt incredibly qualified. It was the same principle, and come on. She couldn't do worse than he would have with Ms. Fourakis' cleaver.

"Towel over your shoulders," Dara said. She ran warm water in the sink, then dipped her hands. She turned to wet his face. She did laugh, then. His expression was priceless—irritation verging on a real, live pout. Wetting her hands again, she swept them across his cheeks and his jaw.

"So far, this is the same," Cade said. Then he recoiled when she pressed the button on the shaving cream can. Menthol foam swirled in her hand. Jerking his head back, his nostrils flared when she moved to put it on him. "That's not."

Amused, Dara waited for him to still. "Do you want me to nick you to pieces? No? Then chill."

The cream stung a little, sharp and minty on his skin. It was true, he had mint in his shave kit at home, but not this much. This made his eyes water, but he tried not to squirm too much. He watched her in the mirror as she rinsed her hands, then took up one of the sticks. Peeling a cap off its head, she dipped it beneath the tap and turned to him.

"Hold on," she said. She looked around, then took two thick decorator towels off the top of the medicine chest. Centering them on the floor, she stepped up and grinned. It didn't perfect the difference between their heights, but it was good enough. Rinsing the razor again, she put a hand up to steady his head.

"Hold still."

They both stiffened when she pressed the blade to his face.

Anxious laughter bubbled from Dara, but she was careful as she cut the first stroke from his sideburns to his jaw. The blade tugged a little, and Cade wasn't sure she knew what she was doing when she caught her breath and held it.

But she finished the first stroke, then swept the razor under the water again. Rising once more, she held the razor away from his face before starting the next strip. "You okay?"

Cade nodded. Now that she'd shown him how all this stuff worked, he could have finished the job himself. Selfishly, he liked how close she had to stand to him. He liked her hands on his face, and the warmth of her breath on his lips.

"Good, here we go again."

He waited until she stopped to say, "You were mad at the boy in the yard."

Peering at him curiously, Dara dipped and rinsed again. "Yes, I was. And he'd better hope he doesn't run into me again."

"You weren't mad at me," Cade said

Befuddled, Dara stopped for a moment. "Why would I be?"

"Because I hid. I watched you."

"Oh. Ohh." Dara slumped. Razor held loosely, she swiped the back of her hand across her brow. Steam drifted lazily from the sink, starting to haze the edges of the mirror. "I don't . . . It's hard to explain. I mean, if you get curious about somebody here in town, I wouldn't start following them around. But . . . I wasn't afraid of you. You had lots of chances to hurt us, and you didn't."

"I could have."

"But you didn't," Dara said. "I mean, sometimes you just

have to trust your instincts. My dad says people worry about being polite, so they don't pay attention to their gut. They let people talk them into situations they don't want to be in."

"I didn't say anything."

Struggling with the explanation, Dara turned in a tight circle to gather her thoughts. Then, suddenly, she captured his hands and brought them to her face.

Her skin was so soft against his rough fingers. Their worn, uneven warmth ghosted against her cheeks.

"I knew you were there. And let's be honest. I had Josh there with me. If I'd been by myself, maybe I would have been afraid. But I wasn't. My first instinct was curiosity, not fear. We were so far out, at least it felt like it to me. And I just . . . I was never afraid of you."

"Then why didn't you come see me yesterday?"

Letting go of his hands, Dara sighed. Stroking the razor under the water again, she lingered there a long time. When she came back up again, she evened out the foam on his face with a careless stroke. Putting the blade to his skin once more, she carefully edged the corner of his mouth.

"Yesterday was a mess. It had nothing to do with you."

"Your father was on the news," Cade said helpfully.

"Oh, you're learning to watch TV," Dara replied. "Awesome. Yeah, he . . . there are a lot of people who want to know who you are. And they're exactly zero interested in taking 'We don't know' for an answer."

Trying not to move his lips, Cade tipped his head back so Dara could shave the notch beneath his mouth. The blade stung there, pulling more than cutting. When she moved away, he said, "You don't know."

"Right, but nobody believes that."

"They're very stupid people, then."

"More skeptical," Dara murmured. Trailing her fingers down his one smooth cheek, she studied it. For what, Cade wasn't sure. But she seemed to find it, because she nodded to herself before starting on the other side.

Watching her, Cade asked, "So I'm the mess?"

"A little bit." She smiled at him, as if to brush it all away. "And me. And Josh. Plus a dash of my sister, and my parents . . ."

The word tasted bitter on his tongue. "Josh?"

"Don't you start, too," Dara said. A few more strokes and she'd cleared all the foam from his face. She gave him a cloth to wipe off, then reached for the can again. As she shook it, she considered him critically. "Lean against the counter. Pretend you're a statue. Please tell me you know what a statue is."

Curling a fist under his chin, Cade froze. He'd seen a picture of this statue in one of his father's books. The posture made Dara laugh, which warmed Cade from the inside. Breaking the pose, he moved out of her way.

The steam swirled around him. Cooler air in the hall kept it from getting too hazy. It left the rest mobile. Almost alive. Twisting around him sinuously, the steam clung to his shoulders, his arms.

Bracing his hands against the counter, he bared his throat to her. All at once, he could feel the breath in his throat. The pulse pounding away beneath his jaw.

Her touch stung in the best way. Clutching the counter tighter, Cade resisted the urge to catch her hips. Pull her closer. Instead, he closed his eyes and focused on the details. Her chest brushed against his, careless, incidental contact.

Then she pressed a red-hot mark on his chest with her palm. She was steadying herself, her breath reedy as she put the blade down on bare, vulnerable flesh.

"Why'd you get so quiet?" she murmured.

Something in his chest wound tight. Was there a right answer? He didn't know, so he told her the truth. "I'm listening to you breathe."

With that, Dara stopped. Razor pressed against his throat, chest brushing his, she stopped. At first, her breath thinned. Then it failed completely. He couldn't know for sure, but he thought that the winding in *his* chest had started in hers. Her touch trembled.

When he looked down at her, she broke away. Nervous again, she splashed water all over the counter in her rush to rinse the razor. It flicked onto the mirror, and down the front of her shirt. It beaded her skin like sweat. He wanted to wipe it away with his hands. Instead, he offered his towel.

"Okay?" he asked.

Cutting off the taps, she took the towel. Clutched it, actually. She wasn't doing a very good job of drying herself. Too brightly, too cheerfully she said, "Just . . . totally jonesing for those cookies."

Cold swept in, now that Dara had pulled away. Gooseflesh broke across Cade's chest, and he wrapped one of the big towels around his shoulders again. It wasn't warm enough, or soft enough. It didn't cling to his skin the way Dara did. It didn't smell as good. But he made do, and followed her to his room with another question.

"What's jonesing?"

THIRTY-ONE

Side by side in matching maroon hoodies, Cade and Dara slipped out the back door and headed for the park. It was too pretty out to stay barricaded in Ms. Fourakis' house.

After the shaving, things felt a little too close inside walls, as well. A new hunger clawed Cade from the inside, taunting him with desires he couldn't quite define. He suspected Dara would have no problem with naming them—she just didn't want to say them out loud.

Yet.

The reporters had started to swarm, so their escape included cutting through several gated backyards. Halfway through one, they accidentally antagonized a chained-up Pomeranian. Cade wanted to stare it down. When Dara pointed out its tether, Cade deflated.

"Dog bully," she teased, slipping her arm in his.

"Cade bully," he replied.

Clayton Park looked as small as it was in the daylight. Bedraggled swings swayed in the wind. The teeter-totter thumped forlornly, driven into the ground by a kid with a stick almost twice her size. A handful of middle schoolers had claimed the metal dome as their headquarters. They cast poisonous glares at Dara and Cade as they walked by. In fact, Dara thought she heard one of them hiss.

Incredulous, Dara said, "And that's why I quit babysitting."

"They got too big to sit on?" Cade asked innocently. Then he burst out laughing when Dara started to explain the concept of child care for cash to him. When she realized he was teasing her, she veered and bumped him.

Then, tugging him by their joined elbows, she led him to the swings. Their sneakers scuffed through thinning mulch, and a cedarish scent paired with the dusty air of aging rubber. Dara dropped herself on one of the black seats. Wrapping her arms around the chains, she waited for him to sit beside her.

"So," she said when he did. "Tell me something cool."

As she pumped her legs, Cade simply dangled in his swing. He made no attempt to take flight. Instead, he trailed his fingers up the silver chain. His pinkie fit perfectly inside one link.

Since he didn't know what she wanted from him, he considered his options. Then he pointed to a huddle of low, fat birds on the sidewalk.

"I could catch one of those with my bare hands."

Throwing her head back, Dara laughed. Her hoodie slid

down, and she said, "So could I, they're pigeons."

"No." Cade moved, as if to prove it, but Dara hauled him back.

"You don't want to. They're nasty."

"They're tiny. I wouldn't feel their beaks at all."

"Nooo. They're licey and dirty." She smiled over at him brilliantly. "Are you impervious to parasites?"

Cade buried a shudder. "No."

Still smiling, she stretched a hand toward him when she swayed past. "Swing with me."

The physical principles were the same, whether the swing was made of rubber or woody vines. It wasn't that Cade didn't know how. He did. But he wanted to watch her more. Her hair slipped loose of her hood. It tangled around her ear, a wonderful, perfect shell of an ear.

Taking her hand, Cade let Dara drag him up to speed. Metal creaked above. Friction drew sweat to his palms, different from regular sweat. It smelled tangy, like rusting iron.

It reminded Cade of artifacts he'd found in the mining town. Lanterns softly orange with age, their glass long smashed and oil drained away. Picks and tweezers . . . once, he'd found an iron stem sticking out of the ground.

When he dug it out, he discovered it belonged to a frying pan. It felt almost soft with rust, like it might disappear entirely if he was too rough with it. But after a brisk rubdown with sand and walnut shells, it was solid underneath. Blackened all over. Weighty and good.

However long it had sat abandoned, it was brand-new to

Cade. Better than his parents' griddle for a lot of things, it became one of his treasures. Even now, it hung in his cave. Probably needing a new scrub, Cade realized. Which in turn, made him realize he didn't know how long he'd been away.

That pang hooked in his chest again, and he jerked himself out of the thoughts before they consumed him.

"Hey there, sailor," Dara said. Her smile was curious now, softer. It gentled her gaze. "What are you thinking about?"

Cade watched her full lips form the sounds, then turned his attention to the trees in the distance. The deceptive trees, not very deep, very full of trash. Plastic bags and shattered glass; what a terrible place. Dragging his heels in the dirt, he slowed to a stop. "I know everything about my home. I'm the only one. Everyone else is gone."

Slowing herself, Dara twisted the chains. Still in motion, her swing gyrated toward his. Her knees bumped his. Their ankles tangled. She had this talent for making him look. It was like she wanted him to fall into her eyes.

"Tell me something." She grabbed his swing, anchoring them together. "Then you won't be alone."

Alone.

She didn't realize how big that was. How true. And rather than climb back into the closet with a potted plant, Cade shoved those feelings aside. Today was a good day. Bacon for breakfast again and no tests. The prettiest girl at his back door with cookies. In his bathroom, wearing steam and touching his face . . . good day. It was a good day.

Seizing on his best, favorite thing, he said, "Honey doesn't come in plastic bears. It comes from beehives. Honeycomb."

"Pretty sure everybody knows that," Dara said, not unkindly.

"But you don't know how to find a hive in the wild, do you?"

"I don't. Fair enough. Proceed."

Cade drew a meandering path in the air. It was supposed to be a bee, which he explained as he locked their ankles together. "Worker bee, starving. Flying everywhere to find nectar and pollen."

"Is he busy?" Dara asked with a crooked smile.

"Very," Cade replied, ignoring her joke. "Now, they don't fly in straight lines. If you followed him all day, you might end up miles from home and starving. So you only follow him for a while. Then you . . ."

He clapped his hands together. Completely unexpected and wonderful, her squeak delighted him.

"Messing with me, nice." Dara wrinkled her nose in disdain. "Very funny."

"Not funny, not done. Listen. You follow him, then you catch him. Gently, you'll ruin him if he stings you. Now, if he was flying east, you walk west. Vice versa. North, south. Anyway, walk at least a hundred steps, two hundred is better, in the opposite direction. Then let him go and follow."

"I'm not falling for that again."

Cade leaned toward her, hooking his knee behind hers, catching the chain of her swing in one hand. Pulling her closer, his brow brushed hers. Their noses nearly touched. "You've never heard of triangulation? I guess I really am alone."

Caught on a hitched breath, Dara didn't move away. Instead,

she knit her brows and glanced down. Like there was very important information printed on the knees of her jeans. But really, she was thinking about what he'd said, making it make sense. After a second, she raised her head. Now her mouth rounded, her eyes, too. There was a new light on her, and she laughed—surprised, not amused.

"That's really how you find a beehive?"

Cade raised his finger again. This time, he trailed it through the air in a gentle spiral, and touched it to her hand. As if the bee had landed there, cradled between them. It was their bee. Their secret. She smelled like sugar and the wind and shaving cream.

Voice suddenly warm as his blood, Cade raised his head and said, "It really is."

And with that, he let his imaginary bee fly home.

The second time Dr. O'Toole called the police department, he was incredibly apologetic.

"I know you must be getting a lot of calls about this case," he said. "And it's entirely possible you've already investigated this lead and discarded it. I didn't expect anyone to call me back . . ."

Reaching for a pencil, Deputy Krause asked, "What was your name again?"

"Dr. Jupiter O'Toole, PhD, not MD."

What kind of name was that? The deputy scribbled it down, then leaned back in her chair. She trained her gaze on the front windows. Any minute, she expected Deputy Bates to come back in with a cardboard box full of Chinese takeout. The taste of chicken fried rice taunted her—so close, but still an eternity to wait.

Distracted by the potential of lunch, Deputy Krause said, "PhD not MD, all right. Did you have a tip you wanted to report, sir?"

Dr. O'Toole's voice was soft, dusty like powder. It soothed, belying his distress. "Yes. I called previously, because I'm an epidemiologist at Case Western Reserve. Eighteen years ago, I was working with Dr. Liza Walsh on the World's Plagues project."

"Mm hmm."

"We were mapping every outbreak from 1600 to the present day. With that data, we planned to build a model that would predict the next outbreak before it happened. I specialize in etiology, she specialized in exposure assessment, you see, and . . ."

Chicken fried rice, so far away, the deputy thought. Out loud, mildly, she said, "This is what you told us when you called before?"

"Yes." There was a pause. Papers shuffled. Then Dr. O'Toole said, "But since I called, I have new information. I checked my records. Dr. Walsh and her husband had Jonathan in the summer of 1997. They disappeared, spring of '99."

"Is there a missing persons report?"

"Well, no," Dr. O'Toole said. "I mean, yes, the university reported her missing. But when the police went to their house, it was empty. Nothing left behind. There was no family that I'm aware of, and the police said people were entitled to move without leaving a forwarding address if they wanted to. So nothing came of it."

Light flooded the office, a reflection of a car passing by. The deputy sat up a little straighter. But the door didn't open. Silently, she cursed Bates and asked the doctor, "And what makes you think this is related to our Doe, sir? The names aren't the same."

"Well, I heard on the news that the first question he asked when he was evacuated from the forest was 'how many people are left?' Which piqued my curiosity. And the drawing looked a bit like Dr. Walsh. Since I called last, I double-checked my records, and the dates line up. But mostly . . ."

The deputy waited for him to fill in his own silence. She gave up on watching for lunch, and hunched over her note-pad. Scribbling in quick details about the call, she hummed. To remind him that she was listening. To get him to quit taking up her time.

Finally, Dr. O'Toole said, "Found it. I've been watching the news coverage, and I was certain when I saw the picture of the boy. I've got pictures from his first birthday party. If you compare them, you see the resemblance.

"That's why I called back, I had more to offer than I did before. I do truly believe Jonathan Walsh and John Doe are the same person. Could I . . . would it be possible for me to send the photos to you? I had my wife scan them."

"Sure," Deputy Krause said. "Let me give you the email address."

Then she proceeded to give him Deputy Johnson's address, because he was lead on the case, second to the sheriff. He could go through it when his shift started at eleven.

Thanking Dr. O'Toole, Deputy Krause rolled her chair back

and hung up the phone. Dropping the message on the department assistant's desk, she headed outside. It wouldn't make the food get there any faster, but she went to stretch on the front walk just in case.

THIRTY-TWO

*T*he kitchen smelled like pizza when Dara let herself in.

Oil stained the corner of a delivery box, proof that it was the best pizza of all: greasy and halfway to cold. Locking up, Dara pushed her hood down and helped herself to the last two slices of pepperoni.

Groaning in pleasure, she slumped against the fridge. With another bite, she slid down and savored it. She had no idea how hungry she was until the first taste of mozzarella and sauce. The perfection of grease and sweet filled her mouth and she sighed again.

"Glad that's you I heard," Sheriff Porter said. He brushed her away from the fridge. Pulling open the stainless steel door, he searched the drawers inside systematically. "I have handcuffs and I'm not afraid to use them."

"Ha," Dara said.

Bottles rattled, and Sheriff Porter finally emerged with a beer. Closing the fridge door, he offered the bottle to his daughter. She lit up, and he smiled. Watching her do the counter trick pretty much always made his day.

She rested the fluted edge of the cap against the edge of the counter. Then she gave the cap a thump. It flipped into the air as the bottle wheezed a steamy breath.

"Don't forget to tip your bartender," she said, smiling like a loon.

It was a dumb, simple thing. Something he'd taught her when she was barely old enough to see the top of the counter. When she was little, it used to earn her quarters from her friends' parents during summer barbecues. Now it was just a leftover, something they alone shared.

Reclaiming his bottle, Sheriff Porter took a thoughtful sip as Dara picked up her pizza again. "So how's Sofia?"

Dara made a face like she might hedge. But she told the truth anyway, no point in lying about it. "I went and saw Cade, actually."

"Huh."

"Daddy," she said, resigned to her exasperation now.

The sheriff shared that exasperation, and whinged back at her. "Daraaaa."

That teased another smile from her. Polishing off her appetizer, Dara took her turn and brushed her father away from the fridge. This time, she rummaged. Leftover chicken, lunchmeat . . . in her heart, she knew she was looking for more pizza. Or, irrationally, something hot and delicious that she wouldn't have to make herself.

"He's doing better," she said. "And you'll like this, he shaved."

Sheriff Porter nodded. "I do like that."

"He didn't cut his hair."

"I like that less," Sheriff Porter said, amused. "So you were at Kelly's all afternoon with him?"

Another hedge. Then Dara emerged with a carton of eggs and a bottle of hot sauce. "We snuck down to Clayton Park."

Though he wasn't wearing his uniform, the work version of Dara's dad suddenly appeared. It showed in the angle of his gaze. That, and a particular tightness swept over him. It was a shield, the one he put on before the badge. The attitude that kept most people from giving him a hard time. "Why'd you have to sneak? Were there reporters out there?"

"A couple out front," Dara admitted. "But Mr. Anderson had a hoodie that fit Cade, and we just went out the back. Nobody saw us."

"Good. I wish somebody'd drive a truck up on their front lawn a couple nights in a row."

Dara snorted. "Recursive story is recursive."

When Sheriff Porter looked over, his baffled expression was almost comical. Dara laughed under her breath and greased her pan. There was no point in explaining memes to her dad. By the time he caught on to the intricacies, they were long over.

Soon, the satisfying crack and sizzle of eggs filled the kitchen. The pizza scent faded, replaced by breakfast at night. *One of the best scents in the world*, Dara thought.

Then she wondered if Cade had ever tried it. If he could even conceive of it. Pretty sure he didn't have a toaster in the middle of nowhere. Or bacon, or OJ—citrus definitely didn't grow in the wilds of Kentucky.

"What would it be like if you'd never had orange juice?" Dara mused aloud.

"Less heartburn," Sheriff Porter quipped. Considering the question, he added, "I don't know. That's like asking, what if you never had food from Ethiopia? I never have, but I expect I don't know what I'm missing."

Scraping her pan, Dara said, "I couldn't do it. Live in the forest. Even if I could give up my phone, and the internet, I mean . . . how do you even survive? I'd die without AC in the summer."

Sheriff Porter laughed. Loudly, and long. "No you wouldn't. I didn't have it growing up. My mother still had an outhouse until she was ten or eleven."

"Are you serious?"

"You have no idea." Sheriff Porter finished his beer and tossed the bottle in the recycling. "Now, sugar, let me ask you something. And I don't want you to get bristly on me. It's just a question."

Being warned not to bristle put Dara on instant alert. She kept her attention on the pan, but shrugged. The gesture told him to go ahead, ask away—but it didn't make promises. She'd bristle if she wanted to.

"Has he said anything to you? Anything that could help me help him?"

Dara sighed. Taking her pan from the fire, she turned to

him. "You know what? I honestly don't know that he needs help. He's healing. He's smart. Why can't he just go home?"

"I'd take him myself if I knew where that was."

"Um, and you know. He told you where he lived." She shrugged. "I'll work on visualizing no AC. Why don't you try imagining a world outside your categories and boxes?"

"And there's not a single thing come out of that boy's mouth to make you doubt?"

Dara hesitated. She carefully and precisely maneuvered her food from the pan to her plate with the spatula. It was something to concentrate on until she could sort out her thoughts. Or her feelings.

Finally, she dumped the pan in the sink and turned to lean against the counter. "I don't doubt him, no. There's a lot I don't know, but that doesn't mean the rest isn't true."

"Give me something. Anything. Help me believe him."

Cradling her plate, she picked at the eggs. It's not that she knew so much. It's that she didn't necessarily trust her father with the things she knew. And that, more than anything, felt like crap. He was her father. This was her family. Ignoring the strange, liquid beating of her heart, she hung on a moment of silence.

Then, she said, "He knows a lot about colds. Not in a home remedy way. He sounds like a doctor or something. A scientist, when he talks about them. Calls it rhinovirus. Did you know people *only* get them from other people?"

Drawling slowly, Sheriff Porter said, "As a matter of fact, I did not."

"You can't get it from a cat or a dog . . ." Dara trailed off. What if she'd said too much? She felt both better and worse for telling Sheriff Porter that little bit. And yet, it was like she couldn't stop herself. Starting for the hallway, she turned back and added, "But maybe if you shared a spoon with a rabbit. Possibly."

Sheriff Porter watched his daughter dart from sight. He didn't know what to do with this little dab of information, but it felt important. He filed it mentally, something to think about in the shower and on the drive to work. Anywhere, everywhere, until inspiration hit him. Until it suddenly made sense.

That's how crimes got solved; that's how he would figure out who this Primitive Boy really was.

The next day, Cade couldn't stop looking at the pencil-sketched innards of a human chest.

Trailing a finger along the pericardium, Cade rested his brow against the poster. He'd never seen these labels before, but they were familiar. Written in the kind of Latin his mother spoke, her secret language. No matter how often he grasped at a memory of her face, it was her voice that surfaced.

She wouldn't want him to be here. Or maybe she would have. Far away from the place where she raised him, he saw her inconsistencies more clearly. Vaccines that were both necessary and useless. Antibiotics—dangerous and essential. Even people, the whole world: dead and not dead. Beautiful and terrifying.

It used to make sense to Cade. Mom said it, it was true.

Roasting hot, Cade returned to the paper-covered table. The big, tinted windows let in too much light, not soothing at all. And they blasted the shadows away. Everything was antiseptic white and smelled like chemicals. Mom's paradoxes aside, Cade was pretty sure he hated hospitals and clinics all on his own.

Thankfully, someone knocked on the door. Dr. Rice came in a moment later, looking nothing like the doctors in the hospital. No white lab coat. No metal dangling from his neck. He wore a T-shirt that said ASK ME ABOUT MY ZOMBIE T-SHIRT, though it was mostly hidden under a plaid button-down.

"Hey there, Cade, just finished looking at your labs from the hospital," Dr. Rice said. He flicked through a folder, then set it aside. "Everything's looking good, how are you feeling?"

Cade shrugged. "Fine."

"Can I take a look at your chest and your foot?"

Another shrug. Cade watched him pump an astringent gel into his palm, then scrub it over his hands. The smell burned off quickly, but it stung Cade's eyes until it did. Powder dusted in the air with a new pair of gloves. So many layers and layers, Cade thought. Holding himself very still, he let the doctor peel off the bandage on his chest.

Humming, Dr. Rice touched the edges of the wound gently. "I hear you won this fight."

"I think it was a tie," Cade said.

Warmth filled Dr. Rice's laugh as he moved on to the bandage on Cade's foot. Even through the gloves, his touch was warm. "No signs of infection, healing up nicely. We're going to want to get you some physical therapy for that shoulder but I think you'll live."

"Good."

Dr. Rice was both fast and slow. He didn't seem rushed, but he managed to listen to Cade's chest and belly, check his pulse, reflexes in his knees and elbows, and get a peek into his ears and throat before the sunlight shifted. Then he sat down, rolling his stool to the counter to write in the file and ask more questions.

"All right, says here we need to stick you a whole bunch. When was your last booster shot?"

"When I was a baby, I guess?"

"You don't remember getting updates when you were eleven or twelve?"

Cade shook his head. *MMR*, his ghost mother whispered like a nursery rhyme. *DTaP, IPV, my sweet little boy. Hib, HepB, Varicella, boo.*

With a wry smile, Dr. Rice said, "If that's the case, we're not going to be friends when you leave, I'm afraid."

"Then tell me about your zombie shirt now," Cade replied.

"All right, but remember, you asked."

The doctor grabbed the hem of the shirt. When he pulled it up, a painting of a decomposed face stared out. Bloody, gangrenous flesh, and rotted teeth—behind the fabric, Dr. Rice moaned something that sounded like *braaaaiinnns*. As quickly as he'd pulled the shirt up, he replaced it.

His face was flushed, an impish smile dancing on his lips. "I don't get to do that a lot."

Cade smiled because it seemed expected. He wasn't sure why the doctor thought a corpse face was so funny. Dead bodies were dead. They melted back into the earth, fed new trees that grew from the soil. He could ask Ms. Fourakis about zombies on the way back to her house. Or maybe he could find the answer himself on her tiny tablet phone.

"All right, my assistant is going to replace your dressings and get your shots updated. Do you have any concerns? Questions for me?"

"No."

"Should we talk about sexually transmitted infections?"

At that, Cade laughed genuinely. "No."

"Sure?"

"More than," Cade replied. Retying his robe, he watched Dr. Rice gather his things and head for the door. Just before he left, though, Cade asked, "Is there a cure for AIDS yet?"

That question broke Dr. Rice's light demeanor. Just a crack, enough to reveal a curious, thoughtful man beneath the irreverence. Holding the door open, Dr. Rice studied him for a long time. Then he said, "I'm afraid not. Do you need to be tested, Cade?"

Pulling the robe onto his shoulders again, Cade shook his head. "No. I was just wondering."

The door closed with a whisper, and another one threaded through Cade's memory.

They got smarter, Cade. Bacteria, viruses . . . they're clever, clever things. They learn. They adapt. When they figured out how to break our immune system, that was the tipping point. No matter how much we planned and prepared, oh, especially when we did. We taught them to destroy us.

Tightening his robe against the cold, Cade pushed those thoughts down, as far as they would go.

THIRTY-THREE

School was the worst it had been since Dara came back from spring break in an ambulance.

It was sick how much she missed being whispered about. At least when it was classmates, she knew they were just curious. Barely anything happened in their small town. Of course people were interested.

Then Jim Albee showed up just off campus. His presence broke the seal. Hunkered in the passenger seat of Sofia's car, Dara covered her face as they slow-rolled into the parking lot. They had to, because the street was full of deputies and reporters, news vans and satellite trucks.

"You've got to be kidding me," Sofia said. "That's CNN."

"They already know everything! What do they want?"

Sofia shook her head, waiting for the deputy in front of her to turn his sign from Stop to Caution. Rubbing her own temple, Dara peered out her window. Sofia was right.

Where the local stations usually milled together, a couple of national stations had set up camp as well. Yellow police tape clearly marked the line: on this side, free-for-all. On that side, trespassing like crazy.

So far, it looked like the reporters were staying well in free-for-all territory. Which was fine. The lights and cameras were so alluring, students streamed that way on their own.

"What is their deal?" Dara demanded. "It's *not* that interesting!"

Sounding a little guilty, Sofia said, "I've been watching some of it, and you're so wrong. On TV, it's the best soap opera ever."

"Sof!"

"Well, it is." She inched forward. "You've got Team Primitive Boy, and they're hard-core subscribed to the truth. They're like, he says he grew up in the forest with his parents, then that's what happened. We like them. That's our team."

"Uh-huh." Dara wondered if she had any aspirin in her purse.

"And there's Team Hoax. Or Team Delusional, as I like to call them. They're, like . . . okay, get this. One website took the pictures of Cade's clothes, the ones he was wearing when they brought him to the hospital? And they're doing, like, these epic Photoshop exposés."

"Buh?"

"These seams prove he had a Singer Sew-Tastic Model 42 Derp! That leather is way too evenly tanned, he bought it online!"

Still fumbling for aspirin, Dara stared at the chaos surrounding her school. It was like a Breaking News Story play set, complete with cordless microphones and real digital camera grip. Tossing a bitter pill onto her tongue, she swallowed it dry because there was no way she was taking a sip of Sofia's mocha espresso. She was tense enough.

Oblivious to Dara's quiet, Sofia slapped her hands against the wheel. "And oh my god. Team Missing Link. Cade is Bigfoot. Or a Neanderthal. Maybe a Neanderthal Bigfoot. So yeah, those guys. I like them. They're cryptid-crazy. And, Dare—"

"Stop," Dara said.

"But I haven't told you about Team National Security!"

Wrenching off her seat belt, Dara unlocked her door. "The car, stop the car!"

Sofia did, and Dara flung herself into the bright spring morning. Head pounding, the ache spread faster as her pulse rose. Stalking across the lot, she bounced off a car that was trying to sneak in the exit. Though they honked, she ignored it. Jerking her hoodie up, Dara glowered through her sunglasses as she walked up behind Josh.

Clapping a hand on his back, she interrupted the interview he was giving. "Can I talk to you?"

The reporter looked like he might wet his pants. "Wait a second, are you Dara Porter?"

"No, I'm Taylor Swift," Dara snapped.

She walked away, and was glad Josh followed. It's not like she could make him do it. Inside, she trembled. A sick, acid burn swirled in her stomach.

Equally angry, Josh shoved his hands deep into his pockets. It's how he kept himself from waving his hands. Since he was a big guy, that made people nervous and she knew it. Dara felt his tension. It tuned hers even higher.

When they were fully on school property, she ducked behind an SUV. From there, the reporters couldn't overhear, or train their cameras on them. She hoped.

"What are you doing?" she demanded.

"Trying to help you!"

Dara boggled. "What made you think I wanted you to talk to the press?"

"I'm trying to tell them what really happened," Josh said. His eyes flashed, and he bounced on his feet. It was an exercise he always did before a match to pump up and tune out. "They're freaking crazy. They're making up all this sh—"

Dara cut him off. "It doesn't matter."

"Are you crazy?"

"I don't think they want the truth," Dara said. Tightening the strings on her hoodie, she peeked around the bumper. There hadn't been any flashing lights before. Now, the cruisers all had their red-and-blues going. "It's like . . . it's like an idea they can build a story on, it has nothing to do with us. Or Cade. Or anything that really happened."

Josh slumped against the SUV. Thumping his head back against the windshield, he actually made the truck shift slightly. "What did really happen?"

"You were there," Dara said, confounded. Incredulous.

Grinding his teeth together, Josh closed his eyes. Nostrils

flaring like a bull's, he gave a curt shake of his head then pushed off the truck. Hands loose, he dragged them through his hair, then spread them out helplessly. "I wasn't."

"Josh, you drove. You . . ."

"Like you said, I was there. And yeah, I drove. I carried that guy I don't know how many miles. Big freaking deal, Dara. When it counted, when it mattered, he saved *you*. It sure wasn't me. He got you out of the way, and I had to hide. I was two feet from that thing on the ground."

Words foundered on her tongue. She felt the impact again. The sick twist of her stomach. The bright flashes of pain in her ribs and her knees. Cade flew. He flew and dropped her, and . . . she'd seen Josh on the ground. Flat, facedown. Why hadn't she thought about this before? In detail? Headache raging, Dara surrendered a helpless look.

Her memories had already started to set. They were firm, immovable pieces of a play that had shown only once. Heat flashed beneath her hoodie, raising a sudden, unbearable sweat. She wanted to peel down to the skin and just breathe.

Instead, she said, "Yeah, he pushed me out of the way, but he went back. He knew you were down there. If all he wanted to do was save me, he could have, and he could have run."

Offsetting his jaw, Josh said, "Uh-huh."

"What is the matter with you?"

"You really wanna hear it?" Josh asked. He didn't wait for her to reply. He backed her against the SUV. There was nothing dangerous about him. Crackling with anger, he bit out his words in a low, hard voice. "It used to be *my* job to take care of you! That's who I was, that's what I did!"

"I don't need you to take care of me," Dara snapped.

Furious, Josh pushed off the SUV. "It's not about you, Dara. I needed it!"

"If it's not about me," she demanded, "then what difference does it make?"

Josh stopped short. All the difference in the world, he thought. But he realized he could scream it or whisper it, or write it in poems or in fireworks—she didn't get it, and she never would.

"Forget it," he said.

He walked away from her and they both felt the break. It was imperfect and jagged, and they pulled away on their own, individual halves. It was the first time he'd left without looking back; it was the first time she didn't want him to.

"This is crazy," Ms. Fourakis said.

She stood in her own front window, glaring at the intruders in her street. They were worse than kids playing hit-and-run. At least they knocked on the door, then ran away. These guys, in all their slick, too-shiny suits, knocked. And knocked again. And pounded, and peeked in windows.

"I'm sorry," Cade said.

Resigned, Ms. Fourakis joked, "You should be. You're more trouble than you're worth."

Cade listed ever so slightly in the chair and gave her a look. She understood why. She'd signed the paperwork to get him what seemed like fifty thousand shots all at one time.

Micro-fine needles—it felt more like he'd sat in some fire ants.

"My very own teenager," Ms. Fourakis said. She patted him on the shoulder as she passed by, back to her amused self. "How'd I get so lucky?"

When she couldn't see, Cade smiled.

Everyone else around him, even Dara sometimes, sparked with tension. It was constant. He didn't think they even knew it. But it was like watching animals just outside the ring of his firelight. The ones waiting for him to drop a scrap, or forget to tie up his cooler. Only the people stood much closer. And Cade wasn't always sure what they wanted.

Except for Ms. Fourakis. He had nothing for her, and she didn't care. She still smiled at him, and made him watch movies over dinner. When Branson came, she sat nearby and rescued him from weird questions. She made it possible to relax.

And she let him play with her toys. Cade turned her cell phone over in his hands. He was getting pretty good at it. Fingers sliding across the surface, he made it bleat and squeal. Then he touched a blue box that didn't usually make a sound at all. This time, an alarm sounded.

Ms. Fourakis popped her head out of the kitchen. "Don't buy anything else from the app store."

With a sheepish smile, Cade nodded. It was his fault she had three different campfire icons now.

Skimming past a familiar sort of drawing, Cade stood slowly. Someone pounded at the door, and in response, he pulled the shades closed. Still holding the phone aloft, he turned it to Ms. Fourakis as he entered the kitchen. "What's a zombie?"

"Braaaaaaaaains," Ms. Fourakis replied. For the first time, something hooked the edge of her smile. She didn't hesitate before speaking. Instead, the hesitation filled her voice. "They're the living dead. They get infected and they die, then they come back. And then all they want to do is eat your brains and turn you into a monster, too."

Cade poured himself a glass of water. "Are they funny?"

"No, scary." Then, Ms. Fourakis backed up on herself. "Sometimes. They're supposed to be scary, but they're kind of funny, too. The CDC has a zombie survival guide."

A primal spark of fear lit in Cade's chest. He knew what the CDC was. Where it was, what they did there. That was the place where the fall started. Engineered, but not intentionally. According to Cade's mother, everyone had good intentions. She included herself in that. Shaking a sealed box in the back of their cave, she sighed as its contents rattled ominously. *There's the road to hell right there,* she said.

Steeling himself, Cade asked, "So they're real."

"No! Oh kiddo, no!" Abandoning her bag of chips, she slung an arm around his shoulder. Shaking him, gently, she enveloped him in her earthy, herbal scent. "They're monsters. Imaginary monsters."

"Then why is there a survival guide?"

Ms. Fourakis rasped a hand over his dreads, then let him go. "Because nobody believes the flu can kill you. It's scary to think about natural disasters. It's easier to plan for something terrible if the terrible thing is a game."

Before he could stop himself, Cade said, "My mother had a plan."

Casual as she picked up her chips, Ms. Fourakis rattled the bag and offered it to him. "Did she?"

THIRTY-FOUR

Deputy Krause whistled under her breath as she walked into Sheriff Porter's office.

With a desk full of leads, she probably should have chained herself to the desk. The interest in the Doe case refused to slack off, and that loser Johnson kept forwarding his leads back to her. Instead of following up on the phone call from Dr. O'Toole, Johnson sat on an email from him until it was good and ripe. Then he bounced it to Krause.

Annoyed, Krause almost batted it right back. But curiosity got the better of her—this email message had photos attached. Something about them nagged her, so she wanted to run them past her boss.

"How about that?" she asked. Sliding a couple of blurry 8x10s from a folder, she handed them to Sheriff Porter.

Enlarged from email attachments, and printed on the office's near-dead laser jet, the grainy pictures didn't look especially compelling.

They could have been taken anywhere, probably by somebody's grandpa who didn't realize he had to hold still to get a clear snap.

Sheriff Porter abandoned his laptop to take a look. "Friend of yours?"

"Nope."

Turning the desk lamp toward himself, Sheriff Porter flooded the photos with light. He leaned over them, spreading them out and scanning each face. Two men flanked a woman and a particularly gleeful baby. Streamers hung in the background, hints of a balloon bouquet, too.

Something felt familiar in the snapshot. He wondered if it was just a generic kid birthday. He'd seen so many, they blurred into a single, buttercream-and-chocolate-cake memory. One by one, he blotted out the faces on the picture with his fingertip. Not familiar, not familiar . . .

When he stopped, Deputy Krause leaned in. "Sir?"

Sheriff Porter tapped the woman's face. "Who is this?"

"Liza Walsh. Had some guy named *Jupiter* send these in. He says he thinks that chick is our Doe's mother."

That was it. Sheriff Porter saw it, then. The same oval face and neat hairline. Strong eyebrows and the tilt of her head. He'd seen that face, a version of it, in his own basement. On a kid who climbed on furniture and stole books of poetry. Now that Sheriff Porter had a reference, he realized Cade's expression hadn't been sullen. It had been reserved.

Emotion darted through him, both elated and cautious. For no reason except his gut told him so, Sheriff Porter believed this was the break they needed. *The* lead. A list of tasks filled his head. He had to talk to Swayle and Kelly Fourakis before the media sniffed out the lead. Or before "some-guy-named-Jupiter" sold his story to the *National Enquirer*.

"Do we have better copies?" he asked.

"I can get some."

Already dialing his phone, Sheriff Porter couldn't stop staring at the picture. "Do that, would ya?"

When a knock came at the back door, Dara was thrilled to ditch her AP history to answer it. The reporters preferred to swarm on the street out front. And since the back fed off the kitchen, she figured she had plenty of weapons in case one of them had decided to push their luck and sneak in from the alley.

Rising on her toes, Dara tried to look out the half-moon window. Too short to get a good view, she took her chances and opened the door.

"Hi," Cade said. Sweat freshened his face, his skin ruddy from exertion.

"Get in before somebody sees you," Dara replied. She caught his wrist, hauling him inside. Quickly as she could, she closed the door. Then, she threw all three locks and collapsed against the frame. The quick burst of panic left her light-headed.

She was glad he couldn't hear her pulse. Or see the way her skin tightened everywhere. His presence was a lightning rod, and she shivered from the snap and pop of it.

"How did you get here?" she asked.

Rather than answer that question, he pulled off the bag he wore and offered it to her wordlessly. Dara nearly dropped it when she took it. It was crazy heavy, and when she pulled back the flap, she saw why. It bulged with groceries—a weird assortment. Crackers and peanut butter, a bunch of bananas, two potatoes . . . she reached in, and pulled out a box.

Brow raised quizzically, she shook it at him. "Instant oatmeal?"

Cade took the box, and tore open one end. Then he waved it beneath her nose. "Smell the apples?"

Well, she smelled dehydrated apples and sugar and cinnamon. It seemed to mean something to him, so she nodded. Reclaiming the oatmeal, she slipped it back into the satchel. Then, gently, she asked, "Did you want me to make something for you?"

He shook his head. "No, it's for you."

Groceries. Huh. She didn't want to hurt his feelings, so she started to unpack. "Thanks. This is really sweet."

"If you run out," he insisted. "So you're not hungry."

Setting the bananas on the counter, Dara stopped unpacking. Now a buzz blended with her tingling, a warm blush that raced her throat and her ears. She'd never been hungry—not really. The occasional *OMG, I just got home from school and I will die if I don't get pizza rolls* kind of hungry. Starving for dinner because she forgot to eat lunch, maybe . . . glancing at him, she couldn't help but notice his anxious expression.

"You get enough to eat, right?" she asked carefully.

"Ms. Fourakis says I can help myself."

"I meant before." She couldn't quite say *at home* yet. A life in the forest didn't fit her mental image of home. How could it be that, without warmth and windows and doors to lock up tight at night?

The thrill of camping had been how dangerous it seemed— though she hadn't counted on how dangerous it really was. She'd worried about people in the woods, not the animals. Dumb mistake. She wouldn't make it again.

Cade rolled a shoulder. "If I hunt enough and dry enough, yes."

Producing a peanut butter bar from the bag, Dara tore it open. Snapping it in half, she offered Cade the first piece. "That's not a real answer. That's like me saying, as long as I go to bed early, and I fall asleep right away, I get plenty of rest."

With shameless pleasure, Cade crunched into the candy. Wolfing it down, it was gone in two bites and his gaze trailed toward the other half in Dara's hands. He didn't ask for it, though. Instead, he shrugged. "There's plenty in the summer and fall. Winter is hungry. Spring, too."

Half the year. Dara was suddenly aware of the pantry. The fridge. The massive amounts of food just sitting around in her house. And guiltily, she thought of how many times they ended up donating canned goods. Usually at Thanksgiving, or when the post office had their food drive in the spring. Boxes and boxes of things they just had laying around and nobody got around to eating.

"Bite," Dara said, offering him the rest of the peanut butter bar. Then, to brush off the importance, and maybe it was only important to her, she nodded toward the stairs. "I have to finish my homework. But you could hang out with me?"

"I'll see where you sleep?"

With a laugh, Dara led him toward the stairs. "If that's what thrills you, sure."

"Here," Dara told him, sliding open a drawer in her desk. "I have some neat stuff in here."

Pursing his lips, Cade just stood there.

"I have to finish these review questions," she said. "Then we can bust out of here and go to the park or something."

The park interested Cade, but the review questions didn't. Though she had a book open, it was oversized. Full of pictures, and not as interesting as the place she slept. He moved along the edges of her room thoughtfully. She had hundreds of pictures on her wall. Plucking at one, he frowned when it stayed stuck fast.

Wondering if she'd notice, Cade watched her. Her hair fell to hide her face. Her pencil skimmed a sheet of paper softly. It whispered, without ceasing. So Cade tugged the corner of the picture again, then bounded toward the window when he freed it. Success!

This window had a bench in it. So did Ms. Fourakis' front window, but she'd filled it with plants. Drinking in the sun there, they flourished. But nothing kept Cade from this seat. Climbing right up, he pushed the curtains out of the way.

Sunlight flooded over him, warm and clean.

His ill-gotten prize clutched in his hand, he watched Dara's back as she worked. Satisfied that she wouldn't turn to catch him, he lowered the square to study it. In black-and-white, Sofia hung upside down from a strange wall. It was pocked with blobs, and it looked like someone just out of view clung to it.

Sofia dangled from a rope. The helmet made her hair stream in odd directions. But it was her smile that fascinated Cade. It was so bright, it seemed like it was in color. In his head, he heard her laughter. Though he didn't understand the scene or the significance, he felt her glee.

That was sheer happiness. Unrestrained. Cade wondered if he'd ever laughed like that. Glancing up again, he wondered if Dara ever had.

She must have sensed him looking, because she patted the open drawer again. Singsonging, like she was trying to tempt him, she said, "I have Happy Meal toys."

Unsure what those might be, Cade tucked the picture in his pocket. Then, reluctantly, he slid from his perch. The room engulfed him in everything Dara. It smelled like her, it felt like her. Or, at least, the way he imagined her. Velvet and warm, a hint of strength.

Walking on Dara's bed, he picked up a teddy bear to smell. Then, he dropped it, and hopped to the floor. He couldn't help himself. Though the drawer was open, and she obviously wanted him to look in it, he leaned over her shoulder to consider the open book.

"What are review questions?" he asked.

"History," she said. "Wanna help?"

Cade shook his head, then smiled when she laughed. It was soft and it made him smile. History definitely wasn't his subject. Since she'd invited him twice, he decided to paw through the open drawer. It was a jumble of bright plastic. None of it seemed important, but it made a nice sound when he stroked his hand through it.

From the tangled pile, he produced a plastic tiger. Its paint was faded, the stripes still black, but the eyes orange with flecks of white. Experimentally, he sniffed it, then bit the base. He was right. Plastic, nothing special. Turning it over, he considered the strings beneath the base. They didn't seem important, but there was a button. He shook the toy, then pushed the button. The tiger collapsed.

Cade threw it back in the drawer before Dara realized he'd broken it. Rummaging for something else, he found a miniature car. Cars! Lines smooth and bright, it was a perfect replica of the parking lot cars. Better still, he understood how this worked. He'd found a tin cart in the mining village. Short two wheels, it hadn't rolled very well. But it was fun to slide through the dust.

Setting this car on the floor, Cade flicked it. To his disappointment, it only spun in place. "Broken," he muttered to himself.

With a curious sound, Dara looked up from her book. "What?"

Cade held the car up. "It's broken."

Turning in her chair, Dara took the car from him. Placing

it on the floor again, she pulled it backward until it started to click. Then she let it go and it careened across the hardwood. Crashing beneath her window, it flipped over. Tiny wheels still whining, it spun to a slow stop.

"It's fine," she said. Reaching into the drawer, she pulled out another. Pull, and zip! It bashed into the first one, and disappeared beneath her bed.

Clambering after it, Cade looked back at her. "I'll try."

"Go for it," she said. Her homework was getting less and less done by the minute. She waited expectantly as Cade perched in the window seat. Leaning way over, he pulled both cars back and let them go at the same time. Amazing! He watched Dara pluck them up casually, disappointed that she didn't let them crash.

But he wasn't disappointed when she climbed out of her chair. Joining him on the floor, she leaned her head toward his. Offering him one of the cars, she wound hers up and said, "You can't tell anybody about my secret stash."

The cars veered off and Cade thumped after them. He punched through the air, grabbing them before they sped beneath the desk. They weren't as fast as squirrels or rabbits. They were easy to catch. Bringing them back to Dara's side, he considered keeping them both for himself. But, they were hers, so he gave her the green one. It wasn't as fast. "They're secret?"

Bobbing her head, Dara set hers to race again. "Well, yeah. I'm a little too old for toys, don't you think?"

"You have lots," Cade replied.

"One drawerful isn't *lots*."

They let their respective cars go. It became Cade's job to retrieve them, and he was happy to do it. They went fast, and that excited him. Then he thumped across her floor or over her bed to find them. It wasn't the same as running and racing through the forest, but it was good to move again.

When he returned her green car, Dara shook it at him. "I rule you."

Cade smiled. "This is true."

THIRTY-FIVE

When Cade turned up the next day, Dara put away another bag of his purloined groceries. With a mental note to herself to return them secretly, she caught him by the arm and led him upstairs. Anticipation radiated from him, a spark that leapt from his skin to hers.

"I want to take your picture again," she said.

Cade agreed with a shrug. His feet barely made sound on the steps. He moved lightly, slipping down the hall and into her room. Immediately, he took to the window seat, the highest perch in the room besides the top of the dresser.

Pulling out her gear, Dara stole looks at him through her hair. Silhouetted against the window, he watched the back-yard like he was hunting. Did he ever relax? Even when he was drugged at the hospital, he struggled against it. But this wasn't his home, was it? She didn't think she could settle into an alien world all that comfortably, either.

"Do you like it here?" Dara asked suddenly.

Cade looked to her. His eyes pierced beneath his dark brows. There was no doubt he saw *her*. "Your room smells like you."

Dara blushed. She didn't know if that was humiliating or exhilarating. He was sitting there, *smelling* her. Like he did every single thing in the store, every bite of food he put in his mouth. The back of her neck prickled. There was no way she was brave enough to ask if she smelled good to him.

"Okay, this time we're going to get it right," Dara said. She raised the camera, deciding to save the tripod for another time. He wouldn't be Cade if she made him hold still. "When I say one, two, three, you smile. Ready? One . . . two . . . three."

Stretching his mouth unnaturally, Cade looked like a lunatic. Like, if the reporters outside wanted a picture to go with their exposé *Is the Primitive Boy Dangerous?!* that would be the face on it, right there. She let the camera drop down as she laughed.

"I smiled," he said defensively.

Waving a hand, Dara raised the camera again. "No, no, you did, and it was great. Most of the time, when you pick up a camera, people expect you to say cheese!"

Cade frowned. "Why?"

"To . . ." Dara trailed off. "They just do. Pictures usually mean smiling. But I actually just want you to be you. I'm not interested in posed shots. I want to see who you are."

Quiet, Cade seemed to consider this. Then he dug into his

pocket. Hopping down from the window seat, he approached her. *He rolls his hips,* Dara thought. *That's how he walks so quietly.* Then she blushed again, for justifying herself to herself. She was just one big box of lame today.

Cade thrust a picture at her. "I stole this."

Curious, Dara glanced down. Sofia, falling off the rock wall. That was a good day. The lacrosse team had won regionals, and they all went for pizza and games at AdventureLand. Dara tagged along because who didn't like pizza and a little light indoor recreation?

Smiling, Dara asked, "Why this one?"

With a shrug, Cade leaned over to look at it again. When he came closer, she smelled *him,* too. There was Ivory soap and fabric softener, definitely. But something else, below it. Warm, and spicy maybe. Like a handful of sage, rubbed soft. He startled her when he lifted his head again.

"It's Sofia," he said simply.

That was his whole explanation, but there was depth in his voice. He got it—he looked at that snapshot and saw what Dara saw. Not just a memory frozen in time, but the wholeness of someone. Their essence, the picture wasn't *of* her. It *was* her.

Cradling her camera to her chest, Dara nodded. "Exactly." It was a small town. She'd never expected anybody else to understand her photography. Even though her parents were supportive, they didn't get it. To them, the stiff, posed Christmas pictures were just as great as the real ones. They didn't see a difference . . . but Cade did.

"Dara?"

She must have been quiet too long. Flashing him a smile, she gave him the picture back. "You can keep it. I can make another print."

His careful hands when he tucked it back in his pocket— she couldn't stop looking at them. She felt too full, too warm. If she moved closer; maybe if he touched her . . . shoving those thoughts aside, Dara did take his hand.

"Come on. I can't take pictures of you inside."

Eating chicken fried rice straight from the carton, Sheriff Porter walked the length of the conference table.

He had a better copy of Krause's picture sitting dead center. Scraps of paper, printed sheets, surrounded it. He wasn't a man to take somebody's word for it. So even though Dr. Jupiter O'Toole was all hopped up and ready to talk, Sheriff Porter wasn't quite ready to talk to him.

Instead, he'd been making calls. The funny thing about the internet, he discovered, was the dead spot. Right around the nineties, when it was getting started—the real world didn't intrude there.

"Kills me," he told Krause as he paced back to the head of the table. "I can read the Gutenberg Bible online, but I have to get a fax from Cleveland to find out about this missing persons report."

Perched on the wall heater, Krause stirred her Happy Family with a fork. "But hey. It's here now."

And it was. The Walshes up and disappeared without a

trace. Their bank account had been frozen, not because it was empty. But because nobody had withdrawn from it in seventeen years. The same thing with their credit cards. The house they'd been living in was rented, so nobody cared when they left. Their cars, paid for.

Sheriff Porter leaned over the report from campus police. It said nothing. Literally. Dr. Walsh's research was the least controversial science in the world. She didn't kill little bunny rabbits, or stick electrodes into prisoners' brains. She wasn't trying to find the missing link. All she did was track diseases.

"You know there's a difference between RNA viruses and DNA viruses?" Krause asked thoughtfully.

Her work was done for the moment. She'd gone and dragged down every lead connected with the Walsh disappearance. Extra pictures lined the whiteboard, headshots mostly. Not a lot about Mr. Walsh, but Dr. Walsh had quite a paper trail. She even found a copy of her dissertation. *Polymicrobial Respiratory Tract Infections and Rhinovirus in Preindustrial Populations*, which she quit reading three pages in.

"Mmm," Sheriff Porter replied.

He didn't care about her research. He didn't even care that her research plus a little bit of crazy might have added up to dropping off the grid completely. Why never really mattered much. That was something for reporters and novelists to worry about. He only needed the truth: was Dr. Walsh Cade's mother?

Because that would take him to the next step. Finding family—well, Krause already found some family. An estranged sister in New Mexico on the father's side, some second cousins in California. He couldn't make them take custody of Cade, but he could try. The courts liked it when family stepped up. So did Sheriff Porter. It made everything a lot easier.

"How do we get a positive ID out of this?" Sheriff Porter asked idly.

With a laugh, Krause plucked up a bite of her lunch. "You could try asking the kid again."

Yeah, that was hilarious. Rolling his eyes, Sheriff Porter put his carton down and paced the length of the table again. If he just kept looking, something would jump out. The answer was there, just like it had been in the picture.

It was there, and he'd find it.

The vicious pack of middle schoolers still roamed Clayton Park, so Dara and Cade skirted around them. Dara was out of breath. The walk from her house wasn't long, but it was a challenge.

The reporters mostly stayed on the streets. That meant Dara and Cade had to stick to alleys and backyards. There had been some fence hopping involved. Nothing for Cade, a challenge for Dara.

Her face was pink, and he liked that she kept grabbing his arm. He held her up so she could catch her breath. Her fingers dug in. She left marks on him, none that she could see. Pretty and flushed, her skin seemed to beg him to touch it. Skim fingers down her throat. Cool her face with his palms.

This time, they stayed on the paths in the woods. In daylight, it was easy to see that this was no forest. When he squinted,

Cade made out the houses on the other side. Listening closely, he heard people all around. Laughter and voices. A lawn mower roared to life in the distance.

People, everywhere. Thinking about it stole his breath, not in a good way. His skin crawled. He wanted to run. So he turned his attention on Dara. It was easy to block everything out when he was with her. Every inch of her fascinated him.

She still wasn't *aware*. At least, she didn't realize the way he looked at her. Didn't know he wanted to catch her, touch her. Keep her, that was the one she'd never pluck out of his head. It was a thought. Only a thought, one he didn't dare to let grow.

"All right," she said. "I'm just going to start shooting, and if you end up in my pictures, great. Wander around or something. Just, you know. Chill."

Whatever that meant. He guessed it was something like *relax*. So he grabbed the lowest bough of an oak tree, and hauled himself into it. At home, the cliffs and the cave and the fire kept him safe from predators. He relaxed there easily.

Away from it, he could only settle when he could see every-thing. When nothing could slip up behind him. Sometimes he'd end up sharing a perch with a rat snake, but they were harmless enough. They only wanted to find nests with eggs, or better yet, baby birds in them. Cade was far too big to digest.

Dara snapped away, her camera *tick-tick-tick*ing as she went. Beneath that, there was an unpleasant whine. It bored right into Cade's brain, like he'd trapped a mosquito in his ear. He watched her lean into flowers, then swing around wide. Suddenly, she pointed the camera right at him.

"Ignore me."

"No thank you," he replied.

He didn't expect her laughter. Once it came, he wanted more of it. Testing the strength in his arm, he reached for the next branch up. Then suddenly, he shot up the tree. The sneakers didn't let him grip, so he had to pace himself. But the oak shook with his weight, a few leftover acorns raining down.

Did she see him? He heard the ticking all the way up here. Looking out, he saw the neighborhoods. Matching houses, long rows of them, all the same. Then past them, a few taller buildings that must have been the town. Up high, with the wind on his face, he saw all of Makwa. It reminded him of the mining town. The grids on the ground, the houses spaced just so.

Laughing again, Dara sounded a little worried. "Get down from there!"

This wasn't his forest. The trees didn't grow so thick or wide as they did there. But he wanted her to see him. To admire him, or at least get the picture she wanted. He could be exactly what she wanted. Dropping a few feet, he smiled when he landed on a good, thick branch.

He didn't hesitate. He ran down it, leaping when the branch became too thin to bear his weight. Dara's gasp filled the air, and he flew through it. Panic shot through him. He had to land on his good foot. Catch with his good hand. This wasn't something he usually thought about.

The maple bowed when he landed on it. Green leaves hissed around him. Seed spinners cascaded down, fluttering all around Dara on the ground. She was beautiful down there in a storm of them.

Clinging to the trunk of the tree, Cade finally caught his breath.

She looked up. She saw *him*.

THIRTY-SIX

*T*oday, they weren't staying in. After trading afternoons in her bedroom and his, with quick, sneaking trips to the park, Dara was ready to show him something new.

Spring threatened to turn to summer. The trees had unfolded all their buds, and daffodils waved from their neat, front-yard beds. Finally warm enough to ditch the hoodies, Dara wore hers anyway. The minute Cade turned up at her back door, she slipped a pair of sunglasses on his face.

"Come on," she said. They followed their intricate map, over the fence, across the alley. Then Dara led him down a new street entirely. Heading for the corner, she grabbed his hand and beamed back at him. "You're going to love this."

Today was the day she finally planned to show him the *ultimate*.

Hustling Cade along, she glanced at her phone. Then, the bus turned the corner. She couldn't remember ever being this excited about public transportation, and yet, there it was. Bouncing a little, she nudged Cade along. Hydraulics groaned, the whole bus sinking like it was exhausted.

"Get on," she said as the bus doors folded open. "Put these quarters in the black box by the driver."

Unfortunately, Cade didn't understand *quick*. He wanted to look at the fare box. Listen to it. His face lit up when the coins slipped in, and the digital face suddenly changed, counting the money. When the transfer ticket popped up, he laughed.

Plucking it from the box, Dara slipped it in his hands and (gently!) pushed him into the nearest seat. After paying her own fare, Dara dropped next to him and smiled when the bus rumbled into motion again.

"This," she told him, "is the County Access Express. It'll take you anywhere in town. Here, grab a map."

To be fair, the buses in Makwa weren't as impressive as, say, the New York City subway system. But it was still grander than anything Cade had ever seen. Smoothing open one of the maps, Dara hung over his shoulder. She traced their route on the green line, and secretly, got a little high on the scent of his skin.

"See, we're going to pass Clayton Park in a few minutes," she told him.

Curling her hands on his shoulder, they both turned to look through the tinted windows. Her nose brushed his hair. A thrill ran through her; he smelled like a campfire. Just a little, sweet and warm. Her fingers tightened and she made herself smile when he glanced back at her.

"What's wrong?"

Dara smiled. "You're missing it."

Clayton Park appeared, that same pack of feral middle schoolers roaming its borders. Today, they slumped on the climbing castle. Shoelaces untied and disaffected smiles, they were as tough as a bunch of kids with an eight o'clock curfew could manage.

Cade said, "I think they live there."

"I think you're right."

When he turned, he caught her face too close to his. Their noses almost touched, and he didn't shrink away. Instead, he teased with dark, dancing eyes. "They wouldn't be the first."

Smoothing the map, Dara tried to keep it on her lap. She failed, a little. Her fingers skimmed the curve of his denimed knee. There was too much adrenaline in her system for something as simple as a bus ride to the mall.

Hanging on him like a thrift store coat, she told herself sarcastically. Rearranging herself, Dara backed off—but not all the way. "Okay, coming up is downtown. There isn't a lot of it, so don't get too excited."

"Too late," Cade said, amused.

For the rest of the trip, she pointed out landmarks. The sailors' monument sulked in bronze. The courthouse had a tree growing from the side of it, a seedling sprouted in an accidental planter. A block away from that, two benches and a tree memorialized a couple of seniors who'd died in a car accident. In the fifties.

It was a small town, and soon they were on the other side of it.

"Grab the string," Dara urged Cade. She pointed at the grey cord in the window.

Though he looked confused, he did as he was told. A loud ding rewarded him, and the digital sign at the front of the bus shifted to read "Next Stop Bear Creek Mall."

Spilling into the parking lot, Dara laughed when Cade stopped to thank the bus driver and shake his hand. As he stepped into the sunlight, he reached for his sunglasses. Dara held him back.

They were lucky to get out of the house unseen. And it was easy to stay unseen when there weren't any people nearby. But Bear Creek Mall was the opposite of deserted.

"We don't want anyone to recognize you," she explained.

She savored the excuse to slip her fingers through his. And she let him walk *slowly* through the parking lot. She wasn't sure why row after row of completely ordinary cars intrigued him so much. But they did, and she may have had something to buy, but this trip was for Cade.

Even with the warm-up, the cool blast of air that greeted them when they walked into the mall was completely unnecessary. Except as advertisement. A waft of cloying, saturated sugar washed over them. They'd come in near the caramel corn store and the cookie outlet.

"What's that?" Cade asked, slipping away from her.

Bolting straight for the caramel corn store, he stopped by

the popper. He watched it spill fresh corn into a bin. It was obvious from the way he stood that he was sniffing the air. Since he couldn't touch the food, he backed away. The novelty store flashed, beckoning.

Though he was curious, he refused to step inside. The strobe light ball at the front door made him blink and jerk his head back. Dipping down, he stared at a basket full of rolling, mechanical ferrets.

They banged into the bin's walls, and into each other. Raising a hand, Cade steadied himself. Then he plunged into the bin and pulled one of the toys from it. It still twisted in his hand. Tethered to a ball, the artificial fur flapped like a weirdly desperate flag.

Reaching for her purse, Dara started to laugh. "Do you want it?"

"No."

Cade watched the toy flail for a moment more. Then he dropped it and backed away. He seemed almost disgusted by it. The bin of battery-powered puppies disturbed him even more. Their wheezing barks, so exact, unnerved him.

Hurrying away from them, he turned to Dara. "Don't people keep pets anymore? Real animals?"

Poor thing. Dara took his hand again, squeezing it gently. "Yes. Those are just for fun."

"I wasn't having fun," Cade replied.

"Then we're definitely skipping the arcade."

She'd kind of planned to anyway. It had a lousy selection of games, the floors were sticky, and everything cost fifty cents.

She didn't mind wasting a quarter for two minutes of hard-core blinking action, but she drew the line at half a dollar.

"Down there is the *good* movie theater," she told him. "There's an indie theater upstairs in an old Hot Topic."

Cade looked at her blankly.

"It's a clothes store."

The look didn't dissipate. Unsure which part had lost him, Dara added, "Like, art movies. Black-and-white stuff in other languages. Mostly about French women who smoke cigarettes and die in tunnels. It's weird."

Still skeptical, Cade nodded. Drifting toward a plate glass window that displayed tablets and phones, he told her, "According to Ms. Fourakis, you can see the exact moment they fall in love in *The Notebook*. That's a movie, by the way."

He said it so earnestly. Dara wanted to throw her arms around him, and pet him. She reminded herself to tell Sofia later. It was too good to keep to herself. Fixing the exact tone of his voice in her head, she repeated "That's a movie" to herself for mental safekeeping.

Then, aloud she said, "Come on. I have a surprise for you."

Reluctant to abandon the brightly glowing gadgets in the window, Cade anchored himself and held on to her hand tight. She could take a few steps away, but he wasn't following just yet. He asked, "What is it?"

"I want you to see it first. I want to see if you recognize it." When he seemed unmoved, she tugged his hand and added. "Please?"

When he relented, it seemed like a much bigger victory than

it was. Peeking over at him, she was startled to see hints of copper and bronze in his brown eyes. The bright mall lights stripped away his shadows. His face suddenly had new dimensions, unexpected details.

If she'd been looking at him with her photographer's eye all this time, she would have noticed. But it turned out she'd been looking at him with something else entirely. Though he held her hand tighter than ever, each step felt light. Almost like floating; almost like flight.

She couldn't wait to show him the surprise.

THIRTY-SEVEN

*I*t was extraordinary.

Skin tingling, Cade stood at the bottom of an enchanted staircase. It gleamed in silver and glass, rising gracefully to the second floor. When he concentrated, he could block the mall from his senses. With his focus steady, he heard the whisper of a hidden machine. Smelled oil and warmth, the same scent he noticed when he passed a still-warm car.

Dara trembled behind him. Her excitement crackled. He felt it leap between them, and he turned with a huge smile.

"Escalator," he said.

Suddenly, Dara was in motion. She herded him onto the steps. The mechanicals vibrated gently. It wasn't audible. It was a physical hum, one that tuned through him as they glided upward.

"Step off, step off," Dara said when they reached the top. She laughed nervously, all but leaping to the landing. "You don't want to get your shoes caught. It'll eat them, seriously."

Cade didn't ask how a machine could eat anything. He didn't want to know. All he wanted was another ride. Bounding to the down side, he grabbed the rails on both sides. It was just as smooth sliding down. Faster than he expected, but he could admit he didn't know what to expect.

When he hit the first floor, he got back on. Dara came down at the same time. It was thrilling, realizing they would meet in the middle. Nearly there, she leaned on the inside rail. A glow warmed her face. There was a brand-new light in her eyes. And for once, no shadows at all.

"Okay, so this is how an escalator works," she said, talking fast before they passed each other completely. "There's an engine under there, connected to two gears, one at the top, one at the bottom. A chain connects both gears . . . get back on!"

Racing down again, he laughed when she started up. The anticipation was sweet, and he held a hand over the gap. They'd touch in the middle, and she was already talking.

"All the steps are separate! They have their own wheels! They roll on the chain that's looped at both ends. When they come out at the bottom, they're right side up."

Their hands met, warm fingers slipping together, then apart. She passed him so swiftly. He expected to see her hair flowing behind her. Though it washed her shoulders when she turned to look at him, there was no wind to touch her face. To tease color into her skin, to carry her scent to him.

Dara stopped on the landing, and waited for him to catch up. "And when they go back inside, they turn upside down. The handrail is made out of rubber. It has its own drive, timed to match the stairs."

Hands spread, Cade stood in the middle of his step. Even though he knew it was just a machine, it felt like ancient magic. The ground moved *for* him, raising him to the heavens. It was such a small thing. A metal contraption that lifted him between two floors. Inside a building, no less, one with steel beams stretching its length.

But he couldn't help remembering what his mother had said about the Egyptians and the Maya. Two cultures, both building pyramids to lift them to the heavens. People were beautiful . . . Dara, waiting for him at the top, was beautiful.

The machine carried him to her. Seamlessly, he stepped off the escalator and caught her face in his hands. His only guides were a few books and instinct, but they were enough. He caught her mouth beneath his. Like a bird, she startled. Then she gentled, pressing back against him. Plush lips parting, she twisted her fingers in his shirt.

Everything was heat. He felt liquid and fierce, branded with all her details. The soaring sweetness of her kiss sharpened his hunger for the next. This fit. It was the perfect fit, and both his worlds fell away. For that moment, there was no wild. No mall, no police, no social workers. No bee hollow or horseshoe falls. No questions, no confusion. No lies.

He murmured her name; she whispered his back.

They belonged.

If the power pack in Channel 43's remote camera hadn't blown out, it never would have happened.

The only place in this backwater to get a replacement was the mall. The reporter, camera operator, and producer flipped a coin because none of them wanted to schlep to the other side of Greater Makwa.

In fact, they all wanted to head back to Knoxville. The State Police weren't talking, the Primitive Boy was apparently a ninja, and they could only run so many freaking interviews with kids from the local high school. They'd burned out their weirdo ration when they interviewed an old woman who claimed the boy was her long-lost niece.

Without anything new to cover, they were wasting their time. The nationals had more resources. They'd sprung for helicopters and hiking experts to try to find the Primitive Boy's secret forest hideaway. Turned out that was a lot like parachuting into Death Valley and trying to find one particular cactus.

So the producer from Channel 43 trudged into the mall with a station credit card. They'd do one more stand-up in front of the sheriff's house, then pack it in.

Texting home, he stopped to check the directory and headed for the escalators. He had to dodge a couple of kids goofing off on them. That's how small the town was. Riding the people mover at the mall counted for entertainment.

Four hundred dollars later, the producer left the camera shop, phone already in hand. Texting with just his thumb, he was halfway through a message to the station director when he stopped. At first, he thought he was hallucinating. Too much motel coffee and not enough sleep or something.

Slipping out of sight, he peered at the escalator kids. He was sure, he was almost freaking positive . . . He raised his phone and took a picture. Sending it quickly to his reporter back at the scene, he added a quick text. *I'm not crazy am I?*

The chirp came back instantly.

THAT'S THEM STAY THERE WHERE ARE YOU?

Dara paid for her panoramic lens, clutching it to her chest.

Though she wanted to look up, a shy weight kept her from looking at Cade directly. Not that she needed to look at him. When their elbows brushed, they sparked—flint against a stone. Her stung lips distracted her. The slightest touch stirred the sensation of the kiss again. Even when she spoke, she felt a low, luxurious buzz.

She wanted to laugh. Not at him; at herself. For thinking he was so perfect and pure and innocent. For believing he couldn't figure out what to do with his hands or his mouth, or his anything. Shivering in pleasure, Dara said, "One more ride down, then we'd better get back."

"Okay."

"If it's all right with everybody, maybe we can go get pizza with Sofia tonight. It's kind of awesome, I think you'll like it."

"Okay."

Freer with his hands now, Cade threaded his fingers beneath

her hair. His rough fingertips skimmed the nape of her neck. One finger curling, he stroked behind her ear, then trailed it against her ear.

Did he have any idea what he was doing to her? Her blush showed, impossible to hide. She wondered if he could hear her breath go shallow. If he noticed the prickles racing her skin. She tightened everywhere. It was a lush sensation and way too intimate for the middle of the mall.

Brushing his hand away, she rubbed her cheek against his shoulder in vague apology. "You're making me crazy."

Cade shared a secretive smile with her. "You've been making me crazy since the first time I saw you."

Dragging her lower lip through her teeth, Dara looped her arm in his. They stepped onto the escalator, drifting down to the main level. This was complicated, and possibly unfair. But it didn't feel wrong, and she wanted to *know*. Pressing closer to him, she asked, "And when was that, exactly?"

"The day you put up the tent."

Incredulous, Dara laughed. "No."

"I was checking my traps, and I heard you singing. Your hair was . . ." He waved a hand, miming a ponytail in motion. "The sun came through the trees exactly the right way. You were like gold."

Blush deepening, Dara led Cade toward the exit. The thick candy smells in the air had thinned some. Now it was a pleasant impression, and one she was almost reluctant to leave behind. She turned to look back, to the top of the stairs where everything changed. And then she frowned for no reason. She didn't see anything unusual. It was just like the atmosphere changed, and she wasn't sure how.

"What's wrong?" Cade asked.

Shaking her head, Dara said, "Nothing. Just kind of gobsmacked. The first day we got there, huh?"

"You knew I was there."

"What? No I didn't. Not until you laughed at the river."

Cade pressed his thumb gently against her back. He drew it down the curve of her spine, before letting his hand fall to rest on her hip. "Yes, you did. He talked you out of it, but you heard me. You were almost aware."

"Almost, huh?"

It looked like Cade might lean in to kiss her again. Instead, he just looked at her. His thoughts flickered behind his eyes, mysterious to her. When he finally glanced away, his features softened. His mouth soft, his brows knitted, he nodded. Squeezing her closer, he said, "I was always there. You just needed to look up."

Simple advice. Rules for tracking Cade in the wild. Amused, Dara steered him around the novelty shop that had unnerved him so much earlier. Peering into it, she tried to see it from his perspective. The masks on the walls hung unnaturally. A lot of lights, a lot of shrieking, beeping sounds.

When she pictured herself swallowed inside a box, nothing but strobes and sirens, she felt it. A quiver of uneasiness. It squirmed in her belly, and made her fold closer to Cade. Because she thought she knew why, she didn't look up.

Instead, she let Cade hit the automatic doors first. He

enjoyed stuff like that way too much. Putting on her sunglasses, she followed him outside. The shift from artificial light to the natural glare of the afternoon was abrupt. She blinked, her eyes watering. Cade was a shape in front of her for a moment.

Suddenly, his shoulders angled. He reached a hand back, grabbing for Dara. "The people with cameras are here."

"Crap," Dara said.

She squinted, and her head went a little dizzy. Cade wasn't kidding, the reporters were there. And not just one of them. Not just that jerk Jim Albee. White vans filed into the parking lot and there were people already on the move. Heading for them. Right for them, a terrifying cloud.

"We can go back through," she said decisively.

"Hey Dara," a man said behind her.

Whipping around, she stared blankly at someone she'd never seen. By the rumpled polo and the eager expression he wore, she guessed he was with the press. "Sorry, that's not me."

The man didn't back off. He kept looking just past them, cagey and abrupt. "Don't be scared. We just want five minutes of your time. Yours too, Cade. We've been dying to talk to you. My name's Mark—"

"No." Dara cut him off. "Talk to my dad. Leave us alone."

Slipping an arm around Dara's shoulders, Cade tried to shield her with his body. It was a sweet gesture, but it didn't make her feel safer. He had no idea how to get away from the mall. And honestly, neither did she.

"Hey," Mark said. "Two minutes. An exclusive, and I can

help you. Come with me right now, and I'll help you ditch the rest of those jackals."

They didn't answer. Instead, they moved at once. Under Cade's arm, Dara broke for the door. Her plan was simple. Get inside, get to the bathrooms. Block the doors and call her dad. Without an escape car, and half the reporters in Kentucky between them and the bus, it was the best they could do.

Edged with desperation, Mark grabbed for Dara. He fell short. His fingers ripped the bag from her arms. Suddenly, Dara felt like she was in the novelty box. Too loud. Too bright. Everything happening too fast. Her heart didn't pound. It filled her chest, and shuddered to a stop.

The lens shattered when it hit the ground. The trapped chime of the glass didn't start Dara's heart. But it made her move. She scrambled for it. At the same time, Mark darted for it, too. Before either reached it, Cade snatched the bag from the ground. He was faster than both of them.

That's when Mark made the mistake of reaching for Dara again. "Hey, I'm not trying to hurt you," he insisted.

But he reached. He grabbed, and Cade lunged. Plowing into Mark's chest, Cade knocked him off his feet. A pair of glasses flew off in a wide, glittering arc. Gabbling voices approached, high-pitched. Excited. The air sharpened with it, thin and electric.

In the rush, Cade grew. His shoulders spread, his back widened. His face, so soft just a few minutes before, had turned feral. Body rising and falling, he was terrifying. Opening his mouth, his teeth flashed. He roared.

The terrible sound echoed in the entrance alcove, off glass and steel. Caught by the microphones on the cameras rushing toward them.

"Don't hurt me, don't hurt me," Mark cried. He threw his arms up to protect his face.

At that, Dara grabbed Cade's shirt and dragged him inside. Everything stretched at wrong angles. Their sneakers squeaked on the faux-granite floor, high-pitched screams that dogged their escape.

A wave rushed up behind them, a human one. Already, their narration rang out, breathlessly describing the scene. *Shocking attack. Flurry of violence.* There was a story now. They wouldn't stop coming.

But Dara let adrenaline lead her. She had a plan. It wasn't a good one, but she had it, they just had to run. Lock in. Call Dad. It was that easy.

They just had to stay ahead.

THIRTY-EIGHT

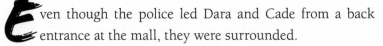ven though the police led Dara and Cade from a back entrance at the mall, they were surrounded.

Gritting his teeth, Cade kept his head down. Swarmed by bodies and microphones, he felt like he was coming out of his skin. Like one more touch from the wrong person, and he'd split and spill out of his own flesh.

"Back up," Deputy Krause shouted.

It was her job to lead them through the parking lot. Two more deputies flanked them. They made a good shield but it didn't stop the reporters. Talking over each other, they pressed from all sides. Without touching, they still managed to invade. Shoving microphones toward them, they shouted questions.

"Can you tell us what you were thinking?"

"Did you feel like you were in danger?"

"Who are you really?"

"Dara, Dara! Cade!"

Though they had an escort, the police cruisers seemed so far away. Their lights doused, they were just blue shapes in the distance. Doors thrown open, waiting for them. *They just need to let me go,* Cade thought. He had enough adrenaline left to knock the rest of them down.

Beside him, Dara made a plaintive sound. He felt sharper when she did that. He tasted her fear, and it made him want to bare his teeth. In the tangled rush, he caught her hand and squeezed it.

Back home, he could have carried her away. Swung off, far above the danger on the ground. They could sit in the glow of his fire. Listen to the birds and the breeze. Here, he was help-less. Wound tight enough to snap, he glowered at the reporters.

"Dara! Hey, hey! Dara, over here!" one of them shouted, worming to the front of the pack. "Your father's the sheriff. Do you think you'll get special treatment?"

"Leave her alone," Cade growled. He surged, but the depu-ties kept him caged between their bodies. Cameras snapped, loud as cicadas. Now, Dara tightened her hand in his. Pulling him closer, she looked up with haunted eyes.

Her color drained out; she shook her head. It was subtle. More the connection of their gaze than an actual movement. But her lips parted, making the shape of words that got lost in the noise of the crowd. Her meaning was clear, though. *Stop.*

How could he stop? He didn't *want* to. He had it in his bones and blood to knock them all down. But for Dara, he put his head down again. Black asphalt flashed between his feet. Soon, roughly, the deputies shoved them in the back of a police car.

The doors slammed closed. It muffled the mob, but it didn't silence them. Huddled against an oily, plastic seat, Cade wrapped his arms around Dara. Tucking her head beneath his chin, he rounded his back to close over her. Casting black looks out the window, he clung to her.

All he wanted was to protect her. He didn't realize he was posing for pictures. Writing the next day's stories. Selling papers, with every furious look.

Sheriff Porter's station was chaos.

The phones wouldn't stop ringing. The deputies had to keep backing people off the front walk. Not just the reporters this time.

Somebody had posted a grainy video clip online, *The Primitive Boy goes nuts at Bear Creek Mall!* It seemed like anybody who'd been halfway interested in the case had converged at once.

He put Duncan on phone tree duty, calling in a couple more bodies to help with the crowd. Krause and the other probies back on the phone. Deputy Lo had the producer from Channel 43 in the interrogation room, giving a statement.

There wasn't a mark on the guy, but he was angling to turn pressed charges into an exclusive interview somehow. Since Dara was his daughter, and she was smack in the middle of all this mess, Sheriff Porter kept his distance.

Throwing open the conference room door, Sheriff Porter

slammed it, too. He ignored the way both kids jumped. Slapping folders onto the table, he demanded, "What were you thinking?"

"He jumped us," Dara said, already out of her chair. "He actually *grabbed* me."

"I'd do it again," Cade added.

"Just shut up, for god's sake."

Refusing to stay silent, Dara came around the table. "All we did was go to the mall. I told that guy to talk to you. I mean, I told him I wasn't even me. We turned around to go back inside and he grabbed me."

Sheriff Porter held up a hand. "I know exactly what happened. It's on the internet, Dara! The Dalai Lama knows what happened, by now."

"Then why are you yelling at us?"

"I am the sheriff," he said, slapping one hand into his other. "No matter what I say, no matter what that video says, even if that jackass decides not to press charges, people are gonna talk. I cannot do my job when everybody in Kentucky is pulling stories out of thin air about me and this office."

Cade bristled. He started to stand, but Dara dropped a heavy hand on his shoulder.

"Don't," she warned.

"I'll put you in handcuffs, son. Don't think I'm lying." Then he turned to Dara. Red splotches stained his face. They crept into his hair, and scalded the curves of his ears. This was a whole new kind of mad, one Dara had never seen. "And don't you give me that look. I'm in here right now so I don't beat him with a phone book for touching you."

That frankness surprised everybody. But it had the intended effect. Cade sat down again, though he kept his fingers tangled in Dara's. And Dara settled some. She threw her shoulders back, trying to shuck off the tension.

With everyone settled, Sheriff Porter glanced out the window in the door. "Branson Swayle's on his way to sit with Cade until we get this straightened up. Dara, your mother's going to fetch you shortly."

"I want to stay," she protested.

"That's too bad."

Though it sounded like it pained him to say it, Cade swore, "I'll be okay."

Turning back from the window, Sheriff Porter approached the table. Since the kid was already worked up, he might be too distracted to guard himself well. Talking to him was usually like talking to a wall. The sullen looks and long silences helped nobody, and Sheriff Porter wasn't stupid. Even when they didn't like to talk, agitated people could tell you a whole lot by the way they acted.

"Look," Sheriff Porter said, leaning over the table. He met Cade, eye to eye, as he flipped open the folder. "I want you to understand something. I appreciate you trying to take care of my daughter."

"Daddy, seriously," Dara said.

He ignored her. "Seems to me like all along, that's all you've wanted to do. Am I right?"

Suspicious, Cade hesitated. But slowly, he nodded.

"Well, now you've seen this mess, and you've got to know it's because we still don't know what we need to know about you."

"Stop it!" Dara said.

Sliding a picture from the folder, Sheriff Porter laid it down in front of Cade. He didn't slap it, or move sharply. His voice was buttery, soothing even. Though his daughter was currently losing her mind over it, he knew he had Cade's attention. Tapping the picture, he looked the boy in the eye and asked, "Does this mean anything to you?"

Cade froze. Loosening his hand from Dara's, he scrabbled his fingers across the picture. It took three tries for him to pick it up. When he did, he pushed his chair back. Holding the picture a little too close, he seemed like he was trying to retreat. Hide in a corner or something.

Excitement welling up, Sheriff Porter watched him, silently.

"What?" Dara asked. She tried to get closer. "What is it?"

Drawing his feet into the chair, Cade curled the picture against his chest. "This is mine."

Sheriff Porter wanted to whoop. Instead, he crossed his arms over his chest and nodded thoughtfully. "So it does mean something."

"Yes," Cade said flatly. "Where did you get it?"

Holding up a hand to stay Dara, Sheriff Porter asked, "You don't know?"

"No. You made it bigger. It's different."

Sheriff Porter gestured at the far right side of the photo. Mirroring Cade's posture, he didn't move closer. He just kept his focus, looking right at him. Ignoring everything else around him. Including his daughter's anxious murmuring. "Actually, that man right there, on the right side? He sent this to us. He knows you. He knows your mother. He knows your real name."

A soft gasp filled the conference room. Arms wrapped tight around herself, Dara said, "Cade?"

"His name's Jonathan Walsh," Sheriff Porter told Dara. Not unkindly, he looked over both of them as he opened the conference room door. "He's been missing since he was a year and a half old."

Cade folded the photo against his chest and shook his head. "I wasn't missing."

"I think we have different definitions of missing, son," Sheriff Porter said, and walked out.

Dara's mouth felt full of ashes. They burned, drying out her throat, turning her voice into a croak. Everything had crashed around her, and Cade. God, poor Cade had been smashed. His expression was wrecked, eyes red-rimmed, and his jaw set so hard. He climbed further in the chair, until he sat on the back of it, his feet tucked into the seat.

Gingerly, Dara approached him. "Cade?"

He didn't answer. He stared past her, a gargoyle in flesh. Rolling the picture ever tighter, his knuckles paled.

"Can I see it?" she asked.

That's not what she wanted to ask. The better question was, *Is it true? Have you been lying? What's really real here?* But she was afraid—not of him, but for him. Once, she'd lain on top of him, trying to hold his life in. She felt the ghostly sting of his blood on her hands. Maybe she always would. So she was gentle with him, and she waited for an answer.

After a moment, he let her take the photo. With hawkish eyes, he watched her smooth it out. She felt him following her gaze as she studied the faces in the snapshot.

It didn't look super old. From the clothes, it obviously was a while ago. But the faces were bright and young. The woman in the picture didn't look into the camera. Her gaze was shifted slightly, to take in the baby in her arms.

Swallowing hard, Dara looked over the top of the picture. "Who are these people?"

Cade looked to the door. It was still closed. Quietly, he said, "That's my mom and my dad. And me. I don't know who the other man is."

Unexpected weight dragged Dara into a chair. "Well then, who's Cade?"

"Me. It's my middle name," he said flatly. "They never called me Jonathan."

Dara wasn't sure where to start. Or to finish. All of her questions seemed to track across each other, none of them the right place to start. Studying the baby in the picture again, she saw Cade in the round face and shock of dark hair. "This is really you."

"Yes."

"But this is at someone's house," Dara said.

"Yes."

With one last look, Dara tried to memorize the faces. Then she handed the picture back to him. Her hand shook a little. His was incredibly steady; it shied from her touch. The knot rose in her throat again, and Dara rubbed at the weight in her chest.

"What happened to them? Did they kidnap you?"

Picture reclaimed, Cade folded into himself again. "No. Everyone was dying. We went into the woods to be safe. The best way to avoid a pandemic is to avoid people. Far away, so you don't get infected, too. Far away so the survivors don't hunt you down . . ."

A chill swept through Dara's blood. What he was saying was crazy. Completely insane, but she didn't dare tell him that. Instead, she nudged him with a neutral, "I don't understand."

"That's what my mom told me," Cade told her. He went away in his eyes, a light fading. A connection dying. When he spoke again, it was obvious he was quoting someone else. Someone he'd believed in. "'We left at the apex of statistical inevitability.'"

Dara reached for him. "Cade . . ."

Very quietly, he said, "I think she lied." And then, instead of reaching back, he turned away.

THIRTY-NINE

*T*hat evening, Dara watched.

She huddled in her bed, hooded by her comforter. Remote in hand, she clicked through the six o'clock news on every station. Her bedroom looked like a slow motion rave. Light blared from the screen, then a blip of dark as she moved up the guide.

They all had it, clips of Cade standing over the reporter.

That's what they played in the background while they talked: Cade rampant, teeth bared, eyes black with fury. It looped on the screens behind the anchors, again and again. If they showed the whole clip, the whole *truth*, she thought bitterly, it was only once. The part that made him a monster, that was all they cared about.

"Serious concerns tonight," one anchor said. She *did* look

seriously concerned. Because hey, it was completely possible that Cade might break into the studio at any minute.

Next station. This anchor wasn't so much concerned. He looked like he might be fighting a smile, actually. Touching the desk in front of him, he peered into the camera. " . . . revealed a darker side to the story today . . ."

"Bite me," Dara said, and changed the channel.

"—rumors of a psychiatric hold—"

". . . close to the investigation say they're closer tonight to IDing the John Doe known as the Primitive Boy."

Sitting up stiffly, Dara raised the volume. She wasn't even sure what station she was on anymore. It played the monster video clip, too, but then it faded into a picture. *The* picture, the one Cade had held in his trembling hands at the station.

Dara slid to the end of the bed, leaning in like she might get the news faster if she was closer to it. She clung to the footboard, nails grating against the wood.

"This undated snapshot may be the key to unlocking the mystery. Though not confirmed, our sources indicate they have positively identified at least two people in the picture, Dr. Jupiter O'Toole and Dr. Liza Walsh.

"A leading epidemiologist at Case Western Reserve University, Dr. O'Toole reported his partner, Dr. Walsh, missing in 1999. Now police believe that Dr. Walsh may have disappeared voluntarily with her family—including a toddler whose age and description purportedly match the description of the Primitive Boy.

"Details are sketchy at this hour, but we'll be following

the story as it develops."

Dara snapped the TV off. Rolling off the bed, she snatched up her phone and dialed her father. A vicious mix of emotion roared through her. Anger, because why couldn't they play the whole clip? Why didn't they tell the whole world that a grown man had tried to grab her just to get a quote? Humiliation, because instead of decking the guy herself, she froze.

Pacing past the windows, Dara listened to the line ring. Outside, the reporters swelled. Hungry for more, their lights turned the front lawn into a movie set. Inside the house, tension reigned. Everything was on the verge of explosion. One wrong word, one snide look, would strike the match.

"I'm busy," Sheriff Porter said as a greeting. He wasn't lying. Dara heard the tumult on the other line. Loud voices, all buzzing at once.

"Somebody leaked the picture," Dara said abruptly.

"I don't have time for this, Dara."

"Make time! Oh my god, listen to yourself!"

Sheriff Porter sighed. "I have to go."

"Aren't you going to do something about it? I know Cade didn't tell them, and I sure didn't. That means somebody *there* is . . ."

"We leaked it."

Going numb, Dara clutched at the window frame. "What? Why?"

"Dara," Sheriff Porter said. His irritation came through the line just fine. And with it, his exhaustion. He sounded so weary when he said, "All they do, all day long, is dig for information. They run one story, everybody else will pick it up. All the amateur-hour detectives on the internet will get in on it."

"But you're making it worse!"

"No, sugar, I'm getting answers as fast as I can. I've got six people on this, and that's all I can spare."

Wordlessly, Dara hung up. When she closed her eyes, she heard the reporters outside. They hummed and hummed, ever present. Layered over that, her mother's footsteps on the stairs. Lia's music playing tinnily from her room.

The rest was the roar inside her own skin. Her heart. Her breath. It killed her that Cade was blocks away all by himself. Barricaded into a house full of things he didn't know how to use. Smothered by systems he didn't understand.

The whole world was staring at him. Stripping him, carving him into pieces, to get what they needed.

She tried to think of her happy place, her imaginary dark-room. But tonight, she couldn't summon the scent of developer that she'd never really sampled. The process wouldn't come to her; she'd read about it online, but never done it. She didn't know what it felt like to wash color prints in pure darkness. The red of the imaginary safety light kept transforming, becoming Cade as he bled for her.

He suffered, and she suffered, and there was nothing any-one could do to fix it.

Ms. Fourakis forced Cade to come out of his room.

Standing at the door, she talked to his back when he refused to look at her. Gentle, but persistent, she told him that everything was screwed up, but it would get better. Everything was scary, but it would get better.

"And I'm going to show you the best movie ever made again," she finished. "You're going to watch it. Tonight, we're chilling. Nothing hard. Nothing important. We'll tackle the big stuff tomorrow, all right?"

Looking back slowly, he refused to move. "I'm fine here."

"Hey kid, I get it. But you can't do anything about it tonight. And I can't let you sit in the dark on top of my nana's antique dresser. So come on."

Cade jumped down. He didn't look at Ms. Fourakis as he passed her. She couldn't see through his skin. She didn't know that he was full of poison right now. That it ate him from the inside, twisting his guts and burning in his throat.

Because Ms. Fourakis wanted him to, Cade took a bowl of stew. The ceramic warmed his hands. Steam rolling from it touched his skin, a bright, hot spot when everything else was numb.

"Doing okay?" Mr. Anderson asked. He clapped a chestnut hand to Cade's shoulder. With a gentle shake, he waited for an answer. Actively. It was so obvious now that they'd been working hard to *listen* all this time, waiting for him to say something important.

Cade didn't feel like participating. He shrugged, then Cade settled into his favorite place in the living room. There was a corner where the pothos cascaded down the wall. The plant's leaves smelled faintly sweet, like freshwater and life. The forest smelled that way sometimes, when there was rain in the air.

Mr. Anderson stepped into the couch, sitting on his feet beside Ms. Fourakis. They leaned toward each other, naturally and unconsciously. With gentle fingers, he stroked her hair back, so nothing lay between them. Though their attention occasionally strayed toward Cade, mostly, they stayed in their own circle.

The stew cooled in Cade's bowl. After a while, he set it aside. Pulling his knees to his chest, he watched the movie by default. None of it registered, really.

In his head, he was somewhere else entirely. A middle world, one that only existed inside of him. Because this place wasn't home. And what he used to think was home wasn't real.

"This is, watch this, watch," Ms. Fourakis said, her gaze fixed on the screen.

Mr. Anderson laughed. "Shh. I am."

Quiet only a moment, Ms. Fourakis drew a sharp breath. "No, but watch. You can see it, the exact minute he falls in love with her. Watch, watch."

"I am," Mr. Anderson replied.

Even though they weren't doing anything but eating dinner and watching the best movie ever made, they were joined. In an invisible way, by threads no one could see. But somehow, Cade was sure, threads no one else could sever.

He turned his attention to the screen, too. What did that moment look like? Who were these people? Were they really falling in love?

Rain beat down on them, was it real rain? he wondered. These people were actors, he knew that. At the end of the day, they stopped pretending. They went home to their own lives. Did that mean they knew who they were?

"Watch," Ms. Fourakis wheezed, tense with anticipation.

There was a look. Cade tightened his arms around his knees, watching the actors. Watching them make something up on the screen. It didn't exist until they made it exist. And it fooled him, just like everything else. When the actors kissed, he felt the currents that rose up when he touched Dara.

They were fainter without her. More like a memory of the sensation. A rush and relief, a spark and then the darkness. Cade turned his head. Not to look away, but to feel the thin, jade leaves of the plant brush against his cheek. That was real. He knew that for sure.

He was healing. Faster than he expected, definitely faster than he might have at home. His chest still hurt, but he could raise his arm again. The pain in his foot had faded entirely. If he had to, he could fish. It didn't take all of his strength to forage.

Dara was the only reason to stay. Sometimes he got lonely in the forest, but he'd never been hunted. His parents had lied to him, so what? Frustrated, Cade thumped his head against the wall and wondered what kept Dara here.

He'd lived in her world. What would it take to lure her into his? The right way, he thought sullenly. Not the way idiot Josh had done it, too stupid to tie up the food. Too dim to light a fire. It would be different with him.

He could show her the places deeper in the forest that no one had seen but him. He'd watched her at the falls. They'd consumed her, left her trembling. Even when she wasn't taking pictures, she was drinking it in. Every detail—he was sure if he asked her, she would have been able to describe it down to the last glimmering drop.

Beyond the falls, a two-day walk from the old mining village, there was a valley full of wild orchids. Their buds would open soon, turning pink-and-white faces to the sun. There were thousands of them.

After a rain, they shivered. Their stems were so thick, their leaves so stiff, that they whispered. It sounded like words; Cade had lain there with them before, trying to make out their words.

There was that secret place, and he could imagine Dara in it. And in the mining town; in the shadow of the cliffs. Among the stone ruins of the last people to disappear from the earth. Those weren't lies. Those people really had lived and loved and then ceased to be.

"Did you see it?" Ms. Fourakis said. It wasn't a question; she sounded drunk and sweet. Leaning into Mr. Anderson, she looked over at him.

And Cade did see it, again. Better than in the movie, natural and alive, just like the plants and trees and rivers back home. The question was whether Dara would see it when he looked at her next.

FORTY

Dawn streaked the horizon, a fine scarlet line that promised rain later. Though the airfield smelled of diesel,
the trees that surrounded it threw off the scent of coming rain.
Leaning against his police cruiser, Sheriff Porter watched the
puddle jumper land at the municipal airport.

When the small, white plane finally stopped, a door popped
open to reveal stairs. They sank slowly to the ground. Then,
after what seemed like hours, Dr. Jupiter O'Toole emerged. He
walked like he talked, thoughtfully and slowly.

Time to meet and greet. Sheriff Porter approached him,
hand already out to shake.

"Thanks for coming all this way."

"Anything I can do to help," Dr. O'Toole said.

He was much older than the man in the picture. Afro shot

with silver now, Dr. O'Toole also boasted bifocals. Fine lines traced the edges of his lips. Though his face was still smooth and round, the seventeen years that had passed between the picture and this moment were unmistakable.

Leading him to the cruiser, Sheriff Porter took the box Dr. O'Toole carried off the plane. "Hope you don't mind going right to the station."

"No, of course not."

"Since he recognized the picture, we're hoping that talking to you will get him to open up. I've gotta tell you, anything would help. Especially now that it looks like he was telling the truth."

Dr. O'Toole slid into the passenger seat with a sigh. "I can't even imagine."

"Me either."

Sheriff Porter packed the box into the truck. It rattled a little, and he looked forward to opening it. Dr. O'Toole, being a meticulous man, had cleaned out his partner's desk when it was obvious she wasn't coming back. And very neatly, he taped it closed, and marked it with the date and her name.

The last of her worldly effects, perhaps. Maybe something they could swab for DNA, to make the ID on Cade stick. More important, Sheriff Porter hoped to find a connection. A scrap, a name, a number. Somebody living who was related to the kid.

Because if he really had spent all this time living in the middle of nowhere, he needed someone to take over. Get him therapy. Get him integrated, and into school. Teach him how to get along before he turned eighteen and the system cut him loose.

He got behind the wheel, and looked over at Dr. O'Toole. "Hungry?"

"I could eat," Dr. O'Toole replied.

The cruiser purred when Sheriff Porter started the engine. Because he had the sirens and the lights, he could leave through the back roads. Leaking the picture to the press was going to make things easier in the long run. But it gave them a blood trail to follow, and he wanted to keep the doctor to himself for the time being.

Drumming his fingers against the wheel, Sheriff Porter glanced over. "Can I ask you something? Off the record?"

"Of course."

"What do *you* think happened?"

Dr. O'Toole brushed his hands down his slacks. It was obvious he wasn't trying to deceive with the hesitation. More like he wanted to say the most accurate thing possible. Sheriff Porter appreciated that. After all these messy, hazy half truths, he looked forward to some nice, concrete facts.

"You must understand, Liza is a wonderful woman. I enjoyed working with her immensely. But I think it started to overwhelm her. If you can't separate yourself from your work, that happens sometimes. As soon as you know how much can go wrong, you anticipate it. I'm sure that happens in your line of work, as well?"

"Oh yeah," Sheriff Porter agreed.

"So, you really must understand. We spent—I still

spend—all day thinking about a catastrophic viral event."

"An epidemic."

"*Pandemic*," Dr. O'Toole corrected gently. "In the 1600s, disease could only travel so far. It decimated cities because that's where all the people were. But it was contained in cities, for the same reason. If you got cholera in London, sheriff, I would have been perfectly safe in Edinburgh. Your contaminated water would have never crossed my lips."

Turning onto a gravel road, Sheriff Porter slowed to keep the ride as smooth as he could. He wasn't sure, exactly, where the doctor was going with this. But he'd hear it through, and that meant saying just enough to keep him going. "All right."

Dr. O'Toole nodded, as if agreeing with himself. Then he went on. "This morning, I was in Ohio. If I have a virus inside me right now, a perfect mutation that will spread because we shook hands, I just gave it to you. To everyone on the plane. To everyone in the airport.

"Are we going to have breakfast in a restaurant? I'm going to expose all those people. Then we'll go to your place of work, and I'll infect the deputies there. The people in the hotel.

"Then, they will go home. Perhaps this perfect virus has no symptoms for . . . two weeks. So you feel fine when you go on vacation with your family to Florida. The pilot who flew me here flies to Juneau to go whale watching. Our waitress honeymoons in Singapore.

"When we finally get sick, all of us, it's not just our enclosed community. When we start to die, this perfect disease won't burn through our neighbors and die out. It will grow and grow, because we carried it farther and faster than we ever could have in our history.

"If this virus truly is perfect, it will have a little more than a fifty percent mortality rate. If it kills too many, too quickly, it will die too. So imagine, then, sheriff. Half of everyone you know is dead in a month, simply because I got up this morning and got on an airplane."

Uneasy, Sheriff Porter glanced at him. "You're creeping me out, I gotta say."

"And I haven't told you one eighth of one thousandth of one millionth of what Liza and I knew when we were building our model. So when you ask me, what do I think might have happened, I think it's better to ask you: What does a *sheriff* think about, late at night, as he waits for his first child to be born?"

The car went quiet. Nothing but the sound of the engine, and the gravel crunching beneath the tires. Licking his dry lips, Sheriff Porter flipped on the turn signal and pulled onto the main highway. "I wanted to take her away so nobody'd ever hurt her."

"I had no idea how overwhelmed Liza was," Dr. O'Toole admitted. "But I understand exactly how she got there."

"You're ruining my life," Lia complained.

Dara peeked out the front window again. Because of their dad's bright idea to leak the picture, things were even worse. The street in front of their house was choked with vans. People walked through the alley behind their house, staring up at them.

The neighbors on either side of them had put up No Trespassing signs, and Dara was pretty sure they were off the Christmas card list. Probably permanently.

Dropping the curtain, Dara turned to her sister. "Do you want to get out of here?"

"Duh."

"Then come on."

It was crazy, and Dara didn't care anymore. Grabbing her purse, she plucked her keys off the wall and headed into the garage. Her third-hand Honda wasn't a tank or anything. But basic rules of self-preservation stated that when faced with four cylinders and a driver who had ceased to care, a person would get out of the way.

Lia followed Dara, hopping into the passenger seat without a question. Things were about to get interesting.

"Seat belt," Dara said.

She started the car before opening the garage door. Incredibly dangerous, and ordinarily, totally unnecessary. But she wanted to be able to hit the gas the second the door lifted. The reporters had proved at the mall that they could swarm. Today, they wouldn't get a chance.

Foot still on the brake, she hit the gas hard. The tires screamed and smoke billowed around them. The reporters scattered, and she dropped the brake. The car shot out of the driveway. The tires shrieked again when Dara pulled hard to the right. It wouldn't do any good to escape, just to crash into Mrs. Bickham's stone garden wall.

Lia reached across her and punched the garage door remote.

Then she flipped the radio on, turning it all the way up. Pounding bass filled the car, Lia's whoops, too.

"Holy crap, that was awesome!" she shouted.

Too keyed up to talk, Dara just nodded. She figured she had a head start on the news vans. They had to gather everything up if they wanted to chase her. She'd drop her sister at Mom's office, and then . . .

And then what? There were probably reporters at Ms. Fourakis' house, too. And Cade was probably already at the police station. She didn't want to sic all these lunatics on Sofia, and it wasn't safe to be in public, either. The mall had proved that.

Rolling through a stop sign, Dara tried to swallow her rising panic. There was no way she could go to Josh's. The only thing waiting there was the official breakup. It was already too late to fix, and she was tired of spreading misery.

So it was a fact: she was trapped. Unless she wanted to drive until she ran out of gas, she had nowhere to go.

Quietly, she hated herself, because she wished for something terrible to happen. An explosion at a factory, or a celebrity suicide, or . . . something. Anything more interesting than the Primitive Boy in Kentucky. Anything.

She stopped short of Mom's office when she saw a single news van in the parking lot. Pulling up to the curb, she left the engine running. Pulling a twenty from her purse, she pressed it into Lia's hand. "Go. Be free."

Lia opened the door. "My life is still ruined, you know."

"Whatever," Dara replied.

Once Lia closed the door behind herself, Dara pounded the gas and sped away—to nowhere.

Already, there were too many people in the room. They stank of cologne and soap, coffee, too. Greasy breakfast things that turned Cade's stomach. Clutching the arms of his chair, Cade forced himself to keep his feet on the floor. He forced himself to keep his head up.

"If you need a break," Branson said, sliding up next to him, "just say the word. You're not in trouble, and this isn't an interrogation. We're here to help you."

Somehow, Cade doubted that. He had ears. He could hear them in the next room talking about next of kin and foster care. They wanted to find a stranger to keep him permanently. Far from here, locked up in houses with windows and doors. Not one of them wanted to consider letting him decide.

The door swung open. Sheriff Porter walked in with Ms. Fourakis. And then, behind her, the man from his picture. Jolting inwardly, Cade made himself hold still. These people had no intention of being fair to him. Listening to him. Anything. So he wouldn't tell them anything they could use. He would behave, and be quiet. He could make his own plans when they weren't looking.

"Cade, I think you know everybody here." Sheriff Porter nodded. "This is Dr. O'Toole, he worked with your mother."

Flattening his lips, Cade stared at him impassively. It felt like holding an ember in his palm, a slow heat turning to pain. He just had to endure it. This Dr. O'Toole probably had answers.

Maybe he'd share them. Somehow, Cade doubted it, though. Everyone said they wanted to help. None of them really did.

Dr. O'Toole shook his head, wonder struck. "You look just like her. My dear boy . . ."

Cade only blinked. There was no question he paid attention. He followed everyone with his eyes, quick and certain to track them in the room around him. They couldn't stop him from listening; they couldn't force him to talk.

Stepping in, Sheriff Porter slid a box onto the table. "Now y'all know we're still piecing this all together. I think we all agree our best bet is to sort out a timeline. The lab boys pulled a couple rubber bands and a hairbrush out of Dr. Walsh's personal possessions, so we're going to rush a DNA test."

"Your part is already done," Branson assured Cade. "You remember, when they swabbed your cheek."

Cade gritted his teeth. If Sheriff Porter noticed, he didn't mention it. Instead, he went back to answer the knock at the door. Taking a couple heavy sacks from an assistant, he turned to slide breakfast onto the table. Cade smelled bacon in there. Eggs, too. And he'd already learned what happened when he took food from Sheriff Porter.

Generous still, Sheriff Porter said, "If you want a few minutes alone with Dr. O'Toole, son—"

"I don't," Cade said.

The abruptness of the reply seemed to dismay Dr. O'Toole. But he waved a hand, brushing up a wavering smile. "I'm sure this has been very confusing for you."

"Why don't we get started, then?" Branson drew his chair to

the table. With swift fingers, he split open a package of small, blank cards. Producing a pen, he wrote *1997* on the top of the first. Beneath the date, he scribbled *Jonathan Cade Walsh, b. August 19, Cleveland, OH.* Capping the pen, he looked back at Cade. "Does that sound right to you?"

It didn't. He knew the name, the Jonathan name. But he didn't know what a Cleveland, OH was. What Walsh was. August was a month of the year, named after a Roman emperor. But he'd never kept time that way. He had seasons in the forest. Cycles. His birthday was the hottest month of the year, just as the birds gathered to fly south.

Disappointed, Branson gave him another encouraging nod. "It's okay, Cade. You're doing fine."

Cade closed his eyes. He was so sick of *fine*.

FORTY-ONE

*T*he tank was almost empty, and Dara drove past Clayton Park for the fortieth time.

So much for her great escape. All she'd done was waste a week's worth of gas, and listened to the same six songs on high rotation. The clock read just past noon. With more optimism than the situation warranted, she headed up the street that would take her to Ms. Fourakis' house.

She almost left when she saw the reporters outside. Where did they all come from? It seemed like they were multiplying, and they were everywhere. Her patience had run out back when it was just a jerk posting to Tumblr in Sofia's backyard. Suddenly, Dara ceased to care.

Instead of sneaking up the alley, she drove right up to Ms. Fourakis' house. Sunglasses on, check. They weren't much, but it felt like they protected her. Enough that she got out of the car in front of everybody. Keys in hand, she headed purposefully for the door. She was a magnet. The moment they realized who she was they rushed toward her.

Mentally, she brushed them away. Physically, she pushed up to the door. They trailed her, crushing behind her in a way they never would have dared in front of the sheriff's house. It was hard to ignore being touched by so many strangers at once. Feeling them breathe and move behind her like a single-bodied beast.

She refused to look back. Instead, she knocked on the door. Lightly, at first, then harder. Realistically, she knew no one would answer. If someone did, it probably wouldn't be Cade.

But she was tired. Tired of hiding and running and fighting to just *be*. There was something wrong with the world when she had to break out of her own house in the morning.

No one answered.

Dara steeled herself with a deep breath, then turned around. A mural of faces blurred in front of her. She couldn't even pick out their individual voices anymore. They were a wall to scale. A gate to jump. Squaring herself off, she put her head down and pushed through them.

They moved—to be honest, she was surprised. But they did, parting for her as she strode back to her car. More predictably, they swarmed around when she got back inside. Like they hadn't heard about her wild ride just a couple of hours ago— didn't they realize she wasn't fooling around anymore?

Throwing the car into gear, she slammed her hand on the

horn. With the high-pitched blare clearing the way, she pulled onto the street, and didn't bother with her signal at the corner.

Sheriff Porter stood in the station parking lot to give the latest update. After thirty-six hours, he was a little punchy, and probably the wrong guy for the job. But he wanted to do it; throw these guys some meat and send them off to look for leads in cities other than his.

The prepared statement was short, and he didn't pretend he wasn't reading from it. If they wanted theatrics, they'd have to get them somewhere else. Every few lines, he'd raise his head. Another act, pretending like he cared if they got it all down.

"With information gathered from many sources, and the cooperation of concerned citizens, we believe we have identified our John Doe. The state lab will be conducting DNA tests, and we expect results in the coming weeks. Because John Doe is a minor, we're declining to name him at this time.

"However, we can give you a brief sketch of what we believe to be the facts at this time. In the spring of 1999, we believe John Doe's parents sold their possessions and abandoned their home in Ohio. It appears they decided to move into the Beaver Creek Wilderness Area of Daniel Boone National Forest.

"At this time, we can't comment on their motives for doing so. Nor can we comment on their current whereabouts. We do not believe they will be found alive, nor do we believe they were the victims of foul play."

Stopping for a sip of water, Sheriff Porter peered into the cameras. He saw slices of his own face, reflected in black glass over and over. He wondered if they could see how tired he was. If they realized he could drop on the spot, if they'd just pack up and leave. Probably not. The folks with the cameras never slept.

After clearing his throat, Sheriff Porter shook the statement and picked up where he left off. "John Doe has given us no reason to discount his version of events. As incredible as it sounds, it is our belief that he spent the majority of his life in Daniel Boone National Forest, unaware of the civilized world just outside its borders.

"The courts will assign him a legal guardian sometime this week. We'll finish our investigation, confirming his identity. However, at this point, CHFS will take over. This is a case for the family courts, and we ask that you let the system do its job."

It was standard to thank people for coming to a presser. Even more standard to open it up to questions. Sheriff Porter no longer cared about standard. He tipped his hat to them, and stepped down without a backward glance.

They squalled their protest, but the nice thing about the station door was that it cut down on outside noise considerably.

The shadowy figure above Dara's bed reached out to touch her. Shaking her, not gently, it leaned closer. Listerine wafted across her face. With another shove, the creature pushed her over and said, "Lord Greystoke is in the backyard."

Squinting, Dara struggled to sit up. Flailing one hand, she shoved Lia. Slow to process, Dara took in the glowing numbers on her clock and the alcoholic stench of her sister's breath.

Then she forced one eye open a little wider. Peering at Lia, Dara asked, "Who?"

Disgusted, Lia walked away. "Don't you ever read?"

"Meh meh meh ever *read*?" Dara repeated under her breath, annoyed.

Throwing her covers aside, she tugged her cami down to cover her belly and padded toward the window. Thinking twice about the outfit and the fact that there were still footprints all over her front lawn, she pulled on her robe. Then she lifted the shades.

There, in the bluish haze of their security lights, stood Cade. Wrapped tight in someone else's peacoat, he looked strange and formal. The only reason she knew it was really him was because of his hair. Bound with a black band, his dreads streamed down his back in a tight column. His face was bare, heart-shaped, and his dark brows framed a thoughtful expression.

A thin light appeared, then stretched across the yard. It swept over him. Raising a hand, he shrank, but he didn't retreat.

Dara's heart pounded. Taking the stairs two at a time, she practically skidded into the kitchen. To her relief, it was Lia at the back door and not one of their parents. Pressing past Lia, Dara turned back and said, "Flip the inside lights before we get in trouble, will you?"

"You're welcome for turning off the alarm," Lia replied.

Then she doused the kitchen overhead, and the yard was mostly shadowed again. The security lights would blink off as soon as people stopped moving near them. Plotting her path carefully, Dara hurried across the wet grass. She trailed her hand along the fence. More than a couple sneak-in-sneak-out party nights told her she was far enough from the sensor here.

Shivering, she did wish she'd put on shoes. As she drew closer to Cade, she asked, "How did you get here?"

Cade looked to the rooflines. It took Dara a moment to realize what he meant. When she did, her mouth dropped open. How many calls had her dad's office gotten about intruders on the roof? she wondered. Turning back to Cade, she caught his arms, squeezing them gently. "Are you okay?"

"I wanted to see you again."

Dara led him beneath the willow tree then gently pushed him almost against the trunk. It was a good place to hide from the lights. And from the prying looks of any neighbors or parents (or random, rabid journalists) that might wander by. The thin, new leaves didn't offer much cover. It was the elegant fall of branches, instead, that shielded them.

"I tried to see you this morning. The station was overrun, your house, too."

"It wasn't a good day," Cade replied.

The hurt in his voice wounded her. It shone in his eyes, even the way he held his head. Dara wanted to rush up to cover him, wrap him in her arms, and take him somewhere safe. Wherever that was. If it even existed.

Gingerly, she trailed her nails against his hands, up his wrists. When she spoke again, it was gently. Quietly, as if the air was too delicate to break with too much sound. "Do you feel that?" she asked.

Adam's apple bobbing, Cade said, "Yes."

"I feel it, too."

Night whispered around them. Wind through trees, and the soft kiss of cars rolling by in the dark. Far at the other end of town, a train whistle lowed. Its plaintive cry echoed, mourned by the sweet cry of new spring frogs.

Tracing her thumbs against the tender curve of his wrists, Dara dropped her gaze. She was afraid if she looked up that she would kiss him. That wasn't going to comfort him; that would be for her. Selfish and greedy, when he needed something more than that. Still, his current wrapped around her. He was heat lightning, racing along her skin. Tingling on her lips.

"Dara," he murmured.

She felt him lean closer. If he were more experienced, he might have known how to nudge her into looking up. That he could sway his hip and bump against hers. Or if he slipped his hard, worn hands up to her throat, he could have tipped her chin back and kissed her anyway.

"I wish I could make this better," Dara said. She threaded her fingers through his and took a step back. "I'm going to try. I'll talk to my mom. She's better with working outside the system. I don't want you to go away. I don't want . . ."

Cade started to protest. Then suddenly, instead, he seemed to solidify. He wouldn't let her look away, but he didn't chase this time. His hands in her hands, they hung together. Knotted between them. "What do you see when you look at me?"

Confused, Dara shook her head. "I see you. I see Cade."

It seemed that wasn't the answer he sought. His features smoothed, making him strange and flat. The lightning died, no longer passing between them. He let his hands slip away, and he said, "I have to go."

"Wait, I don't— What are you really asking me? You're standing here, and you're amazing. And confusing. And broken, god, you look so broken. I want to fix that. I want to . . . I want to kiss you, and I want you to kiss me back, and I want you to stay. When I looked out the window, I hoped it would be you."

He kissed her, quick and hard. It rasped across her mouth, a taste of need and desperation that evaporated when he pulled away.

"Wait," Dara said, catching his shoulder. "At least let me drive you home."

Cade ducked from beneath her grasp. Firm, certain, he turned to face her, backing toward the alley. Smooth, unreadable, his expression didn't change. It was tender, but resolved. Stoic, even. And when he stepped into full darkness, he faded away completely.

Cold rushed in, taking the place of his hands. His presence. His everything, once rushing to surround her—it bled away. She felt like the only person in the world.

The last person.

FORTY-TWO

Something crashed on the roof.

Josh grabbed his Little League bat and charged down the hall. Most of the crazy was happening elsewhere. After the first rush of stories, people forgot he'd been involved at all. It was much freaking better that way.

But they *had* had a couple run-ins on their lawn. Plus, some beady-eyed douche bag from the *Makwa Courier* had stolen their trash. Josh didn't put it past them to break into the house in the middle of the night.

Since his dad weighed one sixty soaking wet, Josh felt like it was his job to run off the predators. That was always going to be his job, now. He'd never hide again.

When Josh hit the living room, he stopped. Listened. Everything was quiet, then something scrabbled down the side of the house. Blood pumping, Josh unlocked the front door. Then, after charging himself up with a couple of bounces, he threw it open. A flash of pale, an impression of a person startled him. Josh swung.

Cade caught the bat.

"What do you want?" Josh demanded.

Knot after knot tightened in Josh's back. Yeah, he'd seen the news. The video of this jag with his hands all over Dara. The werewolf, wild-man act, uh-huh. Josh knew exactly what Dara meant now, when she said she wanted to take *care* of him. Josh wanted to take care of him, too. Right then, he was more than a little sorry he'd missed his chance with the bat.

With a subtle gesture, Cade indicated a shadowy car at the corner. A faint glow filled the cab. It was just enough light to reveal a woman with a laptop and a collection of empty takeout containers. At that moment, she had her head down, apparently searching for something in her lap. Cade pressed a finger to his lips, *shhhh*.

Everything about the guy made Josh want to do the opposite. To yell and get that reporter's attention. Flip on every light in the house and invite the circus to come get a piece of the Primitive Boy.

But there was something about his expression tonight. Cade stared at him. He studied him, not like prey. Like he recognized him, something more than just his face. That's probably why Josh jerked Cade into the house. Closing the door, Josh reclaimed his bat and waited for his explanation.

"Well? I know you speak English, spit it out."

Down the hall, Josh's mom stirred. Stepping into the hall, she called softly, "Honey?"

"It's nothing," Josh replied. Less than nothing. *Just somebody who's gonna explain himself real quick before I kick him to the curb in the dark.* Out loud, he added, "A cat got in the trash, I'm cleaning it up."

"Oh, good. Thank you for honoring our family."

Then the bedroom door shut, and Josh scowled at Cade's raised eyebrow. "Don't even think about my mother."

"I'm not."

What time was it, anyway? Josh leaned to look at the clock. After three. He had no idea why he was standing in his living room with this guy in the middle of the night. At all, really. He looked him over, then came back to his stupid, wide-eyed face. At least he wasn't running around in Josh's clothes anymore. "All right, you gonna explain what you want?"

Cade's expression flattened, like a hand wiped over his skin and planed it smooth. His nostrils flared, and it all happened in a millisecond. A complete change, without hesitation. Thrusting his hand out, Cade looked at Josh expectantly.

"You want me gone. I need to go. Will you help me?"

The hand hung between them. It was hard to tell if he was messing with him. Josh still wasn't sure if there was a difference between the myths on TV and the actual guy standing in front of him. Not for a second did he believe the whole innocent babe in the woods routine.

But on the off chance that Cade was being straight up with

him, Josh said nothing. Nope. He shook his hand, then went to get his keys.

Two hours of sleep wasn't enough. Even at his college peak, Sheriff Porter needed at least three to get through the day.

Ordinarily, he wouldn't let a deputy chauffeur him around. He was a public servant, and he was a hands-on sheriff. He just didn't want to risk falling asleep and crashing a cruiser. Nothing like more police incompetence to keep a story alive.

As they rolled up to Kelly Fourakis' house, the deputy hit the siren—once, twice. Just a couple quick blasts to get the reporters out of the way. Sheriff Porter climbed out. He held his hand up, his own personal wall. They could yammer at him all they wanted, he had nothing to say.

Ms. Fourakis met him at the door. She pressed a mug of coffee into his hands, and ushered him inside. Her house was never loud, but it seemed unnaturally quiet this morning. The rooms felt too big, the space too open.

Leading Sheriff Porter down the hall, she said, "He was quiet when we got home yesterday, but I thought he was going to be all right."

Cade's bedroom was made up perfectly. The covers had been smoothed, and pillows placed at the head. Stacks of neatly folded towels sat at the foot. The toiletries basket rested next to it, its contents carefully rearranged.

Ms. Fourakis picked up a thin green book from the dresser and handed it to the sheriff. There was a note on top, in clean, even handwriting. Block letters, perfectly shaped.

"'Please return this to Dara's father. It belongs to him,'" Sheriff Porter read.

His stomach sank. This whole situation was six kinds of nightmare. He didn't feel guilty for the way he'd handled it. Nobody in their right mind would have believed Cade's story without some proof.

Once he got some, he went along. He changed his whole mind-set, shifting from seeing the boy as a somebody to suspect to someone who needed protection. And now that neglected, half-feral kid had run away. All of a sudden, two hours of sleep sounded indulgent.

"He watered my plants," Ms. Fourakis said, rubbing the back of her neck. "Wrote a thank-you note. I have no idea when he left."

With an optimism he didn't feel, Sheriff Porter said, "Well, he can't drive. He probably doesn't know how to hitchhike, and he doesn't have any money. How far could he have gotten?"

The answer to that question was fifty-three miles in a Ford F-150, and six more miles by foot. If Sheriff Porter was lucky, he'd have twenty-four hours to hide the disappearance from the press—and his daughter.

On Monday, a silvery peep interrupted English class. Right in the middle of a lecture about symbolism, actually. When the teacher went to answer the intercom, one of the guys in the back of the class thumped his desk.

"I bet this *means* something," he said.

Laughter filled the class. Everyone had perked up, stirring the lazy heat that surrounded them. The school only used the

PA for morning announcements. Since a call on the intercom could be for anyone, everyone rippled with curiosity.

"Miss Porter," the teacher said as she hung up the phone. "Please collect your things. Your father's waiting for you in the office."

There was a murmur of disappointment from everyone else as Dara closed her book and shoved it in her satchel.

At least it's Dad, Dara thought as she slipped into the cool, quiet hallway. Though she didn't dwell on it anymore, there was always a worse possibility. That it would be Mom in the office; that Dad wouldn't be coming home anymore.

She was surprised when she got to the front corridor. The office was framed in glass. Inside, Sheriff Porter leaned against the front desk, but he wasn't alone. Two other deputies flanked him, along with Cade's social worker.

That couldn't be good. And after last night, she was afraid to go inside. If something had happened to Cade, she didn't know what she would do. Their stilted conversation played again in her head. After he left, she'd gone through it obsessively. She couldn't help feeling like she'd missed something.

It was something she was going to sort out after school. Today, she planned to turn up at his back door instead of the other way around. Her homework was going to wait. She intended to hold his hands. Hold his gaze. Really, really get him to talk to her. This all had to be too much for him.

Though she couldn't wrap her head around it, she thought she'd started to understand just how scary Makwa had to be to Cade.

How much his mother had messed him up—what kind of mom lied like that? She had to be completely insane to convince her kid that the whole world had died from the flu. And what about his dad? That guy had to be some kind of lunatic, too, to go along with it.

Lost in her own thoughts, Dara startled when the office door opened. Her father stood there, waiting for her to get it together and come inside.

"What's wrong?" Dara asked.

Sheriff Porter didn't answer until they got to a private room. She felt surrounded, like they were trying to intimidate her into being honest. Though the sheriff was her dad, he'd shifted into hundred-percent cop mode.

"When's the last time you saw Cade?"

Reflex wanted her to lie. But instinct told her not to. She'd grown up listening to her dad talk; she was steeped in law enforcement. That meant she knew there was never good news when people asked when you last saw someone. Swallowing hard, Dara said, "Saturday night. Like, three in the morning. He came to the house."

Already, the deputies were taking notes. Sheriff Porter leaned against the table, taking the lead with the questions. "What for?"

"We hadn't seen each other yet," Dara said. She sat down. Unconsciously, she braced herself. It was bad, she could tell. But she forced back tears. She refused to cry out of anticipation. It felt slick and out of control. It made her chest hurt, so she crushed her feelings down. "We usually do, every day."

"Did you talk about anything unusual? Did he seem off?"

Dara couldn't take it. She couldn't go through an interrogation like this. Pretending that it wasn't her father asking the questions; acting like Cade was just some acquaintance. Twisting her hands in her lap, Dara asked, "Daddy, what happened? Is he hurt?"

For some reason, the social worker thought it was a good time to cut in. His milky voice grated, too smooth and too practiced. "He ran away, Dara. We're all very concerned about him."

It felt like falling. Though she knew she was anchored in the chair, Dara felt like everything had dropped from beneath her. The walls pulled away. The fluorescent lights buzzed right in her head. He'd told her, and she hadn't even realized it. That kiss had been good-bye.

"Did he say anything to you?" Sheriff Porter asked.

Slowly, Dara shook her head. "Just that . . . it was a bad day. I told him I was sorry I couldn't fix it."

Sheriff Porter and the social worker exchanged a look. Right there in front of her, like they thought she couldn't see them. She let her anger spring up. She didn't want to cry in front of them. It was going to be ugly, the kind of sobs that ripped and burned. A flood of tears that would choke her and leave her gasping.

"I don't want to have to go around and round with you," Sheriff Porter said. He wasn't mad, just resigned. He stroked a hand over her hair, and gave her a look that said, *Honey, please just make this easier for everybody.*

"He didn't tell me he was leaving," Dara said. It was strictly the truth. He'd never said those words. Standing up again, she pulled away from her father.

"We talked about us, all right? How I felt. We kissed, and then he left. He was wearing jeans and a blue coat and tennis shoes. His hair was tied back, and that was three o'clock in the morning, and that's all I know."

"Dara," Sheriff Porter said.

"I was in the middle of a test. I have to go."

Grabbing her stuff, she bolted from the conference room. Being interrogated by her father had become scary regular. If he had to be the sheriff with her, she didn't want to be his little girl. She wouldn't let him use her vulnerability against her. Or Cade. Not today, and not ever again.

I should have patched up his foot and taken him back that night, she thought, slamming into the bathroom door. Slapping every stall door to make sure they were empty, she barricaded herself in the last one. Locking up, she stepped onto the toilet seat so no one could see her.

Then, finally, she cried.

FORTY-THREE

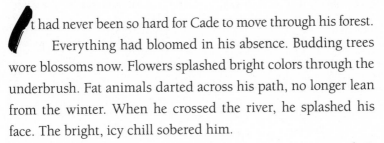

It had never been so hard for Cade to move through his forest.

Everything had bloomed in his absence. Budding trees wore blossoms now. Flowers splashed bright colors through the underbrush. Fat animals darted across his path, no longer lean from the winter. When he crossed the river, he splashed his face. The bright, icy chill sobered him.

Tempted to drink, he sucked his own tongue instead. It wasn't safe unless he boiled it, and he didn't have his travel pack. It was back in Makwa somewhere. Maybe the police station, or still at the hospital.

Instead, Cade searched for dew collected on leaves. Tipping the plants, he collected as much as he could in his hand. It wasn't nearly enough, and it was salty with his sweat. Aching everywhere, he pushed on.

Legs quivering, he forced himself to keep moving. The rubber-soled shoes made him clumsy. More than once, he tripped. And more than once, he cried out. Grabbing at branches for balance tore at the still-tender wound on his chest. Climbing over houses had been a stupid, stupid idea. He could admit that now.

When the bee hollow came into view, he almost collapsed. Every aching, agonized bit of him cried for it. Just for a minute, just to lay down beneath the trees. Rest his hand on the bark. Feel the warmth inside.

But he was afraid if he didn't get back to the cave now that he never would. It was later in the year, but the nights were still cold. Plenty of spawning animals had marked their territory. Bear cubs and coyote pups feared nothing. They knew their mothers were close behind. He couldn't fight off a bluegill in this condition, let alone a bear.

He pressed on, because there was no point in coming home, just to die. But it was strange. When he finally reached his cave, he didn't fall onto his empty pallet. Everything was where he'd left it. Still packed, the travois waiting to follow the river south. To safety. His fire pit's walls remained strong and tall. Vines crept over the mouth of the cave, hanging like a spring-green veil.

Staggering inside, Cade followed the narrow passage back. Beyond his sleeping place, past the nook where he used to keep his books and his tools. Farther back, where the air cooled, and the walls wept. This had been his mother's space. Plastic bins lined the walls, and Cade had never touched them.

Today, he did.

Peeling one open, he tossed the lid aside. A hurt cry escaped his lips. His mother's scent wafted up. It dug a jagged wound through him. It was cruel, that any part of her was left. That he wanted her back in spite of the lies. He missed her gentle hands on the back of his neck. He missed her songs, and her stories.

He missed his family.

Cade scrubbed an arm across his face. Then he dug into the box. Grey plastic squares. They had a metal flap on them, and a logo imprinted into the side. Zip Disk. When he shook one, it rattled. Behind the metal flap, he found a thin film of plastic.

His mother's handwriting labeled each one. It was faded, but legible: *World Plague Model-Sub-Sahara, WPM-South-Central Asia, WPM-London Cholera Maps, WPM-Zaire EBOV.* There were hundreds, all marked with different locations. Different plagues.

Cade dug deeper. He found plastic folders filled with notes and diagrams. Someone had stapled hideous pictures of bodies contorted with disease to dry explanations of the lesions, point by point. There were papers. Magazines. A newsletter, showing his mother and Dr. O'Toole in a lab, surrounded by maps and anatomical models.

When he finally got to the bottom, Cade dropped the newsletter and stared.

This. This is what she saved.

There weren't more baby pictures or more books about beautiful things. Instead of bringing love letters, or the best movie ever made, she brought disease. The very thing she'd run from, and that was the only thing she kept. It infected her, now it infected this place.

Cade kicked the bin over. With the last of his strength, he picked up the next and smashed it against the wall. Plastic shattered. Falling to his knees, Cade grabbed a rock. He crushed the disks. Smashing them to pieces, throwing their parts deeper into the cave.

When he ran out of strength, he dragged himself to the front of the cave. He didn't quite make it to the pallet. He collapsed beside it, the stone still clutched in his hand.

Rubbing Dara's back, Sofia sat sentinel while her best friend had a total nervous breakdown on her bed.

It wasn't the first time Dara had smeared snot and tears on her pillow. She must have broken up with Josh sixty-two times since freshman year. And every single time, Sofia put her back together. That was her job, too. Another sacred duty.

Sofia wasn't sure she could cure this one with salted caramel ice cream and a rousing game of *screw that guy, he sucks!* Though secretly, that's exactly how Sofia felt. Screw Cade for leaving without a good-bye. Dara deserved one.

And so do I, Sofia thought huffily. She let him hide in her house. They were Wii buddies. She let him totally screw up her iPhone with his monkey paws, and he just up and left.

But those were inside thoughts. Secret, keep-them-in-her-head thoughts. Secrets to be deployed later. After the rawness healed, and everybody moved forward to real lives that had nothing to do with crazy 24/7 news coverage and broken hearts.

"Ready for a mop up?" Sofia asked.

The tissues were at hand, and she offered a sympathetic

smile when Dara rolled over. Stuffing Dara's hand with Kleenex, she let her swab her face. Then, she replaced the nasty bundle with a nice, new, clean one.

"How about some pizza therapy?" When Dara shook her head, Sofia offered, "We could go find Kit and beat him with the lacrosse stick some more."

That made Dara laugh. Not long, or hard. But enough to break the misery for a moment. Sofia plastered a hand on Dara's forehead, looking down into her sad, puffy face. The girl was not a good crier, not by a long shot.

With a groan, Dara peeled herself off the bed. Padding into Sofia's bathroom, she turned on the tap. Water splashed, and Sofia slumped on the bed. The usual tricks probably wouldn't work. It's not like she could say, "Hey, you're going to be fine. And when he sees you being fine, he will *suffer.*"

Well, she could have said it. But it wouldn't have made very much sense. No, Cade had wreaked a special kind of havoc on her best friend. Sofia kind of hoped he'd gone back to the jungle. Because if he had, she could wish for him to get ticks. And lice. With a lovely parting gift of rhinovirus. That was the change she wanted to put into the world.

"I think I know where he is," Dara said, reemerging. She dried her hands on her shirt, slumping to lean in the door frame.

"Does it matter?"

"It does to me."

Ugh. The statute of limitations on talking smack about the guy who just trashed her best friend's heart wasn't up yet. Not even close. And Sofia was pretty sure it was going to take a monumental effort to keep her mouth shut. "Honey, I know you feel responsible for him . . ."

"I do," Dara agreed. "But it's more than that."

Don't call him a jackass, Sofia warned herself. To Dara, she said, "Here's the thing, Dare. Let's say everybody's in love, it's healthy, you were going to settle down and have his litter of puppies . . ."

"Ew."

"Right, I know." Sofia nodded, wildly agreeable. "But look, he bailed. He had his reasons, whatever, I don't care. You don't leave without saying something. So much for Mr. I'll Fight a Bear for You, everything got crazy and he ditched!"

Brows furrowing, Dara blinked at Sofia. Then she melted, sliding over to the bed to flump beside her. Throw her arms around her even. She pressed her face to Sofia's shoulder and rocked her with a hug. "Aw, boo, you're hurt, too."

"Get offffff," Sofia said, trying to peel her way out of Dara's embrace.

"No, but you are. I'm sorry."

"Don't you be sorry," Sofia said. "You're not the one who blew."

"Awww, Sof."

"You let somebody beat you at Mario Kart, and look what it gets you."

Sofia succumbed to the wallowing. It was good to share things, sometimes. Though she knew she didn't have near as much invested into Cade, her feelings *were* hurt.

It's not like the last couple of weeks happened in a bubble.

It spilled out through town—in her brother's bedroom, and on the side of her house. In her car, in parking lots, in big old box stores that didn't, Cade had pointed out, seem to sell boxes.

Resting her head against Dara's, Sofia nudged. A bump to say *hey, I'm here, you there?* She smiled, just a little, when Dara nudged back.

Things weren't okay, but they would be.

FORTY-FOUR

*A*n eerie quiet seemed to dog Dara. Sitting at her computer, she flicked a finger against the mouse. She toyed with opening a single file on the desktop. A specific file—all the photos from the camping trip.

Uneasy, she wondered if she wanted to do this to herself. A tremor passed through her finger, and suddenly, the file was open.

Once again, she was struck by the stillness in the photographs. No portraits, no selfies. The fleeting images in this set featured tiny red mushrooms. The curve in an ancient oak. Rainbows on mist, and trees full of sunlight.

This time, she looked up. Above the frame of the photo, into the forest beyond. It wasn't empty; she knew that now. It was alive with so many secrets. Cade was there, somewhere.

Maybe in every single shot.

With a sharp pang in her belly, she realized he was out there again. The first time, his parents carried him in the forest. They wanted to protect him from the world. And now, he'd gone back—why? To protect himself?

Closing the folder, she didn't hesitate. Instead, she dragged it into the trash bin, and erased it forever. The still air in her room suddenly felt stifling. A walk, what she needed was a walk. Heading down the front stairs, she was careful when she opened the front door.

Stepping into the sunlight, she shielded her eyes and watched as the last of the news vans pulled away. There was one left at the corner. Far enough away that Dara felt safe walking onto her own front lawn.

Scraps of trash littered the street like confetti. Black tire tracks stained the curb, but there was no permanent damage. It was like the siege had never happened. Just for fun, and how sad was it that she considered this fun, she decided to get the mail.

It was stuffed with magazines and bills. Kind of funny that the postal service still delivered the mail, even when the Porters couldn't get down the drive to check it. Fingering through the envelopes, a glint of metal on the ground caught her eye.

Dara picked up the brass button. Unremarkable, in every way, she put it in her pocket anyway. A souvenir from the plague year in her yard.

When she looked up, she realized the last reporter was heading straight for her. For a moment, she was torn between running and standing her ground. But there was no camera this time. No microphone. And the reporter actually stopped a few feet away. It was nice to have some space.

"Hi, Dara?" the reporter asked. "I know I'm probably the last person you want to see . . ."

"It's okay," she said. And it was.

Now that Cade was gone, they couldn't do anything anymore. They had nothing to chase, and no story to tell. Since Dara had no intention of talking about the secret things—their private moments—it didn't matter if somebody from a small town paper wanted to get a quote.

The reporter rewarded her with a thoughtful smile. "Thanks. Thank you for that. I was just wondering if you had any thoughts about where Jonathan Walsh might be right now."

None, Dara thought. Because she didn't know a Jonathan Walsh. That name belonged to a face in an old photograph. To another time, and another life, and other people's decisions. That was a little boy who'd once had a birthday party with balloons and cake, friends and family . . . then disappeared entirely.

Jonathan Walsh was a stranger. He always would be. So without the slightest bit of guilt, Dara shook her head. "I don't. I have no idea, I'm sorry."

There was never just one question. The reporter nodded, then followed. "Now that the hunt is on, do you have something you'd like to say to him when we find him?"

Just then, the wind kicked up. It was cold, and it carried

blossoms off the trees. White flecks swirled through the street, beautiful to look at. But they smelled off—that was the ugly trick to a flowering pear tree. Pristine, pale, and pretty—bound up with the scent of decay. Dara tried not to breathe it. And she tried not to react to the word *when*. The certainty of it.

The press had driven away, but they hadn't disappeared. They had to follow the story. And now, the story was Primitive Boy escapes! As if he'd busted out of the zoo to prowl the countryside.

Folding the mail against her chest, Dara looked past the reporter. All down the street, petals fluttered to the ground. It was never going to stop. It might change shape, there might be new details, but this would never stop until there was nothing left to find.

Because she was quiet a little too long, the reporter prodded. "Dara?"

That was it, then. She'd have to end it. She hoped her thoughts didn't show on her face, but even if they did, who could translate them? They were too specific. Exact and unknowable, they fired her from within. Her bones and body were ready to move, run even. But first, she spoke.

"I don't think you'll find him, so no. Thank you, though."

Dara refused to hear anything else. She jogged up the walk to her door. And just outside it, she pulled the brass button from her pocket. Then she flipped it into the yard, to disappear among the mulch. She didn't need a souvenir.

And she was going to make sure no one else had one, either.

— —

Nature moved faster than most people realized.

Cade was plenty aware of it. Rolling to his feet at dawn, he ached. But he couldn't laze around. In his absence, animals had moved into the cave. Marked with urine and scat, it had to be scoured out.

Cutting down a fir branch, Cade shook the spiders from it. Then he carried it inside, brushing the cave floor and the walls. Evergreen sweetened the air, but only a little. It would take air and exposure and time to really improve it. After the long run home, he realized he didn't have the strength to move south. Not yet.

So he unpacked his things, and slept a little. When he woke, he started to clean.

Cade kept his arm as still as he could. It was awkward, trying to work left-handed. But the thick, scabbed edges on his chest pulled when he moved. Beneath that, the muscle felt dangerously liquid. Bright sparks of pain shot up occasionally, threatening to spread. He'd done too much—climbing, trying to swing through the trees.

Stupid, he thought.

He should have known a wound like that hadn't really healed yet. Just because the surface had closed didn't mean it was better.

In town, he'd never had to exercise it. Food came on plates, and stairs walked for him. He'd been in a cocoon. Now he was soft and weak, and had to wait out the injury. Hopefully, when fall came, he'd be able to hunt. Until then, he'd have to make do with fish and foraging.

Lifting the furs on his pallet, he sighed. Bugs scurried out, hiding from the light. He hadn't been there to shake them out, or to dust them with dried cedar and sweet fern.

They weren't ruined, but he'd have to clean them before bed. That meant more fir branches to beat them, rope to hang them in the sun. The very thought of it exhausted him, and he was so, so hungry.

"Should have brought some bacon," he told himself. Ms. Fourakis' fridge had been full of things. Bacon would have been good. Yogurt, too. Or cheese, or leftover dim sum. A piece of spinach pie. Even the eggs. Rows and rows of eggs, just sitting there. His stomach clenched with a growl.

Walking outside, he used a notched stick to lift the cooler from its rope. It wouldn't be bacon, but it would be *fine*.

Peeling open the lid, he recoiled. A pungent, sour cloud engulfed him. The wild onions and leeks he'd collected weeks ago were ruined. Blackened with mold and disintegrating, they reeked. Next to them lay a pouch of pemmican. Sometimes it went bad, but Cade prayed. Not to any god in particular, just to the universe: *Please, please, please.*

He untied the pouch, then gagged. A whiff of rancid grease was like a punch in the nose. So much for prayers—the universe didn't meddle in the affairs of physics. Rot was rot, and his entire store of food was ruined. The cooler toppled when he stood. Just great. Something else to clean up, something else he had to replace.

Rising slowly, he took in his camp. Small and compact, well-hidden. But the back of the cave was full of shattered secrets.

Everything else had started the slide toward ruin. Though he didn't want to admit it, his *home* was gone. He needed to move on. He needed his strength to do it, he needed food to make the journey. But he couldn't stay long.

Eventually, the rangers would stray across his path. They weren't infected. He didn't have to worry about that anymore. They probably wouldn't shoot him. They didn't need to steal his supplies. He understood that now.

Cade's chest tightened, anxiety that refused to subside. It was different because they *knew* about him. The whole, living, teeming world did. There were other people who remembered him now. Dr. O'Toole, Sofia. Josh for sure; that long, silent ride in the dark had imprinted them on each other. It was a pact they alone shared.

And Dara.

The words had been on his lips. He'd almost let them slip out. *Come with me,* he'd longed to murmur. *Stay with me and be with me.* But then she'd said *stay.* So beautiful with her eyes green like spring, so alive and matched to him perfectly.

It was never clearer than at that moment. She couldn't imagine living in his world. It wasn't possible, even thinkable. And she couldn't fathom how foreign and alien her world was to *him.* There was no middle. He couldn't stay; she wouldn't leave.

So it was time to move.

"Soon," he said.

He told the trees and the sky, and the fire pit that was wet from rain and needed to be shoveled out. He had to pack his furs and his tools. He needed water, enough food to get deeper into the woods. More rest, because his chest hurt and he didn't have a cabinet full of pills to fix that.

Weary, he picked up his water bladders and headed for the river. Soon, he said, and he meant it.

"Tampons," Sofia said.

"I'm not staying out there for a year," Dara replied.

Ignoring her, Sofia stuffed some into the backpack. It already bulged like a tick. Rolls of clothes competed for space with a flashlight and a box of granola bars. Bug spray, bear spray, rope, all tied up in plastic garbage bags. Water purification tablets, Swedish steel, sunblock, and Benadryl.

This time, she had real maps, too—paper ones. A compass and pencils, and a wind-up emergency radio. Finally, her cell phone, and a booster antenna. It was amazing how much she'd learned by doing it wrong the first time.

She thrummed with nervous tension. Everybody from the park services to CNN were out there looking for Cade. They had a head start, and a crapload of equipment. More than that, they had an uncontrollable desire to get to their quarry first.

But Dara had participated in a search before, when a man with Alzheimer's had wandered away from his home in the night. Regimented, planned searches were slow. Methodical, they followed grids because that was the best way to cover all the ground.

Lucky for Dara, she didn't need to cover it all. Just the right bits of it. She pulled the laces tight on her boots, running over a mental checklist. "Hopefully, I'll come back out near Whitley

City. I'll text you with my GPS coordinates."

Humming, Sofia rearranged the backpack a little. Then she straddled it. Without her weight, that thing was never going to zip up. Just another service provided by Dara's friendly neighborhood best friend. "You're my very own little geocache."

"I know, right?"

"Yay for me," Sofia replied with a grunt. The bag *would* close, or else.

"I emailed you a bunch of notes and stuff. If you don't hear from me in, like, three days, give it to my dad."

Sliding off the backpack, Sofia sprawled on the bed. "I really hate the sound of that."

"Then pretend I didn't say it. For at least three days."

"Oh, aren't you so very hilarious?"

Dara flashed her a smile. "I try."

Hopping to her feet, Dara looked herself over. She had her layers. She had her supplies. She even had her evacuation plan. A sudden heat swept over her. Her skin flushed, and her breath thinned, but she pulled the backpack on anyway.

Tightening the straps, she tried to calm herself. There was still an hour drive to get through, and she would need that adrenaline.

Footsteps echoed in the hall, and Dara turned to find Lia peering past the partially open door. Bounding over, Dara pulled the door open rather than slamming it shut. This so surprised Lia that whatever sarcastic comment she was about to let loose just faded away.

The sisters looked at each other. It was the ideal moment

for Lia to lord over Dara. There was so much blackmail packed in Dara's clothes and her obvious intentions. It wouldn't just be car rides to school and back. This was enough leverage to *own* Dara. Rides everywhere! Never-ending free passes off dishwasher duty. Party covers for *life*.

Lia slowly tipped her head back. They stared at each other. Not really waiting. Letting the quiet happen. Waiting for things to balance.

Hands on her hips, Lia wrinkled her nose. "Nice boots."

"Thanks," Dara replied.

Sofia slid from the bed, but she knew better than to screw with delicate sister dynamics. Instead, she gathered her purse and her keys. La la la, nothing to see over there by the window, even though she couldn't help but listen.

"So anyway," Lia said, waving lazily. "You'll never guess who called."

"Do I want to know?"

Lia made a face. "Kit. He said all the news vans are down at the rally point, but he'd forgive me if I would come give him the inside scoop."

"Jerk," Dara muttered.

"I was thinking maybe I'd go give them an interview. I mean, I have unique insight, don't I? I'm completely objective, and I eavesdropped on you guys all the time."

Dara stiffened.

"And it's going to save them so much time if they start looking in the right place. I mean, you said yourself that his best bet was to start hitching I-75 North to Ohio."

It was a perfect lie. Totally plausible. Why wouldn't she tell Cade how to get to Cleveland? Everyone wanted to believe he belonged in cities—they'd want to believe he fled to find his home. Dara threw her arms around Lia and squeezed her until she squeaked.

Then she pulled away and cleared her throat, playing along. "God, you're such a creeper."

"Freak," Lia replied lovingly.

Then she stood back and watched her sister head off to destiny. *Or whatever,* she thought, and rolled her eyes.

FORTY-FIVE

Dara was pretty sure that somebody had once said you never step into the same river twice. Or the same ocean. Whichever it was, it was true for the forest, as well.

The last time she'd hiked into Daniel Boone National, Josh had been at her side. The trees were still mostly bare, which made it easy to see down the long paths worn through the underbrush. Since they hadn't seen animals, they assumed there weren't any.

Wrong. All wrong. And now, the forest was a jungle. A thin one, to be sure. But nothing looked the same. Thick, woody vines bloomed with new leaves. There were blossoms now instead of buds, and the canopy was thick and green. The sky was nothing but stuttered glimpses of blue, mostly obscured.

Moving slowly, Dara stopped to test her memory. Had they

passed that twisted tree last time? Was that the boulder where they jogged left? The compass kept her from turning in circles. She marked the maps every half hour. And whenever she heard a noise nearby, she looked around—and up.

Sweat soaked through her clothes. There would be no breaks—she'd decided that as soon as she climbed out of Sofia's car. Now that she knew how dangerous it could be, she sharpened her focus. She got a new burst of energy when her thighs started to burn. It was uncomfortable, for sure. But she recognized it: that subtle incline that led to her camp with Josh.

Dara crested a hill and stopped short. A ruined toothpaste tube lay on the path. In the elements, it had faded. But she knew it belonged to her. In the rush to save Cade, they'd abandoned their entire camp. The deputy who'd returned her camera had left everything else behind.

Now, laced with anticipation and fear, Dara walked into her past.

The tent was in pretty good shape. Faded and wet, but still standing. Something had knocked over the stones that made their fire pit. Boxes rotted, plastic bottles bled from chewed edges. The cooler was there, and she shuddered to think what that looked like on the inside. But that was camp. On the surface, just a bunch of litter.

But Dara saw the stone she'd dropped on the bear. It was ridiculously big; how did she ever move that? Long gouges rent the ground. The blood was gone, long devoured by insects. But she didn't need to see it to know that it had been there.

She could barely breathe. Suddenly jittery, she circled. She stared into the brush and up in the trees. Down along the tree line, then up again. Breaking out her water, she took long, deep gulps. It wasn't very cold, but it made her stomach clench anyway. Her body urged her to run! Run away fast, far away, never come back!

"Shut up," she told it.

Kicking at trash, she yelped when something pale flipped up. Muddied, faded, the ivy and bees pendant that the stranger—that Cade—had left for her lay on the ground. It had weathered without her. Kneeling down to pick it up, she marveled. It felt insubstantial, delicate. All at once, an edge of calm settled around her.

Cade had found her once. Now it was her turn to find him.

She tucked the pendant in her pocket, then pulled out her cell. With the signal booster, she got one whole bar—just enough to text Sofia. *HALFWAY THERE STILL OKAY.* Her bread crumbs were digital. The phone chugged plaintively. After a too-long moment, it bleated. Message sent.

And now, the hard part. Snapping the lid off her antihistamine, she popped two just in case. Normally, that would have sent her straight to naptime. She was way too keyed up for that today, though. Pulling on a pair of gloves, she climbed to the top of the ridge.

Scanning the horizon, she saw butterflies and dust motes. A particularly daring squirrel darted past her. Ache crept into her bones as she waited, but there was no way to hurry this. Her heart leapt when she heard a heavy murmur nearby.

There it was. Her quarry, a drowsy bee, lacing through the air.

It drifted purposefully, dropping onto each flower in a copse before humming off to the next. Careful to stay behind it, Dara followed. Grasses whispered against her jeans. The rhythm and cry of the wild surrounded her—she was trying to melt into it. As the sun shifted, Dara felt like she'd seen every snowdrop and crocus in Kentucky.

New sweat wetted her hands. They felt humid in the gloves, itchy, too. But she kept them on because now she had to do the hard part. All her life, bees had been something to avoid. Summer picnics full of soda cans, had to keep them covered. Lia had drunk a bee once. It stung her mouth, and she'd swelled up, fleshy and thick.

Dara held her hands apart. Suddenly, an old playground song played in her head. *I'm picking up my baby bumblebee, won't my mommy be so proud of me* . . . Stifling a bit of hysterical laughter, Dara took a deep breath. Another. The bee landed on a new flower and Dara approached.

Against all instinct, she moved slowly. Cupping her hand beneath the flower, she closed her fingers one by one. Trapping the bee in the blossom, she plucked it from its stem. With her heart raging, she stood. To be honest, she was waiting for the sting. It didn't come. Instead, she felt its buzzing. Its warmth.

Dara didn't know if she was talking to the bee or herself when she said, "You're okay." But they both were. Checking her compass, Dara turned directly east and started walking. It wasn't quite noon and she hoped that bees liked to be home by dark.

As dusk slipped in around him, Cade surveyed his camp solemnly.

It was possible to be home and homesick at the same time, it turned out. He was erasing himself. His family. When he left, Mom and Dad would sleep alone under their cherry tree by the river. The fragmented remains of his mother's research would stay, seeding the cave—maybe forever.

Picking up a stone from his fire pit, he chucked it into the woods. Charcoal smearing his hands, he reached for the next stone and threw it in the opposite direction. The truth about his world might have changed, but the rules hadn't. Leave no trace—nothing for people to find. Nothing for anyone to remember.

Ash blended with his sweat. He tasted it, bitter on his tongue, and it gritted across his skin. It was hard work, and he was trying to favor his good side. Still, it was impossible to do everything one-handed.

After he'd dismantled the pit, he considered his palms. They were covered in ashes from the last fire his father had built. The first fire he'd tended entirely by himself. He'd lived in this place four years, and now it was time to leave it. Carefully, he pressed four fingers to each cheek. He wanted to take something with him, however temporary.

Scattering the rest of the ashes, Cade swept the clearing in front of the cave. He'd already tied up his furs and his tools.

They waited for him on the travois. Hunger crawled through his belly, so he slaked it with water. There probably wouldn't be any food until he made a new camp.

That never used to bother him. Now it did, and his mouth watered for things he'd never be able to find in the wilderness. Not just the delicious garbage, but treats like oranges. Would he ever have an orange again?

The rumble of his stomach distracted him so much, he didn't notice the trees go quiet. The steady song of frogs and birds trailed off. All that remained was the shifting of branches, and the wind in the trees.

Lashing his iron pan to the travois, Cade stopped abruptly. The underbrush rustled. His ravenous hunger made him reach for his knife. It could be a wild hog, perhaps a piglet.

That would feed him for days. He could carve new fish hooks from the bones, make salve from the fat. He was praying again, for a piglet, for a boar. Dropping low, he crept toward the sound. His feet fell silently, and he wrapped his hand tighter around the hilt of his blade.

Excitement loosened his limbs. The sound was coming from the bee hollow. Wild beasts of all kinds loved the hollow. The ground was always thick with dropped fruit. The bark was sweet—plenty of animals were happy to eat the bees or the honey.

A light flared. Not a candle or a flame, not lightning. Something electric. Cade dropped to the ground, disguising himself in the brush. It wasn't an animal—not one to eat, anyway. Only human beings carried flashlights. It wasn't even that dark yet, so it had to be an outsider. An absolute stranger.

Slowly, Cade backed through the brush. He couldn't be seen. Mentally, he went over his path. The remains in his camp. If he lashed the travois to his back, he could move faster but not as far. Which was more important? Thoughts spinning out madly, Cade pushed to his feet. Time to run.

Then a voice rang out. "Cade!"

Silence and ice swept over Cade. He stopped, dead still in the stretching twilight. It was a bird, he told himself. An owl. A hawk—their cries were the right pitch. He imagined his name in it, he wanted it to be true and he was hungry, he had to be hallucinating.

Twigs snapped behind him. The light bobbed, then stopped. So did the footsteps. Cade turned. He had only a moment to register gold hair and green eyes. Then he crashed to the ground, smothered in heat. Sugared skin. Soft hands on his face. Lips on his.

Dara.

Split through, Cade rose into the kiss. Banding arms around her, he clasped the back of her neck. Lifting to seek her mouth, his chest rumbled with unspoken words. He tasted hers, too, slipped to him on a sudden shock of tongue. Fingers tangling in her hair, he pulled her down until she blanketed him. Until nothing separated them, not even a breath.

"I didn't think it would work," she whispered, and kissed him again. "I can't believe I really found you."

Cade dropped his head back. She filled his sight, and his blood, and his imagination. Tracing a rough finger along her cheek, his chest hitched. And he trembled, under the stark rush of sensation. The numbness fled, and now everything was bright and visceral. Pain and pleasure at once, fear and need. Love.

Pressing her hands to her face, Dara drew back and gazed into his eyes. "I want to see where you live."

FORTY-SIX

It felt strange and victorious to have Dara in his camp.

Quietly, he hated that it came so late. It was dirty now, a place he was leaving. She should have seen it when he had skins tanning, and his bone and shell chimes inside. When he had plenty of food, and his books displayed in the stone niche inside.

But he refused to give in to regret. She was here now. Shaking the herbs out of his furs, he spread them out to make room for them both. Then, he stoked the fire and put water on to boil. She'd want to wash her face.

"You spent four years here?" she asked softly. He saw it in her eyes, confusion laced with hesitation.

"It was nicer before," he told her.

Taking her hand, he was overwhelmed by a rush of desire.

Need. He wanted to ask if she was going to stay. It would make a difference. She was used to walls and windows and beds. He'd peel supple poplar branches to make a bed for her. Lash it with cattails and lavender, so it smelled sweet.

"You left so fast, I was afraid you'd be hungry." From the depths of her bag, she produced granola bars. Beef jerky, trail mix. Then she pulled out a cloth bag. Unzipping it, she caught his eye with a smile. "You said you have a frying pan. I brought bacon to go in it."

Springing over her, he grabbed his skillet, and then the plastic packet in her hand. With a few quick flashes of his knife, he had the package open, and thick slices of bacon arranged in the pan on the fire. Sucking the grease from his fingers, he pretended not to see her surprise.

"That smells good," she said.

"Yes."

"So," she said after a moment. She turned to survey the camp. "I kind of expected more stuff."

Cade shook his head. Where would he keep stuff? The travois was over-packed as it was. But he had a feeling she didn't mean things, not physical objects. She looked for hints that this was home for him.

Gently, he took her hand. Turning it over, he kissed the inside of her wrist. The skin there was delicate, soft beneath his lips. He longed to lick it, to bite her. Just to leave a faint mark. Proof that he'd been there. Instead, he led her into the cave.

There was just enough light from the fire to show her his drawings. There was art here. Beauty. It wasn't the same as her gleaming glass world, but it was just as good. With every step, his bones begged her to stay.

"This is amazing," Dara said. She reached out to touch one of the drawings, but stopped short. It was like she realized it was impermanent, or too precious to risk smudging.

Holding her hand up to the prints, she measured herself against them. Then, she sank to study other drawings. His favorite, the fleet, slim shadow of a deer, leapt across the wall. There were birds there, leaping fish and bees.

He wasn't surprised that she stopped at the human figures. Those were older drawings, blockier. But they were certain enough that his mother's face, his father's, too, rose up from the darkness. Firelight animated them; their eyes followed, lashes lowered. Their lips turned in smiles, directed at each other.

Dara sat heavily, and looked up at him. "I've never taken a picture as real as this."

"You have," Cade said. He followed her down. The stone floor of the cave was cool, and she had kissed him. So he tangled around her, breathing warmth on her neck, banding his arms around her to keep her close. "Sofia on the rock wall."

Shaking her head, Dara said, "It's not the same. How can you stand to leave this behind?"

A pang tightened in his chest. Burying his face against the back of her neck, he surrounded himself in her scent. With the warmth flowing from her hair. Its silken glide against his face was a kiss. Not as sweet as the one on her lips, but still wondrous. "My memories will last."

Alone in the half dark, they clung to each other. Without

clocks, the stars stretched long above them. Wood smoke carried the savory scent of meat, swirling it toward the heavens. Honeysuckle bloomed in the distance. The forest rose up, a dark cloak to keep them from the rest of the world. Drawing her back, he leaned over her shoulder to find her mouth.

To share a breath with her, a kiss, and the night in the place he called home.

Dara woke with dawn. She shivered, trying to burrow against Cade but the cold had stolen her will to sleep. Yellow sunlight dripped through the trees, haunting and beautiful. Dara slipped a hand beneath Cade's shirt. His back was hot to the touch; his body strong and hard.

A tremor passed between them. As he woke, he reached for her. Possessive hands washed up her back, too. Rough, they teased her skin. They demanded a kiss, another touch. Her hem rucked up and she caught her breath when her belly brushed against his.

The reporters seemed so far away now. Her father probably still dreamed in his bed, sure that his eldest daughter had spent the night at her best friend's house. Locked in. Safe. Nearby. Dara wondered, only briefly, what would happen if she stayed.

Tangled together beneath furs and beside a banked fire, it would have been easy to forget everything else. Waking up to him like this, disappearing into the quiet . . . it was fantasy. Perfect in her thoughts, but in reality, she wasn't prepared. She knew it. She hated to admit it. More than that, she hated to say it.

"Dara?" Cade asked. He read her better than anyone.

"I have to go," she said, then she kissed him fiercely. Splaying both hands on his face, she pressed closer, whispering against his lips. Each word felt like bloodletting. "I didn't want to talk about it last night, but I have to now. They're coming. Everybody, the reporters and the police . . . you have to run."

"I know."

Dara sat up. Where was her pack? Her hair fell in her face. Skin protesting the cold, she climbed from beneath the furs to find it. When she did, she slung it open. Voices howled in her head, parts of herself urging her to go with him, the reasonable bits roaring that she couldn't. She couldn't listen to any of them. As wrong as it felt, she had to do this, and get up, and go home.

"Dara," Cade said. He rose behind her, heat radiating from his skin.

Turning, she thrust a compass at him, bundles of paper. "Run south. Everybody thinks you're hitchhiking to Cleveland, so you have a head start. Go as far as you can, as fast as you can. They won't be able to follow you into the mountains."

The compass lay in his hand like a stone. Cade stared down at it. "I've never seen mountains. I always wanted to."

His desolation cut through her. She felt cruel and irrational, even though she knew she was making the best sense she could. Digging into the bag again, she handed him a cell phone.

"It's disposable," she explained. "For when you get somewhere safe. You'll probably have to go into the open to get a signal. But my number's in there, just press one. That's all you have to do. Promise me."

Slowly, Cade looked up. "Why?"

"Just promise me."

Though sunlight streaked across his face, his eyes were full of shadows. All the other thoughts she had, about cutting his hair to disguise him, giving him new clothes—it fled from her thoughts. Because when she looked at him, she saw everything he'd already lost. It was easy to hate herself for taking more, but she had to. Forcing herself to stay calm, she repeated, "Promise me, Cade."

"I promise."

As soon as he said it, she swept in for one more kiss. This one lingered, a slow, sure claiming. It had to last her; she needed her lips to sting with his kiss as she pressed back through the forest, back to her ordinary life in Makwa. It had to be enough for both of them. When she broke away, he reached after her.

Dara shook her head. Climbing to her feet, she zipped her gear and hauled it onto her shoulders. "I have to get back now. If anybody realizes I bailed, they're going to know where I went."

Following her, Cade seemed determined to make this hard. He caught her, held her tight. And he pressed his brow to hers. When he murmured, his voice slipped into her veins, sizzling through her body to her heart. "I love you."

It was a moment suspended. She longed to keep it, to let it play out until the bubble burst. But there was too much at stake. With one last kiss, she hoped she'd imprinted herself on his skin, too. "I love you, too. And that's why you have to run."

"Stay with me," he said.

"I can't, not yet," Dara told him. She pushed away, stronger than he was. Backing into the forest, she raised her hand—a good-bye. Tears streaked her cheeks, but she didn't look heartbroken. No, she was determined. Certain. Sure.

His voice broke when he asked, "When?"

With one last smile, she swore, "I'll find you. I promise."

And then, she was gone.

EPILOGUE

It wasn't Sheriff Porter's idea to let Dara stand next to him during the press conference.

At five thirty, six, and eleven, her raw, tear-streaked face played on every station, exposed to the world. It was her face that landed on the morning paper, dissected with sidebars. Was she sorry? Grieving? Traumatized?

They didn't really care. It was just something else to talk about. A little sidebar to the main story, which was that the Primitive Boy was dead. In his gravelly voice (described by the *Indianapolis Star* as *weary gravitas*; the *New York Times* called it *appropriately solemn*) Sheriff Porter told the world that Jonathan Walsh was dead.

There were witnesses. Dara Porter, the daughter who brought the Primitive Boy out of the forest in the first place.

And three very shocked fishermen, whose truck she stopped in the middle of the road.

Panicked, they said. *Crying and hysterical,* translated the newspapers.

But they all believed, the Parks Department and the Sheriff's Department, the State Police, and just about anybody else with a badge and a vested interest. They believed her when she said she found him burning up with fever. They believed her when she said she did her best to drag him out of the woods.

They put a blanket around her shoulders and carried her away in an ambulance, in the middle of the nastiest spring thunderstorm any of them could remember. Four days passed before it was safe to send people into the depths of the national forest again. Hikers, campers (bloggers, reporters) were advised to note the GPS coordinates if they found remains—under no circumstances should they attempt to remove the Primitive Boy from his grave.

It was a warning made on account of protocol. Nobody expected to find a body—four days! Four days in the rain and the elements and the wild. No one said it, but everyone believed it: what remained of the Primitive Boy was probably bubbling in a coyote's belly and feeding the beetles.

And it was *always* the Primitive Boy.

His birth name was barely remembered. Even when magazines dug up the very strange history of Liza Walsh, interviewed old friends and colleagues, they still called her son the Primitive Boy. That was the story. They wouldn't let go.

That's what made it easy for Cade to make his way into the

Cumberland Mountains. On his own, he decided to cut his hair. When he passed through a regular hiking trail, he traded a couple of furs for a down coat and some boots. They fit all right. What mattered was they weren't primitive.

Neither was he. He had maps and a compass, and a paygo cell phone. And as he stepped into his first dark night in the mountains, he looked up. The stars shifted with the seasons, but they never changed. When he gazed at Orion, Dara gazed at him, too. That hunter, wearing the skins of an animal, standing against the elements, stretched between them.

It was the light that blinked, the one that streaked across the horizon, that would connect them. Cade pressed the number one on his cell phone and sent a message not to the stars, but to the satellite.

The satellite caught it and tossed it back, over trees and mountains, valleys and rivers. Over miles and miles, in the blink of an eye. Cade waited, breath caught in his throat, listening to the distance. The silence went on, but not endlessly. Barely a moment passed.

Dara answered. She would find him.

ACKNOWLEDGMENTS

*M*any thanks to . . .

Vincent Racaniello, PhD, for answering my questions about rhinovirus in the wild. His Virology blog (www. virology.ws) was an invaluable resource while writing this novel.

Kimberly Morgan, Public Affairs Specialist for Daniel Boone National Forest, who helped me accurately hide Cade and his family.

Edgar Rice Burroughs, for the original—first and best—Tarzan of the Apes.

Anne Hoppe, Sarah Shumway, and Jim McCarthy, for taking a chance on a book with no magic in it at all.

J. Wescott and W. Lorraine, the cornerstones of everything I do. You make all things possible.